warning, he smiled, and his spirit welled up around her.

THE SPIRIT REBELLION

The Legend of Eli Monpress Book 2

RACHEL AARON

orbit

www.orbitbooks.net

ORBIT

First published in Great Britain in 2010 by Orbit

A CIP catalogue record for this book
is available from the British Library.

ISBN 978-0-356-50011-9

Typeset in Minion
Printed and bound in Great Britain by CPI Mackays, Chatham ME5 8TD

Papers used by Orbit are natural, renewable and recyclable
products sourced from well-managed forests and certified
in accordance with the rules of the Forest Stewardship Council.

Mixed Sources
Product group from well-managed
forests and other controlled sources
www.fsc.org Cert no. SGS-COC-004081
© 1996 Forest Stewardship Council

FSC

Orbit
An imprint of
Little, Brown Book Group
100 Victoria Embankment
London EC4Y 0DY

An Hachette UK Company
www.hachette.co.uk

www.orbitbooks.net

To my parents, for more reasons
than I can fit on one page

PROLOGUE

High in the forested hills where no one went, there
stood a stone tower. It was a practical tower, neither
lovely nor soaring, but solid and squat at only two stories. Its enormous blocks were hewn from the local stone,
which was of an unappealing, muddy color that seemed
to attract grime. Seeing that, it was perhaps fortunate
that the tower was overrun with black-green vines. They
wound themselves around the tower like thread on a spin-
dle, knotting the wooden shutters closed and crumbling
the mortar that held the bricks together, giving the place
an air of disrepair and gloomy neglect, especially when it
was dark and raining, as it was now.

Inside the tower, a man was shouting. His voice was
deep and authoritative, but the voice that answered him
didn't seem to care. It yelled back, childish and high,
yet something in it was unignorable, and the vines that
choked the tower rustled closer to listen.

Completely without warning, the door to the tower, a

heavy wooden slab stained almost black from years in the forest, flew open. Yellow firelight spilled into the clearing, and, with it, a boy ran out into the wet night. He was thin and pale, all legs and arms, but he ran like the wind, his dark hair flying behind him. He had already made it halfway across the clearing before a man burst out of the tower after him. He was also dark haired, and his eyes were bright with rage, as were the rings that clung to his fingers.

"Eliton!" he shouted, throwing out his hand. The ring on his middle finger, a murky emerald wrapped in a filigree of golden leaves and branches, flashed deep, deep green. Across the dirt clearing that surrounded the tower, a great mass of roots ripped itself from the ground below the boy's feet.

The boy staggered and fell, kicking as the roots grabbed him.

"No!" he shouted. "Leave me alone!"

The words rippled with power as the boy's spirit blasted open. It was nothing like the calm, controlled openings the Spiritualists prized. This was a raw ripping, an instinctive, guttural reaction to fear, and the power of it landed like a hammer, crushing the clearing, the tower, the trees, the vines, everything. The rain froze in the air, the wind stopped moving, and everything except the boy stood perfectly still. Slowly, the roots that had leaped up fell away, sliding limply back to the churned ground, and the boy squirmed to his feet. He cast a fearful, hateful glance over his shoulder, but the man stood as still as everything else, his rings dark and his face bewildered like a joker's victim.

"Eliton," he said again, his voice breaking.

"No!" the boy shouted, backing away. "I hate you and your endless rules! You're never happy, are you? Just leave me alone!"

The words thrummed with power, and the boy turned and ran. The man started after him, but the vines shot off the tower and wrapped around his body, pinning him in place. The man cried out in rage, ripping at the leaves, but the vines piled on thicker and thicker, and he could not get free. He could only watch as the boy ran through the raindrops, still hanging weightless in the air, waiting for the child to say it was all right to fall.

"Eliton!" the man shouted again, almost pleading. "Do you think you can handle power like this alone? Without discipline?" He lunged against the vines, reaching toward the boy's retreating back. "If you don't come back this instant you'll be throwing away everything that we've worked for!"

The boy didn't even look back, and the man's face went scarlet.

"Go on, keep running!" he bellowed. "See how far you get without me! You'll never amount to anything without training! You'll be worthless alone! WORTHLESS! DO YOU HEAR?"

"Shut up!" The boy's voice was distant now, his figure scarcely visible between the trees, but his power still thrummed in the air. Trapped by the vines, the man could only struggle uselessly as the boy vanished at last into the gloom. Only then did the power begin to fade. The vines lost their grip and the man tore himself free. He took a few steps in the direction the boy had gone, but thought better of it.

"He'll be back," he muttered, brushing the leaves off

his robes. "A night in the wet will teach him." He glared at the vines. "He'll be back. He can't do anything without me."

The vines slid away with a noncommittal rustle, mindful of their roll in his barely contained anger. The man cast a final, baleful look at the forest and then, gathering himself up, turned and marched back into the tower. He slammed the door behind him, cutting off the yellow light and leaving the clearing darker than ever as the suspended rain finally fell to the ground.

The boy ran, stumbling over fallen logs and through muddy streams swollen with the endless rain. He didn't know where he was going, and he was exhausted from whatever he had done in the clearing. His breath came in thundering gasps, drowning out the forest sounds, and yet, now as always, no matter how much noise he made, he could hear the spirits all around him—the anger of the stream at being full of mud, the anger of the mud at being cut from its parent dirt spirit and shoved into the stream, the contented murmurs of the trees as the water ran down them, the mindless singing of the crickets. The sounds of the spirit world filled his ears as no other sounds could, and he clung to them, letting the voices drag him forward even as his legs threatened to give up.

The rain grew heavier as the night wore on, and his progress slowed. He was walking now through the black, wet woods. He had no idea where he was and he didn't care. It wasn't like he was going back to the tower. Nothing could make him go back there, back to the endless lessons and rules of the black-and-white world his father lived in.

Tears ran freely down his face, and he scrubbed them away with dirty fists. He couldn't go home. Not anymore. He'd made his choice; there was no going back. His father wouldn't take him back after that show of disobedience, anyway. Worthless, that was what his father had written him off as. What hope was left after that?

His feet stumbled, and the boy fell, landing hard on his shoulder. He struggled a second, and then lay still on the soaked ground, breathing in the wet smell of the rotting leaves. What was the point of going on? He couldn't go back, and he had nowhere to go. He'd lived out here with his father forever. He had no friends, no relatives to run to. His mother wouldn't take him. She hadn't wanted him when he'd been doing well; she certainly wouldn't want him now. Even if she did, he didn't know where she lived.

Grunting, he rolled over, looking up through the drooping branches at the dark sky overhead, and tried to take stock of his situation. He'd never be a wizard now, at least, not like his father, with his rings and rules and duties, which was the only kind of wizard the world wanted so far as the boy could see. Maybe he could live in the mountains? But he didn't know how to hunt or make fires or what plants of the forest he could eat, which was a shame, for he was getting very hungry. More than anything, though, he was tired. So tired. Tired and small and worthless.

He spat a bit of dirt out of his mouth. Maybe his father was right. Maybe worthless was a good word for him. He certainly couldn't think of anything he was good for at the moment. He couldn't even hear the spirits anymore. The rain had passed and they were settling down, drifting back to sleep. His own eyes were drooping, too, but he shouldn't sleep like this, wet and dirty and exposed. Yet when he thought about getting up, the idea seemed impossible. Finally, he decided he would just lie here, and when he woke up, *if* he woke up, he would take things from there.

The moment he made his decision, sleep took him. He lay at the bottom of the gully, nestled between a fallen log and a living tree, still as a dead thing. Animals passed, sniffing him curiously, but he didn't stir. High overhead, the wind blew through the trees, scattering leaves on top of him. It blew past and then came around again, dipping low into the gully where the boy slept.

The wind blew gently, ruffling his hair, blowing along the muddy, ripped lines of his clothes and across his closed eyes. Then, as though it had found what it was looking for, the wind climbed again and hurried away across the treetops. Minutes passed in still silence, and then, in the empty air above the boy, a white line appeared. It grew like a slash in the air, spilling sharp, white light out into the dark.

From the moment the light appeared, nothing in the forest moved. Everything, the insects, the animals, the mushrooms, the leaves on the ground, the trees, the water running down them, everything stood frozen, watching as a white, graceful, feminine hand reached through the cut in the air to brush a streak of mud off the boy's cheek. He flinched in his sleep, and the long fingers clenched, delighted.

By this time, the wind had returned, larger than before. It spun down the trees, sending the scattered leaves dancing, but it did not touch the boy.

"Is he not as I told you?" it whispered, staring at the sleeping child as spirits see.

Yes. The voice from the white space beyond the world was filled with joy, and another white hand snaked out to join the first, stroking the boy's dirty hair. *He is just as you said.*

The wind puffed up, very pleased with itself, but the woman behind the cut seemed to have forgotten it was there. Her hands reached out farther, followed by snowy arms, shoulders, and a waterfall of pure white hair that glowed with a light of its own. White legs followed, and for the first time in hundreds of years, she stepped completely through the strange hole, from her white world into the real one.

All around her, the forest shook in awe. Every spirit, from the ancient trees to the mayflies, knew her and bowed down in reverence. The fallen logs, the moss, even the mud under her feet paid her honor and worship, prostrating themselves beneath the white light that shone from her skin as though the moon stood on the ground.

The lady didn't acknowledge them. Such reverence was her due. All of her attention was focused on the boy, still dead asleep, his grubby hands clutching his mud-stained jacket around him.

Gentle as the falling mist, the white woman knelt beside him and eased her hands beneath his body, lifting him from the ground as though he weighed nothing and gently laying him on her lap.

He is beautiful, she said. *So very beautiful. Even through the veil of flesh, he shines like the sun.*

She stood up in one lovely, graceful motion, cradling the boy in her arms. *You shall be my star*, she whispered, pressing her white lips against the sleeping boy's fore-head. *My best beloved, my favorite, forever and ever until the end of the world and beyond.*

The boy stirred as she touched him, turning toward her in his sleep, and the White Lady laughed, delighted. Clutching him to her breast, she turned and stepped back through the slit in the world, taking her light with her. The white line held a moment after she was gone, and then it too shimmered and faded, leaving the wet forest darker and emptier than ever.

CHAPTER
1

Zarin, city of magic, rose tall and white in the afternoon sun. It loomed over the low plains of the central Council Kingdoms, riding the edge of the high, rocky ridge that separated the foothills from the great sweeping piedmont so that the city spires could be seen from a hundred miles in all directions. But highest of all, towering over even the famous seven battlements of Whitefall Citadel, home of the Merchant Princes of Zarin and the revolutionary body they had founded, the Council of Thrones, stood the soaring white spire of the Spirit Court.

It rose from the great ridge that served as Zarin's spine, shooting straight and white and impossibly tall into the pale sky without joint or mortar to support it. Tall, clear windows pricked the white surface in a smooth, ascending spiral, and each window bore a fluttering banner of red silk stamped in gold with a perfect, bold circle, the symbol of the Spirit Court. No one, not even the Spiritualists, knew how the tower had been made. The common story was that the Shapers, that mysterious and independent guild of crafting wizards responsible for awakened swords and the gems all Spiritualists used to house their spirits, had raised it from the stone in a single day as payment for some unknown debt. Supposedly, the tower itself was a united spirit, though only the Rector Spiritualis, who held the great mantle of the tower, knew for certain.

The tower's base had four doors, but the largest of these was the eastern door, the door that opened to the rest of the city. Red and glossy, the door stood fifteen feet tall, its base as wide as the great, laurel-lined street leading up to it. Broad marble steps spread like ripples from the door's foot, and it was on these that Spiritualist Krigel, assistant to the Rector Spiritualis and bearer of a very difficult task, chose to make his stand.

"No, here." He snapped his fingers, his severe face locked in a frown even more dour than the one he usually wore. "Stand here."

The mass of Spiritualists obeyed, shuffling in a great sea of stiff, formal, red silk as they moved where he pointed. They were all young, Krigel thought with a grimace. Too young. Sworn Spiritualists they might be, but not a single one was more than five months from their apprenticeship. Only one had more than a single bound spirit under her command, and all of them looked too nervous to give a cohesive order to the spirits they did control. Truly, he'd been given an impossible task. He only hoped the girl didn't decide to fight.

"All right," he said quietly when the crowd was in position. "How many of you keep fire spirits? Bonfires, torches, candles, brushfires, anything that burns."

A half-dozen hands went up.

"Don't bring them out," Krigel snapped, raising his voice so that everyone could hear. "I want nothing that can be drowned. That means no sand, no electricity, not that any of you could catch a lightning bolt yet, but especially no fire. Now, those of you with rock spirits, dirt, anything from the ground, raise your hands."

Another half-dozen hands went up, and Krigel nodded. "You are all to be ready at a moment's notice. If her dog tries anything, *anything*, I want you to stop him."

"But sir," a lanky boy in front said. "What about the road?"

"Never mind the road," Krigel said, shaking his head. "Rip it to pieces if you have to. I want that dog neutralized, or we'll never catch her should she decide to run. Yes," he said and nodded at a hand that went up in the back. "Tall girl."

The girl, who was in fact not terribly tall, went as red as her robe, but she asked her question in a firm voice. "Master Krigel, are the charges against her true?"

"That is none of your business," Krigel said, giving the poor girl a glare that sent her down another foot. "The Court decides truth. Our job is to see that she stands before it, nothing else. Yes, you, freckled boy."

The boy in the front put down his hand sheepishly. "Yes, Master Krigel, but then, why are we here? Do you expect her to fight?"

"Expectations are not my concern," Krigel said. "I was ordered to take no chances bringing her to face the charges, and so none I shall take. I'm only hoping you lot will be enough to stop her should she decide to run. Frankly, my money's on the dog. But," he said and smiled at their pale faces, "one goes to battle with the army one's got, so try and look competent and keep your hands down as much as possible. One look at your bare fingers and the jig is up."

Off in the city a bell began to ring, and Krigel looked over his shoulder. "That's the signal. They're en route. Places, please."

Everyone shuffled into order and Krigel, dour as ever, took the front position on the lowest stair. There they waited, a wall of red robes and clenched fists while, far away, down the long, tree-lined approach, a tall figure riding something long, sleek, and mist colored passed through the narrow gate that separated the Spirit Court's district from the rest of Zarin and began to pad down the road toward them.

As the figure drew closer, it became clear that it was a woman, tall, proud, redheaded, and riding a great canine creature that looked like a cross between a dog and freezing fog. However, that was not what made them nervous. The moment the woman reached the first of the carefully manicured trees that lined the tower approach, every spirit in the group, including Krigel's own heavy rings, began to buzz.

"Control your spirits," Krigel said, silencing his own with a firm breath.

"But master," one of the Spiritualists behind him squeaked, clutching the shaking ruby on her index finger. "This can't be right. My torch spirit is terrified. It says that woman is carrying a sea."

Krigel gave the girl a cutting glare over his shoulder. "Why do you think I brought two dozen of you with me?" He turned back again. "Steady yourselves; here she comes."

Behind him, the red-robed figures squeezed together,

all of them focused on the woman coming toward them, now more terrifying and confusing than the monster she rode.

"What now?" Miranda groaned, looking tiredly at the wall of red taking up the bottom step of the Spirit Court's tower. "Four days of riding and when we finally do get to Zarin, they're having some kind of ceremony on the steps. Don't tell me we got here on parade day."

"Doesn't smell like parade day," Gin said, sniffing the air. "Not a cooked goose for miles."

"Well," Miranda said, laughing, "I don't care if it's parade day or if Master Banage finally instituted that formal robes requirement he's been threatening for years. *I'm* just happy to be home." She stretched on Gin's back, popping the day's ride out of her joints. "I'm going to go to Banage and make my report." *And give him Eli's letter*, she added to herself. Her hand went to the square of paper in her front pocket. She still hadn't opened it, but today she could hand it over and be done. "After that," she continued, grinning wide, "I'm going to have a nice long bath followed by a nice long sleep in my own bed."

"I'd settle for a pig," Gin said, licking his chops.

"Fine," Miranda said. "But only after seeing the stable master and getting someone to look at your back." She poked the bandaged spot between the dog's shoulders where Nico's hand had entered only a week ago, and Gin whimpered.

"Fine, fine," he growled. "Just don't do that again."

Point made, Miranda sat back and let the dog make his own speed toward the towering white spire that had been her home since she was thirteen. Her irritation at the mass of red-robed Spiritualists blocking her easy path into the tower faded a little when she recognized Spiritualist Krigel, Banage's assistant and friend, standing at their head. Maybe he was rehearsing something with the younger Spiritualists? He was in charge of pomp for the Court, after all. But any warm feelings she had began to fade when she got a look at his face. Krigel was never a jolly man, but the look he gave her now made her stomach clench. The feeling was not helped by the fact that the Spiritualists behind him would not meet her eyes, despite her being the only rider on the road.

Still, she was careful not to let her unease show, smiling warmly as she steered Gin to a stop at the base of the tower steps.

"Spiritualist Krigel," she said, bowing. "What's all this?"

Krigel did not return her smile. "Spiritualist Lyonette," he said, stepping forward. "Would you mind dismounting?"

His voice was cold and distant, but Miranda did as he asked, sliding off Gin's back with a creak of protesting muscles. The moment she was on the ground, the young, robed Spiritualists fanned out to form a circle around her, as though on cue. She took a small step back, and Gin growled low in his throat.

"Krigel," Miranda said again, laughing a little, "what's going on?"

The old man looked her square in the eyes. "Spiritualist Miranda Lyonette, you are under arrest by order of the Tower Keepers and proclamation of the Rector Spiritualis. You are here to surrender all weapons, rights, and privileges, placing yourself under the jurisdiction of the Spirit Court until such time as you shall answer to the charges levied against you. You will step forward with your hands out, please."

Miranda blinked at him, completely uncomprehending. "Arrest? For what?"

"That is confidential and will be answered by the Court," Krigel responded.

"Powers, Krigel," Miranda said, her voice almost breaking. "What is going on? Where is Banage? Surely this is a mistake."

"There is no mistake." Krigel looked sterner than ever. "It was Master Banage who ordered your arrest. Now, are you coming, or do we have to drag you?"

The ring of Spiritualists took a small, menacing step forward, and Gin began to growl louder than ever. Miranda stopped him with a glare.

"I will of course obey the Rector Spiritualis," she said loudly, putting her hands out, palms up, in submission. "There's no need for threats, though I would like an explanation."

"All in good time," Krigel said, his voice relieved. "Come with me."

"I'll need someone to tend to my ghosthound," Miranda said, not moving. "He is injured and tired. He needs food and care."

"I'll see that he is taken to the stables," Krigel said. "But do come now, please. You may bring your things."

Seeing that that was the best she was going to get, Miranda turned and started to untie her satchel from Gin's side.

"I don't like this at all," the ghosthound growled.

"You think I do?" Miranda growled back. "This has to be a misunderstanding, or else some plan of Master Banage's. Whatever it is, I'll find out soon enough. Just go along and I'll contact you as soon as I know something."

She gave him a final pat before walking over to Krigel. A group of five Spiritualists immediately fell in around her, surrounding her in a circle of red robes and flashing rings as Krigel marched them up the stairs and through the great red door.

Krigel led the way through the great entry hall, up a grand set of stairs, and then through a side door to a far less grand set of stairs. They climbed in silence, spiraling up and up and up. As was the tower's strange nature, they made it to the top much faster than they should have, coming out on a long landing at the tower's peak.

Krigel stopped them at the top of the stairs. "Wait here," he said, and vanished through the heavy wooden door at the landing's end, leaving Miranda alone with her escort.

The young Spiritualists stood perfectly still around her, fists clenched against their rings. Miranda could feel their fear, though what she had done to inspire it she couldn't begin to imagine. Fortunately, Krigel appeared again almost instantly, snapping his fingers for Miranda to step forward.

"He'll see you now," Krigel said. "Alone."

Miranda's escort gave a collective relieved sigh as she stepped forward, and for once Miranda was in complete agreement. Now, at least, maybe she could get some answers. When she reached the door, however, Krigel caught her hand.

"I know this has not been the homecoming you wished for," he said quietly, "but mind your temper, Miranda. He's been through a lot for you already today. Try not to make things more difficult than they already are, for once."

Miranda stopped short. "What do you mean?"

"Just keep that hot head of yours down," Krigel said, squeezing her shoulder hard enough to make her wince.

Slightly more hesitant than she'd been a moment ago, Miranda turned and walked into the office of the Rector Spiritualis.

The office took up the entirety of the peak of the Spirit Court's tower and, save for the landing and a section that was set aside for the Rector Spiritualis's private living space, it was all one large, circular room with everything built to impress. Soaring stone ribs lined with steady-burning lanterns lit a polished stone floor that could hold ten Spiritualists and their Spirit retinues with room to spare. Arched, narrow windows pierced the white walls at frequent intervals, looking down on Zarin through clear, almost invisible glass. The walls themselves were lined with tapestries, paintings, and shelves stuffed to overflowing with the collected treasures and curiosities of four hundred years of Spiritualists, all in perfect order and without a speck of dust.

Directly across from the door where Miranda stood, placed at the apex of the circular room, was an enormous, imposing desk, its surface hidden beneath neat stacks of parchment scrolls. Behind the desk, sitting in the Rector Spiritualis's grand, high-backed throne of a chair, was Etmon Banage himself.

Even sitting, it was clear he was a tall man. He had

neatly trimmed black hair that was just starting to go gray at the temples, and narrow, jutting shoulders his bulky robes did little to hide. His sharp face was handsome in an uncompromising way that allowed for neither smiles nor weakness, and his scowl, which he wore now, had turned blustering kings into meek-voiced boys. His hands, which he kept folded on the desk in front of him, were laden with heavy rings that almost sang with the sleeping power of the spirits within. Even in that enormous room, the power of Banage's spirits filled the air. But over it all, hanging so heavy it weighed even on Miranda's own rings, was the press of Banage's will, iron and immovable and completely in command. Normally, Miranda found the inscrutable, uncompromising power comforting, a firm foundation that could never be shaken. Tonight, however, she was beginning to understand how a small spirit feels when a Great Spirit singles it out.

Banage cleared his throat, and Miranda realized she had stopped. She gathered her wits and quickly made her way across the polished floor, stopping midway to give the traditional bow with her ringed fingers touching her forehead. When she straightened, Banage flicked his eyes to the straight-backed chair that had been set out in front of his desk. Miranda nodded and walked forward, her slippered feet quiet as snow on the cold stone as she crossed the wide, empty floor and took a seat.

"So," Banage said, "it is true. You have taken a Great Spirit."

Miranda flinched. This wasn't the greeting she'd expected. "Yes, Master Banage," she said. "I wrote as much in the report I sent ahead. You received it, didn't you?"

"Yes, I did," Banage said. "But reading such a story and hearing the truth of it from your own spirits is quite a different matter."

Miranda's head shot up, and the bitterness in her voice shocked even her. "Is that why you had me arrested?"

"Partially." Banage sighed and looked down. "You need to appreciate the position we're in, Miranda." He reached across his desk and picked up a scroll covered in wax seals. "Do you know what this is?"

Miranda shook her head.

"It's a petition," Banage said, "signed by fifty-four of the eighty-nine active Tower Keepers. They are demanding you stand before the Court to explain your actions in Mellinor."

"What of my actions needs explaining?" Miranda said, more loudly than she'd meant to.

Banage gave her a withering look. "You were sent to Mellinor with a specific mission: to apprehend Monpress and bring him to Zarin. Instead, here you are, empty-handed, riding a wave of rumor that, not only did you work together with the thief you were sent to catch, but you took the treasure of Mellinor for yourself. Rumors you confirmed in your own report. Did you really think you could just ride back into Zarin with a Great Spirit sleeping under your skin and not be questioned?"

"Well, yes," Miranda said. "Master Banage, I *saved* Mellinor, all of it, its people, its king, everything. If you read my report, you know that already. I didn't catch Monpress, true, but while he's a scoundrel and a black mark on the name of wizards everywhere, he's not evil. Greedy and irresponsible, maybe, and certainly someone who needs to be brought to justice, but he's nothing on an Enslaver. I don't think anyone could argue that defeating Renaud and saving the Great Spirit of Mellinor were less important than stopping Eli Monpress from stealing some *money*."

Banage lowered his head and began to rub his temples. "Spoken like a true Spiritualist," he said. "But you're missing the point, Miranda. This isn't about not catching Monpress. He didn't get that bounty by being easy to corner. This is about how you acted in Mellinor. Or, rather, how the world saw your actions."

He stared at her, waiting for something, but Miranda had no idea what. Seeing that this was going nowhere, Banage sighed and stood, walking over to the tall window behind his desk to gaze down at the sprawling city below. "Days before your report arrived," he said, "perhaps before you'd even confronted Renaud, rumors were flying about the Spiritualist who'd teamed up with Eli Monpress. The stories were everywhere, spreading down every trade route and growing worse with every telling. That you sold out the king, or murdered him yourself. That Monpress was actually in league with the Spirit Court from the beginning, that we were the ones profiting from his crimes."

"But that's ridiculous," Miranda scoffed. "Surely—"

"I agree," Banage said and nodded. "But it doesn't stop people from thinking what they want to think." He turned around. "You know as well as I do that the Tower Keepers are a bunch of old biddies whose primary concern is staying on top of their local politics. They care about whatever king or lord rules the land their tower is on, not catching Eli or any affairs in Zarin."

"Exactly," Miranda said. "So how do my actions in

Mellinor have anything to do with some Tower Keeper a thousand miles away?"

"Monpress is news everywhere," Banage said dourly. "His exploits are entertainment far and wide, which is why we wanted him brought to heel in the first place. Now your name is wrapped up in it, too, and the Tower Keepers are angry. Way they see it, you've shamed the Spirit Court, and, through it, themselves. These are not people who take shame lightly, Miranda."

"But that's absurd!" Miranda cried.

"Of course it is," Banage said. "But for all they're isolated out in the countryside, the Tower Keepers are the only voting members of the Spirit Court. If they vote to have you stand trial and explain yourself, there's nothing I can do but make sure you're there."

"So that's it then?" Miranda said, clenching her hands. "I'm to stand trial for what, saving a kingdom?"

Banage sighed. "The formal charge is that you did willfully and in full denial of your duties work together with a known thief to destabilize Mellinor in order to seize its Great Spirit for yourself."

Miranda's face went scarlet. "I received Mellinor through an act of desperation to save his life!"

"I'm certain you did," Banage said. "The charge is impossible. You might be a powerful wizard, but even you couldn't hold a Great Spirit against its will."

The calm in Banage's voice made her want to strangle him. "If you know it's impossible, why are we going through with the trial?"

"Because we have no *choice*," Banage answered. "This is a perfectly legal trial brought about through the proper channels. Anything I did to try and stop it would be seen as favoritism toward you, something I'm no doubt already being accused of by having you brought to my office rather than thrown in a cell."

Miranda looked away. She was so angry she could barely think. Across the room, Banage took a deep breath. "Miranda," he said, "I know how offensive this is to you, but you need to stay calm. If you lose this trial and they find you guilty of betraying your oaths, you could be stripped of your rank, your position as a Spiritualist, even your rings. Too much is at stake here to throw it away on anger and pride."

Miranda clenched her jaw. "May I at least see the formal petition?"

Banage held the scroll out. Miranda stood and took it, letting the weight of the seals at the bottom unroll the paper for her. The charge was as Banage had said, written in tall letters across the top. She grimaced and flicked her eyes to the middle of the page where the signatures began, scanning the names in the hope she would see someone she could appeal to. If she was actually going to stand trial, she would need allies in the stands. However, when she reached the bottom of the list, where the originator of the petition signed his name, her vision blurred with rage at the extravagant signature sprawled across the entire bottom left corner.

"Grenith Hern?"

"He is the head of the Tower Keepers," Banage said. "It isn't unreasonable that he should represent them in—"

"*Grenith Hern*?" She was almost shouting now. "The man who has made a career out of hating you? Who blames you for stealing the office of Rector out from under him? He's the one responsible for this 'fair and legal' accusation?"

"Enough, Miranda." Banage's voice was cold and sharp.

Miranda blew past the warning. "You *know* he's doing this only to discredit you!"

"*Of course I know*," Banage hissed, standing up to meet her eyes. "But I am not above the law, and neither are you. We must obey the edicts of the Court, which means that when a Spiritualist receives a summons to stand before the Court, no matter who signed it or why, she goes. End of discussion."

Miranda threw the petition on his desk. "I will not go and stand there while that man spreads *lies* about me! He will say anything to get what he wants. You know half the names on that paper wouldn't be there if Hern hadn't been whispering in their ears!"

"*Miranda!*"

She flinched at the incredible anger in his voice, but she did not back down. They stared at each other for a long moment, and then Banage sank back into his chair and put his head in his hands, looking for once not like the unconquerable leader of the Spirit Court, but like an old, tired man.

"Whatever we think of Hern's motives," he said softly, "the signatures are what they are. There is no legal way I can stop this trial, but I can shield you from the worst of it."

He lowered his hands and looked at her. "You are my apprentice, Miranda, and dear as a daughter to me. I cannot bear to see you or your spirits suffer for my sake. Whatever you may think of him, Hern is not an unreasonable man. When he brought this petition to me yesterday, I reacted much as you just did. Then I remembered myself, and we were able to come to a compromise."

"What kind of compromise?" she said skeptically.

"You will stand before the Court and face the accusations, but you will neither confirm nor deny guilt."

Miranda's face went bright red. "What sort of a compromise is that?"

Banage's glare shut her up. "In return for giving Hern his show, he has agreed to let me give you a tower somewhere far away from Zarin."

Miranda stared at him in disbelief. "A tower?"

"Yes," Banage said. "The rank of Tower Keeper would grant you immunity from the trial's harsher punishments. The worst Hern would be able to do is slap you on the wrist and send you back to your tower. This way, whatever happened, your rings would be safe and your career would be saved."

Miranda stared at her master, unable to speak. She tried to remind herself that Banage's plans always worked out for the best, but the thought of sitting silently while Hern lied to her face, lied in the great chamber of the Spirit Court itself, before all the Tower Keepers, made her feel ill. To just be silent and let her silence give his lies credence, the very idea was a mockery of everything the Spirit Court stood for, everything *she* stood for.

"I can't do it."

"You must do it," Banage said. "Miranda, there's no getting out of this. If you go into that trial as a simple Spiritualist, Hern could take everything from you."

"It's not certain that Hern will win," Miranda said, crossing her arms over her chest stubbornly. "Tower Keepers are still Spiritualists. If I can tell the truth out in the open, tell what actually happened and show them Mellinor, let the spirit speak for himself, there's no way they can find me guilty, *because I'm not.*"

"This is not open for debate," Banage said crossly. "Do you think I like where this is going? This whole situation is my fault. If you had another master, this would never have grown into the fiasco it is, but we are outmaneuvered."

"I can't just sit there and let him win!" Miranda shouted.

"This isn't a game, Miranda!" Banage was shouting, too, now. "If you try and face Hern head-on, you will be throwing away everything we worked together to create. You're too good a Spiritualist for me to let you risk your career like this! You know and I know that you are guiltless, that your only crime was doing the right thing in difficult circumstances. *Let that be enough.* Don't fool yourself into thinking that your fighting Hern on this will be for anything other than your own pride!"

Miranda quaked at the anger in his voice, and for a moment the old obedience nearly throttled her with a desperate need to do what Master Banage said. But Mellinor was churning inside her, his current dark and furious, his anger magnifying hers, and she could not let it go.

Banage must have felt it, too, the angry surge of the great water spirit, for she felt the enormous weight of his spirit settle on top of her as the man himself bowed his head and began to rub his eyes with a tired, jeweled hand.

"It's late," he said quietly. "A late night after many long days is no time to make weighty decisions. We'll pick this up tomorrow. Maybe after a night's rest you'll be able to see that I am trying to save you."

Miranda's anger broke at the quiet defeat in his voice. "I do see," she said, "and I am grateful. But—"

Banage interrupted her with a wave of his hand. "Sleep on it," he said. "I've given orders for you to be under house arrest tonight, so you'll be comfortable at least. We'll meet again tomorrow for breakfast in the garden, like old times. But for now, just go."

Miranda nodded and stood stiffly, mindful of every tiny noise she made in the now-silent room. As she turned to leave, she stopped suddenly. Her hand went to her pocket and fished out a white square.

"I'd almost forgotten," she said, turning back to Banage. "This is for you."

She laid the envelope on his desk. Then, with a quick bow, she turned and marched across the great stretch of empty marble to the door. Pulling it open, she plunged out of the room and down the stairs as fast as her feet could carry her.

Banage watched the door as it drifted shut, the iron hinges trained after centuries of service to never slam. When the echo of her footsteps faded, Banage let go of the breath he'd been holding and let his head slump into his hands. It never got easier, never. He sat for a while in the silence, and then, when he felt steady enough to read whatever she had written him, he let his hand fall to the letter she had placed on his desk.

When he looked at the letter, however, his eyebrows shot up in surprise. The handwriting on the front was not Miranda's, and in any case, she never addressed him as "Etmon Banage." Curious, he turned the letter over, and all other thoughts left his mind. There, pressed deep into the soft, forest-green wax was an all-too-familiar cursive *M*.

Banage dropped the envelope on his desk like it was a venomous snake. He sat there for a few moments staring at it. Then, in a fast, decisive motion, he grabbed the letter and broke the seal, tearing the paper when it would not open fast enough. A folded letter fell from the sundered envelope, landing lightly on his desk. With careful, suspicious fingers, Banage unfolded the thick parchment.

It was a wanted poster, one of those mass-copied by the army of ink-and-block spirits below the Council fortress. An achingly familiar boyish face grinned up at him from the creased paper, the charming features older, sharper, but still clearly recognizable despite more than a decade's growth. His mocking expression was captured perfectly by the delicate shading that was the Bounty Office's trademark, making the picture so lifelike Banage almost expected it to start laughing. Above the picture, a name was stenciled in block capitals: ELI MONPRESS. Below the portrait, written in almost unreadably tiny print so they could fit on one page, was a list of Eli's crimes. And below that, printed in tall, bold blocks, was WANTED, DEAD OR ALIVE, 55,000 GOLD STANDARDS.

That's what was printed, anyway, but this particular poster had been altered. First, the 55,000 had been crossed out and the number 60,000 written above it in red ink. Second, the same hand had crossed out the word WANTED with a thick, straight line and written instead the word WORTH.

"Eli Monpress," Banage read quietly. "Worth, dead or alive, sixty thousand gold standards."

A feeling of disgust overwhelmed him, and he dropped the poster, looking away as his fingers moved unconsciously over the ring on his middle finger, a setting of gold filigree of leaves and branches holding a large, murky emerald as dark and brooding as an old forest. He stayed like that for a long, silent time, staring into the dark of his office. Then, with deliberate slowness, he picked up the poster and ripped it to pieces. He fed each piece to the lamp on his desk, the heavy red-stoned ring on his thumb glowing like a star as he did so, keeping the fire from spreading anywhere Banage did not wish it to spread.

When the poster and its sundered envelope had been reduced to ash, Banage stood and walked stiffly across his office to the small, recessed door that led to his private apartments. When he reached it, he said something low, and all the lamps flickered, plunging the office into darkness. When the darkness was complete, he shut the door, locking out the smell of burnt paper that tried to follow him.

CHAPTER
2

Eli Monpress, the greatest thief in the world, was strolling through the woods. His overstuffed bag bounced against his back as he walked, and he was whistling a tune he didn't quite remember as he watched the late afternoon sunlight filter through the golden leaves, bringing with it a smell of cold air and dry wood. So pleasant was the scene, in fact, that it took him a good twenty paces to realize he was walking alone.

He stopped on his heel and spun to see Josef, his swordsman, sitting twenty paces back in the middle of the path with Nico, Josef's constant shadow, sitting beside him. Beside her, Josef's famous sword, the Heart of War, stood plunged into the hard-packed dirt, and beside it lay the enormous sack of gold they'd liberated from Mellinor's sadly destroyed treasury. Despite the fine weather, none of them looked happy.

Eli heaved a dramatic sigh. "What?"

Josef stared right back at him. "I'm not taking another step until you tell me exactly where we're going."

Eli rolled his eyes. *This again.* "I told you before. I told you this *morning*, we're going to see a friend of mine about getting Nico a new coat."

"I didn't ask what we were going to do when we got there." Josef folded his arms over his chest. "I asked you, *where are we going*? We've been walking vaguely north for almost a month now, and since yesterday we've been walking in circles around the same four miles of woods. This is the second time today we've passed that beech tree, and I'm tired of lugging your ill-gotten gains." The sack of gold jingled as his large fist landed on it. "Admit it," the swordsman said, giving Eli a superior sneer. "You're lost."

"I am not." Eli threw out his arms, taking in the scant undergrowth, rocky slopes, and slender, white-barked trees of the small valley they were in the middle of climbing out of. "We're in the great north woods, which the Shapers call the Turningwood, and the Council of Thrones doesn't have a name for because we left the Council maps a week ago. Specifically, we are in the Thousand Streams region of the Turningwood, a name you might appreciate, considering all the valleys we've had to climb through. Even more specifically, we are in the northeast corner of the Thousand Streams, where the streams are slightly less numerous. A little farther north and we'd be in the foothills of the Sleeping Mountains themselves, and a little farther east and we'd hit the frozen swamps on the coastal plain. So, as you see, I know exactly where we are, and it is exactly where we are supposed to be."

Despite such a grand display of navigation, Josef did not look impressed. "If we're where we're supposed to be, why are we still walking?"

Eli turned and started up the hill again. "Because the house of the man we are looking for isn't always in the same place."

"You mean the man isn't always in the same place," Josef said, making no sound of following him.

"No." Eli panted as he reached the crest of the valley. "I mean the house. If you don't like it, complain to him."

"*If* we ever find him," Josef said.

Eli shook his head and started down the other side of the hill, wishing that the swordsman would apply his stubbornness to something useful, like being a perfect gold carrier, or finding them something tastier than squirrel to eat. By the time he'd reached the bottom of the next valley, Josef had still not crested the ridge of the one before. Eli grimaced and kept walking, though more slowly and with one ear out for the sound of jingling gold, which would tell him if this was just a Josef bluff or if he was actually going to have to go back and push the man up the hill. Fortunately, the decision was rendered moot when he took another step forward and found nothing but air.

He yelped as the world spun upside down and sideways. Then, with a sharp pain in his ankles, it stopped, and he found himself hanging high in the branches of a tree. Blinking in surprise, Eli looked down, or up, depending, and saw he was strung up by his ankles in the branches of a large oak. That much he'd been prepared for, but how he was hanging took him by surprise. Instead of ropes, a knot of roots with dirt still clinging to them bound his feet, ankles, and lower legs. They moved as he watched, creaking with a sound very much like snickering. He was still staring at the roots and trying to figure out what had just happened when he heard Josef come over the hill. Eli craned his neck and started to yell a warning, but it was too late. The second Josef was off the rocky ravine, a snaking cluster of roots erupted from the ground and grabbed his feet. The swordsman flew into the air with a lurch and came to rest neatly beside Eli.

"Well," Eli said. "Fancy meeting you here."

Josef didn't answer; he just scowled and bent over, wiggling his foot. There was a flash, and a long knife dropped out of his boot before the roots could tighten. The swordsman caught it deftly an inch from Eli's face and bent over, reaching for the closest root.

"I wouldn't do that," Eli said, glancing up, or down. "It's a bit of a drop."

Josef followed his gaze. The ground swung dizzyingly a good thirty feet below them, but the drop was made even longer by the enormous hole the roots had left when they'd sprung. Josef shook his head in disgust and stuck the knife into his belt. "I thought you were friends with trees."

"For the last time, it doesn't work like that," Eli said. "That's like saying, 'I thought you were friends with humans.' Anyway, don't be a grouch. We've found it! This is the Awakened Wood that guards the house."

Josef sighed. "Wonderful. Fantastic welcome. Is your friend always this friendly, or are we a special exception?"

Before Eli could answer, a woman's voice interrupted.

"Eli Monpress." The words were heavy with laughter. "I wouldn't have thought we'd catch you."

Both men craned their necks. Directly below them a tall young woman in hunter's leathers stepped out from behind the tree they were dangling from, a smug smile on her tan face. She was very young, not more than sixteen, and lanky, as though she hadn't quite grown into her limbs yet. She crossed her long arms over her chest and stared at them as though daring Eli to try and talk his way out of this one. Eli opened his mouth to oblige her, but he never got the chance. From the shadows behind the girl, a pair of white, thin hands in silver manacles shot out and closed around her throat. The girl's eyes bulged and she dropped to her knees as Nico flickered into sight behind her.

"Release them," Nico said in a dry, terrifying voice. "Now."

"No, Nico!" Eli shouted. "She's not going to—"

The rest of it was lost in the girl's roar as she ducked and tumbled forward, using Nico's own iron grip to take the smaller girl with her, slamming them both into the ground with Nico on the bottom. As soon as she was on top, the girl elbowed Nico hard in the ribs. Nico gasped, and her grip faltered. The girl shot up, rolling gracefully to her feet. When she turned around, she had a long, beautiful knife in her hands, the blade glowing with its own silver light.

Nico was back on her feet in an instant, and for a breathless moment the two watched each other. Then the girl in the hunting leathers shook her head and slid her knife back into the long sheath on her thigh.

"I begin to understand why you needed that coat," the girl said, not taking her eyes off of Nico. "Let them down, gently please."

The tree made a sound like a disgruntled sigh and lowered its roots, releasing Eli and Josef just a little higher than would have been a safe drop. The men landed hard in the dirt, and while Josef was on his feet almost immediately, Eli took a bit longer to get his breath back.

"Hello, Pele," he coughed, trying to discreetly determine if his back was broken. "Always a pleasure."

Pele arched an eyebrow. "Can't say I feel the same." She glared at Nico, who was still watching her from a crouch. "Must you always bring such trouble?"

"Trouble is my element," Eli said, sitting up. "And is that any way to greet a customer?"

"Your custom is usually more trouble than it's worth," she said with a frown. "Get up. I'll take you to Slorn."

"Wait," Josef said. "You mean Slorn as in Heinricht Slorn? The swordsmith?"

"He makes a lot of things besides swords," Pele said crossly. "But yes, that Slorn, and he's going to be testy if you make him wait. Now follow me, quickly. We've wasted enough time rolling in the dirt."

"And whose fault was that?" Eli muttered, but the girl was already disappearing into the woods, slipping between the trees like a passing sunbeam.

"You never told me you knew Heinricht Slorn," Josef said, walking over to where he'd dropped the Heart of War. He almost sounded hurt.

"I couldn't," Eli said, picking the leaves out of his hair. "Not talking about him is part of knowing Slorn. He'd never sell me anything if he thought I'd been spreading his location about, or the fact that he really exists. Most people think he's a myth made up by the Shaper Wizards to sell more swords. When that tree sprung, I was half afraid he was going to have the Awakened Wood toss us out altogether because I'd brought you two. But, seeing he sent his daughter out to greet us, I think it's safe to assume we've captured his interest enough to at least get our pitch in."

"Daughter, huh?" Josef said, picking up the Heart and sliding it into its sheath on his back. "She's pretty good to throw Nico around. Must be some kind of family."

"That's one way of putting it," Eli said, wincing as he stretched his bruised back. "We should get moving, though. Pele was right about Slorn's hatred of waiting. The man is brilliant, but..." He paused, brushing the dirt off his coat as he searched for the right word. "Eccentric."

Josef snorted. "Funny way of putting it, coming from you."

Eli just gave him a look and set off through the trees.

Though she'd entered the woods only moments before them, there was no sign of Pele's passing. Eli, Josef, and Nico stumbled in the direction she'd gone, following the dry streambed that was the best they could do for a path. Now that Pele had come out to greet them, the trees were whispering openly, and what they had to say made Eli's ears burn.

"Honestly," he muttered, kicking a sapling as they passed. "She's *right here*." He looked over his shoulder. "Don't listen to them, Nico! They're just a bunch of prejudiced, gossipy old hardwoods with nothing better to do."

The trees rustled madly at this, but Nico just kept walking with her head down, giving no sign that she heard his voice or theirs. Eli looked away. The girl was looking bad. She'd been unusually quiet since they'd left Mellinor, even for Nico, and while she'd been eating as normal, she seemed to be getting thinner. Eli didn't know if that was just the effect of seeing her without her bulky coat all the time, or if he just thought she was larger than she was, but he'd heard Josef talking to her about it as well, at night when the swordsman thought he was asleep. Also, no one, wizard or otherwise, could miss the way her manacles danced on her wrist, jittering across her skin even when she was sleeping. That was new since she'd lost the coat, and Eli didn't like it one bit. Overhead, the trees were whispering again, and Eli gritted his teeth, picking up the pace as they pushed through the thickening woods.

Fortunately, they didn't have much farther to go. The woods opened up just a few steps later, and they found themselves at the edge of a sandy-bottomed valley. At the center, sitting crooked on what had been the sandy bank of a now-dead stream, was a house. It was two stories and heavy-timbered, with a shingle roof and a tall chimney made of river stones. It was a handsome house and well constructed, but quite normal looking until you got to the foundation. There, things took a turn for the bizarre. Where a normal house would have sat on the ground, or stood on stone supports, this one crouched on four wooden legs. They were made of the same dark wood as the cabin, beautifully carved with scales and lifelike wrinkles right down to the clawed feet. At first glance, this could have been passed off as eccentric architecture, but then the legs moved, like an animal shifting its weight, and the house shifted with them.

"No matter how many times I see it," Eli said, "I never get used to it." He set off across the sand, dragging Josef, who was still gawking, along behind him.

Thanks to the legs, the house's doorstep was a good

five feet off the ground. The gap was covered by a set of rickety stairs that would have been suspect in a normal building, let alone a moving one.

"I hate this part," Eli said, grabbing the rope banister as the house shifted again. "I'm already feeling seasick."

"Just go," Josef said, giving him a push. Eli grunted and stumbled forward, pulling himself up enough to knock on the door.

It was opened immediately by a scowling Pele.

"Took you long enough," she said, stepping back. "Come in and don't hang on the stairs. They're set to go any day now."

"Ever the charming and comforting hostess," Eli said as he lurched into the house. Josef and Nico followed more gracefully, and Pele shut the door behind them.

They were standing in a tiny entryway lined with pairs of oiled boots and racks of heavy coats. Eli pressed himself against the wall, partially to make room for Pele to get by and partially to steady himself against the sway of the house as it rocked on its spindly wooden legs. If the motion bothered Pele, she didn't let on; she simply turned and motioned for them to follow her down a long, narrow hallway riddled with doors to other rooms. They passed a sitting room stuffed with books, a small kitchen with a warm hearth and a heavy table piled with chopped vegetables, and even a stone-tiled bathroom complete with an iron tub and a barrel full of steaming water. As they walked, Eli could hear the house adjusting to accommodate their presence, the scrape of chairs scooting themselves under tables when they passed the kitchen, or open books slamming shut on the library desk. Josef must have heard it, too, for the swordsman's hands went to rest on the blades at his hip. Eli let him be nervous. Explaining the complex ecosystem of Slorn's house was more work than he had the patience for at the moment.

The long hallway ended at a closed door. Pele stopped and knocked softly. Almost instantly a deep voice inside rumbled, and Pele pulled the handle.

Almost too late, Eli remembered this was Josef and Nico's first time visiting Slorn. A warning of some sort was probably wise.

"Remember," he whispered over his shoulder as they stepped through the door. "Don't stare."

Josef gave him a confused look, but then they were walking through the door and his eyes went wide as Eli's meaning became clear.

They were standing at the end of a long, well-lit room with a cheery fire in the hearth and a dozen lamps swinging from the tall rafters. Long as the room was, it was mostly taken up by a heavy table large enough to seat eight full-grown men, but which was currently covered with everything from pieces of driftwood to incredibly intricate parts of unknown machinery. At the table's head, an enormous man sat hunched over, working an iron ingot between his enormous hands like a potter works clay. At first glance, he could have been one of the giant, northern woodsmen, but with one slight, important difference. At his shoulders, where his neck should have been, rose the furry head of a black bear.

It was a sharp change, human skin suddenly giving way to black fur, as though the man's own head had been chopped off and a bear's put in its place. But other than the horrible wrongness, it was a natural transition. The man part of him looked like any other man, and the bear part looked like any other bear. His nose was black and wrinkled and it quivered under his slow breathing. Yellow teeth glinted in a jaw that could crush a man's head, but his dark, wide-set eyes were calm and thoughtful as they watched the iron yield to his hands. Although Eli knew what to expect, a shudder ran from his feet to his head. No matter how many times it happened, seeing Slorn was always a bracing experience.

"You're staring," said a gruff voice, more growl than speech. The bear looked up, his dark eyes passing over Eli's shoulder to the man behind him. "I heard Monpress tell you not to do that."

Eli heard the creak of leather as Josef's hands tightened on the knives at his hip, and the bear-headed man made a low rumbling sound that was eerily close to a chuckle. "Don't insult my house with those dull blades, swordsman. Unless you mean to draw the monster on your back, or the monster at your side"—his dark eyes flicked to Nico, who was pinned to Josef's arm—"I suggest you calm down."

Josef relaxed slightly, and the bear grinned, a disturbing sight. "Come," Slorn said. He tossed the iron down and motioned to the bench. "Sit and tell me how I might get rid of you."

"Now, Heinricht," Eli said, plopping down at the table across from him, "is that any way to treat your customers?"

"I'm a craftsman," Slorn said, resting his furry chin on his knuckles. "Not a shopkeeper. Get to the point."

Eli leaned forward. "You see that timid little thing beside my swordsman?" he whispered conspiratorially. "I need you to make her a new coat."

Slorn's dark eyes flicked over to the girl who was huddling in the doorway, as far from the bear-headed man as she could get, her eyes wide and disturbingly bright. They stared at each other for a long minute, then Slorn gave Eli a tired glare.

"When you asked for a cloth that could hide a demonseed's presence," he said, "and manacles to hold it down, I made them. I did it in thanks for the great service you had done me, and I asked no questions. But the debts between us are paid, Monpress. I took the risk of letting you find me today out of respect for our history together, but understand that doing what you ask now will put me in a very tenuous position. What compensation have you brought to make it worth my while?"

Eli's smile brightened, and he motioned to Josef. The swordsman hefted the sack of Mellinor's gold, which he had lugged halfway across the known world for this purpose, walked over to the table, and set it down with a very satisfactory thump. Eli reached out and undid the leather strap, letting the gold spill out in a glittering cascade.

"A king's ransom," he said smugly. "Well, part of one. There's enough in there to buy you a castle, though it'd be up to you to put legs on it. I think that should more than cover one little coat."

Slorn looked at the pile and then at Eli. "I asked you what compensation you'd brought. All I see here is a lot of money."

Eli's smug expression faltered just a hair. "Surely even the great Heinrich Slorn needs to buy things on occasion."

"If I wanted *money*"—Slorn spat the word with disgust—"I could get more than this from far better company." He leaned back, folding his arms over his massive chest. "What else did you bring?"

"False hopes, apparently." Eli sighed. "Look, bearface,

we're in a bit of a bind." His hand shot out and grabbed Nico's wrist, pulling her out from behind Josef and pinning her arm to the table before she could react. He pressed it down, letting the sound of the manacle rattling against the wood make his point for him.

"I don't have to tell you what that means," he said softly, meeting Slorn's dark, animal stare. "You made them. If you don't want gold, tell me your price and I'll steal it for you, but if you're not going to help us, just say so and we'll get out of your fur."

Nico tugged her hand out of Eli's grasp, but he didn't look at her. He kept his eyes on the bear-headed man, who was scratching his muzzle thoughtfully.

"Perhaps we can come to an arrangement," Slorn growled at last. "I've been doing some work on my own, and I think I can make your girl a coat better than the one before. Something made to withstand your"—he paused, looking them over—"harsh lifestyle. In return, however, I want you to do a job for me."

Eli arched his eyebrows. "And what kind of job would this be?"

"Something right up your alley, I'd think," Slorn said. "I'm afraid that's all I can tell you before we have an agreement."

Warning bells sounded in Eli's head, and he gave the crafter a suspicious look. "It's not usually my policy to make deals without knowing what I'm getting into."

Slorn shrugged. "If you don't like it, you're free to go and find a coat elsewhere. Better decide quickly, though. Your demonseed is starting to make the furniture nervous."

As if on cue, the bench they were sitting on started to

rumble and tried to tip backward. Josef slammed his feet and leaned forward, pinning it with his weight. Eli shook his head and turned back to the bear-headed man.

"You make a good point," he said. "All right, we'll take your job, *but*"—he pointed his finger directly at Slorn's snout—"you're making the coat first. Nico's an important part of my team. I need her in peak condition if we're going to do a job, especially one you won't tell me about beforehand."

On the other side of Josef, Eli heard Nico straighten up, and a warm feeling of satisfaction went through him. Perhaps the girl wasn't as unfeeling as she made out.

Slorn, however, did not look convinced. "How do I know you won't just run off?"

Eli clasped his chest. "You wound me! I would never risk losing your good opinion, or all the nice toys you keep making me."

"Fair enough," Slorn said, standing up. "You have your deal. Pele, take the girl upstairs and measure her. I'll start on the cloth tonight."

Pele nodded and pushed off the wall she'd been leaning on. She looked at Nico and jerked her head in the direction of the tiny staircase that led to the house's attic. "This way."

If possible, Nico's face went paler. She looked at Josef, almost like she was asking permission, but the swordsman just stared right back at her. Biting her thin lip, Nico left Josef's side and crept up the stairs after Pele, keeping her arms crossed over her chest and staying as far from the walls as she could. When she reached the tiny landing, she gave Josef and Eli one last terrified look before Pele ushered her into a brightly lit room and shut the door behind them.

"They won't be long," Slorn said, moving across the room with surprising lightness for such a tall, broad man. "We need to move quickly. The manacles were never meant to do their job alone."

"I thought the coat was just a cover," Josef said, standing up. "A front to hide what she is so the spirits won't panic."

"That's part of it," Slorn answered. "But demons feed on all parts of a spirit, including fear. In the absence of its cover, the seed has been gorging, and not just on the fear around the girl, but on her own as well. As it eats, it grows, and as it grows, the girl's fight to keep her mind becomes harder and harder." The bear-headed man knelt down by a chest that opened instantly for him, the lid popping up of its own accord. "I cannot undo the damage that has already been done, but I can slow down the process by hiding what she is, cutting off the demon's food source and allowing Nico to regain some measure of control."

He stopped searching through the trunk and turned to look at them, his bear eyes dark and sad. "You understand, of course, that this is only a delay. No matter how many layers of protection we swaddle the girl in, so long as she lives, her seed will continue to grow. Whether it comes tomorrow or a year from now, the end will be the same. The demonseed will eat her, body and soul, and there will be nothing you can do."

He was looking at Eli as he spoke, but it was Josef who answered, and the vehemence in his voice made them both flinch.

"Nico is a survivor," the swordsman said. "When I found her, she was a breath away from death. I waited for her to die, but she didn't. She kept breathing. Every breath should have been her last, but she always found another. She'll beat this, too, bear man, so make the damn coat."

Slorn stared at him in abashed silence, but Josef ignored him and stood up. "I saw a bath on the way in." He slid the Heart of War from his back and dropped it on the table with a resounding gong from the iron and a painful shudder from the wood. "If Nico asks, that's where I'll be. If anyone else needs me, they can wait."

With that, he turned and stomped off down the hall. Slorn watched him go, looking as astonished as a bear could. Eli just watched from his seat at the table, grinning like a maniac.

"He certainly doesn't mince words," Slorn said, turning back to the chest.

"No," Eli said and grinned wider. "That's why I like him."

Slorn shook his head and turned back to the chest.

Eli watched him for a moment, but he could see the work settling on the bear-headed man's shoulders like a vulture, and he decided it was time to move somewhere more comfortable before Slorn forgot him completely.

"I'm going to freshen up as well," he announced. "I presume the guest bedroom is still in the same place?"

"More or less," Slorn said. "Top of the stairs, third door on the right."

"Third door, much obliged." With a gracious nod, Eli gathered his bag and set off up the stairs, leaving Slorn alone in the great room. On the broad worktable, the enormous pile of gold glittered in the fire light, forgotten by everyone.

CHAPTER 3

Gin was asleep in the flower bed that surrounded the low building where Miranda kept her chambers when she was in Zarin. His legs kicked in his sleep, sending the well-turned dirt flying, and his shifting patterns swirled in strange, spiraling shapes across his body, all except for the patch between the shoulder blades. There, the wound from his fight with the demon girl Nico stood out like a red brand beneath the dried layers of green polluce the stable master had smeared over it. It looked better than before, but it would never be part of his patterns again. Even in his sleep, he seemed to favor the wound, cringing away from it whenever he rolled over.

Suddenly, his dream running stopped. He lay perfectly still, except for his ears, which swiveled in quick circles, each moving independently from the other. The night was as quiet as a city night could be, but Gin jerked up, his orange eyes wide open, watching the corner of the building. A few moments later, Miranda flew around it. She saw him at once, and ran toward him, moving strangely, keeping her breathing almost too regular and her face down so that the last evening light couldn't touch it. This was probably to keep Gin from seeing that she was crying, but his mistress had never fully appreciated just how much his orange eyes could pick up, especially in low light.

Still, he played along, rolling over and sitting up properly as she came near, his tail wrapped around his paws. Miranda didn't slow when she reached him, didn't say a word. She slammed into him and slumped down, and though she never made a sound, the salty smell of tears filled the air until he had trouble breathing. After several silent minutes, Gin decided to take the initiative. After all, if they needed to escape, it would be best to do it now, before the lamps were lit.

He lowered his head until he was level with hers. "Are you going to tell me what's wrong?"

Miranda made a sound somewhere between a curse and a sob. Gin growled and nudged her with his paw. "Don't be difficult. Spit it out."

"It makes me so angry!" Her answer was a whip crack, and Gin flinched. Miranda muttered an apology, scrubbing at her eyes in a motion he was probably not supposed to notice. "It's just...How could they do this to me? How could they betray me like this? All my life, from the moment I understood that the voices I heard were spirits, all I've wanted was to be a Spiritualist. To do good and defend the spirits and be a hero and all the stuff they tell you when you start your apprenticeship. And now here I am, on trial for making the decisions the Spirit Court trained me to make. It's not *right*!"

That last word was almost a wail, and she buried her head in her hands. Gin shifted anxiously. He hadn't seen her this upset in a long time.

"Try to remember that I've been in a stable having cold, foul-smelling gunk smeared on my back all evening," he said. "Could you be a little more specific?"

Miranda leaned back against him with a huff and, in a quick, clipped voice, told him everything. The arrest, her meeting with Banage, the accusations, and Hern's compromise.

"A compromise, can you believe it?" she said, digging her fingers into the dirt. "Extortion is more like it."

"Being a Tower Keeper doesn't sound so bad," Gin offered.

"It *wouldn't* be," Miranda said, "if I were getting the promotion for any reason other than Hern playing on Master Banage's sense of duty toward me! Oh, I hate to think what other concessions Master Banage had to make to get that out of Hern. The man is a slime."

"But if Banage already made the concessions, why not take the offer?" Gin said, sweeping his tail back and forth. "The problem is the Tower Keepers thinking your actions reflect badly on them, right? So let them have their trial. If you're right and Hern's only doing this to make Banage look bad, why give him more fodder by fighting? He can't find fault if you keep strictly to the role of the dutiful Spiritualist."

Miranda gave him a sideways look. "That's a very political answer for a dog who always says he doesn't understand politics."

"I don't understand politics," Gin growled. "But I understand pride, and that's what this is really about.

Sometimes the price of doing the right thing is higher than we realize when we do it. Knowing the consequences, would you have acted differently in Mellinor?"

Miranda froze and thought for a second. "No," she said firmly.

"There you have it," Gin said with a shrug. "So pay the price. Take the out Banage bought you, appease the Tower Keeper's pride, and move on."

"I will not," Miranda said. "Maybe it is about pride, mine as much as anyone's, but I cannot, *will* not, bow to Hern's bullying. Those things he accuses me of *did not* happen, and I will not stand by while he smears my name and my spirits with his lies."

"So, what, you're just going to throw Banage's help away?" Gin growled. "What about the part where losing this trial could lose you your spirits? Your pride is your own, and I respect your right to beat yourself bloody over it, but we're not something to be thrown away so cheaply."

"That won't happen," Miranda said fiercely, gripping her hands until her rings cut into her fingers. "Trust me, we've got right on our side. We won't lose, especially not to Hern."

Gin looked at her, his orange eyes narrowed to slits. "And would you bet all of us on that?"

Miranda didn't answer. They sat in silence for a while, staring out at the darkening streets. Gin sat very still, watching in the way that spirits watch. He could see each of Miranda's spirits, the flow of their souls pulsing softly with the beating of her heart. Each spirit shone softly with its own unique color, and below them, buried deep within Miranda's own bright soul, Mellinor's spirit turned in his sleep. The Great Spirit was enormous and alien even to Gin, ancient beyond comprehension, yet it was also a part of Miranda now, and dear to him because of it, even beyond the natural reverence he owed a Great Spirit. Each glowing spirit, even Mellinor, had a tendril reaching out from its core. These were the bonds, the strong, deep network of binding promises, at the center of which was Miranda. All of them, even the tiny moss spirit, had abandoned their homes to follow her. From the moment they'd sworn their oaths, she'd become their center, their Great Spirit, their mistress, worthy of service. The thought of being taken from her made him afraid in ways he hadn't felt since he was puppy. Yet the Spirit Court could do that, if it chose. Miranda's oath had forged the bonds, but every one of those promises had been made under the authority of the Court. So long as Miranda believed in that authority, the Court owned her rings and the spirits inside, even him. As with all human magic, it all came down to will. So long as Miranda wasn't willing to go against the organization she'd pledged her life to, they were all bound to the Spirit Court's whims. Still, the choice was Miranda's, and despite what he'd said, Gin knew her well enough to know her decision. So he waited patiently, watching as the city lamps flickered on, the tiny fire spirits winking to life as the lamplighters walked the districts, filling the dark streets with soft, dancing light.

When Miranda answered at last, her voice was small but steady. "Gin," she said, "I have always lived my life according to principle. I believe more than anything that there is right and there is wrong, and that the gap between them is wider than any words can bridge. No amount of good intentions or clever plans can turn one into the other. What we did in Mellinor, for Mellinor, was the right thing. I will not sit by and let anyone say it wasn't."

"Does that mean you're going to fight?"

"Yes," Miranda said and smiled, tilting her head to look up at him. "To the great inconvenience of everyone involved."

"The life of principle is never convenient," Gin said with a toothy grin. "At least not that I've seen."

Miranda laughed, and Gin got up with a long stretch. "Now that that's decided," he growled, "you should get inside. You're crabby when you haven't slept."

Miranda stood up stiffly, brushing the dirt off her trousers and looking forlornly at the deep rut Gin had made in the flower bed. "The garden committee is going to kill us."

"Eh," Gin said, shrugging. "You're already on trial for treason. What more could they do?"

Miranda rolled her eyes at that, but she was smiling. As Gin nosed her toward the door of her building, she caught his muzzle in her hands and gave him a serious look.

"Thank you," she said, "for being a pushy ass."

"What else am I here for?"

Miranda shook her head and walked into her building, trudging up the stairs to the tiny suite of rooms the Spirit Court allotted all traveling Spiritualists. Gin watched her until she was out of sight, then moved out to the alley to watch the light come on in her window. The lamp flickered, and then, a minute later, the room went dark again. Satisfied that things would be fine until tomorrow, Gin ambled back to his flower bed and flopped down, resting his head in a soft, sweet-smelling clump of something silver-green with furry leaves, and, after scarcely two breaths, promptly fell back to sleep.

Far away from the low, plain buildings where the common Spiritualists kept their rooms, at the other end of the Spirit Court's district where the architecture took a turn for the large and ornate, Grenith Hern was sitting on his balcony enjoying a bottle of wine. Bright light from his sitting room shone through the open double doors, highlighting the graying gold of his long, straight hair and casting his shadow in perfect contrast on the empty street below, a fine, trim figure in fine, trim clothing. This was not by chance. Hern often sat this way in the evenings, for he enjoyed the picture he presented, and the view of the city was very fine.

From here he could look down the ridge to see the lamps flicker on, one pair at a time. As he watched them, he couldn't help thinking, as he always did when he spent his evenings at home, how, if he were Rector Spiritualis, he would have put every lamp spirit in the city under the control of a single fire, so that they could all be lit at once. The current method of lighting with a pair of lamp lighters walking around telling the lamps when to flare was old-fashioned and inefficient, not to mention a horrible waste of an opportunity to make the Whitefall family owe the Spiritualists a favor for something that would cost the Court very little. Still, there was nothing to be done as he was merely Head of the Tower Keepers, and he certainly wasn't about to give Banage the idea.

Hern sighed at the waste and refilled his glass, his lace cuff holding itself neatly out of the way of the dark wine.

He was just about to take a sip when he heard the sound he'd been sitting on the balcony waiting to catch: the whisper of dust as it moved up the smooth white marble of his townhouse walls. He turned his chair to face the far corner of his balcony as a stream of dark-colored dust began to collect in the tray he'd left out for it. He waited patiently as the dust gathered, forming a thin layer at first, then growing to a large pile. As it collected, a smell began to collect in the air, char and smoke, and it quickly became clear that the powder on the tray was not, in fact, dust, but fine, gray ash.

When the last of the ash had collected, Hern leaned forward, a smile on his slightly lined but still handsome face. "You're early. I hope it's good news."

The ash sighed, sending a smell of burnt hardwood into the air. "For your information, it's been a very difficult day. I will never get used to moving about in such a spread-out fashion, being stepped on and losing bits of myself in the street. It's not to be borne."

Hern made a tsking noise. "Come now, Allio. You're far more useful as a pile of ash than you ever were as a tree."

"I'm glad you think so," the ash snapped, sliding away from Hern in a sulk. "Considering it was your fault I got burned."

Hern shrugged. "You knew the risks when you took the oath. Come, enough complaining. What news do you bring?"

The ash made a grumpy sound, but it gathered itself into a neat pile and began its report. "I put myself in Banage's office, just as you told me. Sure enough, he had the girl brought straight to him. They had quite the argument." The ash rippled wistfully. "Now *those* are Spiritualists. Such conviction, and the spirit the girl had in her, I haven't seen the like since I was rooted in my own forest."

Hern kicked the tray, and the ash quickly got back on topic. "Banage did just what you said he would. He made the offer and left out all the particulars."

"And?" Hern prompted.

"And she didn't take him up on it," the ash finished. "He cut her off and sent her away before she could deny him outright, but I get the impression she's not the kind to take the easy road."

Hern leaned back in his chair, feeling very pleased with himself. "She'll fight for certain, then. I'd bet money on it."

"You'll have to if you want to win," the ash said. "It's one thing to scare old Tower Keepers into signing a paper, but something else again to get them to vote against her in front of the whole Court. You're going to need to put your gold where your mouth is before this is over, I think."

"Ash doesn't think," Hern snapped. "Leave the details to me. Anyway, money won't be an issue. The duke will be coming into town tomorrow, and this is as much an issue for him as it is for me. In the meanwhile, I want you to go to every Tower Keeper who came into town for this event and invite them over. I feel the need to throw a party."

"*Every* Tower Keeper?" the ash said. "Master, I've been out all day. I can't spend all night crawling through town bringing your invitations to *every* Tower Keeper. It's impossible, I—"

"Allio," Hern said, drumming his fingers on his chair, his rings glittering in the light. "I have twenty-one other spirits making demands on my energies. It's very tiring, and I've been thinking I should cut the dross. Now, more than ever, is the time to prove yourself useful. After all, I think I have already been kinder than most, keeping you as my spirit even after the unfortunate burning incident. What a shame if I were forced to give you up now, just because you weren't willing to put in a little extra effort, don't you think?"

The ash swirled on the platter, making little hissing noises. After a few turns, it stopped and lay flat in a defeated heap. "Of course, Master," it said softly. "I wouldn't dream of disappointing you."

"I know you wouldn't," Hern said with a cool smile. "Off with you, then."

The ash bowed and slithered off the platter, disappearing over the balcony's edge with a soft rasp. Hern, however, was already up, walking into his parlor and yelling for his housekeeper to wake up and prepare the kitchen, for he was going to have guests. Once the old woman was roused, Hern locked himself in his office and pulled out the notes he'd prepared for just such an occasion. Making Banage compromise to save his favorite had been sweet, but this promised to be far sweeter, and his face broke into an enormous grin as he leaned over and began to write out his speech.

By the time the first of the Tower Keepers arrived, he was well into his conclusion and feeling more confident than ever that here, at last, was his chance to take something precious from Banage once and for all. When he dropped his pen and went out to greet his guests, he was all confident smiles and charm, and for once, not a bit of it was faked.

CHAPTER
4

The sun was barely over the valley edge when Eli emerged, yawning and disheveled, from the house on legs. As he climbed down the rickety steps, he noticed with surprise that the house was about fifteen feet farther down the dry riverbed from where it had stood the night before. Eli paused a moment, wondering whether he should be concerned that he'd slept right through the move, but he let it go with a shrug. Such things were to be expected when you visited Slorn.

On the flat stretch of sand where the house had stood yesterday, Slorn was already hard at work. He was standing still, stroking his muzzle with long, patient fingers. All around him, laid out in a rough circle with the bear-headed man at its center, was an enormous collection of sewing materials. There were bolts of cloth, enormous spools of thread, skeins of yarn, scissors, buttons, needles, everything you could think of to make a coat. For the most part, Slorn just stood there, still as a statue, but every few minutes he would walk over to one of the objects, a length of silk, say, or a pin poked in a wad of dyed wool, and stare at it hard, like it was the only thing worth looking at in the entire world. He didn't seem to notice Eli, not even when the thief walked up to the edge of his circle and cleared his throat. Eli, quickly tired of not being noticed, left the craftsman to his flotsam and went to look for his swordsman.

He didn't have to go far. Josef was on the opposite side of the house, where the dry river had cut below the tree-lined bank. Nico was with him, as always, perched on a flat white stone with her chin in her hands, watching. She was wearing an outfit that must have been Pele's at one point, a girl's cut sleeve shirt and matching large-pocketed pants that actually fit, for once. It was a nice change from her usual threadbare attire, but her hard look warned off any compliments Eli might have made before she turned her eyes back to Josef.

For his part, the swordsman paid his audience no attention whatsoever. Despite the cold morning air, Josef was shirtless. He'd taken off the bandages as well, and the wounds from his fight with Coriano stood up in red, puckered lines against his pale, scarred skin. The Heart of War was in his hands, its black, dull blade like a hole in the morning light. He held it out in front of him, the muscles in his arms straining against the weight, as though he'd been holding it like that for a long, long time. Then, without warning, Josef pulled the blade back and swung. The enormous sword moved lightning fast, almost too fast for Eli's eyes to keep up with it, flying toward the thin trunk of a sapling. Just before it hit, the blade stopped with a whistle of terrified air, its notched, dull edge quivering less than a hair's width from the sapling's smooth white bark. The tree creaked and shuddered, dropping a snow of tiny, white-green leaves to join the growing pile at its base.

"It's a good thing Slorn's on the other side," Eli said, taking a seat next to Nico. "I don't think he'd like you scaring his trees naked."

Josef pulled back the Heart to its first position. "Daily training is the breath of swordsmanship."

"Profound," Eli said. "But can't you breathe on something less excitable?"

Josef lowered his sword and looked at him. "Do you mind?"

Eli shrugged and leaned back on the warm stone, watching in silence as Josef prepared to take another swing. As the swordsman moved, Eli couldn't help but notice how Joseph's injuries seemed to be dragging on him. Though Josef never flinched or showed any sign of pain, there was a hitch in his movements at the point in the swing when his arm stretched too far, a certain pause in his steady breaths that made Eli supremely uncomfortable.

"Josef," he said hesitantly, "we're going to be here for another day at least; why don't you take a break? Enjoy the scenery or something?"

"I am enjoying it," Josef said as he swung his sword again at the poor, terrified sapling.

"Why are you training so hard, anyway?" Eli said. "Don't most swordsmen let their old wounds heal before they start prepping to get their next ones? You beat Coriano. Can't you let it go for just a little bit?"

Josef stopped midswing and plunged the Heart into the sandy creek bed.

"Eli," he said, leaning hard on the hilt of his sword, "do you know how I beat Coriano?"

Slightly taken aback, Eli guessed, "Thoroughly?"

"I used the Heart," Josef said, nodding to the blade. "So, though he is dead and I am alive, I lost. It was the Heart who beat him, not me."

"But the Heart can't move without you," Eli pointed out.

"Don't mistake the Heart's power for mine," Josef said bitterly. He straightened up, pulling the blade out of the sand and returning it to first position. "All my life, I've had one goal: to push myself as far as I can go. To be the strongest I can be. If I let the Heart win all my battles for me, then what's the point of even holding a sword?"

The question didn't require an answer, and Eli didn't offer one. Point made, Josef turned his attention back to his sword, preparing for the next swing. Seeing that any further conversation was pointless, Eli shoved his hands in his pockets and walked back toward the house in search of breakfast.

An hour later he was bathed, dressed, and helping himself to a plate of fruit, bread, and whatever else he could find in Slorn's pantry when Josef and Nico finally came in. The girl took a seat on one of the stools along the wall, but Josef walked straight through the kitchen to the large water barrel, grabbing a bucket from the shelf as he passed. He dipped the bucket in the barrel, filling it to the brim with the cold water and, after a bracing breath, proceeded to dump the whole thing over his head. Eli jumped back with a yelp, dancing away from the flying water as Josef gave himself a shake.

"You're a wonderful houseguest, you know that?" Eli

said, wiping the water off the table. Josef just shrugged and helped himself to an apple from Eli's plate. He leaned against the heavy wooden table as he ate, staring through the window. Outside, Slorn was still standing in his circle of sewing materials, his bear head warped to monstrous size by the wobbly glass.

"He gives me the creeps," Josef said quietly, taking a bite out of what had been Eli's apple.

"How so?" Eli said. "Is it because of the—" he made a gesture, outlining a muzzle in the air in front of his face.

"More than that." Josef looked around at the small, tidy kitchen. "This whole place has been giving me the creeps since we came in. Rugs that slide out of the way before you step on them, cabinets shutting themselves when they've been left open. It's not natural. And then there's the constant feeling that we're being watched." Josef grimaced. "It's like the whole house is alive."

Well, Eli thought, munching a block of yellow cheese, it had been bound to come up sooner or later. He was only glad he didn't have to give this explanation in front of Slorn. The bear-headed man was a stickler for particulars, and Josef explanations required lots of glossing over.

"Not alive," Eli said, "*awake*. Like an awakened sword, only this time it's cabinets and plates." He held up his empty breakfast plate. "Awakening an entire house is pretty extreme, but that's Slorn for you."

Josef gave him a flat look that was dangerously close to not caring, and Eli tried again. "I know 'wizard stuff' isn't exactly your forte, but try and follow me here. You know about awakened blades, right? Well, this is an awakened house. Unlike a sword, though, a house isn't just one spirit, but hundreds, maybe thousands, all working together. That's how it moves. The legs work with the supports, which work with the nails, which work with the hearth. None of these could move the house on its own, but together they're far more powerful. The secret is getting them to work as a team. It's called 'spirit unity,' and it's a very secret and well-guarded Shaper wizard technique. Even I don't know exactly how Slorn does it, especially with so many small, sleepy, mundane spirits. I've tried asking, but he bites my head off every time I bring it up, something about respecting Shaper secrets."

"So Slorn's a Shaper," Josef said, looking out the window. "I've heard stories, but I've never met one."

"And you're not likely to," Eli said with a shrug. "They keep to themselves. Of course, technically, you still haven't met one. Slorn's an ex-Shaper."

Josef's eyebrows shot up. "What, did he get kicked out?"

"Kicked out or left on his own." Eli said. "I don't know which for sure. But I do know it had something to do with how he got that head."

They both looked out the window where the bear-headed man was still working, this time kneeling in the sand and drawing something with a long stick, muttering to himself.

"How *did* he end up like that?" Josef said softly. "Did the Shapers curse him or something?"

"Powers, no," Eli said, laughing. "There's no such thing as a curse. Slorn's head is his own doing, though, again, I don't know the particulars. I've known Slorn for a long time, but he's tight-lipped about the past. He's had that head the whole time I've known him, though. All I know is that it used to be the head of the great bear spirit that watched over these woods. The bear and Slorn made some kind of deal, and Slorn ended up with a bear's head but a man's body and mind. I don't know why he did it, but I know one thing for sure." Eli pointed two fingers at his eyes. "Those black eyes of his aren't just for show. They're bear eyes, real ones, and they can see as spirits see."

Josef gave him a curious look, clearly not comprehending how impressive this was, so Eli explained further. "You know how wizards are humans who can hear the voices of spirits, right? Well, even the best wizards can't see the spirit world. We can feel it sometimes, especially if the spirits are very strong, but we can't see it. It's like we as a species lack that sense, like our eyes are only half functional, seeing only half of the world. That's why spirits are always complaining about human blindness, because to them, we are blind. Most spirits don't even see as we do. Like this table." He knocked on the heavy wood he was leaning against. "It has no eyes, no sense of vision as we think of it; yet to it, we're the blind ones. But Slorn's different." Eli turned to gaze out the window. "He can see as they see, and that gives him a tremendous advantage as a craftsman. The things he makes are literally on an entirely different level from other goods, even other Shaper stuff, because Slorn is the only human crafter who can actually *see* what he's doing."

Josef pursed his lips. "Why in the world did the Shapers kick him out, then? If he's that good, I'd think they'd be after him like mad."

"They would be," said an annoyed voice behind them. "If they could find us."

Eli, Josef, and Nico whirled around to see Pele leaning

against the doorway, looking cross. Eli relaxed when he saw her, but Josef looked put out, and Nico looked deadly furious. Neither of them was used to people being able to sneak up on them. For her part, Pele just crossed her arms and gave the three of them a sour look.

"Next time you decide to gossip about your host," she said, "don't do it inside his awakened house. When I tell you the walls have ears, it's not a figure of speech."

"Don't be prickly, Pele," Eli said. "If your walls were listening, they know I didn't say anything to my companions I haven't said directly to Slorn's face. Have a little faith in me, darling."

Pele looked skeptical. "Slorn wants to see you outside. All of you."

Eli, Josef, and Nico exchanged a look, then stood up and filed out. Pele brought up the rear, but Eli hung back, letting the swordsman and the demonseed outpace them.

"So," he said quietly, glancing at Pele, "it's 'Slorn' all the time, now?"

"Shaper tradition requires distance between a master and his pupil," Pele said. "Technically, as my father, he shouldn't be teaching me at all, but it's not like there's anyone else." She looked up as they exited the house, staring north at the distant snowcapped mountains. "I don't even remember the Shaper mountain."

"Well," Eli said, putting an arm around her shoulder, "you're not missing much. It's dreadfully boring."

Pele shot him a glare, and Eli removed his arm before she did it for him, hurrying down to the riverbed to stand beside Josef at the edge of Slorn's circle.

Slorn himself was standing at the center beside the carefully stacked pile of materials that had passed his rigorous examination. His bear face was impossible to read, but his movements were anxious as he motioned his guests closer.

"I've finished material preparations for the coat," he said gruffly. "But before I begin the cloth, I'll need to take one final measurement."

"What?" Josef said. "Did the girl miss an inch last night?"

"This measurement can't be taken with tape," Slorn said. "This coat doesn't just hide Nico's body; it hides the nature of her soul, and what lives inside it. For that, I need to take Nico up into the mountains." His dark eyes flicked to Josef. "Alone."

"Why?" Josef said, hand drifting to the Heart's hilt. "What do you need that you can't do here?"

"Those are the terms," Slorn said. "If you don't like them, you can leave."

Josef looked supremely uncomfortable, and Eli was about to say something to deflect the tension when Nico stepped forward, her cracked-leather boots soundless on the packed sand. "I'll go."

Eli blinked in surprise. "Are you sure?"

Nico just gave him a scathing "of course" look over her shoulder before going to stand at Slorn's side. The bear-headed man nodded and turned to Pele. "Bring these"—he pointed to the pile of materials at his feet—"to my workroom. Eli, you and your swordsman can put the rest back into storage."

Eli gaped at him. "What part of our deal says we're your grunt labor?"

But Slorn had already turned and started walking toward the woods, Nico following close behind him. Pele just grinned and started gathering the chosen materials. A moment later, Josef started picking things up as well. When it was clear he wasn't going to be able to get out of this one, Eli sighed and started lugging bolts of cloth into his arms, muttering under his breath about Shaper wizards and the dreadful decline in service. Josef, however, was ignoring him. The swordsman picked up the balls of yarn and yards of cloth with only half an eye to what he was grabbing. His real attention was on the trees, where Nico and Slorn had vanished into the forest's shadow, and nothing Eli said could draw him away from them.

Nico and Slorn moved silently through the forest. They followed no path, but they did not need one. The trees parted for them, the young hardwoods creaking softly as they lifted their branches. Slorn nodded his thanks as he passed. The trees rustled in return but then grew still as Nico walked by.

They walked without speaking until they reached the foot of a steep, leaf-strewn slope. There, Slorn began to climb, his heavy boots moving surely over the slick leaves. Nico followed more cautiously, digging her hands into the wet leaf litter to keep from slipping. They climbed for a long time, and as they got higher, the trees began to change. Slender oaks and birches gave way to heavier, darker trees Nico couldn't name. They clung to the slope in great knots of root and stone, looming enormous and dark, their black leaves blotting out the sunlight until the ground was a dim patchwork of shadows.

As they climbed in the dark, the need to flit ahead through the shadows was overwhelming. Why, something inside Nico whispered, should she crawl like an animal?

She could have been at the top ten times over by now. But Nico forced the feeling down. Such thinking was dangerous. Shadows were the demon's highway, and moving through them, even for a short jump like this, always made her feel like a shadow herself. Without her coat, it was easy to lose focus, to forget to come out of the dark. Easier for the thing inside her to go places it shouldn't, the places in her mind where she hoarded her humanity. A cold, clammy feeling began to wrap around her, and Nico shook her head, focusing her attention to a dagger point on Slorn's back as they trudged on. To stay with Josef, to stay human, she needed to keep her mind clear, sharp. It was only a little longer. She would see what Slorn wanted her to see, and then go back. Easy, simple. She repeated those words again, and deep in the dark behind her eyes, something began to snicker.

Finally Slorn stopped. They were high now, the air cold and heavy with the smell of snow. The strange trees were shorter here, thinner, and Nico caught glimpses of blue sky through the branches. Yet the sun seemed to shy away from them, leaving the thin woods at the top of the slope darker than ever. Everything was quiet. Despite their height, no wind rustled the trees, and no animals moved in their branches. The slope was still, a heavy, unnatural stillness that pressed down on Nico like deep water, and she had the strong feeling she should not be here.

"What you are feeling is the will of the valley," Slorn said softly, turning to face her, his gruff voice grating against the silence. "We woke it years ago and tasked it with keeping things away."

Nico looked around, confused. She didn't see a valley,

just the slope and the strange trees. Slorn saw her confusion, and he motioned for her to look at him, his voice
becoming deathly serious.

"What I am about to show you," he said, "you must tell
no one, not even your companions. If you cannot promise
me this, I cannot make your coat. Will you promise?"

Nico looked up at him hesitantly. No one, not even
Josef, had ever asked her to promise something. She
thought about it a moment, weighing the weight of a
secret against the necessity of her coat and her own growing curiosity, and then she nodded.

Slorn turned and walked up the slope, motioning for
her to follow. Nico did, slowly, fighting against the growing certainty that she should turn around and run while
she still could. She was so focused on putting one foot in
front of the other that she almost didn't see Slorn's shape
flicker ahead of her, as though he'd walked through a
curtain of water. A step later, Nico felt it rush over her
as well, intensely cold and strange, as if the air itself was
moving to let her pass. It was only for a moment, and
then the world around her changed. She was standing
beside Slorn, still on the slope, still surrounded by the
strange trees, only now she was balanced on the edge of
a knife-sharp ledge looking down at a valley that had not
been there a moment before. It was a small, narrow thing,
barely fifteen feet across and maybe thirty feet long, more
like a fissure in the slope than a valley. There were no
trees growing nearby, yet the light was somehow dimmer
than ever. When she looked down into the cleft, shadows
flowed like a river, making it impossible to tell how far
down the crack in the stone went.

Nico frowned. She wasn't used to shadows hiding

things from her. But as she leaned forward to get a better look, a familiar, terrifying feeling crashed into her. It took her over, passing through her senseless body like a spear and landing hook first in her mind. No, deeper. This feeling, the sense of grasping claws, of an endless, gaping, ravenous hunger, of being trapped, of being crushed, was deeper than mind or thought. For an eternity, it was all Nico could do to hold on to the tiny flickering light of herself until, inch by inch, the darkness subsided. Rough, warm hands were shaking her shoulders. She didn't remember falling, but Slorn was helping her to her feet. Already the feeling was fading like a dream, but deep inside her, something curled closer, drinking it in.

"I'm sorry." Slorn sounded genuinely upset. "I didn't know it would affect you like that."

"What is it?" Nico whispered, shrinking away from the ledge. Yet even as she asked, she knew. She knew the demon hunger as well as she knew her own breath. Slorn's answer was to step aside, and very slowly, Nico looked again. The gully was the same; so were the shadows, but the overwhelming wave did not come back. Relieved, Nico stared into the darkness until it gave way, and the dark bottom of the valley came into focus. It was a dry, dead place. The bottom was sandy, as if water had flowed there once, long ago. Now there was nothing but rocks and the scattered leaves of the dark trees lying dry and brittle on the sand. And at the farthest, deepest end, sitting cross-legged on a large, flat stone, was a woman in a long, black coat.

She sat very still, her head bowed so that her hair, wispy and dark, fell to hide her face. Her hands, skeletally thin and pale, were folded in her lap, while at her

wrists, gleaming dully in the dark, a pair of silver manacles trembled. She wore a silver collar at her neck as well,
and rings on her ankles. All of them were shaking, buzzing like bees against her skin so that, even this far away,
Nico could hear the faint, hollow clatter of rattling metal.

The woman gave no sign that she saw Nico and Slorn
on the ridge above her. She sat as still as a doll, the shaking bindings at her wrists the only movement in the gully.
Yet the more Nico stared, the more the woman's very stillness seemed to move and crawl. The cold feeling began to
gnaw at Nico again, and she was forced to look away.

"Is she alive?" Nico said, looking back at Slorn.

"Oh yes," Slorn said, looking down at the woman with
a sad look in his dark, animal eyes. "Very much alive."

"She's a demonseed." It scarcely needed to be spoken,
but Nico said it anyway, as if having it out clear and
simple like that could somehow make the woman in the
dark less terrifying.

"That she is," Slorn said softly. "Her name is Nivel.
She is my wife."

"Your wife?" Nico's voice was trembling now. She
knew very little about things like wives, but it seemed
wrong that the woman should be alone here in the dark
under the open sky, miles away from home.

Slorn must have followed the same line of thought, for
his answer was fast and defensive. "It was her choice," he
said. "She chose to live here in the valley so that when
she awakened she could not hurt her husband, her child,
or anyone else. The valley helps her by keeping innocent
spirits away. No rain falls inside those walls, no trees
sprout, no wind blows."

"Nothing to feed the demon," Nico finished softly. "But how does she live? Humans must eat."

Slorn clenched his fists. "In the five years since I lowered her down there, Nivel has taken neither food nor water. She doesn't sleep and she doesn't move. But her will, her human will, is still there, still fighting. So, in the only way that truly counts, she's still my Nivel. Still human, even now."

Nico didn't see how someone who never ate or slept could be called human, but she held her tongue. Slorn looked down at the woman in black again and his voice grew very sad.

"Over the last decade I have pledged everything: my life, my work, my place as a Shaper"—he raised his hand to his furry face—"even my humanity to finding a way to bring Nivel back from the brink. Yet for all my work, all I've managed is to slow the inevitable. The coats I make, the manacles, these are all just stopgaps, ways to starve the demon, to restrain it and keep it distracted." Slorn bared his teeth. "Ten years and I am no closer to finding a cure than I was at the beginning." He looked at Nico. "Do you understand why I am telling you this?"

Nico shook her head.

"Because, unlike your swordsman, I refuse to give false hope. That's why I brought you here." Slorn took Nico's shoulders and turned her to face the dark gully again. "Look sharply. What you see down there is your future, the unavoidable end. I've heard about what happened in the throne room of Mellinor. I know you've gone over the edge and come back. It's a trick not many can pull off, but no one returns unscathed." His hands tightened on her shoulders. "No one is strong enough to play with the demon and come back every time. No one can hold off the demon forever. Even if you resist with everything you have, a demonseed is something outside of human or spirit understanding. It is a predator, and we, all of us, humans and spirits, are its prey. Just as the sheep cannot fight the wolf, we cannot fight the demon. Eli brought you here for a coat, but I cannot make one for you until you understand completely that it is only a crutch, not a cure. No coat or shackle, no human implement, no magic, no spirit can stop the thing that is inside you."

Nico looked him straight in the eye, shrugging her shoulder out of his grip. "That may be," she said, "but your wife is still alive, and so am I. So long as we're alive, we can fight." It was the first thing Josef had taught her.

"Still alive, as you say." Slorn sighed. "But as for the fight..." He looked down into the valley, and the look of grief on his face was the most human expression Nico had seen him make. "The only way for you to understand is to ask her yourself."

Nico's eyes widened and she turned back to the dark valley. The woman, Nivel, sat still as ever, but then, almost imperceptibly, Nico saw her fingers twitch. Her hand rose from her lap, lifting straight up like a marionette's hand on a string, and the thin, limp fingers curled in a beckoning motion. Beside Nico, Slorn stood perfectly still, watching the woman as her hand fell back to her knees.

Nico swallowed. "Is it safe for me to go down there?"

"Of course not," Slorn said. "Nothing is safe in your condition, but you have less to fear than anything else. So far as I know, demonseeds don't eat each other."

That didn't make her feel any better about dropping

into the dark, but Slorn was settling down on the ground, obviously not going anywhere. Realizing that this was what he'd brought her up here to do from the beginning, Nico decided to see it through. She took a deep breath and then, very carefully, stepped off the cliff edge.

It was a shorter fall than she'd expected, another trick of the unnatural shadows that filled the valley. She landed badly in the sand, but righted herself automatically. Now that she was down in it, the valley was darker than ever. She could see nothing, not even the stone walls of the cliffs that boxed her in. The only sound was the metallic rattle of the woman's buzzing manacles. Nico could feel her own restraints trembling against her skin in answer, matching the rhythm. As the sounds merged, her vision began to sharpen. Not lighten, for there was no more light than before. Even so, she could see clearly now despite the dark. And there, in front of her, was Nivel.

The woman was closer than she'd realized, her bare feet almost touching Nico's legs. Nico jumped back, and the woman in the chair made a thin, hollow sound, like sand blowing over metal. It took Nico a moment to realize Nivel was chuckling.

"You have good instincts."

The woman's voice was a rasp, a mere shaping of breath, as though she'd long since screamed her throat away. Her eyes, bright as lanterns in the unnatural darkness, glittered behind her long, matted hair. Behind them, shapes and shadows flickered in unnatural forms. Even so, meeting the woman eye to eye, Nico felt a strange feeling of kinship and, with it, a strong urge to run away as fast as she could.

"Heinricht gave you the speech, did he?" Nivel said.

"He gives it to every demonseed before sending them to me. Still, you are the first I've seen in a very long time. I thought maybe he'd finally given up." She sighed, a cutting, rasping sound. "My poor, faithful bear."

"Other demonseeds?" Nico said, startled. "He's sent others here?" It seemed impossible. Surely the League of Storms would shut any operation like that down in an instant.

"A few," Nivel said, waving her hand. "We'd hoped to learn something, but the demonseeds we could get were too small and weak to be any use. The League never lets them get too big, you see. But you"—her eyes locked with Nico's—"you're different."

Fast as a shadow, Nivel's hand shot out, grabbing Nico's wrist and dragging her closer. Nico fought by instinct, but the woman's grip was filled with a demonic strength even greater than hers, and Nico found herself on her knees beside Nivel, her face inches from the woman's own. This close, she could smell death and rocks and something else, a sharp, acidic bite that tugged at memories she didn't want to recall.

Nivel's eyes glowed brighter as she looked Nico over before releasing the girl with a suddenness that made Nico stumble.

"You're no usual seed, are you?" Nivel said as Nico picked herself up. "Old, far older than you look, and with a seed that appears to have blossomed many times, yet never freed itself." She tapped her fingers against her knees and a purely human look of inquisitive interest passed over her face. "Tell me, how did you get that way?"

"I don't know," Nico said. "I don't remember anything before Josef found me."

Nivel looked supremely disappointed, and the light behind her eyes flickered. "So it told me before I'd even asked the question. I hate it when the bastard is right."

Nico looked at her, confused. There was no one else in the valley save themselves. Not even a spirit. Nivel caught her surprised look and smiled a pleased smile.

"Well, child," she said, "if you don't know what I'm talking about there might be hope yet."

Nico's heart beat faster. "Slorn said there was no hope. That was why he brought me up here."

"Heinricht's doesn't believe in false assurances," Nivel said, smiling. The expression softened her face until she looked almost human again. "He's always been a realist. But there's a difference between being a realist and being a defeatist. Just because no one has ever beaten their demon doesn't mean you're going to give in, does it?"

Nico shook her head.

"I thought so." Nivel chuckled, the same dry sound as before. "In that case, strange little demon girl, let me give you some hard-learned advice." She caught Nico's eyes with her glowing gaze. "There will come a time when my words mean something to you. I may not have Slorn's eyes, but even I can see you've been using your seed too much of late. It's quickening, growing like a babe in the womb. Someday, possibly very soon, it will wake. When that happens, if you remember nothing else, remember what I tell you here."

Nivel leaned forward, lowering her voice to a bare, scraping whisper, and Nico leaned in to listen.

"Demons," Nivel said, "are predators. Creatures of power and control. But as a human, you are unique among all spirits. Your soul is your own, and you must never give your control over, no matter what. When the voice speaks, do not listen to it, do not take its advice, and do not talk back to it, no matter what it says. Do you understand?"

Nico shook her head.

"You will," Nivel said. "I'm glad I could tell someone. Though we won't meet again, I would feel guilty if I never warned you."

Nico's eyes widened. "Never again? But I've never met someone else like me. I've never had—"

Nivel shook her head. "There are no mentors in this life of ours, child. Even now, the demon inside me is trying to find a way to use you to free itself. In a few minutes, I won't have the strength to keep it back. I have fought this battle of inches for ten years, but it will be over soon. The demon is now as strong as I am. We are perfectly balanced. Yet it can get stronger, and I can't. All it would take is a bite of a spirit. A wind, a few drops of rain"—Nivel's glowing eyes ran over Nico's body—"a little girl, and the demon could shed me like snakeskin and fly free. That's why I told Slorn to put me in this valley, where all the spirits have withdrawn, leaving nothing to eat. Here, I can keep it in check. But," Nivel's rasping voice cracked, "it's been five years since I sat down on this stone, and I'm tired. So tired."

"But you're still alive!" Nico said. "So long as you have that, you can fight."

Nivel laughed, a sad, empty sound. "No one's will is strong enough to hold out alone forever. Just staying alive isn't enough. You need something to live for. A purpose. Mine is Slorn. I left him and Pele alone, and yet he still kills himself trying to find a way to bring me back. I thought that if he was willing to fight for me, to attempt the impossible, then I owed it to stand strong for him. That belief has kept me going far beyond my time. Even so, everything ends."

As she spoke, the manacles on Nivel's wrists began to rattle more incessantly, and Nico winced as the cold, dark feeling began to creep over her again. Nivel took a breath and closed her eyes tight. "You should go now," she said quietly.

Nico clenched her jaw. "I won't say farewell," she said, standing up. Her hand shot out, and she grabbed Nivel's fingers. "We'll meet again, so don't give up."

With that, Nico released her grip and turned around, marching toward the stone wall. When she reached the sheer cliff she began to climb, her impossibly strong fingers finding grips on the most minute cracks and wrinkles in the stone.

Nivel watched her go, cradling the hand Nico had seized, savoring the surprised feeling of the unexpected contact.

I hope you're happy, a deep, smooth voice said in her head. *You just let the death of your world go on her merry way. We should have eaten her when we had the chance.* It sighed deeply. *You'll regret this. Mark my words.*

Nivel just smiled and ignored the voice, as she always had, watching as Nico pulled herself over the edge of the cliff and vanished into the sunlit world above.

High overhead, Nico spilled herself out onto the dry leaves, panting and letting her eyes adjust to the light. Slorn was waiting where she'd left him, sitting solemnly on the dirt.

"So," he said slowly, "you have met the truth of

demonseeds face to face. Do you still want me to make your coat?"

Nico stood up, brushing the leaves off her clothes. "Yes," she said. "Nothing has changed."

Slorn grinned, showing a great wall of sharp yellow teeth. "You have passed the final measure, then. Come," he said and stood up. "Pele and the rest should have things ready by now."

Nico nodded and followed him back down the slope and through the strange, black trees, stopping every few steps to look back over her shoulder, even after the valley had long since vanished from view.

CHAPTER
5

Miranda delivered her decision to Master Banage over breakfast. They argued, but it was the same ground they'd covered the night before, and nothing new was resolved. In the end Banage relented, for what could he do? It was her career and her neck Miranda was risking, and he could not force her to take the easy road. Their parting was short and bitter as Miranda excused herself to prepare for the trial.

Back in her room, she took more care with her preparations than usual. Using Karon's heat to warm the water in the basin, she washed her face and teeth, taking special care with her eyes, which were red ringed and raw from crying and lack of sleep. Next, she dug out the tin of powder her sister had given her ages ago and brushed the white base over her ruddy cheeks, hiding her dark circles as best she could. When she was as pale and serious as she could make herself, Miranda opened the trunk at the end of her bed and began to dress. She'd picked out her clothes the night before, choosing her favorite pair of worn trousers and a soft, light shirt to go under the heavy silk robes that were mandatory for formal Court functions. She had set out her official set this time, blood-red silk with white and gold designs in long, geometric patterns. It was hideous. The fabric was stiff and musty from being in her trunk for so long, but it marked her status as a vested and sworn Spiritualist of the Court even more than her rings did, and that was exactly the impression she was trying to make.

When every one of the robe's impossible buttons was finally fastened, Miranda sat down on her bed and took off each of her rings in turn. With great care, she rubbed each one with a soft cloth, waking and soothing the spirit inside before sliding them back onto her fingers. When the rings were done, she fished Erol's silver-wrapped pearl from his place next to her skin and, after a cleaning coupled with a firm reminder of the dire repercussions of acting out, laid him on top of her robes. Finally, she brushed out her hair as straight as it would go and bound the red mass back in a severe braid so that her face was not obscured from any angle.

Ready as she could make herself, Miranda locked her room and walked down the stairs to the street where Gin was sitting beside the door, waiting for her.

"You know," Miranda said, scratching his head, "since you're not technically a bound spirit, you don't have to come with me today."

Gin gave an undignified snort and trotted off down the narrow walk between the buildings, leaving her to follow.

A group of Krigel's red-robed guards met them at the

side entrance to the tower. Miranda let them lead her and Gin up the low stairs and through the broad side hallways to the back door of the long, opulent room that served as the Court's waiting chamber.

Like all rooms in the tower, the waiting chamber was built on a grand scale, which was good, considering she was there with a fifteen-foot-long ghosthound. Even with Gin, however, Miranda felt as though the room would swallow her up if she let it. It was austere, designed to impress the age and power of the Spirit Court on its occupants, usually minor nobles and representatives from the Council who needed help with flooding river spirits or petulant winds that tore up their crops. Since it was only her this morning, the lamps were dark, and the dim, gray light from the high windows made the room's otherwise luxurious ambiance feel gloomy and cold.

Her guards, who hadn't spoken a word since she'd met them, took their places at the many doors that led into the room, and Miranda, after looking around lost for a bit, took a seat on one of the cushioned benches across from the largest door, which led into the Court itself. She knew from experience that that was where they would come for her. She had waited here once before, the day she took her oaths. Sitting there, she felt the same nervous weight in her stomach. Back then it had felt exciting; now it just made her feel ill.

Through the heavy wood she could hear the shuffling as the gathered Tower Keepers took their places. Muted conversations washed in and out, and over them all rang a smug, laughing voice she'd heard only a few times in her life but recognized instantly. How could anyone forget Hern's superior sneer?

Gin twitched beside her, lowering his head to whisper in her ear. "It's not too late. You can still take the out."

"No," Miranda said. "I need only a majority vote to have all charges against me thrown out. Every person in that room is a Spiritualist, which means every single one of them, even Hern, has taken an oath to protect the Spirit World." She folded her hands tightly in her lap. "What I did in Mellinor was not wrong or abusive, and I have the spirit inside me to prove it. For every ring in that Court, I have a measure of hope that their masters will see the truth and make the right choice."

Gin shook his head as the muted conversations vanished and the room beyond the heavy doors fell into silence as the Court convened. "I hope you're right."

"So do I," Miranda whispered, clutching her rings tighter than ever.

They sat in nervous silence until, at last, the great door opened and the bright light of the Court shone in. Even though she knew it was coming, the shock of the brilliant Court chamber after the dim waiting room threw Miranda off balance for a moment. Then she was in control again, and she marched through the doors and up the steep steps with her head high and Gin right behind her.

The Spirit Court's hearing chamber was a circular room that took up the entirety of the tower's second floor. High overhead, hanging from the tall, arched ceiling, white fires burned in silver sconces without fuel or heat, their sharp light blending with the sunlight that filtered through the tall, milky glass windows. Enormous rings of wooden benches ran along the outer edge of the room, spiraling down from the walls in a series of interlocking tiers, but only the bottom rings were filled. Tower

Keepers sat primly in their formal robes, their ringed hands draped over the high wall that separated them from the open floor and the raised stand at its center, where Miranda would make her case.

Directly across from the doors where she had entered, an enormous bench loomed over everything else. It towered above the polished marble floor, carved from wood so old it had lost all its color and was now solid black beneath the layers of polish. Sitting behind the great bench on a chair as regal as any throne was Master Banage. He was dressed in a coat of pure white with a high collar that framed his face like a snowdrift, making him look ancient and distant, an infallible king of judges. Around his neck he wore the Mantle of the Tower, the regalia of the Rector Spiritualis. It was styled as a chain. Each link was a knot of heavy gold holding a great stone, and each stone held one of the spirits bound, not to any one Spiritualist, but to the Court itself, passed down from rector to rector, the living symbol of the Spirit Court's pledge of protection, justice, and equality to the Spirit World.

It was an awe-inspiring sight that was as much a part of the Spirit Court as the tower itself, and with every step she took toward the stand, Miranda felt the weight fall heavier on her shoulders. The age, the power, the majesty of the Spirit Court threatened to crush her, and no matter how many times she told herself that this was exactly the intended effect, the impact was not lessened. By the time she reached the stand, climbing the three little steps so that she stood at the apex of the court's scrutiny, even Gin's presence couldn't stop her hands from shaking.

"Spiritualist Miranda Lyonette." Banage's voice

boomed down from the high bench, warped into a fearsome specter of itself by the room's strange acoustics. "The Spirit Court has gathered to hear the charges brought against you by your peer, Spiritualist Grenith Hern, Master of the Towers, concerning the incidents that occurred in the kingdom of Mellinor."

Banage looked down at the man who was sitting front and foremost in the first ring of seats. There, dressed in a well-tailored robe of expensive crimson silk embroidered with gold flourishes, was Grenith Hern himself. He was young for a Tower Keeper, scarcely into his forties, and clearly he had been very handsome at one point. His hair, though graying, was still a flaxen blond, and he wore it long and braided down his back like a dandy. However, any appearance of youthful inexperience was banished by the immense collection of rings that glistened on his hands, which he draped casually over the bench that separated him from the open floor. He had necklaces as well, jeweled chains nearly as ornate as Master Banage's, and bracelets glittering beneath the cuffs of his robe.

Banage looked down. "Speak your complaint, Spiritualist Hern."

Hern stood up with a gracious nod and turned to face Miranda, meeting her glare with a warm, confident smile.

"My complaint is one of a most serious nature." His smooth voice rang out through the great room. "I charge that Miranda Lyonette, in violation of her duty and her oaths, did conspire with the noted criminal Eli Monpress to gain access to the spirit known as Mellinor, a Great Spirit overpowered and imprisoned by the dreaded Enslaver Gregorn, and thought destroyed more than four hundred years ago. Despite her orders to apprehend Monpress, Spiritualist Lyonette instead worked with him to win over Mellinor, already weakened and confused from the long Enslavement and imprisonment, with threats and guile. Furthermore, in payment for this assistance, Spiritualist Lyonette bought Monpress time to escape by destroying the throne room of Mellinor, putting countless lives in danger."

Banage gave him a cold look. "This is your charge?"

Hern nodded. "It is."

"And what punishment do you seek?"

Hern turned to look down at Miranda, and his smile became a cruel smirk. "Banishment," he said, low and cold. "Banishment from the Spirit Court by stripping of rings, rank, and privileges, including entry to Zarin or any other safe haven maintained by the Court."

A great murmur went up among the crowd. Miranda let the sound wash over her, keeping her eyes straight ahead. She had expected this, she told herself, but still, hearing the actual words turned her spine to water. When the noise quieted down, Banage leaned forward from his high seat to look down at Miranda and spoke as gently as the acoustics of the room allowed. "How do you answer these charges, Spiritualist Lyonette?"

Miranda met his eyes one last time, and took the plunge.

"I call them nonsense." Her voice rang out through the chamber. "It is true that I was sent to Mellinor to capture Eli Monpress, but when I arrived in Mellinor, I found a far greater crime against the spirits than anything Monpress was capable of. As you should all know, for I went into this at great length in my report, the prince,

Renaud, who lost his throne thanks to Mellinor's ancient prejudices against wizards, had turned to Enslavement to get it back. He awakened and Enslaved a Great Spirit left by his ancestor, the Enslaver Gregorn, in the artifact we know as Gregorn's Pillar, the same artifact I had been sent to Mellinor to ensure Monpress did not steal. Despite my efforts, Renaud successfully shattered the pillar and took control of the weakened Great Spirit of the now-dry inland sea Mellinor. However, with Monpress's help, I was able to free Mellinor from Renaud's control and destroy the Enslaver."

By the time she finished, the crowd was whispering madly. Hern raised his hand, and the noise stopped.

"A fascinating story," he said. "All of which matches what the Kingdom of Mellinor itself reported to the Council, of course. Yet, the question still remains: How did all of this end up with Monpress escaping and you with the Great Spirit?"

Miranda glared at him. "After Renaud's death, Mellinor rightfully demanded that the land Gregorn had stolen from him, what was now the Kingdom of Mellinor, be returned. However, there were, are, people living on that land, and millions of spirits who would perish if it returned to a sea. I could not let that happen. Yet a spirit without its land is a ghost with nowhere to go, and Mellinor had survived too much to die moments after winning his freedom. So we came to a compromise: Mellinor would leave the kingdom to its new inhabitants, and I would give him a new home using the only vessel large enough for a spirit of his power, my own body."

"Your body?" Hern gave her a distasteful look, which he made sure everyone saw. "Highly unorthodox, and very dangerous for both spirit and Spiritualist. Your idea, I take it?"

"Yes," Miranda said. "But then, wouldn't any Spiritualist risk their life to save a Great Spirit?"

"Their own life, yes," Hern said. "But have you thought of what happens if you die like that, Miss Lyonette? With a small ocean inside you?" He held up his hand, gesturing with his jeweled rings. "A *stone* is stable, durable, but humans are fragile creatures. That dog of yours could turn feral and eat you, and in the course flood all of Zarin."

Gin growled savagely, but Miranda put her hand on his muzzle and yanked his fur until he stopped. When she felt sure he wouldn't start again, she released her grip and answered Hern as calmly as she could. "I did my best with the options I had. I had to make a choice that night, and I chose to preserve as many lives as possible, spirit and human. What Spiritualist would do otherwise?"

"What Spiritualist, indeed?" Hern said, his voice growing coy and condescending. "You try to play to our sense of pity, to hide your true intention behind pure motives. But we are not so easily fooled as that poor, befuddled water spirit."

Miranda blinked, astonished by this new attack, but Hern did not let up.

"Do you think we've looked the other way throughout your astonishing career?" he said, looking around the Court. "How could we? You came to the Court from a wealthy Zarin family, finished your training in two years instead of the standard three, and from the moment you took your apprentice's oath, no one would suit you as a mentor save Etmon Banage himself, the new favorite to become Rector Spiritualis."

Miranda clenched her fists. "I don't see how any of this has any bearing on—"

"Don't you?" Hern snapped. "Look again. Your entire life within the Court has been one of achievement and ambition. It's no secret that Banage is grooming you to be his successor. The special missions he sends you on are all highly irregular, and we won't even begin to talk about the misappropriation of Court funds in hiring a bounty hunter, one Coriano, to track down Monpress."

An enormous swell of noise went up at this, and Banage banged his desk for order.

"Hern," he said, "if you have a problem with my policies, you will bring them up with me personally. In this trial, you will limit your statements to the matter at hand."

"Of course." Hern's tone changed again. He was all sincerity now. "I merely mentioned this ugly situation to give our good Keepers a rounded look at the character of the woman whose fate we are deciding." He turned back to Miranda. "After all, when her history of ambition and disrespect for Spirit Court regulations are considered, should we really be surprised that, when the opportunity arose in Mellinor to bind a Great Spirit, something no Spiritualist has done since the oaths were codified, Miranda Lyonette seized upon it?"

Gin snarled, and this time, Miranda didn't stop him. "This is ridiculous!" she cried. "How can you stand there and pull these lies out of thin air? However badly you think of me, what part of my story, of *anything* that has happened, could make anyone believe what you're saying? If I were this ambitious monster you make me out to be, then surely I never would have just let Eli escape!"

"Ah," Hern said, "but that was the deal, wasn't it? Looking the other way in exchange for his help. Of course, you'd fail in your mission, but who could fault you for failing to catch the famously uncatchable Eli Monpress? Such a small blemish is easily overpowered by the prestige of being the master of a Great Spirit. Frame it that way and suddenly your plan is quite understandable. Just another shortsighted and selfish grab for power hidden under good intentions."

Miranda looked around in disbelief as the Tower Keepers nodded. "Where is your proof?" she shouted. "My report, Mellinor's own report, the truth itself, do these mean nothing to you?"

"Proof?" Hern lashed back. "The proof is in your report!" He held up a stack of papers for all to see. "If taking Mellinor was not your final intention, why then did you pair up with Monpress instead of contacting the Spirit Court for backup according to the standard procedure for dealing with powerful Enslavers?"

Miranda flinched. "There was no time."

"No time?" Hern said, astonished. "If Mellinor had time to send a bounty request to the Council, surely you had time to contact a nearby tower? The only reason I can see for your silence was that you wanted to keep your doings a secret from the Court. You paired up with a thief who wouldn't question your actions, and in return you quietly looked the other way while he ran off with half the contents of Mellinor's treasury."

"There are no towers in Mellinor!" Miranda shouted. "Or anywhere nearby. That's why I was sent there in the first place rather than leaving things to the local Tower Keeper. As for looking the other way, I was unconscious when Eli escaped because I had just taken in a Great Spirit! And if you don't believe that Mellinor came to me of his own free will, then I invite you to ask him yourself!"

A great swell of talk rose up from the stands, and Miranda stood in the middle of it, stiff as stone. This was her biggest hammer, and she'd meant to save it until later, but Hern certainly wasn't playing for a long trial. If she was to have any hope of winning, she couldn't afford to dance around. Still, Hern looked cool and collected, giving her a little go-ahead motion with one narrow, jewel-covered hand, and that made her more nervous than any of his earlier bluster.

Banage silenced the court with a wave of his hand. "Spiritualist Lyonette is correct," he announced. "Since the complaint is that she gained the spirit Mellinor under false pretenses, the resolution seems simple enough. We will question the spirit to see if it has been mistreated." He looked down. "Miranda, if you would."

Miranda nodded and closed her eyes, reaching down into the deep well of her spirit where Mellinor slept. He woke as soon as she brushed him, and a strange sensation rushed through her body, as though she were pouring out of her skin. It wasn't uncomfortable, but neither was it pleasant, and it went on for what felt like a very long time.

When the sensation finally faded, the sound of water filled her ears. She opened her eyes and saw Mellinor hovering beside her. The Great Spirit of the inland sea had changed since she'd offered her soul as his shore. He still appeared as a great orb of water, crystal clear and glowing with his own shifting blue light, but he was smaller now, barely as tall as she was. She'd known he had to shed some of his size to live inside her, but actually seeing the once enormous globe cut down to something more manageable was a shock. Still, Mellinor did not seem troubled at all by his new stature. He hovered, turning to watch the wizards in the stands as they gawked openly. The more they gawked, the brighter the light in the water became, and Miranda got the distinct feeling that, diminished as he was, Mellinor was still the largest spirit most of them had ever encountered firsthand, and the ball of water knew it.

Banage leaned forward on the bench. "You are Mellinor," he said, almost hesitantly, "Great Spirit of the inland sea?"

"I was." Mellinor's voice was like a crashing wave. "But my sea is long gone to grass and trees, so now I am Mellinor, beholden to Miranda."

Hern leaped at this. "Beholden? You mean oath bound?"

Mellinor gave him what passed for a dirty look among water spirits. "Formalities are pointless. I accepted her offer of sanctuary and sustenance in exchange for service on the understanding that I am free to leave whenever I wish, which I currently do not."

"So," Hern said, ignoring Mellinor's distaste, "you were given the choice of servitude or . . . what?"

He left the question hanging, and Mellinor's water swirled. "I see where this is going, human," the water spirit rumbled. "I am not bound to answer to you."

"But your mistress is," Hern said. "Answer the question, service or what?"

Miranda felt Mellinor give her a questioning prod.

She nodded and, with a watery sigh, the Great Spirit answered. "Return to the sea. When I was free from the Enslaver, I attempted to reclaim my land. Miranda Lyonette and Eli Monpress stopped me, for it would mean the death of millions of spirits, as well as thousands of your kind. Monpress meant to return me to the sea, and defeated, I would have gone. It was Miranda who stopped him. Had she not offered the Spiritualist's pledge to me, I would be lost right now, my soul pounded to nothingness beneath the waves. Servitude to a good master is a small price to pay for escaping that end."

Miranda beamed at the glowing water, but Hern's smug smile only grew wider.

"So," he said, "just to make sure I have this right. You were given the choice between death at Monpress's hands or service to Spiritualist Lyonette?"

"I don't like how you say it," Mellinor rumbled. "But if you insist on reducing a complex situation to its most base components, then yes, that is technically correct."

Hern turned to look out over the rows of Spiritualists, spreading his arms to encompass them all. "Though it scarcely needs to be spoken," he said in a ringing voice, "I would like to remind everyone present of the first rule of servant spirits, as it is written in the founding codex of our order: 'Servitude of a spirit is by the spirit's choice alone.' *Choice*, my friends, a spirit's informed, free choice is the cornerstone of all the magics of the Spirit Court. What happened that night in Mellinor was not choice. We already have a name for when the only options are death or service." His face clenched in a disgusted sneer. "*Slavery*. That night Spiritualist Lyonette and the thief Monpress put Mellinor in a situation where there was only one outcome. Though he took the oath, Mellinor did not enter her service by his free will, but rather because there was no other choice." He paused gravely for a moment, letting that sink in. "Though it doesn't fit the technical definition," he continued at last, "I think we can all agree there's little else to call it but Enslavement."

"Are you stupid?" Miranda shouted, all her calm crumbling around her. "You heard it straight from Mellinor! He's here because he wants to be! *I saved his life!*"

Everyone was shouting now. Spiritualists shot up from their seats, arguing over each other in increasingly loud voices while Banage shouted for order. Gin was growling furiously, with his ears flat and his claws out, digging into the stone. Only Hern was quiet, watching the chaos as a victorious commander watches the routing of his enemy. Miranda was so angry she could barely see straight, but Mellinor's anger dwarfed her own. It throbbed through their connection like a tide as his surface shifted from calm blue to an angry, choppy, steel gray.

After several minutes Banage finally regained order. When the room was quiet, he nodded at the water spirit. "Do you have anything else to add?"

"Only this." Mellinor's voice was like a breaking glacier. He turned to Hern, and his water grew very dark. "I have been Enslaved, Spiritualist. I know the madness, the agony, and the humiliation better than any spirit who still has their mind intact. If you presume to call my contract with Miranda Enslavement again, then I will exercise that free choice you claim to value so highly to drown you where you stand. And none of those weak flickers you wear so gaudily on your fingers would be able to stop me."

Hern blanched, and Banage let him squirm for a moment before turning to Miranda. "Spiritualist Lyonette, please control your spirit."

Miranda had a choice answer for that, but a look at Banage stopped her tongue. As much as she would love to let Mellinor do what the spirit was aching to do, any hope of beating the charges against her would vanish if she didn't stay to the right side of Court law, which meant no drowning. With great effort, she tugged at Mellinor's connection, and the spirit reluctantly pulled back, but his cold light never lost its focus on Hern until the last wisp of water vanished.

"You have all heard the charges," Banage said. "The accused will now exit the chamber while the Court deliberates."

Dismissed, Miranda climbed off the stand and marched across the open floor, doing her best to ignore the whispers that followed her. Behind her, she could hear Hern chatting with the Spiritualists around him, his voice ringing confident and cheerful over the hum of the crowd. Her heart sank in her chest as she walked through the double doors the apprentices held open for her, returning to the dark waiting chamber.

"That pompous idiot," Gin growled, pacing in cramped, little circles through the long waiting room while the apprentices secured the door behind them. "You should have let Mellinor drown him."

Miranda didn't answer. She plopped down on the bench against the far wall and put her head in her hands. On her fingers, her rings were awake and asking questions, buzzing through their connection. With great difficulty, she sent them firm, reassuring waves of confidence.

Everything would be fine. Slowly, her rings quieted, the smaller spirits first, and finally the larger ones. Even Mellinor settled down under the pressure. Tired from his earlier anger, he burrowed deep into the corners of Miranda's mind where she rarely went, his mood dark and brooding and well suited to her own.

When they were all still, Miranda lifted the pressure and sat back, staring up at the high windows. She rarely lied to her spirits, but she wasn't above withholding a truth, especially one that had not come to pass yet, and things *could* still turn out in the end.

She closed her eyes. Even thinking it felt foolish. Everything would be all right? She didn't see how they could have gone worse. She'd needed to make a glorious defense. Instead, she'd lost her calm and let Hern lead her in circles away from her carefully prepared arguments. Miranda gritted her teeth. She'd let him play her for a fool from the very beginning, from that first night in Banage's office when she'd read his name on the petition.

Miranda leaned back, letting her head thunk against the cold stone wall. She'd been such an idiot. All this time, she'd truly believed that if she could only tell her story, show them Mellinor, prove that Hern's case was completely unfounded, then the Tower Keepers would be on her side. Yet she could see them now in her mind's eye, the robed figures, their faced turned toward each other, whispering, their ringed hands drumming impatiently on the stands. They hadn't come to Court today to be convinced, to test innocence. There'd been no questions, no demanding of proof, no calls for witnesses, nothing. The Tower Keepers who came today had come to see an unpleasant bit of necessary business through, just as Banage had warned her. She clunked her head against the stone wall again, a little harder this time. Stupid, that's what she'd been. Stupid and naive, thinking things would be the way she wanted just because that's how she believed they should be.

She could hear Gin's claws on the stone as he paced. He'd been right that night in the garden. Coming here today, naked like this, with only her spirits and her word behind her, it had been a prideful thing to do. She had gone in with her head held too high to see the shaky ground beneath her feet, and now...

Miranda raised her hands quickly, pressing her fingers hard against her eyes to block the wetness that threatened to roll down her cheeks. She could not be weak, not now. But Hern's voice, smooth and triumphant as he announced the punishment, was circling through her mind.

Banishment from the Spirit Court by stripping of rings, rank, and privileges.

Her hands began to tremble. She had known from the beginning that this was the risk she was taking, but, at the same time, she had not truly understood what was at stake. Banishment she could handle. Rank could go as well, and everything else. But her rings? She turned her hands over, pressing the stones of her rings against her cheeks. She could feel her spirits moving inside them, turning as they slept. Each one was tied to her by a promise, a sacred pledge she'd thought would last until her death. Could she lose that?

The crack of the doors interrupted her thoughts, and Miranda had just enough time to scrub her eyes before two red-robed Spiritualists entered the waiting room. They didn't look at her, only opened the doors and stood at either side, waiting for her with downcast faces. Miranda got up from the bench with a terrible feeling of dread. Had the Tower Keepers reached their decision so soon? Surely not. It had been barely ten minutes. Could they even take the vote that quickly? Yet the young Spiritualists stood waiting to escort her, and Miranda had no choice but to take her place between them. Without a word, they led her up the stairs into the bright light of the Court, and with every step she took, Miranda felt her hope grow fainter.

This time, her walk through the Court was very different. She was the same, marching in with her head high and her face a calm mask over her fear. She was still a Spiritualist after all, at least for the next few minutes. The circular room, however, had changed in the short time she'd been waiting. Before, the first two rings of seats had been nearly full. A slim showing, but still, people had been there. Now, the great Court was almost empty. Only a few Spiritualists sat sprinkled across the benches, mostly faces she knew, Banage's supporters. Everyone else seemed to have left after the vote. Probably too cowardly to stay and watch the aftermath, she thought darkly.

Hern was there, of course, lounging in his chair like a patron at a boring play, though he did look up to give Miranda a smile, which she did her best to ignore, focusing instead on Master Banage. For once, however, the sight of her mentor brought her no comfort. Even beside the snowy whiteness of his collar, his face looked pale and worn. For the first time his hair looked more gray than black, and his blue eyes were sad and tired when they met hers. If she'd had any hope about the verdict, it died then, but she walked to the stand the same as ever, straight and proud, with Gin stalking behind her like a silent, silver mist.

"Spiritualist Lyonette," Banage said when she had climbed the steps and taken her place on the stand. "You have heard the accusations brought against you and given your answer. Your case has been debated by the leading members of the Spirit Court, and we have come to our decision by majority vote. Are you prepared to hear our verdict?"

Miranda gripped the brass railing that surrounded the stand. "I am."

Banage looked down at the desk in front of him. "Spiritualist Lyonette, this assembly finds you guilty of conspiring with the criminal Eli Monpress for the purpose of obtaining the Great Spirit Mellinor under false pretense and in violation of your oaths. As punishment, you are hereby banished from our assembly. Your titles and privileges within the Court, including all pacts, promises, or agreements made in its name, are now considered void. You will surrender your bound spirits and leave this city at once."

Master Banage's voice was soft and calm, yet every word struck Miranda like a hammer, rattling her mind until all she could do was stare at him dumbly. She heard footsteps behind her and turned to see two young Spiritualists she didn't recognize walking toward her, one with a large pile of sand stalking behind her like a tiger, the other walking beside what looked like a centipede made of stone.

They were moving slowly, and Miranda had plenty of time to look down at her hands. Her rings glittered on her fingers, each one shining with its own tiny light, innocent, completely unaware of what was about to happen. Mellinor, however, knew things were wrong. He moved under her mind, a shadow under the water that was her conscious, restless and thrashing. Miranda closed her eyes, feeling the pull of her spirits, the bond of the vows she had made them, the vows that had just been pronounced void. It felt the same as ever, an iron cable tying her soul to her spirits.

Standing there on the stand with the Spiritualists advancing toward her, Miranda faced her choice. Truly faced it, for the first time. Honor the Spirit Court or honor her spirits. When she saw her situation like that, laid bare of all its pomp, she realized she'd already chosen. All that was left was to act.

The thought terrified her, but not nearly as much as it would have an hour ago. After all, a voice that sounded suspiciously like Eli's whispered in her head, *What more could they do to you?*

The approaching Spiritualists were an arm's length from Gin's tail when Miranda turned to face them.

"Eril," she said softly, "distraction."

A great cackling laugh rose up from the pendant on her chest, and Eril burst forth in a blast of wind that nearly knocked her flat. He howled as he circled, overturning empty chairs, scattering papers everywhere, and the room erupted into chaos. Hern shot out of his chair, but his voice was lost in the gale. The other Spiritualists were standing as well, thrusting out hands covered in bright glowing rings, but Miranda had no time to watch them. The Spiritualist with the sand tiger shouted something, and her spirit sprang forward, meaning to trap Miranda in an avalanche of sand. As it leaped, Miranda threw out her hand. A blast of water flew from her fingers, meeting the sand creature head-on. The wall of water engulfed it, and sand flew out in all directions with a rasping scream. The girl who commanded it cried out as well, and another ring on her hand flashed, but Miranda was too quick.

"Skarest," she ordered, and lightning crackled down her arm, jumping in a white arc from her finger to the girl's chest. The Spiritualist flew backward with a great cracking sound, landing in a sprawl on her back across the room.

"Skarest!" Miranda shouted, horrified.

"She'll be fine," the lightning crackled smugly. "Watch your back."

Miranda whirled around just in time to see the other Spiritualist send his stone centipede skittering forward, but even as she opened her mouth to call Durn, her own stone spirit, Gin leaped over the spirit and landed on its Spiritualist. The stone monster froze as the ghosthound picked the boy up by his collar with one claw and tossed him into the benches. The rock centipede scurried over to its fallen master, but other spirits were joining the fray now. Hern had jumped down from the seats onto the chamber floor, his hands wreathed in a strange blue fire that matched the flashing stone at his neck.

Seeing they were about to be horribly outnumbered, Miranda hurried over to Gin. "Time to go!"

"Where?" Gin growled, kneeling down so she could jump on his back. "We're in the heart of the Spirit Court. I'm all for leaving these idiots in the dust, but you picked a really bad place to rebel."

The Spiritualists in the benches had their spirits out now. Everywhere Miranda looked she was ringed in by spirits of every type and size beginning to move down out of the gallery to the floor.

"There." Miranda pointed at the high windows.

"It's too narrow," Gin snapped. "We won't get through."

"Well, try anyway," Miranda said, getting a death grip on his fur.

Gin growled and dropped into a crouch. She could feel his muscles tensing, gathering strength, and then, in a single, explosive motion, he jumped. Miranda had never seen him jump like this. It felt as if they were flying. They soared over the benches, over Hern, who could only watch openmouthed, lifting his flame-ringed hands too late. Gin and Miranda flew past Banage, and Miranda turned to catch one last glimpse of her mentor. What she saw, however, was not what she'd expected. Despite the fiasco going on in his Court, Banage had not moved. He simply sat there at his seat, watching her. Then, without warning, he smiled, and his spirit welled up around her.

She'd felt him open his spirit wide before, but this was different. The stones on his chain of office glowed like sunlight, and Miranda's bones hummed with power. Not just Banage's power, but the power of the Rector Spiritualis, the wizard tied to the interconnected spirit of the Spirit Court's tower and the great sleeping spirits that lay beneath Zarin itself.

Banage flicked his fingers and the room shook with an enormous groan. It lasted only a second, but it was enough. Ahead of them, the too-narrow window they were flying toward suddenly slid away, the milky white glass that was never meant to open dropping down to let them through. It didn't stop there, though. Next, the stone that ringed the window began to peel outward, the white marble bending and curling like an opening flower, creating a hole just large enough for Gin. Miranda barely had time to gawk before they were through, soaring out of the tower and into the clear morning air.

For one glorious moment they flew high and free with all of Zarin spread out before them. Then, in a slow, inevitable arch, they began to fall. Miranda felt Gin's legs kick, then begin to scramble in the empty space, and she realized something was wrong. They were too high, even for Gin, and falling at the wrong angle.

For a single, breathless moment, they tumbled in free fall, the sky and ground swapping places in sickening circles as they hurdled the three stories down toward the cobbled courtyard. Miranda gripped Gin's fur and opened her mouth to scream, but no sound came. Instead, Mellinor poured out of her. Later, thinking back, she could never recall if she had asked him or if the water spirit had acted on his own, but she had never been so happy to see the impossibly blue water.

Mellinor plummeted ahead of them in a great wave, falling to the pavement below and forming a vast pool of water. She watched, her terror overcome by amazement, as the water shaped itself into a great, floating well a dozen feet deep, or tall, depending on how you saw it, and Miranda realized she had better hold her breath.

Gin hit the pool with a great splash, and it was all Miranda could do to hold on as the force of the water threatened to scrape her off the ghosthound. But Mellinor caught her, his water absorbing the impact. She regained her seating just as Gin's feet touched the ground. The water held them a moment longer, until Gin had his balance, and then, with a heady rush, Mellinor poured back into Miranda. She went stiff, gasping for breath as the water spirit returned to her, and she would have fallen off if her fingers had not already been tangled in Gin's fur so tightly. Then Mellinor was back where he always was and they were standing in the courtyard, dry and safe, with the sound of spirits clamoring above them.

Gin didn't give Miranda time to assess the situation. As soon as the water was gone, he burst forward, nearly running over a handful of gawking people. Miranda could only hold on and keep her head down as the ghosthound jumped the wall that separated the Spirit Court from the rest of the city. No one tried to stop them as they ran through the busy streets and made a beeline for the southern wall.

"We'll hit the south fields," Gin said, his voice barely audible over the rush of the wind and cries of the people forced to jump out of their way. "Make a show. Then when Zarin's out of sight, we'll circle back east and lose ourselves in the farmland. Lots of hiding places there. We can rest and decide where we're actually going."

Miranda nodded against his fur, happy to let him decide. She looked down at her fingers knotted in Gin's fur, at the rings that pressed into her skin. Then she looked back over her shoulder at the great tower of the Spirit Court standing straight and white over the city. She regretted it immediately as a surge of emotion choked her throat, and she ducked her head, burying her face in Gin's neck. She did not look at anything again until they were far, far away.

Etmon Banage eased his spirit a fraction, and the stones that Miranda and Gin had just gone sailing through folded in again, the window sliding back into place as though it had never moved. Below him, the solemn chamber was in complete uproar. Hern stood by the empty stand, his hands still wreathed in his blue fire spirit, shouting orders. The other Spiritualists weren't listening. They were busy withdrawing their retinues and helping the poor pair who had tried to confront Miranda get back on their feet.

When Hern realized he was getting nowhere, he marched to the foot of the great bench and glared upward.

"Banage!" he shouted. "Have you gone soft in the head? Why did you let a convicted criminal escape?"

"That window is a priceless part of our tower," Banage answered matter-of-factly. "The ghosthound was going through it, one way or another. Would you rather I let it be broken?"

"Don't play that line with me," Hern growled, pointing a finger wreathed with blue flame. "You knew. You knew she would try to escape!"

Banage arched his eyebrows at the younger man. "You were the one who pushed her into the corner, Hern," he said. "Miranda is a strong, proud Spiritualist. Is it surprising she pushed back?"

Hern gritted his teeth and lowered his hands, the flames sputtering out. "It makes no difference; she's a traitor and a criminal now. We'll hunt her down sooner or later."

"Perhaps," Banage said, unfastening his stiff collar. "But your involvement in this matter is at an end, Hern. I suggest you put it out of your mind."

Hern glared at him. "What do you mean? I'm not finished until that girl's rings are dust."

"The pursuit and apprehension of traitors is the sole

purview of the Rector Spiritualis." Banage removed his heavy chain next and handed it to Krigel, who had stepped forward to help him. "Rest assured, I will give this matter the attention it deserves."

Hern glared murder at him. "I will not let you bury this," he said, his voice taut. "Do not think this is done, Etmon!"

"I would never allow myself such luxuries," Banage answered, but Hern was already off, marching through the chaotic hall, his robes flying behind him like fantastic wings. A handful of the remaining Tower Keepers fell in behind him, leaving the room nearly empty.

"Well," Krigel said when they were gone, "that was a fine fiasco."

"Yes," Banage said, sinking back down into his chair. "I seem to have a talent for making troublesome enemies."

Krigel sniffed. "Any man who wasn't Hern's enemy would be no friend of mine."

Banage nodded absently, staring up at the window.

Krigel followed his eyes. "If you don't mind my saying, sir, that was very unlike you. What possessed you to do it?"

"What," he said, "let her escape? It certainly wasn't the proper thing to do." He paused, and a thin smile spread across his lips. "Let's just say it felt more right than letting Hern win."

"I see," Krigel said. "And are you saying that as the Rector Spiritualis or as her master?"

"Both," Banage said. "She made her choice and she chose her spirits. I can't say I would respect a Spiritualist who chose otherwise, not as mentor or as Rector.

Now"—he stood up—"back to work. Tell me, which traveling Spiritualist reported in last?"

"That would be Zigget," Krigel said. "He stopped in last week and left promptly a day later to investigate reports of spirit abuse by pirates on the Green Sea."

"Good," Banage said, nodding. "Notify anyone who asks that Zigget is now in charge of catching Miranda Lyonette and bringing her to face trial."

"But he's on a boat by now," Krigel said. "Even relaying through the towers, it will take weeks to inform him of his new assignment."

"Too bad," Banage said. "I suddenly have the strong feeling that no one but Zagget is right for this job."

"It's Zigget, sir," Krigel said.

"Whatever." Banage shrugged, looking around at the scattered papers and overturned benches. "Put him on it and make sure Hern knows, and get someone in here to clean this up."

"Yes, Rector." Krigel bowed.

Banage patted him on the shoulder and walked down the stairs and out of the chamber, running his hand along the wall as he went. Beneath his fingers, the stone tower whispered that the white dog and its master were already outside the city, running south and east across the plains. Smiling, Banage pulled back his hand and started up the stairs, feeling much better than he'd expected to feel.

CHAPTER
6

As soon as Slorn announced he would start the coat, he vanished into his workroom and did not come out for food or sleep. The first day of waiting passed quickly enough, but by the second Eli was getting dangerously bored.

"You know," Josef said, "it's a sign of maturity to be able to entertain yourself."

They were sitting around the table in the main room. Josef had all his knives, swords, and throwing spikes laid out by size, and he was carefully sharpening them with a contented look on his face. Nico was sitting beside him, reading some book of Slorn's she'd picked up the day before, one of Morticime Kant's fourteen-volume *A Wizarde Historie*. This activity had surprised Eli for two reasons: one, that Slorn kept that kind of trash in his house, and two, that Nico could read. She'd never given any signs that she was literate before, but there was so little he knew about her, it wasn't safe to assume anything. Anyway, that had been yesterday's realization. Today, he was slumped over the hard chair by the fire, bored out of his mind.

"An active mind requires stimulation," he grumbled, tilting his head to look at Josef. "We can't all be happy sharpening knives all day long."

Josef just kept dragging his long knife over the whetstone with practiced ease and said nothing. Realizing he wouldn't get an argument, Eli swung himself up with an exaggerated sigh and looked again at the sealed door to Slorn's workroom. The only interesting thing going on in the whole house and Slorn was too stingy to let him watch. Still, there was always a way.

"What are you doing?" Josef asked as Eli began to stalk across the room.

"Broadening my mind," Eli answered, carefully laying his fingers on the door. It was good, hard wood, and already awake. Eli smiled and began tapping his fingers against it.

Before he could say anything, the door said, "Don't even think about it."

"Come now," Eli said softly. "Surely dear Heinricht wouldn't mind if I checked in on him. It's not often I get to watch a master at work. Just a peek, what do you say?"

"Absolutely not." The door held itself firmer than ever. "And if you're considering schmoozing anything else, I'll tell you right now you can save your breath. Every stick of furniture in this house is under strict orders to make sure *you* keep out of the way."

Behind him, Nico made a sound almost like a snort. Eli gave her a cutting look over his shoulder before turning back to the door, which had pulled back so far it was digging into its frame.

"I wouldn't dream of getting in the way," he cooed.

"No one wants him to finish quickly more than I do. I just want to learn. How can you deny me that? Come on, I don't even have to see. Just let me listen in." He leaned forward, putting his ear against the gap in the boards. "Slorn loves knowledge above all else. How could he object to just a little listen?"

The door gave a shriek and Eli jumped backward, slapping a hand over his ear to stop the ringing. The door's shriek faded to a loud, off-key humming, and Eli sighed, rubbing his ear with his palm.

"All right," he said. "I get it. You can stop now."

The door hummed louder.

"I guess this is one of those times I should be glad I can't hear spirits," Josef said, looking down at the sword he was sharpening with a smile that was slightly larger than the blade warranted.

"In this house, that's all the time," Eli grumbled. "Does Slorn awaken only the rude ones?"

"I hardly think following orders makes a spirit rude," came a growly voice. The door ceased its humming, and everyone turned to look as Slorn himself stepped into the room looking very tired and very annoyed.

"Slorn," Eli said. "How nice to see you again. I was beginning to worry work had eaten you for good."

"I find it hard to work with so much noise going on." Slorn folded his arms over his chest. "Aren't thieves supposed to be quiet?"

"Only when quietness is called for," Eli said.

"I'm so sorry, Heinricht," the door said. "I was only trying to protect your privacy, and—"

The bear-headed man silenced it with a wave. "You did well. I was coming out anyway."

Eli brightened. "Is it done?"

"Mostly," Slorn said, turning back toward his workroom. "Come in and see, but don't touch anything."

Eli sprang across the room and fell in behind him, giving the grumbling door a dazzling smile as he passed. Josef put down his sword and followed at a more reasonable pace, with Nico bringing up the rear.

Eli had been trying to get into Slorn's workroom since his first visit, and he was not disappointed. The room was in strict order and absolutely full of curiosities. Shelves filled every available bit of wall, and every available bit of shelving was covered with bins of scrap cloth, animal hides, and enormous spools of thread, some of which were glittering, others almost invisible. There were bins of metal as well, all obscurely labeled in Slorn's spidery writing as "resentful" or "pleasant," and one locked chest on the top shelf bore a red sign that read "bloodthirsty— for blade cores only."

There was a large forge in the corner, which was surprising, considering there was no chimney on this side of the house, but it was cold and its anvil had been pushed to the side. Instead, a large loom took up what little floor space there was. It sat empty now, but its shuttles were twitching with exhaustion, coming down off of two days of solid work.

Eli hopped around like a magpie, examining the tool racks, the shelves of materials, the half-finished projects, anything he could get to. Josef, obviously not seeing what the excitement was about, strolled along behind him looking decidedly bored until he spotted something that made him stop midstep. He grabbed Eli's sleeve, pulling the thief away from the chest of glass knobs he'd been gawking over, and nodded toward the wall. Eli followed his gaze, letting out a low, impressed whistle.

There, hanging from a large iron peg, was a sword unlike any they'd seen. To start, it was enormous, larger even than the Heart of War. The blade, guard, and handle were all the same dark metal, a steel blacker than iron with a red tinge that made Eli shudder. Strangest of all was the edge. The heavy, black metal tapered on one side, sharpening, not to a sword edge, but to a row of jagged, bladed teeth. They ran in an uneven line, like teeth in a sea monster's jaw, and every one of them gleamed killing sharp. The sword's surface had a strange, matte finish that made the blade look darker than it was, but when Josef reached out to touch it, Slorn was suddenly there, grabbing his hand halfway.

"I said don't touch," the bear man growled.

"Slorn," Eli said, sliding between the two men with a smile. "I thought you didn't make swords anymore."

Slorn let go of Josef's hand with a low rumble. "I don't, usually. That's a custom order for another client." He glared at the sword. "The rabid piece of junk took me almost two months to finish and it's not friendly, so I'd appreciate it if you left it alone."

Despite the warning, Josef leaned in, more interested than ever. "It must weigh what, two hundred? Two fifty?"

"A ton," Eli said. "Who's it for, a mountain?"

"I have clients who are mountains," Slorn said, "but no. And I was told weight didn't matter, so I didn't bother to weigh it. Can we move on, please? I don't have all day."

He stepped aside, motioning them to the far back corner of the workroom. Eli went cheerfully, Josef less so, but what they saw next put the sword out of their minds.

In the corner stood a dressmaker's dummy half eaten by something that looked like liquid night. Eli blinked and looked again, letting his eyes adjust to the soft light of the workshop, and slowly, the blackness arranged itself into the shape of a woman's coat.

It was a long coat with a wide collar, flared sleeves, and buttoned straps to hold it closed. Silver flashed at the neck, and when he looked harder, Eli realized the flashes were needles. A small army of needles swam through the black fabric, moving in perfect unison, dragging the shiny black thread behind them. Still, despite that all this was happening less than three feet in front of him, Eli had a hard time seeing what the needles were doing. The light from the tall floor lamp seemed to slide around the coat, almost like the yellow glow was deliberately avoiding it. Eli marveled at the effect, wondering what kind of fabulous cloth Slorn had used, but when he looked at the scraps that lay scattered about on the floor, he realized the fabric was actually no blacker than any dark wool.

He mentioned this to Slorn, and the bear-headed man smiled wide.

"That's the new layer of protection I put in." His voice had an uncharacteristic note of bragging in it, the pride of a workman who has just made something unique. "It's not that the coat is so black, but that the lamp can't see it. Watch this."

He grabbed the coat's sleeve and began to move it toward the lamp. The closer he got to the light, the darker and less substantial the coat became.

"How did you do that?" Eli asked, snatching the sleeve out of Slorn's hand to get a better look at it.

"The law of type," Slorn answered proudly. "Most

spirits who emit light are fire spirits in one form or another. They all have the same type. It's like a spirit species." He added that last bit for Josef, who looked completely lost.

"But the law of type merely states that spirits of the same type share strengths and weaknesses," Eli said, giving the coat's fabric an experimental tug, amazed at the strength of it. "What does that have to do with not seeing?"

Slorn chuckled. "Let's just say that spirits who share a type also share the same blindnesses. For example, fire spirits as a whole are very direct. They don't bother with things they can't burn. To take advantage of this, I simply wove the spirits in the coat together in a way that, for the spirits, makes it look like resting water, which is of no interest to flames."

"Wait," Josef said. "So you're saying fire doesn't see water?"

"No," Slorn shook his head. "I'm saying that, since deep, standing water is generally not a threat to fire spirits, they are almost universally uninterested in it, and so feel no need to illuminate it." He gave Josef an amused look. "Why do you think lakes look so black at night?"

"Clever," Eli said, letting the sleeve fall back to its position. "Very, very clever. So we've got a coat that is almost invisible in firelight. That will be very useful in our line of work."

"Doesn't work in sunlight, though," Slorn said, frowning. "The sun's a different matter entirely, so don't get overconfident."

"No worries," Eli said. "I'm confident in my confidence. What else did you put in?"

Slorn shook his head and turned back to the coat. "It's a vast improvement over the previous coat. It's stronger and more flexible, though still thick enough to keep even the most persistent spirits from seeing what's inside, not that they would know to try. To the spirit world, this coat and anything it hides are just a blank, no more interesting than a sleeping nest of small water spirits or a pile of finely ground sand. Plus, the needles are putting a hood in as we speak, so there won't be the problem of losing the hat anymore, though she will look a little out of place in warmer climates."

"She'll look a little out of place anywhere besides a cultist convention." Eli grinned. "Fortunately, we're not concerned with appearances." He looked over at Nico. "What do you think?"

Nico's eyes were wide. "I want to try it."

"Go ahead," Slorn said, stepping aside.

The needles finished the last stitches on the hood as Nico stepped forward. She reached out, almost hesitantly, and took hold of the coat by the collar, gently sliding it off the dummy's shoulder and onto her own. It fell around her like a cloak, seemingly far too big, and yet her hands peeked out perfectly from the long sleeves while the hem ended just below her knees. She gave it an experimental shake, and the coat swirled around her like a current.

"Well?" Josef said.

Nico held out her arms. "It's heavy," she said, surprised.

"Not nearly as heavy as it should be," Slorn said, "considering what's in it. That coat contains almost a hundred feet of cloth, all folded and crunched around itself to give the spirit an actual size and power much greater than its form would suggest. There's wool and silk and steel in the weave, all picked for their complementary personalities and strong sense of duty. Out of that mesh of spirits, I have imprinted a new soul with properties greater than its component parts." Slorn ran his fingers over the smooth, black fabric. "This cloth will stop arrows, knives, and even a sword thrust from anything except an awakened blade. On your shoulders, it's better than any normal armor ever could be, because all the pieces of this coat, the thread, the cloth, the buttons, are part of one awakened spirit given a single purpose: to protect the spirit world from panic and destruction by concealing the demon and protecting the demon's prison"—he nodded at Nico—"you. If you are the strongbox that holds the demon, they are the vault around you, or that's how the spirit sees itself." Slorn smiled. "I made it rather zealous, so you'll have to be careful. The coat will follow you as its captain and obey any orders you give so long as they do not contradict the purpose I used as the foundation of its creation—preventing the demonseed from escaping into the world."

"Wait," Eli said. "Follow her orders? How? Nico's not a wizard."

Slorn looked at him, astonished. "Of course she's a wizard. Only wizards can become demonseeds. Normal human souls are far too flimsy to contain a demonseed to maturity."

A stab of betrayal hit Eli in the gut as he turned to Nico. "You were a wizard all this time? Why didn't you tell me?"

For the first time since he'd know her, Nico looked hurt. "You didn't ask," she said softly. "And it didn't seem important. Besides, it's not like I can talk to spirits casually, being what I am."

Eli opened his mouth to ask more questions, but the murderous look he was getting from Josef was enough to make him close it again. Fortunately, Slorn took that moment to change the subject altogether.

"Now that you've seen the work," he said, "it's time to talk about the price."

"I was wondering when we'd get to that." Eli sighed. "Well, never let it be said that I am a man who doesn't pay his bills. What can we do for you?"

Slorn sat down on the edge of his wooden table. "Have you heard of the Fenzetti blades?"

"Of course," Eli said. "I'm a thief. I've heard of everything you can put a price on, and the price on a Fenzetti is higher than most. There are, what, five total in the world? All held by collectors who won't sell them for love or money."

"There are ten, actually," Josef said, "including the half-finished piece Fenzetti was working on when he died." He raised his eyebrows at Eli's incredulous expression. "What? I'm a swordsman. Fenzetti blades are famous swords. It's not hard to see the connection. What I want to know," he said, shifting his gaze to Slorn, "is why does the world's greatest awakened swordsmith want one? Fenzettis are novelty items, prized for their supposed indestructibility, but they're hardly great works of sword making. Any swordsman, wizard or not, would gladly trade a Fenzetti for one of Heinricht Slorn's blades."

Slorn's mouth twitched. "It's not supposed indestructibility. The swords made by Fenzetti are impossible to break by any known means. Fenzetti was a Shaper wizard, you see. This was hundreds of years ago, far before my time, but he was legendary as one of our most creative craftsmen and guild masters, presiding over an uncommonly experimental and productive period of Shaper history. Now, traditionally, Shapers keep a large stockpile of rare materials for their work, including materials no one else really knows about—things the spirits bring them, oddities, stuff no one else understands. The objects we call Fenzetti blades are made of such a substance. The Shapers named it bone metal, for its off-white color, and for a while it was a subject of great interest among the Shaper crafters. It's not often you get your hands on an indestructible substance. Unfortunately, this indestructibility also made the bone metal completely unworkable. You can't melt it or scratch it, can't crush it or hammer it, and no one has ever successfully woken a bone metal spirit. After a few years of frenzied study, most Shapers wrote bone metal off as an interesting but useless substance. What good is a material that can't be turned into anything?"

"Fascinating history lesson," Eli said. "But when does Fenzetti come in?"

"I was getting to that," Slorn said crossly. "Of all the Shapers, Fenzetti was the only one who ever figured out how to work bone metal. Over a twenty-year span, he made a series of unbreakable swords from the material. Still, even the great Fenzetti could do only crude work with bone metal, and I've heard that even the few pieces he considered his masterworks aren't much to look at. But then"—Slorn grinned—"I'm not exactly looking to hang one on my wall. I want the metal."

"Well, in that case," Eli said, "why not just buy bone metal? Why go through the trouble of stealing a Fenzetti?"

"Because bone metal is so rare in nature it might as well not exist," Slorn said, annoyed. "What bone metal there is, the Shapers keep in their storehouses under their mountain. As I think should be abundantly clear by this point, they're not just going to sell the stuff to me, and I don't think you want to try robbing the Shaper mountain again."

"No," Eli said, laughing. "Once was enough for me, thanks. I guess Fenzetti blades it is. Do you want any one in particular?"

"A large one would be preferable," Slorn said thoughtfully. "But I don't have a particular blade in mind. Whatever you can get quickly will be fine."

"Quickly may be relative," Eli said. "But a deal is a deal, and you certainly did come through on your end."

"Are we settled then?" Slorn said.

"Yes." Eli grinned and stuck out his hand. "One coat for one bone metal blade, even trade."

Slorn shook his hand firmly and then shuffled them out of his workroom, Nico still happily swirling her coat. As they filed out into the main room, they found Pele there waiting for them. Her face was pale and anxious, and her hair was windswept and wild, as if she'd been standing in a gale, though the trees outside were perfectly still.

"Slorn," she said quietly. "The weather's changing."

Eli gave her an odd look. Weather talk wasn't usually something Pele mentioned with that kind of gravity. Slorn, however, stopped midstep and pricked up his round ears, listening.

"You're right," he said, at once as serious as she was. "The pressure is changing." He looked to Eli. "You've got the coat, so you'd best be leaving now. The weather changes quickly here. We need to move the house."

"If you say so." Eli felt uncomfortably like he had just missed something very important. "Wasn't like we had much left to do, anyway."

It took them about five minutes to get everything assembled. The kitchen packed them a bag of sandwiches and fruit that Eli took with such effusive thanks, the counters were nearly quivering with happiness. Josef, meanwhile, packed up his knives suspiciously, keeping his eyes on Slorn and Pele as they went around closing cabinets and shuttering windows. Eli didn't blame him. It was hard to feel the urgency for a storm when the sky was blue and bright.

But as they trundled down the stairs and out onto the dry stream bed, Eli began to feel it too. The pressure was falling, making his ears ache, and though the air was still and calm, he could smell rain. High overhead, the clouds were moving quickly.

Slorn and Pele saw them to the edge of the woods, but the moment Eli, Nico, and Josef stepped into the shade of the trees, their hosts turned and went back inside the house without looking back, as though they were deliberately trying not to see which way their guests left.

When the door shut behind them, the house shuddered. There was an enormous creak of bending wood, and the house's foundations began to move. The four spindly legs straightened and stretched their chicken-feet talons, leaning forward, then backward, so that the house rocked like a ship at sea, and Eli felt sure he was going to be sick just watching. Then, when all the legs were stretched, the house shuddered and took a step forward. The wooden limbs rippled like muscle, and the house was off, walking in long strides down the dry streambed and disappearing into the woods with surprising speed, leaving only a thin line of chimney smoke behind it and no footprints at all.

Josef gave a low whistle as he watched the line of smoke vanish behind the trees. "No wonder the bastard was so hard to find." He looked over at Eli. "So, you're his friend; are the storms here that dangerous or was the bear man spinning a story to get rid of us?"

"I don't think that's the case," Eli said quietly, looking south. There, barely visible over the treetops, the black smudge of a storm front was building on the horizon. That much wasn't so unusual; the weather in the mountains was finicky, but something was off. The clouds around the storm front were drifting south, yet the dark thunderheads were plowing straight north against the wind, and moving fast.

"Come on," Eli said. "I don't think we want to be around when that hits."

Josef nodded and they began to move east, following the streambed, walking as fast as they could go in the loose sand. Behind them, the storm rolled on, veering slightly west in the direction Slorn's house had gone.

The walking house stopped on a rocky cliff at the edge of the Awakened Wood. It turned twice in a circle and then crouched on the cliff's edge. As soon as the house stopped swaying, Slorn opened the door and stomped down the rickety steps, his bear face unreadable. Pele was right behind him, and they took their positions in the high, scrubby field that led up to the cliff.

The storm rolled over the forest, lit from within almost

constantly by arcs of blue-white lightning. The treetops tossed sideways where it passed, yet no rain fell. Slorn and Pele hunched against the wind as it came, howling and heavy with the ear-splitting pressure of the storm. The clouds flew overhead, blotting out the afternoon sun, and the cliff went as dark as rainy midnight. Slorn could feel Pele shivering next to him, and he put a hand on her shoulder, steadying her as they waited in the dark.

Lightning flashed all around them, jumping between the clouds in spidering arcs. Then, with a crack that split all hearing, a single tree-sized bolt struck the ground in front of Slorn, blinding what little night vision he had gained. But no light could blind the world Slorn saw through his spirit sight, and as the clap of thunder followed on the lightning's heels, he saw it appear. A primordial storm, such as had not been seen in the world since creation, stood before them, an epic war of air and water spirits and the lightning spirits they birthed, embroiled in an endless conflict hundreds of miles across. Yet all of this was bound into the shape of a tall man in a black coat carrying a long sword, crushed together by the white mark Slorn dared not look at. The flash of the lightning faded, and Slorn let his normal eyes, the bear's soft-focusing, near-sighted vision, take over. It was best not to look at the Lord of Storms as he truly was for too long.

For a long, awkward moment, no one spoke. Finally, Slorn took the initiative, lowering himself in a small bow. "Welcome, as always, my lord. What can we do for you?"

"Spare me the gracious-host routine," the Lord of Storms said. His voice was impatient, and he was looking around, his flashing eyes seeing through everything. "I'm just here to get our new recruit his sword."

The Lord of Storms stepped aside to reveal another man standing behind him. Slorn's eyes widened in surprise. He hadn't even seen the man until now, though that was due to the Lord of Storm's control over his thunderheads. There certainly was no other way Slorn could have missed the monster of the man who stepped forward. He was taller even than the Lord of Storms, and nearly twice as wide. His head was clean shaven and crisscrossed with pale, puckered scars. His black coat, which was too small, he wore open and fluttering in the wind, the sleeves ripped off to make room for his bulky, overmuscled arms. His face had the strange, smashed look of a brawler's, the bones broken too often to ever sit right again. Yet what made Slorn look away in disgust wasn't his crooked fingers or his sharp-toothed, murderous sneer, but the sash he wore across his bare chest.

It was a strip of crimson fabric tied over one shoulder of his ripped coat. The cloth had several long, telling splatters streaked across it that left little to Slorn's imagination, but even more disturbing was what was sewn into the sash. All across the red cloth, sewn in with surprising care, was a collection of what Slorn could only guess were trophies. There were broken sword hilts, some of them with their spirits still whimpering in pain, bits of jewelry still splattered with lines of dark, dried blood, and other things Slorn didn't look at too closely.

"This must be the one you told me about," Slorn said carefully. "Your new, nonwizard recruit." It had to be. There was no way a wizard could wear what the man was wearing and not go mad.

"Yes," the Lord of Storms said. "Spirit deafness is a bit of a hindrance, but you don't have to hear to kill demons. Sted here has proven he can get the job done, so I've decided to make him a full member of the League." He smiled at Slorn, a terrifying sight. "The sword's the last bit he needs. I presume it's ready?"

"Yes," Slorn said. "Pele, take Mr. Sted here to his new sword."

To her credit, Pele didn't hesitate. She stepped forward and motioned for the enormous man to follow her. As they disappeared into the house, Slorn took the opportunity to broach the subject hanging over their heads.

"So," he said, looking at the Lord of Storms. "It's not often you escort a new recruit to pick up a sword yourself. Is Sted that good?"

"Hardly," the Lord of Storms said. "Sted's a brawler. He was born a brawler and he'll die the same. I only hope we can squeeze a few dead demons out of him before it happens." He turned to face Slorn, and his expression grew murderous, a sure sign that the time for small talk was past. "You need to consider the company you keep more carefully, Slorn."

Slorn crossed his arms. "So long as I fulfill my contract to provide the League of Storms with awakened blades, I am free to pursue whatever other side projects I desire. This is our agreement."

The Lord of Storms sneered. "I allow your little dalliances with that thing you keep up in the mountains only because the Weaver managed to convince my lady you would be the one to find a cure for the demon infestation. That generosity does not extend to Monpress's pet monster. I may be forbidden from interfering in the thief's actions, but that doesn't mean I have to stand by and watch while you sell him tools to hide the demon from us."

So the Lord of Storms had been warned off Eli by the Shepherdess. Slorn had suspected something of the sort. It wasn't like the League to let something like Nico run free. He tucked that bit of information away for future use.

"All I gave Eli was a coat to replace the girl's ruined one," he said. "Surely you don't want the demon terrifying the countryside and causing panics."

"Spare me," the Lord of Storms snarled. "Know this, Shaper: This is not the way of things for much longer. Do you think that boy's my lady's first favorite? Or her last? The time is coming, very soon, when the Shepherdess will grow tired of Monpress's antics. I suggest you think long and hard about where your loyalties fall when that day comes."

"When that day comes," Slorn said slowly, "I know exactly what I will do."

"Good," the Lord of Storms said. "The League of Storms has existed since the world began, and in all that time you're one of the best swordsmiths we've ever had. It would be a great shame to lose you." He paused, and gave Slorn a long, hard look. "Great, but not unbearable. Do I make myself clear?"

Slorn smiled. "Immensely."

Inside the house, Pele lit the lamps with a wave of her hand as she led the way to her father's study. The man behind her, Sted, was talking in a loud, brash voice, as he'd been since she'd closed the front door behind him.

"So," he said, keeping too close behind her. "You're the bear man's what, servant? Lover?"

"Apprentice," she answered curtly, leading him into the den.

"Ah." She could see him grinning. "Thought you looked a little rough for a concubine, but we are pretty far out. Where are we, anyway? The boss wouldn't tell me."

"We're in the Turning Wood," Pele said, coming to a stop at Slorn's workroom door. "That's all I can tell you. Slorn's location is a League secret."

She opened the door to the workroom and led him inside. "I must ask you not to touch anything," she said. "No spirit in this workshop may be touched by outside hands without Slorn's strict permission."

"Why would I want to touch this junk?" Sted growled, glaring at the scraps of cloth left over from Nico's coat. "Where's my sword?"

Pele stood aside and motioned to the black blade on the wall. Sted stopped in his tracks. He stared at the sword, eyes wide. "Is it magic?"

"It is awakened," Pele answered, turning to look at the jagged-toothed blade as well. "Since you are spirit deaf, Slorn made the blade from a stock of ore with a very straightforward personality. This sword has only one desire: to destroy all that stand before it. Not a sophisticated weapon, but we were assured a straightforward blade would be best for a man of your"—she paused—"talents."

If Sted caught the insult, he showed no sign. He reached out greedily for the blade, but Pele moved faster, gripping the handle right before him.

"As I said, no touching." She met his angry glare. "The

sword doesn't know you, and it would be happy to take your hand off. Before I can hand it to you safely, you'll need its name."

Sted snorted. "What do I look like, some duelist fop? I don't bother with names for my swords."

"No, you don't name it," Pele said crossly. "This is an awakened sword. It has its own name." Gasping a little at the weight, Pele carefully took the sword down from its peg, wincing as she always did at the pure blood thirst that permeated the metal. "This is Dunolg," she said, turning the blade so that the hilt was toward Sted, "the Iron Avalanche."

Sted grinned, taking the sword with a steady hand. "A proud name." He gave it a test swing, which was quite unnerving in the tiny room. "It fits," he said, nodding. "Yes, this sword will do nicely. I can feel it. We'll cut anything that dares stand before us."

Pele stepped back as Sted swung the sword again, his scarred face lighting up with ghoulish delight as the wicked, toothed blade cut through the air. It whistled as it swung, a low trill of pure, violent hunger that made Pele sick to her stomach. When she had helped Slorn forge the blade, she hadn't been able to imagine the kind of man who could form a bond with such a monster. Now, as Sted tied the jagged blade to his hip with a length of stained leather, she was sorry she'd found out.

Slorn and the Lord of Storms were waiting in silence when Sted and Pele exited the house. Sted started to say something about his new sword, which he wore proudly on his hip, but one look at his master's face was enough to silence him. Without a word, he took up his place beside the Lord of Storms. When he was in position, the

Lord waved his hand, and then, without a good-bye or a thank-you, they were gone. There was no lightning this time; they simply vanished into the dark. The moment they were gone, the unnatural clouds began to roll away, retreating as quickly as they had come, and sunlight burst back onto the high ridge.

Only when the storm front was far in the distance did Slorn let out the breath he'd been holding.

"Father," Pele said softly, "was it right to give that man *that* sword?"

"Right has nothing to do with it." Slorn ran his rough hands over the fur between his ears. "It was work, Pele, nothing more." With that, he turned and walked back into the house. "Let's move."

Pele sighed. When her father got like this, there was no point in asking for more explanation. She simply hurried after him, climbing the rickety steps as the house began to shudder. As soon as she was inside, the house took off down the ridge, heading north, toward the mountains.

CHAPTER
7

The Spirit Court's tower was not the only great building in Zarin. Across the city, past the dip in the ridge made by the swift Whitefall River, the white-painted stone and timber buildings that made up most of the city took a turn for the elegant. The roads steepened as they climbed up the ridge, cutting back and forth until they reached the highest arch of the city's rocky backbone. There, perched like a coral on a jut of bare rock, stood the Whitefall Citadel, fortress of the Whitefall family, the Merchant Princes of Zarin, and official home of the unprecedented organization they had founded, the Council of Thrones. Though not as tall or as mystical as the Spiritualist's white tower, it was nonetheless magnificently impressive. The castle stood apart from the city, separated from the steep road by a long bridge that stretched across a natural gap in the ridge. Perched as it was on an outcropping, the citadel seemed to float all on its own, a great, airy fortress of flashing white walls and soaring arches. But most impressive of all were the famous towers of Zarin. There were seven in all crowning the inner keep, so tall they seemed to scrape the sky itself with their hammered gold spires.

Despite its grandness, these days the citadel was mostly for show. It remained the symbol of the Council, and its seven towers stood in proud relief on every gold standard the Council mint pressed, but the enormous bureaucracy that kept the Council turning over had long ago outgrown the soaring towers of its home fortress, spilling into the mansions and trade halls of the surrounding slopes. These days, the only people who actually stayed in the fortress were the Whitefall family of Zarin and any actual nobles who deigned to come to Council functions themselves.

On the fifth floor of the citadel's inner keep, where everything was as luxurious as money and station could make it, one such man, Edward di Fellbro, Duke of Gaol, was having tea in his rooms. For most nobility, especially those with lands as rich as Gaol, this act would have involved at least three servants, yet Edward was alone, calmly finishing a modest plate of fruit and bread at the corner of his enormous dining table, which was covered, not in cornucopias of exotic fruits and sweetmeats, but with maps.

They were spread out neatly end to end, maps from every region in the Council Kingdom in different styles and time periods, some old and worn, some whose ink had hardly dried, yet every single one of them was dotted with the same meticulous red markings. Sometimes they were Xs, sometimes circles or squares, and very occasionally a triangle. No matter the shape, however, the same tight, neat notation was listed beside each one, usually a number and a short description, and always marked with a date.

Duke Edward stared at the maps intently, his thin face drawn into a thoughtful frown as he took a sip from his teacup only to notice it was empty. Scowling, he held out his cup, and an elegant teapot on four silver legs waddled over to refill it. The pot trembled as it moved, its worked golden lid rattling softly as it poured. The duke glared at the pot and it stopped rattling instantly, moving back to its spot in the tea service with murmured apologies and careful bows so as not to drip.

Edward saw none of it. His stare was already back on the maps, flicking from point to point in no discernible order. From his posture, he might have stayed like that indefinitely, but a knock on the carved door interrupted his contemplation.

"Enter," he said, not bothering to hide the annoyance in his voice.

The door opened, and one of the Council pages, dressed head to toe in the ridiculous white and silver finery Whitefall made all his servants wear, stepped timidly into the room.

"Spiritualist Hern to see you, my Lord," the boy announced with a low bow.

Edward put down his fork and pushed his plate away. "Send him in."

The boy stepped back, and the duke's unexpected guest sailed into the room. Sailed was the right word. Edward had never met anyone as preoccupied with his appearance as Hern. The Spiritualist was in full regalia today, a tight green coat embroidered with blue and silver in the imitation of peacock feathers, with tall, turned, and pointed cuffs hanging down over the glittering, knuckle-sized jewels of his rings.

"I swear, Edward," he said, collapsing onto a cushioned lounge by the window as the boy closed the door, "your quarters get smaller every time you come to Zarin. And they've got you up on the fifth floor this time, with all those stairs." He pulled out a handkerchief and patted his flushed face. "It's intolerable. I never understood why you don't just take a house in the city like everyone else."

"I see no point for such a useless expense," the duke said dryly. "Besides, the part of my Council dues that covers these rooms is too dear already. A rich lord does not stay rich by indulging in redundant expense."

"So you like to say," Hern said, helping himself to a cup from the tea service, which he held out for the nervous teapot to fill. "What's that you're working on there?" He nodded toward the spread of maps. "Plotting to expand your lands? Going to take over the Council Kingdoms?"

"Hardly," the duke said. "They wouldn't be worth the bother."

"So what are these for, then?" The Spiritualist actually sounded fascinated, a sure sign that he was only trying to get Edward talking and comfortable. It was the same song and dance they went through every time Hern visited, and Edward had long since learned it was faster to just go along than try and force the Spiritualist to get to his point sooner. Besides, he hadn't explained his system in a long while, and explaining something to others was a useful exercise for uncovering faults in execution.

"These," he said, leaning forward and stretching out his hand to tap one of the red markings on the map in front of him, "are the movements of Eli Monpress."

Hern blinked. "The thief?"

"Do you know any other Monpresses?" Edward gave him a scathing look. "You asked, so pay attention. Each red mark denotes where he's been active since he first appeared five years ago." He moved his fingers over the maps without touching them, tracing a path between the markings. "The Xs are confirmed robberies, the circles are unconfirmed incidents that I believe were his work, and the squares are crimes attributed to Monpress, but which I don't believe he had a hand in."

"And how do you make that judgment?" Hern said, blowing on his tea.

"I look for a pattern." Edward was pleased with the question. A chance to talk through his logic was always welcome. "All men have patterns. It's human nature, even for someone as famously unpredictable as Monpress. Look here." He moved his finger over the X closest to him, far south of Zarin, covering the dot that denoted the desert city of Amit.

"Monpress's first crime we know of was here, the theft of the Count of Amit's cash prize for the annual Race of the Dunes. He also stole the winning horse, which he then used as a getaway. He's next seen a few months later"— his finger ran up the maps, heading far north to the very top of the Council Kingdoms—"here." He tapped a red X in an empty spot of the map, somewhere in the wilderness between the Kingdom of Jenet and the Kingdom of Favol. "He ambushed the wedding procession of the Princess of Jenet and stole her entire dowry, including nearly eighty pounds of gold brick, fifty horses, a hundred head of cattle, and all of the bride's wedding jewelry."

"I've heard of that one," Hern said with a laugh.

"The story I heard said he did it all by himself, but surely—"

"I think that was the case," the duke said. "Before the swordsman and the girl came into the picture a little over a year ago, Monpress always acted alone. For the Princess of Jenet, witnesses say he talked the road itself into changing its path, leading the whole procession into a sinking mire that he could reportedly walk over like it was dry land."

"Come, that's impossible." Hern waved his jewel-covered hand. "I've got two top-notch earth spirits, and even I couldn't convince an entire road to move."

Edward raised his eyebrows, tucking that fact away for future use. "Well," he said, "however he managed it, the road story fits Monpress's pattern."

"Which is?" Hern said, slurping his tea.

The duke gave him a flat look. Even if he was only feigning interest, surely Hern wasn't that dense. "Look at the history," Edward said slowly. "Monpress's crimes are always robberies, and not just robberies, but thefts on a grand scale, usually against nobility. They are never violent, save in self defense, and usually leave little question as to who the perpetrator was."

"You mean the calling card." Hern nodded.

"Indeed." Edward reached up to the very top of his maps and unclipped the small stack of white cards he'd pinned there. They were all roughly the same size, and though a few were on cheaper paper, they all had the same basic look: a white card stamped at the center with the same fanciful, cursive *M*.

"They started out handwritten," the duke said, shuffling through the cards carefully so as not to get them out of order. "Then after his third crime, when his bounty was raised to five hundred gold standards, they were all printed. The early ones are still cheap, but for the past two years, he's used a variety of high-quality stocks, though never the same one twice." The duke smiled, tapping the cards on the table to line them up again. "Monpress is vain, you see. He's a glutton for attention. That's the way you can spot a fake Monpress crime."

He spread his hands over the maps, coming to rest on one of the red squares just north of Zarin. "Here," he said. "Two years ago someone broke into a money changer's house, killing one of his apprentices in the process. The thief left a Monpress calling card, and that was all the local authorities needed. However, anyone who's spent time studying Monpress knows that, whoever committed that crime, it wasn't Eli. First off, a money changer's office is far too small a target. Second, the murder of the apprentice, very unlike him, but the real sign here is the lack of flair. It's such a simple, unsophisticated crime. Uninventive. For me, that alone is enough to absolve Monpress of guilt in this matter."

"Impressive," Hern said, making a good show of actually looking impressed. "Are you going to take all this over to the bounty office, then? Earn a little goodwill from the Council? The northern kingdoms are still rather miffed at you for raising the toll to use your river last year."

"I calculate my toll based on the damages their drunken, irresponsible barge captains inflict on my docks," the duke said. "If they have a problem with that, then they are free to reimburse me directly or hire better captains. As for Eli," the duke said, returning the stack of cards to its place at the top of the map, "I would never dream of giving my findings to a group as disorganized and sensational as the Council's Bounty Office. If they think they can just throw money at a problem as complex and nuanced as Monpress and make it go away, then they deserve the runaround he's giving them."

Hern gave him a sly look over his teacup. "Thinking of collecting the bounty yourself, then? I didn't think fifty-five thousand was a large enough number to interest a man of your wealth."

"Do not make assumptions about my interests," the duke said, sitting back. "Only a shortsighted fool thinks he is wealthy enough not to take opportunities presented."

"How interesting to hear you say that," Hern said, sitting up and putting his teacup aside. "As it happens, a new opportunity has just opened up for me."

The duke smiled and mentally calculated Hern's timing. Five minutes from arrival to broaching of actual point, faster than usual. Hern must have something big on the line. "How much?" he asked, tapping his fingers together.

Hern looked taken aback. "Edward," he said, "what makes you think—"

The Duke of Gaol gave him a cutting look. "How much, Hern?"

"Ten thousand gold standards," Hern said, crossing his legs and draping his arms over the back of the couch. When the duke gave him an incredulous look, he just shrugged. "You asked, I answered. I've a rare opportunity here, Edward. Remember what I wrote you a few days ago about forcing Banage to exile his own apprentice to a tower? Well, the girl lived up to her reputation better than I'd thought possible and rejected the deal entirely. Fortunately, I got wind of this before the trial, and just this afternoon I had her convicted of treason."

"Sounds like a done deal," the duke said. "Why do you need my money?"

"Well," Hern said and took another long sip of his tea. "A treason conviction is a serious matter, Edward, especially for a girl as promising and protected as Banage's little pet. It all happened very quickly and I had to make a few promises the night before to see it through."

"I see," the duke said. "And these 'promises' add up to ten thousand gold standards? What happened to the thousand I gave you last month?"

"Gone," Hern said with a shrug. "How do you think I got the signatures for her accusation? Whether they're Tower Keepers or apprentices, all Spiritualists have an obsession with duty, and that makes getting them to do anything very expensive. Frankly, Edward, you got that trial on the cheap. Any other time and it would easily have cost twice that much to put Banage's favorite on the spot. But this Mellinor business was such a mess. People were already nice and scared and looking for someone to blame, and who better than the girl at the heart of it?"

"And what does this have to do with me?" the duke said. "So far, all I've heard is the usual Spiritualist politics, and I have quite enough politics of my own to deal with. Why should I give you ten thousand standards to fund more?"

Hern's eyes narrowed. "Don't get cheap on me, Fellbro. This is as much for your benefit as mine. Fifteen years now I've been Gaol's Tower Keeper, and for fifteen years I've been keeping idealists like Banage out of your land. We don't need to go into what would happen if an investigation of Gaol was requested, but you'd be amazed how fast the Spirit Court's policy of noninterference with sovereign states can vanish if they judge the cause worthy enough. Such an investigation could be especially troubling if they teamed up with your enemies in the Council, who would love to see a return to lax tariffs and rules of your father's time. I have worked tirelessly for years now to keep your secrets, and all I've ever asked in return is a little monetary assistance in my efforts to reform the Court. Ten thousand is pocket change for a man like you. We both know it, so don't try and pretend I'm being unreasonable, or else I may have to start suddenly remembering things about Gaol you'd rather I didn't."

Edward gave the Spiritualist a disgusted look. Still, the man did have a point, and it had been a while since he'd dipped into the Spirit Court management part of Gaol's budget. "You're sure that ten thousand will buy the result you're after?"

"Certain." Hern leaned forward. "Miranda Lyonette was one of Banage's key pillars within the Court. It's no secret he's been grooming her to be his successor. Crushing her is the closest we can come to striking a direct blow at Etmon himself. Even though she managed to flee Zarin before her sentence could be carried out, the deed is done."

"She escaped?" The duke arched his dark eyebrows. "That was careless of you, Hern."

"Doesn't matter," Hern said, shaking his head. "She can't run forever, and in any case, her reputation is ruined. She'll never work as a Spiritualist again, and

Banage is left alone and bereft, robbed of the apprentice he loved like a daughter. The old man is weakening, a bit at a time. Soon, with enough money and pressure, the damage will be irreversible. We'll rip Banage's control of the Court wide open, and then all I have to do is be in the right place at the right time with the right incentives and the Spirit Court will be mine, and, through reasonable extension, yours."

He finished with a smile the duke found discomfortingly overconfident. Using money to sway circumstance in your favor was one thing, but when you started outright buying people to act against their conscience, a situation could quickly slide out of control. Still, he'd requested Hern as his Tower Keeper exactly because the man knew how to play the Spirit Court. If he couldn't trust him now he'd have lost a lot more than ten thousand gold.

"One more question," the duke said carefully. "This Miranda Lyonette, she's the one the Court sent to Mellinor after Monpress, correct?"

"Yes," Hern said. "Her failure there was what got her into this mess."

The duke nodded. "And do you think the Spirit Court will be sending anyone else after Eli while this is going on?"

"No," Hern said. "I think the Court has had quite enough of Monpress for a while."

Duke Edward nodded absently, staring down at his maps. "How fortuitous." He looked back at Hern. "I'll send a notice for the ten thousand to your house after I've warned my exchequer. He'll assist you as usual in collecting the money from my accounts in Zarin. And if you need more, Hern, don't bother coming over. Just send a letter with a documented list as to why. All of this beating around the issue is inefficient."

Hern's eye's widened at that, but his smile never flickered. "Lovely chatting with you too, my lord," he said, standing up with a graceful swirl of his coat.

"Send in the page on your way out," the duke said, reaching across the table to grab a sheaf of blank stationery and an ink pot from his desk.

Hern shot him a dirty look, but the duke was already absorbed in whatever he was writing, his pen scratching in neat, efficient strokes across the paper. With a sneer at being treated like a valet, Hern left the duke's room in a huff, grabbing the first page he saw and literally shoving the boy toward the duke's door before it had even finished closing.

The boy stumbled into the duke's parlor, blinking in confusion for a few moments before recovering enough to drop the customary bow.

"You," the duke said without looking up from his note, which he was folding into thirds. "Take this to the printing office on Little Shambles Street. Give it to Master Scribe Phelps, and *only* Master Scribe Phelps. Tell him that fortuitous circumstances have necessitated an acceleration of my order, and he is to have the numbers outlined on that note ready for distribution at the points written beside them by tomorrow morning. Repeat that."

"Printing office, Little Shambles Street, Master Scribe Phelps," the boy repeated with the practiced memory of a trained page who got this sort of request quite often. "I am to tell him that fortuitous circumstances have necessitated an acceleration of your order, and he is to have these numbers ready for distribution at the points written beside them by tomorrow morning."

The duke handed him the folded note without a word of thanks, and the boy shuffled out, wishing that, just once, the duke would bother to tip for such feats of memory. He never did, but that was part of why Merchant Prince Whitefall charged the old cheapskate double for his rooms.

When the page was gone the duke stood alone at his table going over his plans step by step in his head. He did this often, for it gave him great pleasure to be thorough. Phelps would balk at having to print thousands of detailed posters and have them packed for distribution in one night, but a successful man seized opportunity when it arrived. The Court's interest in Monpress had been the last uncontrollable element. If they were putting off their investigation thanks to this business in Mellinor, now was the time to strike. Accelerating the pace made him nervous, but he fought the feeling down. Surely this apprehension was merely a product of being in Zarin, where things were messy and chaotic. In a week, all his business here would be done and he'd be on his way back to Gaol, where everything was orderly, controlled, and perfect.

Just thinking about it brought a smile to his face, and he reached down for his teacup, newly refilled by the creeping teapot, which had already returned to its place on the tea service. Yes, he thought, walking over to the tall windows, sipping his tea as he watched Hern climb into an ostentatious carriage in the little courtyard below while, behind him, the page hurried toward the gates with the letter in his hands. Yes, things were going perfectly smoothly. If the printers did as they were paid to do, then tomorrow the net woven of everything he'd learned over years of following Monpress would finally be cast. All he had to do was sit back and wait for the thief to take the bait, and then even an element as chaotic as Eli Monpress would be drawn at last into predictable order.

The happiness of that thought carried him through the rest of his day, and if he drove particularly hard bargains in his meetings that afternoon, no one thought anything special of it. He was the Duke of Gaol, after all.

CHAPTER
8

Down the mountains from Slorn's woods, where the ground began to level out into low hills and branching creeks, the city of Goin lay huddled between two muddy banks. Little more than an overgrown border outpost, Goin was claimed by two countries, neither of which bothered with it much, leaving the soggy dirt streets to the trappers and loggers who called it home. It was a rowdy, edge-of-nowhere outpost where the law, what there was of it, turned a blind eye to anything that wasn't directed squarely at them, which was just how Eli liked it.

"Aren't you glad I talked you out of making camp and coming down in the morning?" Eli said, strolling down the final half mile of rutted trail out of the mountains.

"I still don't see why you wanted to come here at all," Josef said. "I passed through here about two years ago chasing Met Skark, the assassin duelist. It was a mangy collection of lowlifes then too, and Met wasn't nearly as good as his wanted posters made him out to be. Still," he said, smiling warmly, "Goin did have some lively bar fights once the locals got drunk enough not to see the Heart, so it wasn't a total waste."

Eli looked at him sideways, eyeing the enormous wrapped hilt that poked up over Josef's broad shoulders. "I don't see how anyone could get that drunk."

"The strained liquor they brew in the mountains is strong stuff." Josef chuckled. "They don't call it Northern Poison for nothing."

Goin was surrounded by a high wall of split and sharpened logs set into the thick mud. The northern gate was closed when they reached it, but the guard door stood wide open.

"Sort of defeats the point of a gate in the first place," Eli said, standing aside as Josef and Nico ducked through.

Josef shook his head. "Can't say I blame them for not bothering."

Eli sighed. The man had a point. Inside the wooden wall, the town was a maze of wood and stone buildings, dirt streets, flickering torches, filthy straw, burly, drunk men, and foul smells. Hardly a high-value target, even for the least discerning bandits.

"Civilization at last," he mumbled, covering his face with his handkerchief. "This way."

He led them deeper into the town, stepping over drunks and dodging fistfights, turning down blind alleys seemingly at random until he stopped in front of a small, run-down building. There was no sign, nothing to separate the building from the dozen other run-down buildings around it. Josef glared at it suspicously, but Eli smoothed his coat over his chest, checked his hair, then stepped forward to knock lightly on the rickety wooden door.

On the second knock, the door cracked open and a hand in a grubby leather glove shot out, palm up. With a flick of his fingers Eli produced a gold standard, which he dropped into the waiting hand. It must have been enough, for the door flew open and a burly man in a logger's woolen shirt and leather pants welcomed them in.

"Sit down," he said, motioning to a fur-covered bench. "I'll get the broker."

Eli smiled and sat. Josef, however, did not. He leaned on the wall by the door, arms crossed over his chest. Nico stayed right beside him, her eyes strangely luminous beneath the deep hood of her new coat.

The large man vanished through the little door at the rear of the building, leaving his guests alone in the tiny room, which was uncomfortably warm thanks to the red-hot stove in the corner and smelled like dust. A few moments later, the man came out again, this time trailed by a tall, thin woman in men's trousers and a thick woolen coat, her graying hair pulled tight behind her head. She walked to a stool by the stove and sat down, looking Eli square in the eye as the large man took up position behind her.

"The fee is five standards a question," she said.

"That's a bit steep," Eli said. "One is traditional."

"Maybe in the city," the woman sneered. "This far out, customers are few and far between. I have to eat. Besides, you don't pay the doorman in gold if you're bargain shopping. Five standards or get out."

"Five standards then." Eli smiled, flashing the gold in his hand. "But I expect to get what I pay for."

"You won't be disappointed," the woman said as the man took Eli's money. "I'm a fully initiated broker. You'll get the best we have. Now, what's your question?"

Eli leaned forward. "I need the location and owners of all the remaining Fenzetti blades."

The woman frowned. "Fenzetti? You mean the swords?"

Eli nodded.

"A tough question." The woman tapped her fingers against her knees. "Good for you I had you pay up front. Come back in one hour."

"No worries." Eli smiled. "We'll wait here."

Neither the woman nor her guard looked happy about that, but Eli was a paying customer now, so they said nothing. The woman stood up and disappeared into the back room. The man took up position by the door she'd gone through, watching Josef like a hawk.

"Well," Eli said, fishing through his pockets, "no need to be unfriendly, Mr. Guard. How about joining us for a game?" He pulled out a deck of Daggerback cards. "Friendly wagers only, of course."

The guard glowered and said nothing, but Eli was already dealing him a hand with a king placed invitingly faceup. The guard's expression changed quickly at that, and he moved a little closer, picking up his cards. After winning the first five rounds, the guard had warmed up to them immensely. So much so, in fact, that he scarcely noticed his luck going steadily downhill after his initial streak. Eli kept things going, asking him innocent questions and distracting him from the cards in his hand, which only seemed to get worse as the rounds went on. To Josef, who was used to Eli's fronts, it was clear that the thief's attention was only half on the game. His real focus was the door the woman had disappeared behind and the strange sounds that filtered through the thick wood. The noise was hard to place. It sounded like a sea wind, or a storm gale, yet the torches outside the tiny, grimy window were steady, burning yellow and bright without so much as a flicker.

Almost exactly one hour later, by Josef's reckoning, the door opened and the woman came back into the room. By that point, the guard had been losing for nearly forty minutes, and four of Eli's five gold standards were back in the thief's own pockets. The woman shot her guard a murderous look, and he jumped up from the bench, leaving his hand unplayed (a good thing, too: his pair of knights would never have beaten Eli's three queens) as he dashed to his place behind her. Eli only grinned and gathered his cards, tucking them back into his pocket before he turned to hear his now greatly discounted answer.

With a sour expression, the woman flipped open a small, leather-bound notebook. "I was able to get the locations of eight Fenzetti blades," she said. "You don't look like the sort who's trying to buy one, so I'll skip over the part about how none of these are for sale. Of the eight I could locate, five are held by the Immortal Empress."

Eli made a choking sound. "The Immortal Empress? Couldn't you start with something in an easier location? Say, bottom of the sea?"

"You paid only for location and owner," the woman said. "Them being impossible to get is your problem."

"All right," Eli said, sighing. "Well, that's five out of the way. How about the other three?"

The woman ran her finger down the page. "One is owned by the King of Sketti."

"Sketti, Sketti," Eli mumbled, trying to remember. "That's on the southern coast, right?"

"It's an island, actually," the woman said, nodding. "Large island in the south sea. Four months from Zarin by caravan, five by boat."

Eli grimaced and motioned for her to continue.

The woman flipped to the next page in her book. "There's rumored to be a Fenzetti dueling dagger in the great horde of Del Sem. It hasn't been seen in eighty years, though, not since Rikard the Mad lived up to his name and started giving out his family's treasure to anyone who promised to banish the demon he was convinced lived in his chest."

Eli frowned. "So that one could be anywhere, really."

The woman nodded and closed her book. "I'd say Sketti is your best option. Would you like to buy another question?"

"Not so fast," Eli said. "You said there were eight known blades. You've only told us seven so far. Where's the last one?"

"Oh," the woman said. "That one might as well be at the bottom of the sea for all the chance you have of getting your hands on it. It's currently held by the Duke of Gaol."

"Gaol?" Eli whistled. "He's supposed to be richer than most countries put together. Rules over a beautiful and boring little duchy like it's his private playground, or so I've heard. Where does the impossible part come in?"

She gave him a look of disbelief. "Where have you been?"

She got up and walked over to a small wardrobe set against the corner. It looked like a simple coat closet, but when she opened it Eli saw it was full of papers, organized into wooden nooks with small, scribbled labels. She dug around for a moment and then returned carrying a rolled-up poster.

"I can't believe you haven't seen these. They've been plastering them up in every city, town, and waypost across the Council Kingdoms for the past week. The printing cost alone must have been a fortune."

Eli took the poster from her and carefully unrolled it. It was very large, twice the size of the bounty posters and covered in splashy block printing surrounding an engraved illustration of the most formidable fortress Eli had ever seen.

"Edward di Fellbro," he read aloud. "Duke of Gaol, Liegesworn of the Kingdom of Argo, so on and so forth." He scanned down the enormous list of titles that always seemed to follow anyone important, looking for the actual announcement. "Ah," he said. "Here we are. It's an announcement for the duke's new stronghold. Look here"—he motioned Josef and Nico over—"'... this new, impenetrable fortress, a wonder of modern architecture and security built on impenetrable bedrock, was created to protect his lordship's priceless family heirlooms, the famous treasures of Gaol.'"

Eli's eyes flicked back and forth, his grin growing wider by the word. "Powers," he cackled. "There's three paragraphs alone on the thickness of the walls!"

"Mm," the broker said, nodding. "It goes on like that the whole way through. People thought it was funny at first, him making such a big deal over it in places that didn't even know there was a Duke of Gaol. Who advertises a fortress, anyhow? But the tune changed after rumors got round 'bout what he did to the first couple of thieves he caught. Cruel doesn't begin to describe it. So, unless you're Eli Monpress, I'd count this target out. No sword, Fenzetti or whatever, is worth that kind of suicide mission. Stick to Sketti."

Eli nodded thoughtfully, rolling the poster back into a tube. "Can I keep this?"

"Sure." The woman shrugged. "As I said, they're everywhere. I'll just get another."

"Much obliged," Eli said graciously, standing up. "Thank you for a very thorough answer, Miss Broker. I'll make sure to recommend your services."

The woman gave him a sharp look. "It's customary to tip," she said. "Especially considering how you managed to cheat my idiot here out of most of my fee."

Eli gave her an innocent smile, but she arched an eyebrow. "I told you," she said. "A girl has to eat, and if you won't play fair by me, then I might be forced to write a letter to these sword owners."

"You make a good case," Eli said, and his hand flashed, sending four gold standards flying across the room in rapid succession. The woman caught them easily, and she nodded her head in thanks as the thief and his companions ducked through the low door and into the night.

"Well," Josef said, walking in step with Eli through the narrow dirt streets, "that was surprisingly informative. If I'd known brokers were so useful I would have tried harder to find one."

"They're everywhere if you know what to look for," Eli said, spinning the rolled-up poster between his fingers. "Though they're really at their best when you're looking for something physical. They don't handle manhunts well. I didn't expect such a thorough answer from a broker in an end-of-nowhere town like Goin, but I guess I should have known better. Brokers, wherever they are, always know what's going on. Someday, when I get bored enough, I'll find out how they do it."

"Well," Josef said, "at least we know where we're going. I've never been to the southern coast, but there are several good swordsmen along the islands I've been meaning to test out. This seems like a good opportunity."

"Josef, Josef, Josef," Eli said. "What are you talking about? We're not going to Sketti. There's no way I'm wasting the half a year it'll take to go all the way down to the south coast, and then come all the way back on what is essentially a pro bono project." He flashed a smile at Nico. "No offense, dear, but your coat isn't worth *that* much. Besides," he said, unrolling the poster again with a gleeful grin, "why would we pass up an opportunity like this?"

"I see several in bold print," Josef said, looking over his shoulder.

"*Look* at this!" Eli cackled. " 'Impenetrable fortress'? 'Impossible to infiltrate'? '*Thief-proof*'? It's practically an invitation!" Eli slapped the paper with the back of his hand. "This, my friends, is a challenge! And I never turn away from a challenge."

"Or a trap," Josef grumbled. "Come on, Eli, think. The only reason to put up a notice detailing your fantastic security is if you're desperately trying to ward off thieves, or fishing for them. Considering he's putting up posters in nowhere mud-hole towns miles from his borders, I'm going with the latter. *Especially* when the bait seems tailored to a certain famous thief with a kingdom-swaying bounty who's well known for his love of impossible targets. Powers, he might as well just hang up some 'Welcome Eli' banners and be done with it."

"You might be right," Eli said, rolling the poster back into a tube. "But that just makes it even more irresistible. Besides, the duke's lands are in Argo. That's barely a week away from here if we acquire some transportation. Even if we just go over to take a look and decide it's impossible, we've still hardly lost any time. Besides, if this trap for me is as transparent as you seem to think, then there are bound to be dozens of bounty hunters hanging around, and you did say you wanted a good fight."

"I wouldn't call most of the trash that comes after us a 'good fight,'" Josef grumbled, but even his gruff tone couldn't hide the spark of interest. "Of course," he added, a few moments later, "we never know when we might run into another Coriano."

"That's the spirit." Eli grinned, clapping him on the back. "Come on, let's go find some food and then see if we can't find a ride out of here. I don't know about you two, but I'm *really* sick of walking."

Neither Josef nor Nico disagreed with that statement, and so the three of them went off in search of a tavern whose kitchen was still open and whose floor wasn't currently a wrestling ring.

As it turned out, finding a meal was the hardest part of the night. The taverns of Goin lived up to their reputation as rowdy dumps where beer counts as food and a broken nose is considered part of a good night out. This worked for Josef, who had a bit of fun tossing the locals around under the guise of "securing a table," but Eli was having trouble finding anything on the dinner boards of the few places that offered food that wasn't a concoction of meat, grease, and dirt. After several hungry, bloody hours, the night rolled around into predawn, and Eli was finally able to buy a sack of day-old bread from a baker who had just opened his shop.

Obtaining transportation was significantly easier. Most of the stable hands were drunk, and the stable locks were old and rusted. With about five minutes' work Eli had them a very respectable-looking covered merchant's cart and a team of sturdy but unexceptional brown horses to draw it.

Josef and Nico both frowned when they saw the horses. Horses were always a risk. They were very sensitive to threats, especially demons, and were prone to panic if Nico came too near. Slorn's new coat was working wonders, however, and the horses barely noticed when Nico climbed up over the driver's bench and into the back.

"I could get used to this," Eli said, jumping up after her. "Remind me to thank Slorn again."

"Don't get too happy," Josef said, climbing in last and taking the driver's seat. "We're not out yet."

He took off the Heart and laid it gently in the cart. Next, he undid all of his scabbards, handing his blades one by one to Nico. Finally, he pulled up his collar and buttoned his cuffs, hiding the scars on his arms and jaw, and slouched over the horses with a petulant expression on his face. Eli nodded in approval. If it wasn't for the strange, watchful look in his eyes, even he would have been hard-pressed to label Josef as anything other than a big farmer with a bad temper.

Their ride out of town was uneventful. If the guards had any suspicions about how a merchant cart that had been driven into town by an old woman the night before was now being driven out by a surly man in his twenties, one look at Josef's shoulders was enough to convince them it wasn't really important. They rode in silence for about twenty minutes before Eli tapped Josef on the shoulder and the swordsman pulled the cart over to the side of the empty road.

"Cover for me," Eli said, hopping down. "I'm going to see if I can't speed things up."

Josef nodded and leaned back, undoing his cuffs and flipping his collar back to its usual flat position. Nico started handing him his belts of knives as Eli undid the harnesses on the cart horses and let them wander over toward the clumps of grass that grew between the wagon ruts.

"There," Eli said, tossing the harness on the ground. "Either they'll find their way home or some deserving soul gets new horses. Never let it be said that I never gave back to the people."

"You're a regular public servant," Josef grumbled, belting on his swords. "What now?"

"Now," Eli said, "we get moving."

He crouched down beside the right front wheel and gave it a friendly pat. "Good morning," he said cheerily.

For a few moments, nothing happened. Then, slowly, the wheel began to creak as it finally woke up. "What's good about it?"

"Well," Eli said, looking around, "to start, it's a lovely dry day on a nice even road with a downward slope. Doesn't get much better, I'd think."

The wheel wobbled. "That's because you're not down here being dragged along by those cloppy-cloppy beasts, going so slowly you got moss in your joints, having mud kicked at you morning, noon, and night. No day's a good day when you're in the rut, I tell ya."

"Ah," Eli said, keeping his voice low so the other wheel wouldn't wake up too soon and spoil the plan. "Today's a bit different, friend. You see, the horses are gone, and I've got a bit of a challenge for you, if you're interested."

"Challenge?" The wheel perked up. "What do you mean?"

"Well," Eli said, "you see that wheel over there?" He pointed at the left front corner of the cart. "He told me, just now, that you're over your prime, off circle, and that he can outroll you any day of the year."

The wheel creaked with fury. "Oh, he did, did he? Put on only last winter and already looking to replace me, eh? Well, I'm sound as any wheel you'll find, and if he wants to try me, tell him he can go ahead. I'll match any horse he cares to try!"

"Oh, we're not talking horses, friend." Eli shook his head. "This is an open challenge. The two of you in a flat-out race, no horse, just you, him, and the open road, winner take all."

"No horses?" The wheel balked. "How'm I supposed to roll, then?"

"Oh, that's easy," Eli said. "You just roll forward."

"What, you mean like downhill?"

"Or uphill," Eli said. "Anywhere! Just roll."

"Don't know 'bout that," the wheel said. "Last time I tried that I fell over. I hate falling over."

"No worries there," Eli said. "The cart will keep you up, and I'll be in the seat acting as the referee and laying out the course. What do you say, want to try a race? Prove who's the better wheel?"

"Won't be much of a competition," the wheel cackled. "Just give the signal and I'll show you how a cart's supposed to move."

"Excellent," Eli said, standing up. He left the wheel muttering threats at its axlemate and leaned toward Josef, dropping his voice to a whisper. "I'm just waking the front two for now. When they catch on, we'll switch the wheels and start again with the pair in the back."

"I have no idea what that means, but all right," Josef said, pulling himself back into the cart. "Just don't get the cart too excited. It's a long trip."

"Won't be when I'm done," Eli said, walking around the cart to the left wheel to start the process again.

A few minutes of excited whispering later, the whole cart began to shake. Eli leaped into the driver's seat and grabbed hold of the bench. "Hang on," he said, grinning at Nico and Josef. "Here we go."

He'd barely finished speaking before the cart launched forward, rattling down the overgrown road at a breakneck pace.

Josef clung to the cart for dear life as the trees flew by and the sky danced overhead. Eli was laughing and shouting directions and encouragement to the wheels, who were spinning as though their lives depended on it as they screamed insults at each other.

"Don't you think this is a little conspicuous?" Josef shouted over the wheels.

"Not at all!" Eli shouted back. "This is nothing

compared to how some Spiritualists travel. If we're lucky, people will think we're Shaper wizards. No one's stupid enough to mess with Shapers, and they ride stuff like this all the time, though their horseless carts are a lot nicer, not to mention smarter. I could never pull this stunt on Shaper goods. Ah," he said, breathing deeply, "I love common, sleepy spirits. They're so open to suggestion."

Josef looked at him blankly, but Eli just grinned wider.

"What? No point in going slow through that if we don't have to, right? Don't worry so much."

Josef had an answer for that, but experience told him to save his breath. The thief would do what he wanted, and this *was* faster. So he made himself as comfortable as he could in the pitching cart and dug out one of his throwing knives. At least the cart gave him a good chance to practice catching his knives in an unstable environment, and Josef wasn't the kind to let opportunity pass.

From her place in the back of the cart, Nico watched Josef as he flipped the razor-sharp knife, catching it first with his right hand, then his left. Behind her, the green forest whirled by in a blur as they bounced at full speed down the road toward Gaol.

CHAPTER
9

They had to switch the wheels only once before they reached the border of Argo. The roads had been quiet and empty, barely more than cart tracks as they skimmed the northern edge of the Council Kingdoms. They had seen no one and, more important, no one had seen them.

"Well, it makes sense," Josef noted as their cart rolled to an exhausted stop by the signpost marking the official border. "That glorified goat track was the worst excuse for a road I've ever seen."

"Why should they keep it up?" Eli said, climbing stiffly off the cart. "It's not like anyone with money goes through there. Who'd take a narrow road through the middle of nowhere now that the Council's opened the rivers? Still"—he patted the exhausted wheels—"across the top of the Council Kingdoms in three days. I'd like to see a riverboat do that."

"No one would ever accuse us of traveling normally."

Josef shrugged, helping Nico down. "Can the cart keep going?"

"No," Eli said. "They've earned their rest. Help me out," he said, leaning down. "After all that, the least I can do is leave them free."

They undid the wheels and left them propped in the rocks beside the cart. Then, with a thankful farewell, Eli, Nico, and Josef set out down the overgrown path into Argo.

"All right," Josef said, setting a brisk pace. "What now?"

"Now, we make for Gaol." Eli reached into his pack and pulled out his map. "Argo is divided into four autonomous duchies, each about the size of a small kingdom itself. Argo's really more like a collection of kingdoms than somewhere like Mellinor, where one king calls all the shots. That's probably why it was one of the first major players to join the Council of Thrones. It was already used to the idea of governance by committee. Anyway, Gaol is the southernmost duchy, taking up the whole of the Fellbro River Valley just before it joins the Wellbro and they both change their names to the Whitefall River as the water enters Zarin's territory. That's part of why Gaol is so rich. The Fellbro River connects the northwest quarter of the Council Kingdoms with everything else. There's enough trade coming down that waterway to keep even the greediest merchant happy, and not so much as a kernel of wheat passes through without Gaol levying some kind of tariff. Now, we're currently in Eol, the northernmost and relatively poorest duchy of Argo. All the attention's on the river traffic, so I expect that if we can stay on foot and on the border here we can just walk into Gaol with no questions asked."

Josef shot him a look. "That simple, eh?"

"With us? Never," Eli said, laughing. "If we can get into Gaol's capital, which, I might add, is also called Goal, thanks to the stupid and confusing naming conventions of the northwest kingdoms. Anyway, if we can get in unmolested, we'll have Slorn's sword and be out of here in a week, tops."

"A week?" Josef said. "You said kidnapping the King of Mellinor would take a week."

"Give or take a major inconvenience," Eli said, shrugging. "Kidnapping was a new area for us. There were bound to be slip-ups. This is good old-fashioned theft, and no Spiritualists in sight to mess it up. I think we'll be all right."

Nico and Josef exchanged a look behind Eli's back as they followed the thief south, down the overgrown road and into the rolling hills of Argo.

It took them two days to reach Gaol's border, mostly because on the second day it began to rain. It was a drenching, cold rain blown down from the mountains, and it made the going miserable. Eli, drowned and sulking with his blue jacket wrapped tight around him, mentioned something about stopping every mile or so, but nothing came of it. The mountain forests had stopped at the Argo border, logged to make room for sheep and cattle grazing, but it was poor land up here and the ranchers' homes were spread thin. They passed a few farmhouses, their inviting plumes of smoke smelling of cooking and warmth, but the travelers didn't stop. Eli had learned his lesson about nosy farmers on multiple occasions, and even a miserable, wet walk wasn't enough to make him try one of those doors.

"Not much farther," he said, tilting his head so the water would have a harder time going down his neck.

"So you keep saying," Josef said. The swordsman paid no more attention to the rain than a bull does, and the water rolled off him with scarcely a notice. Nico kept in step with him, kicking her thin feet so the mud wouldn't build up on her boots. Eli grumbled something about traveling with monsters and kept his own pace, moving his feet carefully so as not to lose a boot in the quagmire the road had become. It was a complicated process, which was why he didn't notice that Josef and Nico had stopped until he ran face-first into Josef's back.

"Powers!" he muttered, stumbling back. "What *now*?"

Josef just nodded at the road ahead of them. Eli squinted into the rain, confused; then he saw it too. About ten feet ahead of them, the rain stopped. The road went on, the hills went on, but the rain didn't. Eli walked forward, sloshing through the mud until he was on the edge of where the weather suddenly cut off. There, in the middle of the road, was a line. On one side, it was a miserable, cold, wet rain; on the other, the weather was sunny and the road was dry.

Squinting through the rain, Eli leaned forward until his nose was almost touching the invisible barrier separating rain from sun. "Well," he said softly, "that's odd."

"That's one way to put it," Josef said.

Eli tilted his head back and squinted at the sky. The disconnect seemed to go all the way up. Even the gray clouds stopped at the line, swirling and turning over on each other at the border as if they'd hit an invisible wall.

"Very odd," Eli muttered.

Josef glared at the division. He didn't like unexplainable things. "Any ideas on what could cause something like this?"

"Well," Eli said, tapping his fingers against his wet chin. "It could be some kind of agreement between the local spirits. I doubt it, though. Spirits have their own politics, but something this precise smacks of human interference."

Josef frowned. "A wizard who likes sunshine, then?"

"That'd be my guess," Eli said, poking at the line between wet and dry with his boot. "Not a Spiritualist, though. They'd consider something like this, I don't know, rude. Not their style at all."

Josef nodded, and they stood there staring at the anomaly for a moment longer. Then Eli shook himself.

"Well," he said, "no point in standing in the drink when we don't have to. That's our road, so we might as well stop worrying and enjoy the sunshine."

He strode forward, crossing the border between rain and sun with only a tiny hesitation. He felt nothing as he crossed, just the welcome warmth of sunlight on his wet shoulders. Now that he was on the dry side, the air was cool and bright and the dry road was solid and even, a welcome change from the rutted mud slick they'd been shuffling through all day.

Once they were all in the dry they shook out their soaked clothes and sat in the thick grass on the roadside while they drained the water out of their boots. Now that they could see the sun, it was clear that the afternoon was quickly passing, so after a short rest, they pressed on, following the road down out of the hills into a green valley.

The land on this side of the rain was very different

from the scrubby hills they'd been plowing through since abandoning the cart. The brown grass and rocky outcroppings had been replaced by orderly orchards and green pastures. The road was well maintained, with neat stone walls dividing it from the farmland and not a single rut in the hard-packed dirt. In the distance, picturesque farmhouses made of gray stone and whitewashed wood nestled between the hills like plump, roosting chickens. Sleek horses grazed in green fields while roosters with deep-blue tails strutted on white fences, crowing occasionally as the sun sank lower.

"It's like we walked into a painting," Josef said. "*Cottages at Sundown* or something."

Eli brushed self-consciously at his dirty clothes. He hated being dirty in general, but being dirty here felt like an insult to the bucolic perfection. "Funny, I figured the richest province in the Council Kingdoms would be a little less pastoral."

Josef shrugged. "Even rich people have to eat."

"I just hope this place has something worth picking up besides the Fenzetti," Eli said. "All I'm seeing is a lot of grass and livestock, and I'm *not* doing horses again. I swear, the more valuable their bloodline, the harder they bite."

"I don't think you have to worry about that," Josef said. "There's the town."

Eli looked up and saw that Josef was right. At the bottom of the hill they'd just crested stood a large, lovely town. Gray stone buildings with steep red roofs stood in orderly squares divided by broad, paved roads. The city was hemmed in on all sides by a high stone wall, though it looked more like an ornamental barrier to separate the city from the country than an actual, defensible position. On the far side of the city from their position, a river hemmed in by bridges and dock houses glittered in the evening light, and above it, sitting on a jut of rock like a crow on its perch, was the duke's citadel.

Even if the poster hadn't had a picture, Eli would have recognized the building. Perfectly square, with tiny windows and a black exterior, it was radically different from the charming buildings that surrounded it. Guards walked the perimeter, tiny glittering figures with polished hauberks guiding thick-shouldered dogs on leather leads. Though it was still early evening, torches burned on the citadel walls, their light reflected by mirrored panels set right into the stone, bouncing the light back and forth so that every shadow was illuminated. These felt like unnecessary precautions, however. Even without the guards and the lights, the thick walls of the citadel positively reeked with inaccessibility. Eli felt his pulse quicken. It was a challenge, a true challenge, and he could hardly wait to begin.

Josef caught his gleeful look and folded his arms over his chest. "We're doing this carefully, remember?"

"Oh, I remember." Eli grinned. "It would be a shame and a waste to do it any way but right." He clapped his hands and turned to his companions. "First order of business, setting up base camp. I'm thinking docks."

"Sounds good," Josef said. "Lots of people go through there. It's hard to remember them all. Even the best guards won't notice three new faces."

"Close to the city, too," Eli said, eyeing the river. "And plenty of escape routes."

"That's settled, then," Josef said, veering off the road. "Let's go."

Eli and Nico followed the swordsman as he left the road and cut straight down the steep embankment toward the river. They hit the water south of town and followed it up, slipping past the wall through one of the dozens of dock gates and up onto the river walk. The river itself was a good fifty feet across and deeply trenched for the large, low-running barges that floated down it. Piers jutted out into the murky green water, connecting the boats to the long, low storehouses that pushed right up to the river's edge. River crewmen were gathered in knots by the iron fire troughs, smoking pipes and roasting fish on skewers over the hot coals. These clusters were few and far between, however, and other than the river men, the docks were empty.

"Better and better," Eli said quietly.

They chose one of the storehouses on the end, a small affair with an older lock, which took Eli five seconds flat to pick, and plenty of dusty cargo that wasn't going anywhere.

"Perfection," Eli said, craning his head back to look up at the last light of evening as it streamed through the tiny, glassless windows high up on the two-story walls. "And with daylight to burn."

"I'll take care of the groundwork," Josef said, setting the Heart down in a corner. "Nico, secure the building. Eli, do whatever it is you do."

"Right," Eli said, plopping down on a crate and kicking off his wet boots. "I'll get right on that."

Josef made a "forget it" gesture as he walked out the door. Nico had vanished the moment Josef assigned her duty, and so Eli was left alone. He took his time wiggling out of his wet coat and fanning out his shirt so the white cloth wouldn't dry crinkled. Finally, when he was beginning to feel human again, he stood up and strolled to the center of the dusty warehouse.

"All right," he said to the empty room. "Let's get started."

It was fully dark when Josef slipped back into the storehouse, carrying a bag of food and a long list of new troubles. But when he opened the door, he realized he wasn't the only one who'd had bad news. Eli was sitting in the far corner of the room, surrounded by boxes and looking more frustrated than Josef had ever seen him look.

He put down his bag and walked over, crouching next to the thief. "What's wrong?"

"It's the boxes!" Eli exclaimed, far too loudly. "They won't talk to me!"

Josef flinched at the desperate edge in his voice. Anything that put Eli this out of whack was going to be a problem.

Eli glared at the boxes. "They won't talk to me at all. Not at all! It's like they're not even spirits!"

"Eli," Josef said slowly, "they are just crates. We'll find something else—"

"It doesn't matter if they're crates or cupcakes!" Eli cried. "They're spirits, and they're not talking. Spirits *always* talk to me, unless they're under an Enslavement not to, but I don't feel anything like that here. Just crates who *won't talk.*"

"Maybe they're shy?" Josef said and sighed. "Anyway, we've got bigger problems than not-talking crates. Something's off in town."

"Off?" Eli said. "Off how?"

"Hard to explain, really." Josef ran his hand through his short hair. "To start, it's spooky quiet. Everything's so neat. Plus, the streets emptied out as soon as the sun went down. No taverns, no drunks, nothing but guards, clean streets, and quiet."

Eli shrugged. "Gaol's a peaceful, quiet town full of decent, boring people. I realize you might not have much experience with those, but it's hardly something to get alarmed about."

"There's quiet and then there's quiet," Josef snapped. "I told you, this was spooky quiet. And"—he reached in his pocket—"these are all over town." He took out a piece of paper and unfolded it, revealing a familiar grinning face above a large, bold number. Fifty-five thousand standards.

"They didn't even get the bounty right," Eli said, grabbing the poster. "I'm worth *sixty* thousand."

"Who cares about the number?" Josef growled, snatching the paper back. "I knew this was a trap from the moment you got all starry-eyed over that poster for the citadel back at the broker's, but the bounty posters confirm it. We should sneak out tonight before it slams shut on our heads."

"Sneak out?" Eli cried. "Josef, we just slogged through two days of rain to *get* here. We're not going to just turn tail and leave."

"Weren't you listening?" Josef said, grabbing Eli's arm. "It's one thing to get caught in an ambush, but it's just plain stupid to stay in one after you've spotted it. Part of fighting is knowing when to retreat."

"As you are so fond of pointing out," Eli said, snatching his arm back, "I'm not a fighter. And we're not leaving."

"You should leave," whispered a quiet voice. "You seem like a nice wizard. We don't want you to die."

Eli spun away from Josef. "Well, hello there," he said. "Looks like you *can* talk!"

The crates around them jumped. "Shh!" the voice hissed. "Not so loud! If we're caught talking to you it's the end for us."

"What?" Josef whispered, looking around.

"It's the crates," Eli whispered back, grinning like a madman. "They're agreeing with you." He patted the swordsman on the back and then leaned in to whisper to the wooden crate. "What do you mean 'the end'? Who would catch you?"

The crate fell silent again, leaving the question hanging. Then, in a voice that was scarcely more than a whisper of dust on wood, it said, "The watcher."

Eli frowned, confused. "Watcher?"

"The duke's watcher sees everything," the crate said, trembling. "We're not allowed to talk to wizards, but you're the nicest, brightest wizard we've ever seen, so please, leave. We don't want you to get caught."

Eli was about to ask another question when a sharp crack from the highest crate on the stack interrupted him.

"Watcher!" the crates cried in unison. "It's coming! Say nothing! Ignore the wizard!"

"Get out of here!" Eli's crate whispered frantically.

"What's coming?" Eli whispered frantically, running his hands over the dusty wood. "What do you mean 'watcher'?"

But the crates had shut themselves down again, and in the silence, Eli heard a low sound.

"What is going on?" Josef said again, more urgently this time.

"Shh!" Eli hushed him, hunkering down among the crates.

Josef gave him a cutting look, and then he heard it too.

It sounded like a strong wind rushing between the buildings, only it didn't rush. The roaring sound lingered, moving up the river slowly, patiently, and in a manner that was wholly disconnected with the entire idea of wind. It hit the wooden walls of the warehouse like a wave, rattling anything that wasn't nailed down, whistling as it tore through the high windows. Then it was gone, moving methodically down the line of dock houses, leaving only the terrified silence of traumatized crates in its wake.

Eli glanced at Josef and the two of them crept back to the center of the storehouse. Nico was there waiting for them, though Eli hadn't seen her come in. She was simply there, and she didn't look happy about it.

"Something just came by," she whispered once they were close.

"So we heard," Eli said. "Did you catch what it was?"

Nico shook her head. "I want to say it was a wind, but I've never felt a wind like that."

Eli bit his lip thoughtfully, but Josef looked like his mind had just been made up.

"So," he said, "we've walked into a trap full of terrified spirits and winds that aren't winds. Is that enough to convince you this job is going to be more trouble than it's worth?"

"One day." Eli faced Josef, holding up one finger.

"Give me one day to scout the situation. Tomorrow night, we'll make the hit or leave. Either way, it'll be done." He looked up at the high windows. "There's something going on here. First, the line in the rain; now this. Surely you're as curious as I am about what's going on here?"

"Of course I'm curious," Josef said. "But I don't let my curiosity get me stuck in situations I can't get out of. That's the difference between you and me."

"Come now," Eli said. "I've never been in a situation I couldn't get out of."

Josef gave him a look. "There's a first time for everything."

Eli chuckled. "Well, if we're going to be compressing three days of prep into one, let's get things rolling. But first, I'm going to secure our position."

"How do you mean to do that?" Josef said. "You just said the spirits wouldn't talk to you."

"For this, they don't have to," Eli said, walking back over to the crates.

"Excuse me," he said, his voice soft and sweet. "I appreciate the warning earlier, and I have one more favor to ask you."

The crates rattled uncomfortably, and Eli put up his hands.

"It's nothing big. In fact, you were probably going to do it anyway. All I want is for you to go to sleep. Just ignore me, forget I'm here, and I swear I won't do anything wizardly to wake you up."

The crates rattled at this, confused, and a splintering voice from the back cried, "How can we sleep? You're a wizard. Now that we're awake, it's not like we can just not notice you."

Eli sat down cross-legged in front of them. "Just try," he said softly.

The crates creaked uncertainly, but Eli didn't move. He simply sat on the floor, his eyes closed, his face calm, as the warehouse grew darker and darker. Presently, the nervous noises from the crates grew quieter, and then stopped altogether. The warehouse fell as silent as any old, forgotten place.

Quiet as a cat, Eli stood up and walked away from the crates and over to the little corner by the door where Nico and Josef were huddled around a tiny lamp, quietly eating the food Josef had brought.

"We good?" Josef said, tossing Eli a round loaf of bread.

"We're good," Eli answered, flopping down beside them.

"So," Josef said. "I know I'll regret asking, but what did you do?"

"I put them back to sleep," Eli said tiredly. "Small, normal spirits are almost always asleep unless a wizard wakes them up. Of course, the problem here is that, once a wizard wakes up a spirit, it's hard for them to go back to sleep if the wizard's still there. It's like trying to go to sleep when someone's in the room waving a lantern around. I simply quieted my presence. Think of it as throwing a blanket over the lantern. The lantern's still there, but it's not such a bother. It's an old trick I learned back in my thieving apprentice days, actually. It's not always good to be noticeable when you're trying to be a thief. So long as I don't do anything wizardly or otherwise make a scene, I should seem almost normal to any watching spirits."

"Great," Josef said, "a plan that depends on you not making a scene."

"I just wish I knew what was going on," Eli said, ignoring him. "The only thing that can get spirits that riled up is a wizard stepping on them, but there's no Enslavement I can feel. I don't think I'd miss it if there was one. It's not a subtle thing."

"So it's a mystery," Josef said, leaning back against the wall with the Heart propped against his shoulder. "Let the Spiritualists deal with it. Spiritual mysteries are what they're there for, when they're not bothering us."

"How can you be so blasé?" Eli said around a large mouthful of bread. "Don't you want to know what's going on?"

"Sure," Josef said. "But wanting to know is a terrible reason to do anything. It only causes trouble, and not the good kind either, the stupid, time-wasting kind. Just let it go. We're on a deadline, remember?"

"How could I forget?" Eli grumbled, lying back.

They sat in silence for a while before Nico leaned forward and blew out the lamp. Lying there, in the dark, Eli meant to think more about the crates and the wind and all the other strange things. He needed to think about them because, despite Josef's cracks about curiosity, the first rule of thievery was never go into a job if you didn't understand the territory. This was a dangerous game, with more uncontrollable factors than he was comfortable with. But, despite his best intentions, the weeks of hard travel pulled at his body, and he was asleep as soon as the light went out.

High overhead, the windows rattled in the dark as the strange wind passed by again.

· · ·

The night air above Gaol was still. Far off on the horizon, lightning flashed from distant storms. Even so, no rain-heavy wind swept the fields of Gaol and the clouds did not cross the duchy border. They knew better.

Down in the streets, however, a wind moved slowly. It sent the tall oil lamps flickering, disturbing the steady pools of light they shed on the paved streets. It dipped into alleys, under barrels, and through attics. It roared as it went, a cruel, howling sound, and never strayed from its path, moving with almost painful slowness until it had made a full circuit of the town. Only then did the wind pick up speed. It turned and rose, flitting over the rooftops and toward the center of town where the duke's citadel crouched on its jutting rise, every bit as sullen and formidable as the posters made it out to be.

The strange wind circled the base of the fortress once and then turned and climbed the glum wall to the top, the only part of the gloomy structure that varied from the blocky architecture. Here, crowning the top of the citadel, was a series of interlocking towers. They were short and hard to see from the ground, but being on top of the citadel they provided a breathtaking view of the city and the countryside around it. At the center of the fortress, nestled between the towers, was a small courtyard garden filled with small, neat plants, all carefully arranged into beds by color and size. It was here the wind stopped, spiraling down and slowing to an almost stagnant crawl before the man who sat on a reed chair at the center of the garden going over a stack of black-bound ledgers by the light of a steady lamp.

The wind hovered a moment, hesitantly, but the man didn't look up from his ledger until he had finished the row. Only then, when each figure had been noted in his short, meticulous handwriting, did Duke Edward look up at the empty space where he knew the wind was waiting. "Report."

"My lord," the wind whispered, "two things. First, Hern has arrived."

"Has he?" The duke set his ledger aside. "That's unexpected."

"He went straight to his tower as soon as he was through the gate." The wind made a chuckling sound. "He doesn't seem very happy about being back."

"Interesting," the duke said. "What's the second?"

The wind's whistle grew nervous. "I caught a blip of something over by the docks this evening."

The duke scowled. "A blip? Explain."

"Well," the wind said, "it's hard to describe to a blind man—"

The duke's glare hardened, and a small surge of power rang through the garden. All at once, the wind found the words.

"It was like a flash," it said. "And then it was gone. I passed over twice but never saw it again. Could have been a hedge wizard, some spirit-sensitive riverboater who never developed his skills past listening for floods."

"But you don't think so," the duke said.

The wind jerked at this, surprised, and Duke Edward smiled. He'd always been good at picking up what wasn't said. It was a useful skill for people and spirits alike.

"I don't know what it was," the wind said, finally. "But nothing ordinary shines that brightly."

"I see," the duke said. "I trust discipline is being maintained."

"Of course," the wind huffed. "Your spirits speak to no one."

"Good," Edward said. "Keep an eye on this blip. Tell everyone that I want tight patrols tonight. The bait has been spread far and wide. Our little mouse may be in the trap already."

"Yes, my lord." The wind spun in the closest equivalent a wind can give to a bow. "Anything else?"

The duke thought for a moment. "Yes, on your next round, send Hern over. I'm curious what he's doing back in Gaol so soon after my investment in his success in Zarin."

"Of course, my lord," the wind chuckled. It had never liked Hern much, and it delighted in the chance to make the Spiritualist come when called like he was one of his own fawning ring spirits.

"Thank you, Othril," the duke said. "You may go."

The wind circled one more time before blowing away. When he was gone, the duke opened his ledgers again and returned to marking numbers.

Nearly an hour later, one of the duke's house servants came into the garden to announce Hern's arrival. Duke Edward had long since finished his accounting and was now using the time to work with his vines. He ordered them one way, then another, sending them twisting up the stone walls of his garden and along the narrow breezeway door that looked out over the dark western hills. He heard Hern enter but didn't turn his attention from his vines until they had worked themselves into the desired double spiral.

When he finally turned to greet his guest, he found the Spiritualist standing in the doorway and looking quite put out.

"So," Hern said slowly, "you wanted something?"

"Straight to the point, this time," Edward said, sitting back down in his chair. "You must be in a foul mood."

"Being ordered from my bed by a *wind* after a long journey has that effect."

"I'll make this quick then," Edward said, his voice clipped and clinical. "I gave you money to dominate the Spirit Court in Zarin. Why, then, are you back in Gaol?"

Hern gave him a cutting look. "Politics isn't like your garden, Edward. I can't force things into the shape I want." The Spiritualist began to pace. "Banage has been working his connections in Zarin tirelessly. You'd think escaping a trial for treason was a heroic effort! The ink on her banishment edict is barely dry, but all I hear is *poor Miranda*, the noble, oppressed Spiritualist who threw away honor and safety to uphold her promise to her spirits. The whole Court is eating it up, even the Keepers who voted against her, and it's making things very difficult." Hern stopped there a moment, reaffirming his composure. Edward, for his part, simply watched and took note.

"As it stands," Hern continued in a tight, calm voice, "Zarin is no longer the optimal place for me to pursue my objectives, so I've returned to regroup. I've got some sympathetic and influential Tower Keepers coming in tomorrow to discuss our next move. It is vital we counter Banage's spin on the facts before he sways the whole Court back under his cult of personality."

"Mmm." The duke nodded, turning back to his vines. "See that you do. I would hate to think that my investment in you was a bad one, Hern."

The Spiritualist stiffened, but said nothing. Edward smiled. It pleased him to know that Hern understood the difference between them here. Hern might have influence in Zarin, but this was Gaol. Here, there was no power, no authority that the duke did not control.

"It is late," Hern said at last. "Please excuse me."

Edward waved, listening as Hern turned and left. When the man was gone, Edward picked up his ledgers and his lamp and walked toward the door. When he reached it, he stopped and turned to his garden. He looked at it for a moment, the well-balanced colors, the sweet fragrance of the flowers, all in perfect order. Satisfied, he said, "Good night."

As soon as the words left his lips, every flower in the garden snapped itself shut. With that, Duke Edward of Gaol took his lantern and went down the empty halls to his bed.

CHAPTER
10

Far, far west of Gaol, far west of everything on the barren coast of Tamil, the westernmost Council Kingdom, Gin ran through the sparse grass with a bony rabbit hanging from his teeth, his swirling coat making him almost invisible in the clouds of cold, salty sea spray. The land here met the water in great cliffs, as though the continent had turned its back on the endless, steely water, and the ocean, in retaliation, bit at the rock with knife-blade waves, eating it away over the endless years into a large and varied assortment of crags and caves, yawning from the cliffs like gaping mouths below the dull gray sky.

Gin followed the cliff line until he reached a place where the coast seemed to fold in on itself. Here, moving his paws very carefully on the wet, smooth stone, he climbed down into a hollow between two pillars of rock. It was narrow, and he had to scramble a few times to keep from getting stuck. Then, about ten feet down, the rock suddenly opened up, dropping him into a large cave.

It was dim, but not dark. Gray light filtered down through the cracks overhead and through the wide mouth of the cave that looked out over the ocean. Little ripples of shells and sea grass on the sand marked the high-tide line, filling the cavern with the smell of salt and rotting seaweed. Gin landed neatly on the hard sand and turned away from the roaring sea, trotting up toward the back of the cave where a small, sad fire sputtered on a pile of damp driftwood. Beside it, hunched over in a little ragged ball, was his mistress.

He dropped the rabbit in the sand beside the fire and sat down.

"Food," he said. "For when you're done moping."

Miranda glared at him between her folded arms. "I'm not moping."

"Could have fooled me," Gin snorted.

She reached for the rabbit, but just before her fingers touched the torn fur, Gin scooted it away with his paw.

"Are you ready to talk about where we're going next?"

Miranda sighed. "We're not going anywhere."

Gin's orange eyes narrowed. "So we're just going to live out our lives in a sea cave?"

"Until I can think of somewhere better," Miranda snapped. "We're fugitives, remember?"

"So what?" Gin said. "If anyone is actually looking for us, it's probably Banage trying to set this mess straight."

"This isn't Banage's problem," Miranda said, meeting Gin's eyes for the first time. "I was the one who decided to do things the hard way, and I failed." She buried her head in her arms again. "If I can't be a good Spiritualist, then at least I'll be a good outcast and vanish quietly, not make a scene to embarrass the Court further."

Gin shook his head. "Do you even hear how ridiculous you're being? Do you think it'll make everything better if you keep playing dutiful Spiritualist to the end?"

"Supporting the Spirit Court *is* my duty!" Miranda cried. "I'm not playing, mutt."

"No," Gin said. "You're hiding and licking your wounds. What good are you to the Spirit Court if you're only using it as a reason to run away?"

"*Run away?*" Miranda's head snapped up. "I don't get to just stop being a Spiritualist, Gin! I have oaths! I have *obligations*!"

"Exactly," Gin said. "But to us first. I thought you'd already made this decision back in Zarin, but now I'm not so sure. What matters more, Miranda, the Spirit Court or the spirits? Will you deny your oaths to us to save Banage's honor? Would he even want you to?"

Miranda looked away, and Gin stood up with a huff. "Just remember, you're doing no one any good hiding in this hole," he growled, trotting toward the cave entrance. "Eat your rabbit. Next time you get hungry, you can go out and catch your own dinner."

Miranda stayed put until he left. When his shadow vanished into the sea spray, she grabbed the rabbit and began to dress it.

Stupid dog, she thought.

She skewered the rabbit on a stick and arranged it over the coals. Gin might be a particularly perceptive dog, but he was still a dog, and he didn't understand. If she made a scene, things would only get worse for Master Banage, and that would be intolerable. Banage had been the one trying to help her, as always, and she'd thrown it back in his face. As Miranda saw it, she had only one option left, one final duty: disappear, fade into the world, and never give Hern another inch of leverage against her master.

Miranda sat back against the cave wall, digging her fingers into the hard-packed sand as the rabbit began to sizzle. Outside, the gray ocean crashed and foamed, throwing cold spray deep into the cave. She grimaced. Gin was right about one thing: They couldn't stay here forever. She had no spare clothes, no blankets, and she was filthy with sea grime and sand. Even her rings had cataracts of salt on them. Still, she didn't know where else to run, or what to do when she got there. When she tried to imagine life separated from the Spirit Court, her mind went blank.

She supposed that was understandable. She'd been in the Spirit Court since she was thirteen, and from the moment she'd taken her vows the Court had been her life. That, she'd always suspected, was the main reason Banage had accepted her as his apprentice over all the others. She was only one who would work the hours he worked. But she'd done it gladly, because when she was doing the Spirit Court's work, she felt as if she was doing something that mattered, something worthwhile. It gave her purpose, meaning, confidence. Now, without the Court, she felt like a block of driftwood bobbing on the waves, going nowhere.

She leaned back, staring up at the firelight as it danced across the smooth curve of the sea-washed stone. The wind blew through the cave, whistling over the rock like it was laughing at her. Then, out of nowhere, a voice whispered, "Miranda?"

Miranda leaped to her feet with her hands out, ready, but the cave was empty. Only the fire moved, the little flames clinging for life in the high wind. She pressed her back against the wall. A trick of the wind? Spirits sometimes mumbled as they went, especially winds, who seldom slept. Yet the voice had been clear, and it had certainly said her name.

She was turning this over frantically in her head, trying to keep a watch on everything at once, when her eyes caught something strange. At the mouth of the cave, silhouetted by the strip of sunlight, a figure landed.

Miranda blinked rapidly, but it didn't change what she saw. With the light at their back, she couldn't tell if it was a man or a woman, but it was certainly human, even though she'd just seen it do something a human shouldn't be able to do. Whatever it was had not walked up or climbed down—it had *landed* in front of her cave. Landed neatly, as though it had hopped down off a step, but that made no sense at all. The cliff was nearly a hundred feet tall.

Even as she was trying to sort this out, the figure ducked under the cave's low entrance and walked forward with quick, sprightly steps. Miranda pressed her back to the wall and sent a tremor of power down to her rings only to find that they were already awake and ready, glimmering suspiciously. As the figure stepped into the circle of the firelight, Miranda saw that it was a man. She placed him at late middle age, maybe older, with gray hair and skin that was starting to droop. He had an intelligent, wrinkled face and large spectacles, which gave him the air of a kindly scholar. This effect was aided by the long, shapeless robe he wore wrapped several times around his bony shoulders so that he looked like someone who'd lost a fight with a bed sheet. Other than the robe and the spectacles, he wore no other clothes she could see. Even his feet were bare, and he took care to walk only on the sand, stepping around the washed-up patches of sharp, broken shells.

Miranda didn't move an inch as he approached. Nothing about him was threatening, yet here was a stranger who'd appeared from nowhere, and she was a wanted fugitive. But even as the thought crossed her mind, she felt almost silly for thinking it. Anyone could have seen that the man wasn't from the Spirit Court. If the lack of rings wasn't proof enough, the fact that he just walked up to a Spiritualist, who had all her spirits buzzing, without a trace of caution completely tossed out all suspicion of Spirit Court involvement. That left the question, what was he?

As he approached, the wind continued to roar, drowning out all other sounds. It blew the sand in waves and whipped the man's robes around him, though, miraculously, they never tangled in his arms or impeded his legs. When he reached Miranda's fire, the man sat down gracefully, like a guest at a banquet, and gestured with his hand.

The moment he moved his fingers, the wind died out, and in the sudden silence, he extended his hand to Miranda.

"Please," he said, smiling. "Sit."

Miranda didn't budge. It took a strong-willed wizard to work with a wind, and she wasn't about to give him an opening just because he was polite. "Who are you?"

"Someone who wants to help you, Spiritualist Lyonette," the man said pleasantly.

"If you know that much," Miranda said, relaxing a

fraction, "then you should know it's just Miranda now. My title was stripped last week."

"So I have been told," the man said. "But such things matter very little to the powers I represent." He motioned again. "Please, do sit."

Curiosity was eating at her now, and she inched her way down the wall until she was sitting, facing him across the fire.

"I'm sorry," the man said, taking off his spectacles and cleaning them on his robe. "I have been rude. My name is Lelbon. I serve as an ambassador for Illir."

He paused, waiting for some kind of reaction, but the name meant nothing to Miranda. However, the moment Lelbon spoke, she felt a sharp, stabbing pressure against her collarbone. At first, she thought the man had done something, but then she realized it was Eril's pendant driving itself into her chest.

Careful to keep her face casual, she sent a small questioning tendril of power down to her wind spirit. The answer she received was an overwhelming, desperate need to come out.

"Eril," she said softly, pulling on the thread that connected them, giving permission. The pendant's pressure stopped and the wind spirit flew out. For once, however, Eril did not rush around. Instead, he swirled obediently beside Miranda, creating little circles in the sand.

"Sorry, mistress," the wind whispered. "Illir is one of the Wind Lords. To not pay my respects to his ambassador would be unthinkably rude."

Miranda tensed. "Wind Lords?"

"Yes," Lelbon said. "The West Wind, specifically."

"And this Illir," Miranda said carefully, "is the Great

Spirit of the west?" It seemed like a tremendous area to be under the control of one Great Spirit, but with spirits it was always better to suggest more power rather than less, so as not to risk offending. From the way her usually intractable wind spirit was acting, Miranda guessed that Illir was not someone you wanted angry with you.

"Great Spirit isn't the most accurate description," Lelbon said with the slow consideration of someone who thrived on particulars. "Great Spirits have a domain: The river controls its valley, an ancient tree guards its forest, and so forth. Winds are different. They can cross dozens of different domains over the course of their day, and since they do not touch the ground, local Great Spirits have little control over them. So, rather than be part of the patchwork of grounded domains, the winds have their own domain in the sky, which is ruled by four lords, one for each cardinal direction. Whenever a wind blows in a direction, it enters the sway of that lord. Illir is the Lord of the West. Therefore, when a wind blows west, it is under the rule of Illir." He smiled at the space where Eril was circling. "Any given wind will blow in all directions during its lifetime, and thus owes allegiance to all four winds. Angering any of them could mean shutting off that direction forever."

"A terrible fate," Eril shuddered. "It is our nature to blow where we choose. Losing a direction for a wind is like losing a limb for a human."

Miranda nodded slowly, a little overwhelmed. She'd never heard of any of this, not from her lessons in the Spirit Court or her travels, and certainly not from her wind spirit.

"Don't look so fretful." Lelbon smiled at her wide-eyed look. "There's no reason for humans, wizard or otherwise, to know the obligations of the winds. Most spirits don't even understand how it works. They don't need to. The winds handle their own affairs."

"So what are you?" It felt rather personal to ask, but she had to know. "Are you human or..."

Lelbon laughed. "Oh, I'm human. I'm a scholar who studies spirits, wind spirits in particular, which is how I stumbled into my current position. The West Wind is an old, powerful spirit, but also rather eccentric and very interested in the goings-on of humans. In return for letting me study him and his court, I serve him as messenger and ambassador whenever he needs a face people can see. Most people find talking to a wind directly to be quite disconcerting."

"That's one way to put it," Miranda said, glancing sideways at the empty spot where Eril was spinning. "But why did Illir send you to talk to me? What does the West Wind want with a former Spiritualist?"

The man pursed his lips thoughtfully. "Your reputation among spirits who care about this sort of thing is quite exemplary, Miranda Lyonette. Particularly your daring rescue of the captured Great Spirit Mellinor."

Miranda jerked. "You know about that?"

Lelbon chuckled. "There is very little the winds do not hear, and it was hardly a small event. Next to that, the technicalities of Spirit Court politics and who is or is not officially a Spiritualist aren't important. All I need to know is would you be willing to do a job for us?"

Miranda sat back. "Thank you for the compliment, but I'm afraid you've come to the wrong person. You would be much better off taking your plea to the Rector Spiritualis in Zarin."

"Ah," the man said. "My master has already determined that the Spirit Court is not in a position to offer the assistance we require, which is precisely why I was sent to find you. Won't you at least hear our offer?"

Miranda frowned, then nodded. After all, what harm could there be in just hearing him out?

Lelbon smiled and leaned closer. "As I explained, the Wind Lords, while very powerful spirits, aren't technically Great Spirits, in that they don't have dominion over a specific area. Even so, they, like all large, elder spirits, have a duty to protect and look after spirits less powerful than themselves. So it has always been. Now, this arrangement seems simple enough on the surface, but in reality it's a delicate balance of responsibilities. The winds are required to act on whatever problems they see in the domains they cross over. Yet, as they have no real dominion over any spirits except wind spirits, this often means nothing more than reporting the problem to the local Great Spirit, who deals with the trouble in its own way, if at all."

"Doesn't sound very reliable," Miranda said.

"That depends on the Great Spirit," Lelbon said. "If they are open to outside assistance, things go smoothly, the problem gets dealt with, and everyone moves on. However, if the Great Spirit does not welcome interference in their affairs..." He trailed off, looking for the right word. "Well, let's say that things can get complicated, which brings us to my offer."

"Let me guess," Miranda said. "Your lord has found trouble somewhere where the local Great Spirit doesn't want him."

"More or less," Lelbon said, smiling. "I can't go into

the particulars of the goings-on. My master is already trespassing on dangerous ground simply by seeking you out. All we're asking you to do is go to the place and make your own assessment as a neutral party. That's the job. We would pay your expenses, of course, and my master would be very grateful."

For a long moment, Miranda was very tempted. It sounded like an interesting problem, and it must certainly be urgent if the West Wind would rather pull her in than wait for the Spirit Court to assign someone. But...

"Strictly for curiosity," Miranda said slowly. "Where would I be going?"

"Are you familiar with the land surrounding the Fell-bro River?" Lelbon said. "The duchy called Gaol?"

Miranda froze. "Gaol?"

"Yes," Lelbon said. "Medium-sized holding, about four days' ride from Zarin."

"I know where it is," Miranda muttered. This changed everything. Gaol was where Hern kept his tower. "Look," she said. "You seem to know a great deal about me, so you know I can't go to Gaol. That's Hern's land. If I was seen there at all, everyone would think I was there for revenge. Anywhere else I could maybe help you, but not Gaol."

"It is precisely because of your history with Hern that we chose you," Lelbon said seriously.

Miranda's eyes widened. "You think Hern is involved?"

"Let me put it this way," Lelbon said, leaning closer. "If he were doing his job as a Spiritualist, would we need to ask your help? We need *you*, Miranda, exactly as you are. No one else will do."

They stared at each other for a long moment and then Miranda looked away. "I'm sorry, I can't. I've muddied the Spirit Court's reputation too much as it is already. If I go and make a scene in Gaol, I'll be no better than the thief Monpress. Tell your master thank you for the offer, but I can't do it."

They sat in silence, and then, slowly, Lelbon stood up.

"Well," he said, "if that's your final decision, I won't insult you with arguments. However"—he reached into the folds of his white robe and drew out a little square of bright, colored paper—"should you change your mind, just give us a signal."

He pushed the folded paper into Miranda's hands before she could refuse and turned away, padding across the sand toward the cave's mouth. Belatedly, Miranda stood up and hurried after to show him out. It was only good manners, though she felt a bit ridiculous playing hostess in a cave. Even so, Lelbon smiled graciously as she ducked with him under the cave's low-hanging lip and out onto the stony beach.

"I am sorry," Miranda started to say, but the man shook his head.

"All I ask is that you think about it. After all"—his soft voice took on a cutting edge—"you are the Spiritualist. You must decide how best to uphold your duty."

Miranda winced at that, but said nothing. Lelbon smiled politely and, after a little bow, walked away down the beach. She watched him go, feeling slightly awkward. After his dramatic and mysterious arrival, she'd thought for sure his exit would be something more dramatic than ambling down the stony beach. But the old man kept walking, his bare feet deftly dodging the patches of stone and broken shells, growing smaller and smaller behind the clouds of sea spray. She was about to turn back into her cave when she caught a motion out of the corner of her eye.

Far down the shore, she saw Lelbon raise his hand, as if he were hailing someone. As his hand went up, a great wind rose, whipping Miranda's hair across her face as it barreled down the beach. It reached Lelbon seconds after passing her, and the old man's shapeless robe belled out around him like a kite. As she watched, his bare feet left the sand. He soared up with the wind, the white of his robe like a seabird against the dull gray sky, and vanished over the cliffs. Miranda ran into the water, hoping to see more of his amazing flight, but the sky was empty, and the old man was already gone.

She was still staring when the sound of something heavy landing in the sand behind her made her spin around. Gin crouched behind her, panting as if he'd run the whole cliff line. "What's going on? What was that enormous wind?"

"Wasn't it amazing?" Eril said before Miranda could even open her mouth. "It was one of the great winds who serve the west. I've never met a wind so large!"

"What was a great wind doing here?" Gin growled, glaring at the sky.

"Trying to give us a job," Eril said, whirling so that his words blasted into Miranda's face. "I can't believe you turned him down! Illir is the greatest of the Wind Lords, and you passed up the chance to do him a personal favor?"

"Wait, what?" Gin looked at the wind. "What kind of job?"

"One we're not taking," Miranda said firmly, sending a poke of power at Eril. "If it had been anywhere else, maybe, but there isn't a spirit in the world who could make me go to Gaol."

As she was saying this, Eril was talking under her in a frantic rush, filling Gin in on the particulars of Lelbon's request. Gin listened, the fur on his back standing up in a ridge by the time the wind finished.

"Is it true?" he said, orange eyes flashing as he looked at Miranda. "You turned down a plea of help from a spirit who sought you out?"

"Don't look at me like that!" Miranda shouted. "I didn't make us fugitives to turn around and walk straight into Hern's backyard! Would you have me make everything we went through in Zarin worthless?"

"Better than making your entire career as a Spiritualist worthless!" Gin shouted back. "We are your spirits, Miranda. We serve you because we believe in you. The Miranda I follow would never turn down a spirit's plea for help."

"Weren't you listening to anything I've said?" Miranda cried. "Master Banage—"

"Banage would never forgive a Spiritualist who turned her back on her oath to the spirits in order to serve the Court." Gin was snarling now. "And you know it."

"That's not fair!" Miranda said. "This isn't that simple!"

"Isn't it?" Gin growled, turning away. "You told me not too long ago that there was right and there was wrong, and no amount of words could bridge the gap between the two. Maybe it's time you considered your own words, and what those prized oaths of yours really mean."

With that, the dog took off down the beach. Miranda could only stare after him, fuming. She felt Eril slide back into his pendant, curling back into place with a long, disappointed sigh, leaving her alone on the long, thin stretch of rocky beach. Suddenly too tired to go back into the cave, Miranda sat down in the sand, digging her bare feet under the smooth rocks and staring out at the pounding waves.

To serve the spirits, to protect them from harm, to uphold their well-being above all else, that was the oath all Spiritualists took the day they received their first ring. Miranda looked down at the heavy gold ring on the middle finger of her left hand, tracing the smooth, perfect circle stamped deep into the soft metal. It was supposed to represent the circle of connection between all things, from the smallest spirits to the greatest kings, and the Spirit Court's duty to promote balance within that connection.

The ocean spray blew her hair wild around her face as she turned to look where Gin had gone. Balance and duty, right and wrong. Even as she thought about it, she could almost feel Banage's disdainful look. After all, Banage's deep voice echoed in her head. What greater shame could there be for the Spirit Court than a Spiritualist who turned her back on a spirit in need?

She reached into her pocket and took out the flat, folded square of colored paper Lelbon had given her. She turned it carefully, unfolding the delicate paper again and again until she held nearly four feet of colorful tissue streaked with reds, greens, and golds in her hands. There was nothing written on it, no note, no instructions, but when she reached the center of the square, the paper ended in a sharp point tied to a long string. Feeling a bit silly, Miranda stood up, careful to hold the fluttering paper out of the water. She walked to the edge of the beach and released the paper into the wind. It whipped up, colored streamer flapping as it soared into the sky, anchored by the string Miranda wrapped around her fingers. For a long moment the colored kite danced in the sea wind, dipping and bobbing. Then, without warning, a wind snatched the kite out of her hand. The bright, colored paper flew up into the sky, turning little cartwheels as the wind blew it off, dancing and dipping westward, over the sea.

Miranda watched the kite until it vanished behind the clouds, and then she turned to find Gin. She didn't have to go far. He came trotting up almost at once, looking immensely pleased with himself.

"I knew you'd come around," he said, tail wagging. "Are we leaving now or do you still need to get something?"

Miranda looked back at the cave. Her little fire had already flickered out, and everything else she had was on her back.

"Don't think so," she said. "Ready when you are."

"I've been ready for the last five days," Gin grumbled, lying down so she could climb up. When she was steady, he jumped, taking the first rocky ledge in one leap. The beach swung crazily below them, and Miranda felt all her blood running to her feet. By the third jump, Gin's claws were scraping on bare stone, and Miranda closed her eyes to keep from being sick. Then they were on flat ground at the top of the cliff face, and Gin was asking her which way to go.

"East and south," Miranda said.

"How far?" Gin asked, loping over the scrubby grass.

"I don't know." Miranda bit her lip. "If we go east, we'll hit the road to the river, but if we cut cross-country, two days' hard running?"

"Right," Gin said, nodding. "We'll be there tomorrow morning."

"Tomorrow morning?" Miranda scoffed. "You can't fly, mutt."

"No?" Gin grinned. "Watch me."

He picked up speed, racing over the low hills faster and faster until it was all Miranda could do to hold on.

"Gin!" she cried over the wind. "You can't keep this up all the way to Gaol!"

"You worry about what we do when we get there," he shouted back. "Leave the running to me."

After that, Miranda gave up and held on. Clinging to the ghosthound's shifting fur, she tried to think of what she'd do when they reached Gaol, but her mind was blank. After all, she didn't even know what they were looking for, and though Lelbon had said the West Wind would help, she didn't know what kind of help a great wind spirit considered appropriate, or if she'd recognize it when it came. Still, being on the road again, running toward a purpose, these made her happier than she'd been since arriving in Zarin, and she contented herself with holding on as the rocky fields and scrubby grass streaked by. Overhead, the cloudy sky grew dimmer as evening approached.

CHAPTER
11

Eli woke up to bright sunlight in his face and Josef's boot poking his ribs.

"Get up," Josef said. "The situation's changed."

Eli sat up, rubbing the grit out of his eyes. When he looked again, Josef was gone. He blinked a few times, trying to figure out if he'd dreamed the whole uncomfortable event, and then he spotted the ladder nailed to the wooden wall of the warehouse beside the door.

It was a hairy climb. The ladder was nailed to the wall with no allowance for footing, and he wasn't actually awake enough for this sort of thing. Still, a few moments later he wiggled through the trapdoor to the sloped roof to find Nico and Josef lying belly down on the wooden shingles, staring across the water. The warehouses, being, as they were, by the river, were at the lowest point of Gaol. From the roof, however, you could see into the city proper, which seemed to be in some commotion.

"The sun's barely up," Eli said, yawning. "What is it, a bakers' riot?"

"Not sure," Josef said, eyeing the crowds that filled the broad streets leading up to the citadel. "Those are hardly bakers, unless bakers in Gaol make bread with swords. I was going to guess peasant riot, but the crowd's far too calm, and nothing's happening at the citadel. So now I'm thinking conscript army, and seeing as we're knee-deep in a thief trap made for Eli Monpress, I'd say that crowd has your name on it."

"Well," Eli said, "they're going the wrong way."

He was right. The well-armed crowd in the street was heading away from the docks, marching uphill toward the keep.

"I wonder," Eli said, standing on his toes to get a better view. "We should head down and find out what's going on."

Josef glared at him. "What did I just say last night about curiosity?"

"Josef," Eli tsked, "this isn't just curiosity; it's ground-work. You gave me a day and a night to pull this job, and I can hardly steal a Fenzetti blade from here. Come on." He smiled, heading for the trapdoor. "Let's get dolled up."

He vanished down the ladder. Nico and Josef exchanged a long-suffering look before getting up and following.

Though years of thievery and natural inclination had given Eli a quick hand and inventive eye for improvised disguises, he always kept the staples on hand. There were some things you simply could not count on improvising. The moment he reached the floor of the warehouse, he ran to his pack and began pulling things out. He had a surprisingly large pile before he found what he was looking for: a small, carefully wrapped package tied with string. Eli undid the knots deftly and the package spilled open, revealing a cascade of golden, flowing hair, the crown jewel of his costume collection.

He shook the wig out a few times, but it needed very little. Wigs of this quality never did, if you stored them right. Eli didn't know how much it had cost, but he guessed quite a bit since its previous owner, the Princess of Pernoff, had seen fit to store it in the safe with her jewels. Eli had relieved her of both that night, and though the jewels were long gone, the wig remained one of his favorite possessions.

Using his fingers, Eli brushed his short hair back until it was flat against his head, and then, leaning over, slid the wig on with practiced ease. When he came up again, he looked remarkably different. The pale golden locks hung in subtle waves around his face, setting off his pale skin in a way his own dark hair never had, making him look delicate and noble in a fragile way, something he took full advantage of.

"Powers," Josef said, jumping off the ladder. "Not that thing again."

"I'll stop wearing it when it stops working," Eli said, pinning the wig into its final position with a half-dozen tiny hairpins. "See if there's anything workable in the crates. I saw one addressed to Freeman's Clothier in Zarin that might have something good."

Josef walked over to the pile of wooden boxes and began reading the faded shipping manifests. He had to move several to get to the crate Eli had mentioned, but when he cracked it open, they were not disappointed.

"Perfect," Eli said, grinning.

Inside was a neatly folded stack of brocade jackets,

obviously intended for some tremendously overpriced shop in Zarin. Eli pawed through them, finally picking out a garish red-and-gold peacock pattern that matched the wig perfectly and, as an added bonus, caused Josef to sigh in disgust. Unfortunately, the only coat in the box that would fit over Josef's broad shoulders was a hideous green monstrosity that he refused to wear. Finally, Josef settled for a thick, black shirt from his own pack.

"I guess that will do," Eli said and sighed. "Just be sure to scowl a lot; that way no one will get close enough to notice the mended stab holes and bloodstains."

"I do wash it," Josef said. "Anyway, it fits me better than the guy I took it off."

Eli gave him a startled look. "I don't think I want to hear any more about your brand of shopping."

Josef shrugged. "It's not like he was using it."

Eli left it at that.

In the end, Josef decided to bring only the twin short swords he wore at his hips and the knives he could hide in his clothing. He and Eli agreed that walking into town covered in blades as he usually was would be asking for trouble, especially when they were trying to be discreet. Of course, this also meant Josef would have to leave the Heart, something Eli had a much harder time convincing him of.

"I don't see why this is a big deal," Eli said. "You hate having to use the Heart anyway."

"That's not the issue here," Josef said, crossing his arms stubbornly. "It's plain stupid to walk into an unknown situation, with armed men gathering in a city we know is a trap, and not bring our best weapon."

"Come on," Eli pleaded. "It's common knowledge you're with me these days. Carrying that thing is like walking around with a giant signpost: 'Here's Josef Liechten! Please stab!' If you're going to bring it, there's no point in disguises at all."

Josef scowled. "I don't think—"

"Just leave it here," Eli interrupted. "It's not like it could get stolen anyway, seeing as you're the only one who can pick it up. Besides"—Eli's voice smoothed to warm honey—"you're Josef Liechten, the greatest swordsman in the world. Surely *you* can take a few armed men without the Heart."

Josef gave him a dangerous glare. "Don't treat me like one of your idiot spirits." He pulled the enormous black blade off his back and dropped it. It fell like a meteor, sticking point-first in the wood floor. "I'll leave the Heart because you make a good case, but don't ever try and con me again, Monpress."

"Point taken," Eli said softly, but Josef was already stalking toward the door.

"You deserved that," Nico said, standing up from the crate she'd been sitting on.

"Thanks," Eli said sarcastically, but his heart wasn't in it. He looked over at Nico. "Sure you don't want a disguise? Just for a change?"

"No." Nico gave him a little half smile. "Nothing in those crates can do this."

She stepped forward into a long shadow cast by one of the dividers that separated the windows and vanished. Eli blinked. He'd seen Nico do her shadow thing dozens of times, but never that cleanly. It was like she'd simply disappeared.

"Slorn did a good job with this coat," she said behind him.

Eli jumped and whirled around. She was several feet away, sitting on a crate a few rows up, shaking her oversized sleeves with a kind of visceral happiness, like a cat playing with a stunned mouse.

"So I see," Eli said. "Shall we go?"

But the crate was already empty, and Nico winked into existence again beside Josef, who was standing impatiently at the door.

"Right," Eli muttered, hurrying to catch up.

The city of Gaol was a beautiful, well-laid-out place. Every road was perfectly straight, every house perfectly kept. Small gardens glowed like jewels behind the low stone walls, and every sign was painted in matching colors without a single scuff or faded letter. Even the paving cobbles were set at perfect right angles with their cracks swept meticulously clean.

Over all of this order flowed a constant stream of ordinary people, men and women, with identical swords belted at their sides. They were moving in close knots, talking together in quiet, nervous whispers. None of them looked happy to be there, but they moved at a good pace, making their way toward the citadel at the city center to join the growing crowd.

"Amazing!" Eli stood on tiptoe to get a better look. "It's like they turned the town upside down, shook out the people, and gave them swords. What is this, community military service?"

"Stop gawking," Josef said, tugging the thief down by his gaudy coat. "You're supposed to be a traveling merchant, remember?"

"I think it's perfectly in character for me to gawk," Eli

said, batting Josef's hand away. "Haven't you ever met a merchant?"

They were walking toward the center of town down one of the main roads. Eli, as the merchant, stayed out in front, while Josef, the hired sword, kept a few paces behind. Nico, as usual, was nowhere in sight, but Josef's practiced eye spotted her flitting in and out of the gloom between the buildings, a tiny, girl-shaped patch of darker shadow. They were following the crowd toward the duke's fortress, its hulking, boxy shape black against the clear morning sky. Ahead, the road opened out into a square that was even more packed than the street they were on. Eli paused, frowning at the armed crowd, and then, quick as a bird going for cover, ducked into the nearest door, forcing Josef to turn sharp if he wanted to follow.

The doorway led to a bakery. It was a tiny shop, just a few benches and a counter separating the actual ovens from the customers. Still, like everything in Gaol, it was immaculately neat. Boards covered in precise lettering detailed the startling variety of baked goods and sweet-meats the shop offered. Hearing the door, the baker pulled himself away from the small window that overlooked the crowded square and came to the counter, a sour look on his flat face.

At once, Eli launched himself into character, his grin growing snide and arrogant as he flipped a handful of silver bits from the local currency casually between his fingers.

The baker's expression became infinitely more gracious at the glitter of silver. "What can I get for you, sir?"

"Hmm," merchant Eli droned, not bothering to look

away from the window. "Give me a half dozen of those little fruit things, and a loaf of whatever's cheap, for my boy here. Something hearty—these swordsmen eat you out of house and home."

Josef didn't have to fake his scowl, and the baker's red face paled. "Of course, sir, at once."

He went over to the shelves and began pulling things down with the hesitant clumsiness of someone who didn't usually do this himself.

"Where are your apprentices?" Eli said, casually leaning on the spotless counter. "I can't imagine you run this shop alone."

"Oh, no," the baker said and laughed. "But you know how boys are. They ran off to the square as soon as they heard the news. The duke's called in the conscriptions, the whole lot, word is." He huffed as he set out the tarts. "I'm just thankful I got dispensation on account of my shop, or I'd be grabbing my sword too."

"Conscriptions?" Eli said. "Why? Is Gaol under attack?"

"Oh, no." The baker shook his head. "Who'd attack Gaol? No, sir, word everywhere is that Eli Monpress robbed the duke's fortress last night."

The silver coins stopped flashing in Eli's hand.

"Really," he said, almost too casually. "How do you know it was Monpress? Did they catch him?"

"No," the baker said, fishing a loaf of brown bread out of the bin. "There's been no official word yet, but if they'd caught the thief, I doubt Duke Edward would bother with conscripts." He gave Eli a wink. "*That's* how we know it was Monpress. Who else would warrant mobilizing the whole country to catch him?"

"Who else, indeed," Eli said. "But it's been hours since the robbery if Monpress robbed the citadel last night. Wouldn't the thief have escaped by now?"

"I don't see how he could have," the baker said, packing Eli's order into a small wicker basket. "The duke closed the gates before dawn this morning. They say Monpress can move through shadows and kill guards just by looking, but that's rubbish. Whatever his bounty, he's human, and nothing human could have gotten through the duke's security."

"Why do you say that?" Josef asked, glaring at the baker from his place on the wall. "The thief got in, didn't he?"

The baker jumped and looked at Eli, obviously waiting for him to discipline his guard, but Eli was staring out the window, studying the citadel and the growing crowd with intense interest. Realizing he wouldn't get any backup from that quarter, the baker sullenly packed the last of Eli's pastries into the basket. When he was done, he had to wait a moment while Eli tore himself away from the window, but the pile of silver Eli tossed on the counter quickly smoothed over any hurt feelings.

"Thank you, sir," the baker said, bowing graciously as Eli swept out of the bakery with Josef on his heels.

The moment they stepped onto the street, Eli veered hard right, and they ducked down a narrow but shockingly clean alley. Nico was waiting for them, and she helped herself to one of the pastries from Eli's basket as soon as he was close.

"What's going on?" she asked, biting into the corner of the flaky tart.

"Someone got here before us," Josef said, leaning

against the wall with his arms crossed. "I'd like to know who."

"I have an idea," Eli said carefully, picking a tart out of the pile. "But I'd have to get a look at the scene of the crime to be sure."

"What?" Josef said. "You mean *inside* the citadel? The one surrounded by armed guards?"

"Well, I certainly can't tell anything from out here," Eli said.

Josef frowned. "You do realize this could all be part of the trap."

"What?" Eli said, his mouth full of sweet pastry. "Fake a robbery so I'd come and investigate? That's a bit of a long shot. Think of it like this: We're here for a Fenzetti blade. Now, if another thief did break in, he either took the blade with him or had to leave it. Either way, we have to go into that citadel, either to pick up the thief's trail or get the blade for ourselves. The way I see it, we've just had the opportunity of a lifetime dropped in our laps. They're getting their orders now, but in a few moments, that whole crowd of citizen soldiers is going to start tearing this town apart looking for Eli Monpress. By going into the citadel, we'll be going to the only place they're *not* going to be looking. No thief good enough to get into the Duke of Gaol's citadel would ever return to the scene of the crime. When you look at it that way, the citadel's the safest place in the city for us to be right now."

Josef gave him a long look, casually sliding a dagger in and out of his sleeve as he thought about it. "That's some twisted Eli logic," he said at last, "but I'll bite. Anyway, sneaking into a citadel sounds a lot more interesting than hiding in a warehouse until dark."

"Ah," Eli said, licking the last of the tart off his fingers. "But that's the brilliant bit of the plan. We won't be sneaking. They're going to let us in all nice and legal."

Josef arched an eyebrow. "How are you going to manage that?"

Eli only smiled and shoved the wicker basket at him. "Just eat your breakfast. I've got to do some shopping. Be back in five minutes."

Josef barely had time to grab the basket before Eli was gone, ducking back out into the street with a flash of fake golden hair and vanishing expertly into the crowd. Josef stood there, holding the basket and watching where Eli had been for a moment, and then he sighed and sank back against the wall.

"Never boring with him, is it?" he said, fishing the loaf out of the basket and biting deep into the warm, dark bread.

Nico shook her head and helped herself to another tart.

Ten minutes later, Eli popped back into the alley carrying a small velvet bag in his fist and grinning like a cat who'd just eaten a coop of canaries. Josef stopped twirling the empty breadbasket between his fingers and straightened up. "What did you buy?"

"Take a look," Eli said and opened the drawstring, upturning the velvet bag over his open hand. There was a faint tinkling sound, and a glittering cascade fell out of the bag into Eli's waiting palm. They were rings. Jeweled rings in a rainbow of colors, all set in gold bands of various thickness. Some of the stones were round and smooth, others were cut to sharp points that refracted the morning light in glowing colors, and not a single one was smaller than the first knuckle of Eli's thumb. They were, in short, the tackiest, gaudiest jewelry Josef had ever seen.

"Powers, Eli," Josef said, picking up a ring set with a ruby that was almost larger than the embellished band it was attached to. "I hope you stole these. I can't imagine paying good money for something this ugly."

"Oh, I paid for them," Eli said, shoving the rings onto his fingers. "But not much, don't worry. They're glass. Fakes. I saw them in the window of one of the stores as we were walking up. They're what gave me the idea for how we're going to get into the citadel, actually. Look." He held up his newly adorned hands and wiggled his fingers. "Remind you of anyone?"

He'd crammed the rings onto every finger, thumbs included. His right pinky actually had two rings, both smaller gold and pearl bands that looked like something a father would buy for his spoiled daughter. But he was right, the effect was familiar, and Josef began to understand.

It didn't seem possible, but Eli's grin grew even wider. "Come on," he said, turning on his heel. "This is going to be the most fun I've had all year."

Josef stepped out after him. Nico, still licking her sticky fingers, kept right on the swordsman's heels.

CHAPTER
12

Gin made good on his boast. He ran like the wind itself, his long legs eating up the miles as they ran cross-country, on road and off. His orange eyes were completely unhindered by the darkness, and he stopped only when Miranda made him, which she did as much to catch her breath and unclamp her aching hands from his fur for a bit as to make the dog himself rest. Still, they made the journey from the western coast to the edge of Argo, the kingdom of which Gaol was the most prominent duchy, with time to spare, crossing the border shortly after dawn.

As they ran, Miranda had plenty of time to worry. She had no money or supplies, just what she'd had with her under her Spirit Court robes the day of the trial, which was precious little. Alone and in exile on the beach, she hadn't given it much attention. Now, however, all she could think was that this was a sorry start to a job. What she needed was some money, a cleaning up, and maybe a writ or other official document that could give her a new identity. As she was, no papers, no money, no authority, her hair thick with salt and her clothes stained with sea spray, she didn't even know if they'd let her through the city gate.

At their second stop, however, something happened that made Miranda realize she wasn't giving the West Wind enough credit. After two hours of hard running, Miranda coaxed Gin to a stop by a creek. While he drank, she stretched her legs, which ached from holding on to the ghosthound so tightly for so long. But as she was bending over to touch her toes, she felt something flutter against her fingers. She jumped in alarm and looked down to see it was a note, the paper money some kingdoms issued for internal use instead of coins or council standards. The note fluttered, and she snatched it between her fingers before it could blow away again. It was from the kingdom of Barat, which she vaguely remembered being somewhere south and west. Miranda studied the note intently before slipping it into her pocket. The number printed on the corner was modest, and she didn't even know if she could find somewhere that would accept it outside of Barat, but it was more than she'd had a moment ago, so Miranda counted it a lucky find and let the matter drop.

The next time they rested, it happened again. This time a small rain of silver coins from Fenulli, a city-state hundreds of miles away, landed inches in front of Gin's nose. After that, every time they stopped, more money appeared, always from countries to the west, and always in small amounts, yet their pile was growing. By the time they reached the Gaol border, Miranda's pockets were bursting, and she was feeling much more confident about

the whole affair. She was still going over the particulars
in her head, how she would change the money, what she
would say if anyone commented ("My father collected
currencies," or "We're a traveling act," which would
explain the dog nicely), when she realized Gin was acting
oddly. They were still at the Gaol border, off the road but
in sight of the signs, standing in a little valley just below
a well-kept vineyard, but Gin showed no signs of moving
on. Instead, he was pacing back and forth, in and out of
the duchy.

"What is it?" she asked, too tired to be as concerned
as she should be.

"Look at the ground," Gin growled, his nose against
the grass. "See anything odd?"

Miranda looked at the ground. It looked like field grass
to her, with a few stones scattered about. Fortunately, Gin
answered his own question before she had to admit her
ignorance.

"The grass is wet here," Gin said, pawing at the ground
on the non-Gaol side of the border, "but dry here." He
jumped the little gully that marked the beginning of the
duchy and nosed at the bright green, but bone-dry, Gaol
grass. "It's like that all through here," he snorted, raising
his head. "Like it didn't rain on Gaol at all. What kind of
weather acts like that?"

Miranda frowned and squinted upward, but the sky
was the same rainwashed clear blue as far as she could
see on both sides of the border. She looked back at the
ground, and her frown deepened. What kind of weather
indeed?

"We are here to investigate strange happenings," she
said. "This would certainly count, but it can't just be

that the rain is acting odd. I don't think the West Wind would need us for something like that. Let's go farther in. Maybe we'll find more oddities."

Gin nodded and they trotted up the hill into Gaol itself. They kept the road in sight but stayed to the ridges and trees, Gin slinking lower and lower as the farms grew denser. Still, everything they saw looked perfectly normal. Idyllic even, so much so that Miranda began to wonder why they'd been sent here at all.

"I never knew Gaol was so pretty," she said delightedly as they crossed a stone bridge over a clear, babbling brook. "Why in the world does Hern spend so much time scheming in Zarin when he's got this to come home to?"

"Well, I don't like it one bit," Gin said. "It's too open and too neat. Even the grass growing in the fields is lined up in a grid. It's unnatural."

"Better get used to it," Miranda said, signaling him to stop at a picturesque stand of shaggy fir trees. "Because you're going to be waiting here while I go change this money and gather information. I saw a sign for an inn and trade house a little ways back. It'll be a start, if nothing else."

Gin snorted. "I'm not going to wait here while you wander off."

"We're trying to keep a low profile, remember?" Miranda said, jumping down. "Ghosthounds aren't exactly inconspicuous."

Gin rolled his eyes at that, but he sat down, which meant he was going to go along. Miranda smiled and checked her pockets one last time. The mix of coins and paper ruffled pleasantly under her fingers. Satisfied, she ran her hands through her windblown, salt-stiff hair and bound it back in a stiff braid. When she was as presentable as she could hope for, she left the trees and made her way down the hill to the large, charming lodge at the bottom, whose bright painted sign advertised lodging, baths, and all manner of trade and services for travelers.

Miranda swerved west and came up to the inn on the road as though she'd been walking on it the whole time. The main building was set back from the road itself, behind a large yard for caravans to turn around in. However, the turnaround was empty this morning. So were the stables, Miranda noted as she climbed up the wooden steps and opened the door to the inn. The building was just as charming inside as it was outside, with large wooden beams across the ceiling, warm lamps hanging on the walls, and a large stone hearth surrounded by benches. Feeling decidedly out of place in her dirty clothes, Miranda put on her most competent face and walked over to the dry-goods counter, where an old man was sorting through a large accounts book below a neatly lettered sign advertising money changing.

"We don't trade any council standards," he said as she approached. "Local currency only."

"I wasn't going to—" Miranda started, then dropped it, fishing her money out of her pockets instead. "Local is fine. Can you change these?"

The man stared at the strange collection of currencies as though Miranda had just emptied a fishing net on his desk and gave her a look sour enough to curdle cheese. "This ain't the Zarin exchange, lady."

"Just change what you can," Miranda said. "Please."

The man sneered at the pile, and then, with a long-suffering sigh, began to sort the notes and change into stacks.

"So," Miranda said, leaning forward just a little. "Quiet day?"

"Quiet?" The man snorted. "Try dead. The duke's called conscription and suspended all travel, or didn't you notice the empty road?"

"I just arrived," Miranda explained. "What do you mean 'called conscription'? Is there a war brewing?"

The man laughed loud and hard. "Council'd hardly allow that, would they? No, the duke can call conscription for whatever he likes. This here is a duchy in the old way. Old Edward owns everything, every field, every house, every business, even this one. We're all of us working for him, one way or the other, and conscription duty ain't any harder than farm work. Anyways, no one would say no to him even if he wasn't landlord and employer. You don't say no to the Duke of Gaol. Not if you want to keep the things what make life worth living."

Miranda grimaced. This duke sounded like a monster. That was one good thing about being here on her own rather than on the Spirit Court's business: She wouldn't have to introduce herself to the duke before getting to work. "Well," she said and smiled. "Why has he called conscription this time? Is there an emergency?"

He gave her a look as if she was stupid. "Didn't you hear? Eli Monpress robbed the duke last night. Stole him clean. Word is the treasury is empty."

It took every ounce of Miranda's discipline to keep her face calm, but inside, she was shrieking with joy. Eli Monpress here? Now? She couldn't even imagine a stroke of luck this fantastic. If she could somehow get her hands on Eli, why, even Hern couldn't keep her out of Zarin.

She looked up to see the innkeeper staring at her, and Miranda realized she must be grinning.

"That's too bad," she said, forcing her face into courteous disinterest. "I hear Monpress has a nice bounty. Did the duke catch him?"

"No word on that yet," the innkeeper said, shrugging. "The citadel's been shut up tight. But look at it this way: Would the duke shut down trade and close the borders if he had the thief in a cell?"

He might, actually, if he'd done any research on Eli, Miranda thought, but she kept it to herself.

"Doesn't matter none anyway," the man continued. "The duke will catch him all the same. This is Gaol, after all." He smiled, pushing a small stack of silver coins across the counter.

"Sixty-four exact," he said. "Take it or leave it, but you won't find better for the paper around here."

Miranda had no idea if that was good or not, but she took the money without complaint. The coins were thin pressed, and each was stamped with a man's face in silhouette, which the block lettering on the edges identified as belonging to Edward, Eighteenth Duke of Gaol.

It must have been a nice bit of money, for the innkeeper's tone softened considerably. "Anything else, miss?"

Miranda thought a moment. "Yes," she said. "I'll need a new set of clothes. And some soap."

The man raised his eyebrows, but he turned around and got a paper-wrapped bar from the shelf behind him.

"Soap," he said, slapping the bar on the counter. "One silver. As for clothes..." He walked over to the corner and opened the first of a series of large chests set against the wall. "My daughter's work," he said, pulling out a stretch of brown homespun. "Five silvers each. Just pick out what you like."

Miranda walked over with a grimace. The chest was full of dresses. Farmer girl dresses. With little motifs of daisies on the trim and sleeves. A quick look through the other chests showed more of the same. The man's daughter was apparently prolific, and very fond of daisies. Seeing this was all she was going to get, Miranda settled on a long, rust-colored dress with a wide skirt that looked like it would do for riding, and, most important of all, long sleeves that went down over her fingers to hide her rings. The color didn't clash with her hair too badly, and the stitching, though large, was sturdy. Satisfied, she paid the man for the soap and the dress, and he even wrapped it up for her for free, cementing her suspicion that she was being vastly overcharged.

Miranda shoved the package under her arm. Before she turned to leave, however, she asked one final question.

"Sir," she said, "did it rain last night?"

"Of course not," the man sniffed. "It's Wednesday."

Miranda gave him a funny look. "What does that have to do with rain?"

"This is Gaol," the man said. "It only rains on Sundays."

Miranda just stood there a moment, stunned, while in her head, several little pieces clicked into place.

"Thank you," she said. "Thank you very much."

The man just made a harumphing noise before going back to his ledger.

Miranda walked up the road until she was out of sight of the inn's windows, then sprinted up the hill to where

Gin was hiding. She'd worried he would be asleep, but the dog was awake and waiting.

"What's going on?" he asked as soon as she ducked under the shaggy treeline.

"Strange and wonderful things," she answered, peeling off her shirt. "Mellinor, could I get some water?"

The water spirit complied, and she was sopping wet in an instant. Peeling the soap out of its waxed-paper wrapping, Miranda began to scrub her face and hair. She relayed her conversation with the innkeeper as she washed, occasionally breaking to ask Mellinor for more water, which he gave immediately, for he was listening as well.

"Eli Monpress! Do you believe the luck?" Miranda said again, leaning over to wring out her hair.

"Lucky indeed," Gin said. "But go back to that bit about the rain. As I've heard it, only a Great Spirit can order the rain, and only then if it's got the cooperation of the local winds. How is a human doing it?"

"Maybe he's Enslaving the Great Spirit of this area," Miranda said, wincing as she picked at a knot of tangles rooted at the back of her neck.

"Preposterous," Mellinor rumbled, giving her a bit more water. "If this place was Enslaved, we would have known miles ago. The whole world would have known. Trust me, a land whose Great Spirit is Enslaved does not look like this."

The water slung outward, taking in the lovely hills, rolling farmland, and flowering orchards. Miranda was going to point out that Mellinor had looked pretty nice to her when she'd arrived, but then she remembered that spirits probably saw something completely different and she kept her mouth shut, washing the last of the soap out of her hair in silence.

"Well, whatever's happening, it's not good," she said, squeezing her hair dry. "Time to ask the spirits what's going on."

She pulled the dress over her head, the thick fabric catching on her wet skin. When the dress was in place, she knelt on the needle-strewn ground and pulled the green stone ring off her little finger.

"Alliana," she said softly, placing the ring on the ground, "say hello to the grove for us."

The moment the ring touched the ground, a circle of bright green moss began to spread over the brown needles. It spread to the base of the nearest tree, the moss's tiny rootlings prodding the bark. But as the moss crept up the fir tree, its quiet, tiny sounds became frustrated.

Finally, almost five minutes later, the moss retreated, and Alliana herself spoke up. "It's no good, mistress," the moss said, sounding quite put out. "I can't get the tree to talk. I couldn't even talk to the sapling sprouting below it. I don't understand; green wood is normally very chatty."

Miranda frowned. "You're saying they wouldn't wake up?"

"No, they're awake," the moss grumbled. "They just won't talk. I don't know what kind of land this is, but its spirits are *frightfully* rude."

Miranda bit her lip. This was an unexpected problem. "Try another tree."

They tried five altogether, but every time it was the same. The trees would not talk. None of the spirits in the little grove would. Finally, Alliana asked to go back to sleep, as this was all too frustrating for her, and Miranda drew her back into the moss agate.

"All right, I give up. What's going on?" Miranda said, sliding the ring back onto her finger. "Could it be Eli? What did he call it, building goodwill with the countryside?"

"No amount of goodwill does that," Mellinor said, flicking a spray of water at the reticent trees. "And I doubt even the thief has this kind of reach. Normally, I'd say Enslavement. I never knew anything else that could shut up young trees once a wizard woke them up, but they don't seem frightened, just worried." The water made a thoughtful splashing sound. "No, something is wrong in Gaol, and I doubt it's only here. The West Wind was right to be worried."

"So what are we going to do about it?" Gin said, tail twitching.

"Start at the top," Miranda answered. "If anyone can tell us what's going on, it's the Great Spirit of Gaol. Since the Fellbro River is by far the largest spirit in this area, I'm going to guess it's either in charge or knows who is, so we'll start with it, and for that, we're going to the capital."

"The capital?" Gin gave her a look. "The river runs all down the duchy's eastern side. Why do we need to go to the capital?"

"Because it's only three miles away, *and* because Eli's in the capital." Miranda smiled, shaking her sleeves until they fell down over her rings, hiding them completely. "Nothing wrong with a little bonus."

"I thought you said Eli had already robbed the duke," Gin said. "Wouldn't he be long gone by now?"

"Come on," Miranda said. "This is Eli we're talking

about. When has he ever just run away? I don't think he even could, not with an entire treasury. Even Nico's not that strong. No, I bet he's hiding in the capital, waiting on his chance to waltz out while everyone goes crazy around him. Who knows, maybe he's still in the duke's citadel." She grinned. "After all, 'the last place a man looks is under his feet.'"

Gin gave a long sigh. "It's a dark day indeed if you're quoting the thief." He lay down. "Come on, let's get going. I did a little scouting while you were gone. If we keep low, we can hide behind copses and hedge walls almost all the way."

Miranda glared at him. "You were supposed to wait here."

Gin just wagged his tail, and Miranda shook her head before climbing on.

"Just *try* and remember to be sneaky," she whispered as they crept out of the fir trees.

"Who do you think I am?" Gin snorted. He slunk up the hill, keeping behind the vineyards until he reached a stretch of trees and bushes that did indeed shelter them for the next few miles, just as he'd said it would.

When they reached the outskirts of Gaol's walled capital, Miranda left Gin hidden in an empty barn. He was much easier to convince this time around. Even Gin admitted there was no way he could sneak into a city, and besides, the night's running was catching up with him. Miranda left him sleeping under the straw in the hayloft, and then, strolling casually out of the barn, she started for the city.

With the embargo on travel, she'd expected it would take some finagling to get into Gaol's capital—a bribe for the guards, maybe, or some wall climbing. But as she got closer, she realized it wasn't going to be a problem. The road was full of people, farmers mostly, from their clothes, and almost all of them wearing swords. These must be the conscripts, she realized. The duke was apparently building himself quite an army. Because of this influx, the guards at the large gate were letting people in without much question. No one, however, was coming out. Miranda held her breath and kept her head down as she passed through the gates, but the guards didn't even speak to her. For once, she was very grateful to be ignored.

Gaol's capital was as lovely as the countryside around it, with a high, thick wall, a grid of neatly paved streets lined with iron street lamps, and tall, close timber and stone buildings with tiled, sloping roofs.

"It's every bit as orderly as the land outside," Mellinor whispered in her ear as she turned onto one of the side streets. "The Great Spirit must be a horrible taskmaster."

"I don't think the Great Spirit's the problem," Miranda muttered. This was a wizard's doing, she was certain. But how, and why? Those were the questions she was here to answer. As for who, though, she had a pretty good idea already. She looked northeast, where the pointed roof of an instantly recognizable tower poked over the rooftops. This was Hern's territory, after all, and as she thought about it, several strange things in Hern's past began to make sense, like how he'd refused year after year to take an apprentice of his own. She'd always chalked that up to self-importance combined with laziness, but if he were hiding something in Gaol, suddenly his not taking an apprentice would be cast in a new light. Same with his stubborn refusal to let other Spiritualists do any studies in Gaol, and his insistence that no Spiritualists cut through the duchy on their way to other places. He'd claimed his duke disliked Spiritualists disrupting his duchy by riding through on strange creatures, and since Hern was powerful and influential, and going around Gaol was a simple matter, no one had thought to question that explanation.

Well, Miranda thought, glaring at the tower, that was about to change. With a final sneer, she turned and started walking downhill toward the river.

As she went deeper into town, the crowd got thicker. Everyone, men and women, was carrying swords. Some moved in orderly groups through the streets, conscripts who'd already received their orders. Others, people who'd come through the gate with her, were still pushing toward the citadel, which seemed to be the heart of the whole operation. By the time she'd reached the edge of the town center square, the crowd was shoulder to shoulder. Miranda pushed her way through as best she could, but it was clear she wasn't going to get to the river this way. She scowled at the wall of backs in front of her and started looking around for a side street she could take down to the water. That's when she spotted him.

There, pushing his way through the crowd not five feet from her, was Hern. He was overdressed as always in a bright blue coat with silver embroidery, and looking hurried. The rings on his fingers glittered dangerously as he elbowed his way past a belligerent, and very large, pair of farmers. Once he was past, he gave the crowd a sneering look and turned down a side street lined with large, beautiful houses. As soon as he was around the corner, Miranda followed him.

"Miranda," Mellinor said in a warning voice. "What are you doing?"

"Think about it," she whispered, sneaking through the crowd. "Hern's secretiveness, strange things going on with the spirits in Gaol, the West Wind asking me, Hern's enemy, specifically to investigate? It doesn't take a genius to put it together."

"That may be," Mellinor said, "but don't forget your own words. You didn't want to take this job specifically because of Hern. I don't like Hern any more than you do, but the world hasn't changed in the last day. You said it yourself: if anyone sees you here, they're going to think it's revenge. Take your own advice, ignore the pompous idiot and keep going for the river."

"The river will still be there in an hour," she said under her breath. "I can't miss an opportunity like this. Think, if I can prove that Hern's behind whatever is going on here, I can destroy his credibility, maybe even get a retrial. It would be even better than catching Monpress. Even if it's just that he knows what's going on and hasn't reported it to the Court, that would be enough to throw mud all over his career." She stood on tiptoe, catching a glimpse of Hern's blond head through the crowd, before ducking down again. "No," she said. "He has to be up to something. The Spirit Court referendum is coming up any day now, and he wouldn't dare leave Zarin and miss the run-up for that unless he had a very good reason. I'm going to find out what that is."

Mellinor didn't like that one bit, but he didn't say anything else. Miranda trailed Hern for two blocks. It was nervous work. All the houses faced the road, and there was no cover for her to hide behind once they left the crowds. But Hern never so much as looked behind him. He just marched in that pompous, hurried way of his until he reached the steps of a large, expensive-looking inn. Here, he went up the stairs, nodding to the boy who opened the door for him, and vanished inside. A moment later, Miranda followed. The boy didn't open the door as readily for her, but a coin changed his mind and Miranda found herself in the opulent entry hall of a wealthy inn in a wealthy town. Hern was at the far end of the room, talking with two men Miranda recognized as Tower Keepers. Just as she spotted them, a well-dressed servant walked over to escort the men up the stairs.

"Miss?"

Miranda jumped, startling the waiter who was hovering at her elbow. "Can I help you, miss?"

"Yes," Miranda said, pointing at the stairwell Hern had just disappeared up. "What's up those stairs?"

"The private dining rooms, ma'am," the man answered skeptically, eyeing her rough clothes.

"Good," Miranda said. "I'd like one. How much?"

"It's fifteen silvers for a private meal," the man said. "We've got grouse and pheasant in a plum glaze, with—"

"Sounds lovely," Miranda said, shoving the money at him. "Show me up."

The man's haughty expression vanished when the money hit his hand, and he cheerfully led her up the stairs. There were several dining rooms, but only one of the doors was closed. She picked the door beside it, and the waiter showed her into a small room with a dining table and a little stand in the corner with water, stationery, and a jug of flowers. Best of all, it had a simple plank wall separating it from the closed dining room next door. She could just barely hear the buzz of voices coming through the wood, and then Hern's haughty laugh.

"This is perfect," Miranda said, nodding. "You may go."

The waiter gave her a confused look, but bowed and left, shutting the door behind him. The minute he was gone, Miranda got down on the floor beside the wall and pressed her ear against the planks. The men's voices drifted through, muted but understandable.

"It's a mess is what it is," one of the Tower Keepers was saying. "We voted against the girl like you said and nothing's changed except Banage is more self-righteous than ever. Also, the tide in the Court's on his side now. My position as head of the committee on Forest Spirit management is threatened."

"You knew the risks." Hern's voice was bored. "But you took my money all the same. You think your committee head position's in danger now, just wait until the Court hears about how you took a bribe to bring down Banage's favorite."

Miranda's eyes widened. She shot off the floor and grabbed the stationery from the table, as well as the ink pot and pen. Here was Hern admitting to everything she'd suspected. She had to get it down on paper so she didn't forget a word.

Both of the Tower Keepers were angry now, accusing Hern of threatening them, trying to call his bluff, but Hern's voice was as calm as ever.

"Gentlemen," he said, "we can go up together, or we can go down together. Your choice."

The men grumbled, and Miranda got the feeling Hern was giving them that same haughty, implacable look he'd given her the day of the trial. It must have worked, for a few moments later he started asking them about the situation in Zarin.

Miranda was writing furiously when the door to her room clicked. She sprang off the floor and into her chair just as the waiter entered with a covered dish.

"First course," he said cheerily. "Mushroom soup with cream and a bread tray. Your main course will be up in just—"

He stopped as Miranda frantically put a finger to her lips. The voices from the other room had stopped as well, listening. Then she heard their door open. They were also getting their first course. Miranda let out a sigh of relief, and then she flashed the waiter a dazzling smile.

"Sorry," she said. "It's been a very long trip. All I want to do is sit quietly for a while." She stood and pressed a stack of coins into his hand. "Don't bother with the other courses," she whispered. "I just want to be left alone."

"Yes, lady," the waiter whispered back taking the coins gladly. "Whatever you like."

She smiled and waved as he left, and then, as soon as the door was closed, she grabbed the soup and a hunk of bread and sat right back down on the floor, readying her pen and paper for whatever else Hern might admit.

Out in the hall, the waiter counted over his new wealth. The crazy lady had given him ten coins to *stop* serving her. Well, he wasn't going to complain, and he wasn't going to let the rest of the dinner she'd bought go to waste. He was hungry, too, and the slow-roasting pheasants had been tempting him all day. Grinning, he put the money in his apron pocket and hurried down the stairs to the hotel's register. It was dangerous to carry this much money around. The other waiters would filch it the first chance they got, which was why everyone gave their tips to the register. Sure, he took a five percent cut, but it was a small price to pay for knowing your money wouldn't vanish altogether.

The register took his coins no questions asked, and, after noting the amount, threw them into the strongbox with all the other cash. He closed the lid, plunging the coins into darkness. The moment the light went out, the coins began to talk. They buzzed like rattler snakes, spreading gossip, telling what they'd heard, but the waiter's coins' story quickly rose to the top. A wizard with rings, powerful ones, spying on Master Hern. The duke must be told!

This was the message given to the strongbox, who in turn told the beam of the wall it was set into, who told the eaves it supported, who told the lamp on its post outside. The lamp, then, did what it had been ordered to do and switched itself on. A moment later, a strange, slow wind blew through the street, circling when it reached the glowing lamp. It heard the story and, judging it important, carried the coins' words over the rooftops, over the growing crowd in the square, and up to the very top of the citadel, where its master waited.

Back in the hotel, Miranda was almost giddy. Over the course of their lunch, and what sounded like a few glasses of wine, Hern had laid out a dozen plans to bring Banage down, any one of which would be a grievous violation of his oaths. She'd gotten them all down, marking the ones that seemed to be already in progress. It was a dizzying list. Hern had apparently been bribing Tower Keepers for years, which explained why Master Banage had been having so much trouble with them. She was not really surprised to hear that Hern had been buying votes, but to actually learn the full extent of his reach from his own lips was amazing, and it was all she could do to get it down. By the time their waiter brought the brandy, she had ten pages of close-scribbled notes full of dates, names, and specifics, and she was almost bursting with the urge to wrap everything up and take it to Banage herself, exile or no.

But as the men in the other room settled down with the brandy glasses, an unexpected knock interrupted them. Miranda jumped, thinking it was her waiter again. But the knock was at the other door, and she heard the scrape of chairs as Hern got up to see what was going on. There was a creak as he opened the door, followed by words too quiet for Miranda to make out, and then the crinkle of paper.

"What is it, Hern?" one of the Tower Keepers asked.

Hern didn't answer. She heard the scrape of his boots as he walked across the room. Not back to his seat, but to the wall that Miranda was crouched against. He was so close she could hear his breath. She held her own, not daring to make a sound.

A moment later, Hern spoke one word. "Dellinar."

Miranda's eyes widened. It was a spirit's name. In the split second after, time slowed to a crawl. She turned and grabbed her papers, shoving them into the pocket of her dress as she called for Durn, her stone spirit. He could stop anything of Hern's, Miranda was sure, buying her time to get to the window. They were only one flight up; she could make it. But even as her lips formed Durn's name, the wall between the rooms exploded in a shower of splintered wood and snaking green vines. The plants sprang like tigers, snapping around her ankles, her waist, and her wrists, slamming her to the floor so hard she saw spots. More vines wrapped around her arms and her head, sliding across her open mouth to gag her. She struggled wildly, but then the vines twined around her throat, nearly cutting off her breath. She looked up and saw Hern kneeling beside her, a wide grin on his face.

"What you feel is my vine spirit about to crush your windpipe," he said calmly. "If your spirits try anything, he will take off your head."

Miranda spat an obscenity at him, but all she managed was strangled sound as the vine twisted tighter.

Hern leaned over so that he was in front of her, and he waved a piece of paper. "Lovely bit of warning," he smiled, glancing down at her scattered notes, which had fallen from her pocket when she fell. "Good timing too. I must remember to thank dear Edward."

There was shouting out in the hall, and Miranda caught a glimpse out of the corner of her eye of soldiers entering the room. "Spiritualist Hern," a stern voice announced. "Duke's orders, both you and the spy are to report to the citadel at once."

Hern glowered. "I have this well under control, officer."

The soldier didn't even blink. "Duke's orders," he said again.

Hern rolled his eyes. "Very well," he said. "But first"—he made a florid gesture with his jeweled hand. Miranda gasped and began to kick as the vines wrenched tight. She reached frantically for her spirits, but it was too late. The plants cut into her skin, binding her limbs and cutting off her air. Her body grew impossibly heavy, and she lay still, her lungs burning for air.

"Pick her up." Hern's voice was very far away. "And mind the vines."

Hands slid under her and she felt herself lifted. Guards' faces blurred across her vision, and then she saw nothing.

CHAPTER
13

The crowd in front of the citadel was thinning, the conscripts getting their orders from a group of guards in full uniform at the gate and moving off in organized packs toward different sections of town. The peasant soldiers organized with remarkable efficiency, and Eli got the feeling that the duke called in conscripts fairly often. Eli waited until the coast was clear, lounging casually on a bench by a fountain in one of the little parks just off the main square while Josef waited tensely behind him with Nico. Eventually, the last of the conscript groups moved off and most of the uniformed soldiers trudged back into the citadel, leaving only a small knot of guardsman and a lone officer at the door.

Seeing his opportunity at last, Eli stood up and walked toward the square, Josef and Nico trailing along behind. Just before he stepped out into the open, Eli paused and closed his eyes. When he opened them again, his demeanor had changed. His posture was perfectly straight, his shoulders square, his face intent and uncompromising. When he stepped out into the square he didn't walk across the cobbles; he marched straight over the open ground to the broad steps at the front of the Duke of Gaol's impenetrable fortress.

The knot of six guards and their decorated officer stood at attention at the top of the stairs before a heavy iron door. They pulled closer as Eli approached, gripping their spears suspiciously. Eli ignored the warning and walked until he was just shy of the first step. There, he stopped and planted both feet with iron stubbornness.

"If you're here for the conscription," the officer said skeptically, "you're too late to avoid the fine. If you give your name to Jerold here, I'll be sure the duke knows you showed up, but—"

"Don't be stupid," Eli sneered, tossing his golden hair. "I'm no conscript. I am the Spiritualist Miranda Lyonette, head of the Spirit Court's investigation into the rogue wizard Eli Monpress. I heard that he struck this fortress last night, and I demand access to the scene of the crime."

The guard just stood there, blinking in confusion. Whatever he'd expected the man marching across his square to say, this certainly was not it. "You," he said slowly, "are Miranda Lyonette?"

"Yes," Eli said, looking extremely put upon.

The guard looked at the guard next to him. "Isn't Miranda a girl's name?"

"How dare you, sir!" Eli cried. "I'll have you know it is an old family name. Honestly, am I to be constantly hounded by the ignorance of others? A girl's name, *really*."

The absolute scorn in his voice did the trick, and the

guard's face went scarlet. "Forgive me, sir. I meant no offense. It's just, well, do you have proof of your identity?"

"Proof?" Eli rolled his eyes dramatically. "You insult my name and then ask for proof? Honestly, do I look like I have time for this idiotic song and dance?"

"Anything will do," the guard said. "Some sort of identification from the Court, or—"

"You know anyone beside Spiritualists who wear rings like these?" Eli held up both his hands, letting his gaudy glass rings catch the sun. "What do you want, a writ signed by Banage himself?"

"That would be good, actually," the guard said as politely as possible. "I really can't let you in without papers of some—"

Eli went positively livid. "You dare, sir! I just made the two-day trip from Zarin to Gaol in under four hours. Do you think I had the time to wait for those Court bureaucrats to give me papers? When you're chasing Monpress, time is of the utmost importance! Already, the trail is getting colder, and for every second you waste I lose hours in the hunt for the thief. If you won't let me in, then I will make sure your duke knows exactly who is responsible for letting his thief get away!" Eli looked about. "Where is your duke anyway? Bring him here at once!"

The guard blanched. "You see, the duke is terribly busy, and without proper identification, I'm afraid I can't—"

"Afraid?" Eli's eyes narrowed. "You'd best be afraid, doorman! Somewhere in that brick of a citadel is a spirit who saw how Monpress did what he did. Even now, that spirit is falling asleep. If it falls asleep entirely it will likely forget what it saw, and if that happens—" Eli paused for a deep, shuddering breath. "You don't even want to know what I'll do, but one thing is certain." His eyes narrowed, pinning the guard captain with a killing glare. "*Should* that happen, I will make sure everyone, from Zarin's highest seats of power to the Duke of Gaol himself, knows that *you* were the reason why."

The guard bowed, his face pale and sweating. "Apologies, Spiritualist Lyonette; I never doubted you were who you claimed to be. But I'm afraid I still can't give you access to the treasury without permission from the duke. If you could wait just a—"

"I will not!" Eli said with a flippant wave of his ringed fingers. "Powers, man, you've already been robbed blind! What are you afraid I'm going to do in there, steal your dust? Just show me and my assistants to the scene of the crime and I can get to work finding your thief, which I'm sure will make your duke much happier than you interrupting him with stupid requests."

The guard was sweating profusely now, and Eli took his chance for the final push. "Listen very carefully," he said slowly, twitching his spirit just a fraction so that the gaudy rings on his fingers glittered with malice. "If I lose the trail because of your delays, you will wish you'd never heard of Spiritualists. Do you understand?"

"Of course, Master Spiritualist," the guard said, waving his men toward the doors. "Right this way."

The pack of guards opened one of the great iron doors, and Eli, Nico, and Josef followed the guard captain into the citadel.

In the sky overhead, the wind that had been circling since Eli first stepped out into the square changed direction, blowing up the stone wall to the top of the citadel and through the window of one of the stubby towers at its crown. The tower was all one room, large and circular, with a long table at its center. A cluster of men stood around it, all dressed in the same drab uniform. Most of them looked like dressed-up farmers taken from their fields and thrust into uniforms, which was what they were. They were the conscript leaders, and they all wore the same quiet, obedient expression as they watched the head of the table where Duke Edward was pointing out markers on the city map carved into the table's smooth, wooden top.

The duke was in the middle of laying out details about how he wanted the perimeter handled, but he stopped midsentence as the wind blew by.

"Is this about Hern again?" Edward said.

"Not this time," the wind answered, blowing in circles above the farmer-generals. "Someone claiming to be a Spiritualist just bullied your idiot door guard into letting him and his assistants into the citadel."

The duke scowled. "A Spiritualist? One of Hern's cronies?"

"No," the wind spun. "I don't think it's really a Spiritualist, either. Didn't even look like a wizard to me. It was a yellow-haired man, said his name was Miranda Lyonette."

The duke's eyes widened. "Miranda?" He pursed his lips. "Considering Hern just sent word that he is escorting *Miss* Lyonette to the citadel as we speak, I find that hard to believe." He scratched his beard. "Whoever it is, I'll investigate myself. We can't afford another contingency at this point. The situation is bollixed enough as it is. Speaking of which, any news from the spy?"

"Not yet," the wind whispered. "I'll go check again."

"Thank you, Othril," the duke said. "I trust you'll notify me if anything else odd happens."

"Of course, my lord," the wind huffed.

Edward waved his hand and the wind flew off back to his patrol, shooting out over the citadel's edge. When he was gone, Duke Edward turned back to his officers, all of whom had waited patiently through what seemed to them to be a one-sided and nonsensical conversation.

"Gentlemen," the duke said. "It seems we have a rat in our cupboard. Those of you already assigned positions, please take your soldiers to their places. The rest of you, come with me." He swept past the table and toward the door. "We have an intruder to catch."

The officers saluted and went their separate ways, calling for their seconds to rally the conscripts as they trundled down the rickety stairs into the citadel proper.

The inside of the fortress of Gaol was not what Eli had expected. As soon as the guard led them through the iron doors, he'd looked eagerly for narrow halls, high ceilings, archer decks, thief catches, all the wonderful things highlighted on the poster. But the hall they entered was low and perfectly ordinary. Little hallways branched off of it leading to barracks, small offices, meeting rooms, and equipment caches. The walls were of uninspiring thickness, the architecture unremarkable, and there was only one portcullis, not five, as the poster had boasted. In short, it was a normal citadel built on a conservative plan, and perhaps a bit on the cheap.

Eli was supremely disappointed.

"*This* is the great citadel of Gaol?" he said, gazing

around in disgust. "Where are the six-foot walls? The multitiered locks? Where are the booby traps? The poster promised traps in every room!"

The guardsman's hairy face turned a bit red. "Well," he mumbled, "that's just advertising. Those posters of the duke's were just a precaution. Tell the thieves how impossible it is and they just give up, right? Far cheaper than actually building some supercitadel. Anyway, I'd say it worked. We've had no trouble from thieves since word got around about how secure the fortress was."

"No trouble until last night," Josef pointed out.

"Well, that's Monpress," the guard huffed. "He hardly counts. Don't worry, though; the duke'll catch him, Sir Spiritualist, make no mistake."

"Oh, certainly," Eli said with disgust, eyeing the hallway, which had now widened out into a large common room. "How did the duke know it was Monpress, anyway?"

"Well," the guard said, "who else could it be?"

"Who else, indeed?" Eli said, smiling, while Josef rolled his eyes.

The officer led them out of the common room through a flimsy doorway and into a hallway even smaller and drabber than the ones before it. Eli glowered at the man's back. So far, the "thief-proof citadel of Gaol" was a monstrous waste of time. If not for the Fenzetti, and if he wasn't so curious about someone impersonating him, Eli would have called the whole thing off the moment they passed the unlocked weapon cabinets. Only when they were almost to the center of the citadel did Eli finally spot something promising. Their guide had led them around a corner and into a small hallway set back from the main thoroughfare. Unlike the others, this hall was long and narrow, with a ceiling tall enough for archer stands to be placed over troops. Best of all was what waited at the end. There, at the far side of the hall, standing beside a large stone hearth and chimney, was an immense metal door. Its surface was perfectly smooth, without even a knob or handle. It was set flush against the stone without groove or crack, no way to get leverage at all. It stood black and impenetrable in the firelight as they approached, and Eli immediately began to perk up. This was more like it.

When they reached the fire pit the guard captain stopped and began to feel around in his pockets, muttering apologies.

"Sorry, sorry," he said. "It's something different every time." He drew out a small sachet wrapped in white paper. He laid it in his palm, weighing it experimentally before lobbing the packet, paper and all, straight into the banked fire. The paper curled and blackened, its edges cracking as sweet-smelling smoke—Eli picked out cinnamon and thyme—rose in a white plume. Then, without warning, the fire burst upward in a full roar, blasting the tiny hall with a wave of heat.

"You again?" a flickering voice bellowed as the fire churned, but the guard just mopped a bit of soot off his balding head, completely unaware that the fire was speaking to him.

The flames slumped down sullenly. "I know," it mumbled. "Open the door, close the door. I never get to sleep. It's been years. I don't know. No rest, no sleep, nothing but work..." The voice wavered like smoke in the wind and then faded as the fire dropped back to its usual size, leaving only the smell of burnt cinnamon. Somewhere below them, machinery began to grind and the great door in front of them rolled aside.

"There you are," the guard said. "That's the magic gate. Don't understand how it works, but I suppose it beats pushing that slab open with your shoulder, eh?"

"Indeed," Eli said, doing his best to convey the absolute disgust he was sure a Spiritualist would have felt at seeing a fire spirit used in that way. It wasn't hard. He felt kind of sour himself. He didn't know what kind of operation Gaol was running, but wizards who overworked their spirits deserved to be robbed blind. He only wished he'd been the one to do it. His thoughts drifted back to the terrified crates, but he forced himself to stop. Whatever was going on here, he didn't have time to deal with it. Anyway, it didn't matter. Once word got out that Eli Monpress had robbed Gaol, the Spiritualists would start showing up in droves. They would deal with whatever abuses were going on in Gaol. That would be his gift to the spirits, and it would have to be enough. Right now, he needed to find out who was taking advantage of his reputation before the situation got out of control. He had a suspicion, but for once he really hoped he was wrong; otherwise things were going to get very, very annoying. Just thinking about it made him feel tired, and he quickly turned his attention back to the task at hand.

The room beyond the treasury door was massive. It was perfectly square, with bright, mirrored lanterns burning high overhead that Eli suspected were also spirit powered, since he could see no way a servant would get up that high to light them. The harsh, brilliant light fell over what must have once been an impressive and large collection, but was now just a neat grid of empty shelves with only telltale holes in the dust to show there had ever been anything there.

"The entire holding of the di Fellbro family," the guard said, almost teary. "Gone."

"Not all gone," Eli said, pointing across the room to where a large golden lion still took up half a shelf.

"Aye," she guard said. "The thief left a few pieces. Some we think were too large for him to carry. Others, well, we honestly don't know why he left them."

Eli nodded and leaned closer. "Confidentially, friend," he said conspiratorially, "how close are your men to catching Monpress?"

The guard's face went red. "Hot on his heels, sir. I can't tell you the details, of course. Security must be upheld."

"Of course," Eli said, smiling graciously. "Thank you, Captain, we'll take it from here."

The captain twisted uncertainly. "Actually, sir, I'm afraid I'll have to stay. I couldn't leave anyone, even a Spiritualist, alone in here."

"Suit yourself," Eli said with a shrug. "We won't be long."

The guard nodded and took a seat on the ledge of the hearth, but Eli had already stopped paying attention to him. He walked across the room to the lion and kneeled down to peer into its open mouth. Josef stood behind him, eyes roving over the empty shelves, while Nico wandered off toward the far end of the room, staring up at the high ceiling.

"So," the swordsman said quietly, "think they're actually close to catching the thief?"

"Not a chance," Eli said, running his fingers over the

lion's mane. "He wouldn't have let us in if they had a lead. For all they know, this stuff just vanished in the night. The guard's probably sticking around because he's hoping we'll give him something he can use. Look here."

His fingers paused their roving just behind the lion's left paw, and Eli bent down almost to the ground, peering intently at the gold with a knowing smile. "Thought so, this is a fake. Actual Golden Lions of Ser have a tiny blessing to the volcano of Ser stamped into their left paws. This one has nothing."

"It's not real gold?" Josef said, drumming his knuckles on the lion's head.

"Oh, no, it's real gold." Eli stood, brushing off his knees. "But whoever robbed this place wasn't your common cat burglar. Look at the shelves, not a one out of place. Even the dust is undisturbed. This room seems completely secure, far more so than anything we walked through to get here. I've been on the lookout since we stepped through the door and even I can't figure out how the thief got in, or got out again with what had to be a wagonload of priceless artifacts. However, I can tell that whoever did this was patient, educated enough to spot a fake, discerning enough not to want one, and very, very good. That narrows the list down quite a bit."

"So you know who it was?"

Eli rolled his eyes. "Let's just say there's only one man I know who can pull a job like this, but if we're going to find him, I'm going to need to see a list of the duke's business contacts."

Josef looked at him, thoroughly confused. "Business contacts?"

"It's our only chance. He certainly didn't leave a clue

here." Eli craned his head around, scanning the shelves. "Well," he said cheerfully, "at least the Fenzetti blade is missing."

"How is that a good thing?" Josef said.

"If the thief took it, we know it wasn't fake."

"Or wasn't here to begin with," the swordsman grumbled.

"No, no." Eli shook his head. "If the broker said it's here, then it's here. Their information is always reliable; that's why you pay through the nose for it."

While he was speaking, Nico appeared beside Josef. The swordsman instantly stopped listening to Eli and turned his attention to her.

"Men with swords are filling the hallway," she said quietly. "And someone is talking with our guard."

Eli spun around. Sure enough, there was their guide at the door in deep, frantic conversation with someone Eli couldn't see. As he watched, whoever it was ran off, and the guard took up position at the center of the door.

"The game is up," Josef said, looking at Nico. "I'll take the front. See if you can't find another exit."

Nico nodded and they broke, leaving Eli staring at empty space.

"What are you planning?" he whispered loudly, trotting after Josef as the swordsman ran for the door.

Josef didn't answer. He reached the door and stared down the guardsman, who had turned to face them, a short sword held in his shaky hands.

"I am sorry, Sir Spiritualist," he said, peering over Josef's shoulder at Eli. "Orders from the top. The other guards are coming right now. I have nothing but respect for your organization, but please, surrender quietly."

Eli stared at the guard as if he'd grown a second head before he remembered his cover story and snapped back into character.

"Surrender?" he shouted, beyond indignant. "I am here on the business of the Spirit Court! I am apprentice to the Rector Spiritualis himself, head of the Eli investigation! When it comes to Monpress, I *AM* the highest authority! And I demand that you tell those men to stand down and let us pass!"

Eli had himself in a fury now, and it was working. The guard was sweating bullets, but he still didn't move. Behind him, the clink of metal boots on stone was deafening as the guards marched down the hall, filling their only escape with a wall of armed men, and not the conscripts from outside either, but professional soldiers.

Eli was about to start a new round of threats when Josef threw out his arm, cutting him off.

Josef looked down at the guard. "You seem like a nice fellow," he said. "Sorry about this."

Quick as a cat, Josef stepped forward, sliding inside the man's guard and pinching his inner arm just below the joint of his armor. The guard cried out in pain, and his sword fell from his now-limp hand. The second it dropped, Josef spun him around and gave him a push. The man went flying into the hallway, straight into the first pack of guards. They scrambled to catch him, but the guard's weight sent them lurching backward. By the time they recovered, Josef filled the door completely. He drew his swords and stepped into a defensive position, spinning the blades in whistling arcs, an enormous grin on his face.

The soldiers in the hall surged forward, swords drawn,

and as they crashed into Josef, the swordsman did what he did best. He planted his feet and, with a great roar, swept his swords, one high, one low, into the crowd. The soldiers, trained to fight in formation, all held their weapons at the same height. Josef's swords sang over and below them, past their defenses. The man on the far left had it worst. Josef's swords slammed into his armor at the shoulder and the thigh, flinging him sideways into the soldier on his right. Josef carried the momentum, throwing himself into the sweep. His weight, the force of his blows, and the unexpected angle were too much for the men, and they smashed into the far wall, grunting in pain and surprise. Swords clattered to the stone as they tried to catch themselves, but it was no use. The moment they were off balance, Josef spun and slammed them again, with his leg this time, beating them against the wall and into the doorman, who'd just finished getting up.

What had been a coordinated charge was now a mess of men on the floor. Josef grinned and fell back to the door, not even winded. The second line of soldiers got their swords ready and were starting to push past their fallen comrades when a whistle sounded. It was a high trill, and the moment it went off, the guards began to pull back.

Josef fell into his defensive crouch, but the hallway was emptying rapidly until only one man stood at the far end. He was tall and thin, with neatly trimmed black hair streaked with gray, and a bored, slightly annoyed expression. His eyebrows arched when he saw Josef.

"So," he said, "you're our Spiritualist?"

"Depends," Josef growled. "Who's asking?"

The man fixed him with a cold stare. "I am Edward di Fellbro, Duke of Gaol."

"The man himself," Eli whispered, peeking around the corner. "Why is he here? Aren't dukes supposed to lead from the back?"

Josef ignored him, tightening his grip on his swords. "Look," the swordsman said. "I'm not going to bother feeding you a story. We're just here looking for the thief, same as you. No need to get nasty. Just back off now before more of your soldiers get hurt."

"Back off?" The duke chuckled. "You're in no position to be giving orders, boy. But I have no mind to waste time and money forcing you out. Surrender now and I'll let you keep your life."

"And if I don't?" Josef said.

Edward just smiled, a cold, thin smile, and moved his mouth, saying something Josef couldn't quite make out.

From his place against the wall, Eli gave a little squeak. "Josef!" he cried. "Get back!"

Josef jumped backward a second before the hearth beside the treasury door erupted in a wall of white-hot flame. Almost before he could recover, two flat stones came sailing through the fire. Josef's sword knocked the first one aside before he'd even realized what it was, but the next one clipped him on the shoulder, and he grunted in pain.

Eli jumped forward, grabbing the stone from where it had fallen and turning it over in his hands. It was a paving stone from the hall outside, and as he touched it, he could hear the rock babbling in terror.

"Josef, watch out," Eli said. "He's a wizard."

"I guessed that," Josef grumbled, rubbing his shoulder. In the doorway the flames were dying down, revealing the duke again. He hadn't moved from his place at the end of the hall, only now he had a pile of paving stones in front of him. They were stacked neatly, leaving a large, bare patch on the floor around him. He smiled at Josef and casually tossed a paving stone in his hand.

"The offer of surrender is still open," he said.

Josef opened his mouth to tell him exactly what he could do with his offer, but at that second, the duke saw Eli crouched on the floor, his blond wig askew. The duke's pale, lined face went white as snow, and he opened his mouth in a shout that drowned out Josef's comeback.

"Eli Monpress!"

Eli jumped and looked just in time to see every single one of the paving tiles shoot forward. They flew from the duke in a flock of loosed fury, flying through the air faster than stone was ever supposed to move. They flung themselves at Eli, and they would have done some terrible damage had Josef not grabbed the thief by his gaudy collar and tugged him down at the last second.

The paving stones whistled inches over their heads, but Eli barely had time to get some air back into his thundering lungs before he heard the duke's voice roaring through the keep. "Spirits of Gaol! Your duke commands you! Crush the intruder!"

"Hold on now," Eli said, looking up from his crouch. "You can't just order a building like—"

The walls began to shake. In the hall, stones ripped themselves from the supports while dropped weapons picked themselves up off the ground. Everything, nailed down or not, began to lift and turn toward the doorway where Eli and Josef were crouching.

"Nico," Josef said. "We need that exit."

Behind them, the room was quiet. Out in the hall, things were beginning to speed forward.

"Nico!" Josef shouted.

At once, she appeared beside them, whether through her shadow stepping or just her terrifying speed, Eli couldn't tell. She flung back her hood, her scraggly black hair standing straight up, her eyes bright as candles, and a familiar wave of fear washed over the room. She pushed Josef aside and turned to face not the hallway or the things flying down it, but the enormous treasury door. Her hand shot out, the silver manacle jerking and shaking on her wrist, and her fingers dug into the iron like it was river mud.

Deep in the stone under their feet, something screamed. Nico ignored it, digging her fingers deeper, her glowing eyes narrowing to slits as she spoke a command.

"Move."

The enormous door moved faster than Eli had ever seen iron move. Bits of stone went flying as it surged forward, slamming itself shut with an impact that shook the keep.

For a moment, everything was silent, then there was dull clatter as the flying object collided with the now-shut door. The duke was shouting on the other side, but the sound was very far away. Then, all at once, the room began to scream.

Eli and Nico both slammed their hands over their ears as the terrible sound swept over them.

"What did you do?" Eli shouted.

"I closed the door," Nico said, her voice thin and strained as she pulled her hood back over her head.

"I can see *that*," Eli said. "My problem is with *how* you did it."

"What?" Nico glared at him, her eyes bright as lanterns. "It worked, didn't it?"

"Oh, sure," Eli said, rolling his eyes. "Solved the crazy wizard problem, but you can't just do that to spirits!"

"You've told me to scare spirits before," Nico said grudgingly.

"That's different," Eli snapped. "Giving spirits a little scare is one thing. It doesn't hurt anyone and it moves things along, but that's not what you did. You sank your fingers into that metal and gave it an order, and that, Nico, is not good. That door can't say no to you when you've got your teeth in its throat. Giving spirits orders they can't say no to is no better than Enslavement, and we don't do that. Besides, now we're trapped in a screaming, panicked vault that, as you mentioned earlier, has *no other exit*."

Nico turned away, scowling. Eli grabbed her shoulder to turn her back around, but Josef stepped between them.

"Save it," he said, sheathing his swords. "Let's find a way out. Quickly. We're losing structural integrity."

He was right. Large streams of grit were falling from the ceiling as the stone arches that held up the vaulted ceiling fought to get free and crush the demon. Chunks of rock clattered down the stone walls, landing in a series of crashes that were only getting louder.

"We're not finished," Eli said, pointing at Nico. Then, without another word, they split to search for some way, any way, out.

"All right," Eli shouted, scanning the shaking walls. "The thief got in, and he didn't take the main door. I can promise you that. Look for something unusual."

"Could you be more specific?" Josef yelled, staring blankly at the quivering wall.

"I don't know." Eli ran his fingers over the shivering,

weeping rock. "Discolored stone, a corner out of place, anything that could mark a secret door or passage, maybe a bricked-over window. I'll take a mouse hole at this point."

"Can't you just do something wizardly?" Josef said, dodging a chunk of stone that fell right where his head would have been.

"I don't exactly think these spirits are in the mood to chat!" Eli shouted back.

Josef gave him a rude gesture just as Nico cried out, "Here!"

Argument forgotten, Eli and Josef ran over to find the girl standing in front of what looked like a perfectly normal patch of wall behind a toppled shelf.

"What?" Eli said, looking around frantically. "I don't see anything."

"Neither do I," Nico said. "But listen, it's not screaming."

She was right. While the other stones were in full-on panic, the patch of wall in front of them, a little eight-brick square, was perfectly silent. Now that Eli looked, it wasn't shaking either. It was a rock amid the chaos, and now that he saw it, he wondered how he could have missed it earlier.

He stepped in close to the stone and ran his fingers across it, very gently. It felt hard, like stone, but different—soapy and almost hollow when he tapped it. A slim grin crossed Eli's face. He raised his foot and, taking aim, gave the wall a good, hard kick. A clean, sharp crack appeared down the middle of the block of wall, and the stone crumbled to dust, revealing a dark tunnel just the right size for a man to crawl through.

"What was that?" Josef said.

Eli waved him away, focusing instead on what was waiting inside the tunnel. A few feet in, leaned carefully against the tunnel's wall, was another square of wall identical to the one he'd just broken, and stuck to it was a small, white card. Eli reached in and snatched the card between his fingers. There was no printing on it, no identification, just a sentence written in neat, masculine cursive.

Thought you would need this.

Eli cursed under his breath and shoved the card in his pocket. "All right," he said. "Let's move."

"What was that?" Josef said again. "Is this a trap? Is it safe?"

Eli gave him an incredulous look. "Anything's safer than this! Get in the tunnel! And watch that square. One whack at the wrong place will cause it to crumble."

Without further hesitation, Josef crawled in, pressing himself against the wall to squeeze by the square of fake wall. Nico followed right behind him, buried deep in her coat. When they were through, Eli paused for a moment and dug around in his pockets, pulling out a large, white card printed with an elaborate, cursive *M*.

"First rule of thievery," he muttered to himself. "Never waste an opportunity."

With that, he tossed the card toward the center of the room. It swooped through the air and landed at the foot of the fake Lion of Ser. Eli nodded and ducked into the tunnel. Crawling on his hands and knees, he turned and, very, very delicately, lifted the square of fake wall. Behind them, the dusty remains of the old fake stones were already indistinguishable among the grit and rubble showering down from the ceiling. Satisfied that they wouldn't be followed, at least not immediately, Eli gently plugged the entrance. The square of fake wall fit perfectly, as he'd known it would, and the tunnel plunged into darkness. Their path secured, Eli turned and made his way down the tunnel after Josef and Nico.

The tunnel ended unceremoniously twenty feet later in the ceiling of a wine cellar. Josef and Nico were already waiting when Eli jumped down, and Josef reached up to press the loose boards on the ceiling back into place behind him, leaving no sign that they'd ever moved.

Eli stood doubled over for a moment, catching his breath. When he'd coughed up enough dust to start a mortar company, he straightened and took off his gaudy red coat, which was now a dull, pinkish gray.

"Come on," he said, shoving the balled-up coat behind an ancient wine barrel. "Let's go."

"We're getting out, then?" Josef said, slapping the dust out of his shirt.

"Nope," Eli said. "We're going to get our Fenzetti."

Josef gawked at him. "Are you mad? The duke knows you're here. The jig is up. Only thing for us to do now is get out with our skins. Anyway, you don't even know where the other thief is. How are you going to find him when there's a whole duchy out there looking for you?"

"I know how to find him," Eli said, taking off his wig and carefully placing the dusty blond mess into his pocket for cleaning later. "He certainly hasn't left Gaol."

"Why wouldn't he?" Josef said. "You said he was smart. Leaving seems like the smart thing to do."

"Ah," Eli said, smiling. "But you're forgetting the first rule of thievery."

"Which one?" Josef sighed. "You have a hundred at least."

"This one is very important," Eli said, stepping up to the cellar door and putting his ear against the coarse wood. "The last place a man looks is under his own feet." He paused for a moment, holding his breath, and then opened the door with a flourish. "After you."

Josef stomped out, followed by Nico. But as she passed, Eli caught the edge of her sleeve. She looked over her shoulder, her eyes still suspiciously bright.

Eli tightened his grip. "I'm sorry if I was rough earlier, but I meant what I said. I know you did it to save us, but you really can't go around doing that to spirits. There's a lot I don't know about how you work, Nico, and I'm sorry I haven't helped you like I should, but there's a big difference between giving a spirit a little scare and giving it an order."

Nico looked away. "I had to. Josef—"

"Josef can't say this because he's not a wizard," Eli said. "What you did back there was as bad as any Enslavement, if not worse. At least in Enslavement there's a battle of wills the spirit could maybe win, but no spirit can win against you. Demon fear is simply too strong. I'm being serious, Nico. Don't do it again, all right?"

Nico clenched her fists. On her wrists, her manacles began to shake softly, but Eli held on to her coat until, at last, she nodded.

"Promise?"

Nico nodded again, and he released her sleeve. Josef was waiting for them on the other side of the door, arms crossed over his chest. "What was that about?"

"Nothing," Eli said and smiled. "Let's get moving."

Josef gave him a skeptical glare, but he nodded and let Eli lead the way out of the cellars. Nico trailed behind, her face hidden by the long hood of her coat.

The wine cellar was at the bottom of a warren of cellars that ran under the keep. Fortunately, the warren let out into the kitchen yard, which was where they made their escape, blending in with the mass of kitchen workers and other menials who were all gathered at the edge of the keep, presumably to watch the excitement. Whistles were blowing everywhere now, and hordes of conscript patrols were racing through the streets and toward the citadel. In all the confusion, no one noticed three more scruffy, dirty people, and they were able to duck down a less-fashionable side street without trouble. Once they were a block from the castle, Eli changed direction, guiding them through the winding streets seemingly at random until he came to a stop in front of a modest building that, if the sign outside was correct, housed a trading company.

"Wait here," Eli said. "I'll be right back."

He flashed them a knowing smile and vanished around the back of the building. Josef, fed up with arguing, slumped back against the wall while Nico took her time brushing the dust off her coat. A few minutes later, Eli emerged from the front door carrying an enormous ledger and grinning like a maniac.

"Powers," Josef said. "How much did you have to bribe a clerk for that bit of work?"

"Nothing," Eli said. "Things are too hot for bribery right now, so I nicked it. I *am* the greatest thief in the world, you know."

Josef rolled his eyes.

"Not like there was anything to it," Eli said, flipping through the book as he walked. "I could have stolen the whole office for all the clerks cared. They were all pressed against the windows like it was going to be revolution in the streets. Gaol must be a boring place if this is all it takes to make the town go crazy."

Eli flipped the pages back and forth and then stopped, tapping his finger on an entry toward the end of the book. "Here we go," he said. "Fennelle Richton, masonry expert and antiques appraiser under contract with the Duke of Gaol for ornamental stonework, currently residing at the Greenwood Hotel. That's by the docks, I think."

Josef looked at the entry, which was one of hundreds that ran down the page. "How do you know this is our man?"

"Fennelle and Richton are the main characters in *The Tragedy of the Scarlet Knight*. It's his favorite opera."

"His?" Josef said. "His who?"

"You'll see soon enough." Eli turned on his heel and set off for the docks, Nico and Josef close behind them. In the distance, voices grew louder as the northern corner of the duke's famous fortress collapsed in on itself in a great shower of rubble.

CHAPTER
14

The citadel shook and rumbled as bits of it collapsed. Edward, Duke of Gaol, ignored the stones clattering to the floor around him, staring instead at the smooth surface of the closed iron door to his treasury. He'd heard of Monpress's demon, of course, but dismissed it as another rumor, one up there with tales of Monpress's ability to turn invisible. That said, to see it in action himself, in his fortress, was a well-deserved lesson in making assumptions.

Even now, minutes after the initial wave, the demon panic was still flooding through the air. The shouts of people outside echoed down the shaking halls, tiny and distant under the rumbling of the terrified stone. The duke ignored them. He simply waited, patiently, with his hands crossed behind his back. The moment the demon panic began to ebb, he opened his spirit.

At once, every stone was still. The duke's will filled the castle, crushing all resistance, stomping down on fear.

He laid his hands firmly on the wall beside him, feeling every stone in the castle as they lay subservient before him. Only then, when he was certain he had every pebble in the citadel's full attention, did he give his command.

"Clean yourself up."

The fortress obeyed. Stones jumped off the floor and refitted themselves into place. Cracks mended themselves, and he felt the citadel groan and shake as the collapsed northern corner shuddered and then rebuilt itself. When the duke lifted his hand from the stone, there was no sign there had been a panic at all. Even the scuff marks on the stone from Josef's fight with the soldiers were gone.

The duke shook his hands with a sigh and turned to face his gawking officers, who'd come running in the moment the citadel stopped moving.

"It's a miracle," one of the young guards whispered.

"No," the duke said. "It's business as usual." He glared at the soldier. "I'm not just some wizard, boy. I'm the Duke of Gaol. Everything here is mine to command, the stones, the water, the winds, and you. Don't ever forget that. Now"—he pointed at one of his officers—"you, take your men and get the courtyard under control. I want the conscripts back in position by the river and everyone else in their houses. Full lockdown. I don't want to see so much as a stray cat on the streets, understand?"

"Sir!" The officer saluted and motioned his men down the tunnel.

Edward looked over the remaining soldiers. "The rest of you, stand by. I have one final problem to attend to, and then"—he smiled—"we're going thief hunting."

The soldiers saluted and stood at attention. Satisfied, Edward turned back toward his treasury. Out of everything in the castle, only the treasury door remained out of place. It alone was still bashed and dirty, and still stubbornly closed. The duke walked forward slowly, deliberately, letting his open spirit go ahead of him as a warning, but the door did not move.

"Why?" the duke asked softly. "Why so willfully disobedient?"

"I can't help it, my lord," the door shuddered. "She ordered me closed. I must obey."

The duke leaned in, his voice very low and very cold. "Whatever Monpress's girl can threaten is nothing compared to what I'm about to do to you if you *do not open*."

The door gave a terrified squeak and began to thrash in its track, but no matter how it fought, it could not roll back.

"Please, my lord," it panted. "Mercy! She struck something deep, I'm afraid. A strange mix of demon fear and wizardry. I've never felt anything like it! Please, just give me a few minutes to overcome the fear and I swear I'll obey. I beg you, my lord!"

The duke waved his hand. "Time is a luxury I do not have." He glared at the stones on either side of the door. "If you cannot open, then I'll find something that will."

He snapped his fingers at the wall beside the door, and all at once, the mortar began to crumble. Stones popped themselves out of their sockets and landed in a neat pile on the floor. Robbed of its support, the door began to wobble. Duke Edward stepped back and motioned for the blocks to keep coming. The door held out for an impressively long time, but soon, as more and more of its supporting structure was removed, not even its will was enough to stand against gravity. It fell with a long, tragic cry, crashing to the floor in an enormous cloud of dust.

The duke turned to his soldiers. "Get some rope and take this hunk of metal outside. Set it up at the center of the square where the rain can hit it. We'll see what a few years of rust can do for its temperament."

The soldiers, spirit deaf and not quite understanding what was going on, ran to obey him. At his feet, the door began to sob, a terrible, squealing metal sound, and something made a little crackling noise at the duke's elbow. Edward looked over and saw his fire, the fire that connected all the hearths in the citadel, flickering hesitantly.

"My lord," it crackled. "Don't you think that's a little harsh? He was wounded by a demon, and—"

"Would you like to join him out in the yard?" the duke snapped.

"No, sir," the fire answered immediately.

"Then don't say another word." The duke straightened up, watching as the soldiers came back with the rope and began looping it around the heavy door.

"If it can't serve as a door," the duke said, "then it can at least serve as an example. Disobedience will not be tolerated."

"Yes, sir," the fire whispered again, but the duke was already off, walking over the poor sobbing door and into his empty treasury.

The cracks and broken stone had been repaired here as everywhere, but the shelves were still in disarray. He put them back with an impatient wave of his hand, noting that the false Lion of Ser and a few of the other cheap pieces were still in place. There was, however, no sign of the thief's escape. Duke Edward walked in a slow circle, scanning the wall, running things over in his mind, but he got no further than he had this morning when he'd first investigated the crime scene. He'd been sure before, but he was now positive that the first robbery had not been Eli's work. So why had Eli come?

Pride was the obvious answer. Monpress was a prideful man. He might have come looking for clues as to who would impersonate him. Yet that seemed too simple an explanation. If his studies had taught him anything, it was that Monpress never did anything simply. Also, it was too fast. The robbery had only happened this morning, which meant Monpress must have already been in town. That made him smile. His bait had worked. At least that part of the plan had stayed on track. His smile faded, someone had sprung the trap early, and he meant to find out who. Still, today's events had convinced him that the situation was salvageable. Monpress was in town. He'd probably been planning his own heist when he heard about the impostor and came to investigate. That certainly matched what he knew of Monpress, but still, something was off.

Edward walked in a slow circle around the room. Eli's exit bothered him. The thief was known for his flash, and the demon trick with the door had certainly been flashy, but after that, nothing. He'd vanished just as smoothly as the thief last night. He briefly entertained the idea that the two thieves might be in league, but he dismissed it almost as quickly. Monpress wasn't the kind to share glory.

He was still walking and thinking when he spotted something white on the floor. He stooped to pick it up, turning it over in his hand. It was a card, marked the same as all his others, with the fine, cursive *M*. Smiling,

Edward slid the card into his coat pocket. Cocky to the last, that was Eli. He couldn't bear to leave any credit unclaimed. But as he straightened up, his eyes caught something else out of place. There, straight ahead, the wall was uneven.

Edward stared at it. He'd ordered all the bricks to square themselves when he'd righted the citadel. Was this more disobedience or just simple incompetence? He stepped in for a closer look, brushing the crooked stones with his fingers. As he touched the smooth cut surface, his eyes widened, and several mysteries clicked into place.

Othril blew in through the front door of the citadel, pausing to stare at the sobbing bulk of the treasury door as the guards struggled in teams of twenty to drag it down the steps. After a moment of gawking, the wind hurried on. It was best not to question things like that, and he had news for the duke that could not wait.

He found the duke in the treasury, which wasn't surprising, staring at the wall, which was. Othril circled uncertainly overhead. Interrupting the duke while he was working was never something that ended well, but neither was withholding a time-sensitive report. He was still warring between those two bad choices when the duke made the decision for him.

"Othril," he said, pointing at the square of wall in front of him. "Look there and tell me what you see."

Othril swooped down to the duke's level and stared at the stone. "Nothing," he said. "I see nothing at all. Why?"

"Nothing," the duke said. "I thought so."

He reached forward and grabbed the stone. The blocks crumbled in his grasp like flaky pastry, revealing a tunnel.

A tremor of panic shot through Othril. It had been his job to inspect the castle. His job to find anything untoward. The duke was not forgiving of failure. Fortunately, Duke Edward looked more annoyed than angry.

"It's a mash-up," he said, picking up a large chunk of the fake wall and crumbling it in his hands. "Tiny specks of stone and sand too small for consciousness, and thus below the notice of awakened spirits, bound together in brittle glue and then stamped to look like a wall." He paused, shaking his head. "It's actually brilliant in a simplistic way. How else would you hide a tunnel from a wizard who knows every spirit in his castle than to make something those spirits can't see? Not Eli's work, of course. Far too subtle. Still," he sighed, "one can't help being a little impressed by such a simple and effective escape."

"Yes, well," Othril said, "about that. I came to let you know that the spirits have reported in and we're ready to move into position." The wind paused. "Do you still want to go ahead with the plan, my lord? If you're certain he's not Monpress, perhaps we should wait."

"No," the duke said, standing up. "We're absolutely going ahead. Monpress is in town, and he's also looking for the impostor. This may well be our chance to catch two thieves for the price of one."

"Monpress is here?" Othril said, astonished. "But I haven't—"

The duke gave him a cold look, and Othril backed away. "Of course, my lord. As you say."

The duke nodded. "What about our other business? Is the Spiritualist secured?"

"Yes," the wind said, used to the duke's sudden subject changes. "And the measures to make sure she stays that way are in place, as you ordered. Hern was gloating the whole time, though his cronies looked less pleased. He swears she's the real Miranda Lyonette, the one who worked with Monpress in Mellinor. She won't wake for another hour or two, but she apparently knows Eli better than most. Are you going to go talk to her?"

"Of course not," the duke said. "In an hour or two, everything should be over. Besides, no amount of information is worth dealing with extremists like Banage and his sympathizers. I have far too many contingencies as it is. No, so far as I'm concerned, she's Hern's problem now. I'm just keeping hold of her for the moment, since Hern can't keep a prisoner to save his life. It's his love of gloating. He gives them too many opportunities for escape."

"What about her dog?" the wind asked. "I've been hearing reports from the countryside about a dog."

"As I said," the duke said, walking out of the treasury, "Hern's problem. Moving on, is the city ready for lockdown?"

"Of course," the wind said. "Has been for hours. All we're waiting on now is for the conscripts to finish clearing the last of the nonenlisted townsfolk back into their homes."

"Good." The duke smiled as he walked down the front steps of his citadel. "It may not be unfolding quite as I designed, but the trap is still in place. Eli will come, mark my words. Just be ready to tighten the noose when you hear the signal."

"Yes, lord duke," the wind said, spiraling up into the cloudless sky as the duke made his way across the square shouting for his officers.

On a black cliff above the gray northern sea stood a great citadel. It was cut from the same black stone as the cliff, or perhaps it was part of the cliff. After so many years it was difficult to tell. It stood tall and sharp, looming over the choppy waves and the desolate strip of shore far below like some great weapon dropped in an ancient battle of giants. Yet it stood alone. There was no town nestled in the rocky field at its base, no houses on the barren hills beyond. Nothing but stone and sand and wind-dwarfed trees and the citadel, its windows dark beneath the grudging noon light that filtered through the ashy clouds overhead.

Midway up one of the leaning towers, sitting at a broad desk that faced one of the larger windows overlooking the sea, Alric, Deputy Commander of the League of Storms, was dealing with the morning's crises. A demonseed had awakened in the desert that spanned the southern tip of the Immortal Empress's domain. So far, it had eaten three dunes, a cactus forest, a small nomad camp, and the agent who'd been sent to deal with it. Alric listened carefully to the wind spirit who'd come with the report, his thin-lined face set in a thoughtful frown as the wind blustered about the size of the demon and how it had already eaten a great desert storm and didn't Alric know they were all doomed?

When the wind finally blew itself out, Alric turned to the large, open book that took up most of his desk, and he flipped to the last page. Taking his sharp pen, he neatly crossed out the name of the now-deceased agent. It was a shame. The boy had shown promise. He flipped forward a few pages and decided to put one of his senior agents on the desert problem. Ante Chejo was an excellent swordsman and a level thinker, and he was from that part of the empire. He would do nicely. Decision made, Alric made a note next to Chejo's name in the great book and called in a runner. The silent, somber-suited man was at his side instantly. Alric gave him the orders and the runner left to find Chejo.

Thanking the wind for the message, Alric sent it to wait in the courtyard with stern assurances that Chejo would take care of things from here on. The wind didn't seem convinced, but it left, blowing out the window in a blustery huff and leaving Alric to deal with the other fires that were already flaring up.

There were rumors of a possible demonseed on the southern jungles of the Council Kingdoms and a new report of something off the north coast of the White Wastes, which was probably just a leviathan but had to be investigated all the same. There were reports piling up from agents in the major cities on demon cult activity, fund movements, and possible candidates for the League as well as the usual panic reports from spooked spirits that had to be investigated, compiled observations from each of the great winds, and equipment requests from the League armsmaster. It was the same rubbish over and over, but they had to be sorted, all the same.

He was about halfway through the morning's work when something fell onto his desk with a clatter. He looked up. It was a bound and capped tube stamped with the seal of their post in Zarin. Alric frowned. It was not unusual for a message to simply appear on his desk. That was part of the system the League of Storms had always used to spread information quickly, set up long, long before he was born. What was unusual was that Zarin would be sending a report now when he'd just received their morning report thirty minutes ago. He popped the seal with his finger and began to read.

Fear pulse reported at midmorning, Gaol. Spirit destruction, mass panic, suspect five weeks or higher. Request backup.

Alric read the message twice in rapid succession before letting it curl back into a scroll. He hunched forward, his frown deepening. This was a problem. A fear pulse was League jargon for the wave of demon panic that was generally the first warning when a new demonseed finally devoured its human host and became active on its own. Yet Merick, his man in Zarin, had placed the demon at five weeks of unrestrained growth, which was simply not possible. No demon could escape League notice for five weeks, especially not somewhere as populated and civilized as Gaol. But Merick was an experienced League member and not one for embellishment. If he said five weeks, then that's what they were dealing with.

Alric pushed the message away and leaned back in his chair to consider his options. There were only two demons remotely that active outside of the Dead Mountain itself, Slorn's wife and Monpress's pet. Alric drummed his fingers on the table. Nivel was well contained, but Eli's creature was another matter. If she was the source of the fear Merick reported, then this was going to be a complicated situation. The White Lady had forbidden the League to hunt that specific demon. The Lord of Storms had made that much clear, though he didn't say why and obviously wasn't happy about it. Still, the League couldn't just ignore a mass panic in a highly populated area. Their mission was to promote order, and order depended on rapid, predictable response. They could cause another panic even worse than the first if they didn't show up. Alric tapped his fingers thoughtfully, turning the problem over in his head. Slowly, a plan began to piece itself together.

Smiling slightly, Alric took the message and carefully slid it under a stack of other finished papers. Powerful as she was, the White Lady could not read minds. He had no proof that the disturbance in the report was Monpress's demon. There was no physical description, no witness reports. All he had was a dire message and a request for aid, and following up on such things *was* his job. If he never let on to his suspicions, how was she to know that the accidental elimination of the Monpress demon was less than accidental? He just had to make sure he put the right agent on the job. Someone strong enough to take on a demon of that size and a good enough swordsman to deal with her guardian, not to mention prideful enough to take on the Heart of War. But at the same time, he needed a man ignorant enough not to realize whom he was fighting, and whose loss wouldn't be a crippling blow to the League when the Lady took her vengeance.

Fortunately, he had just the man in mind.

Smiling slightly more than was appropriate, Alric summoned a runner. The dour man appeared instantly, stepping into Alric's office through a narrow slit in the air. It opened soundlessly, a cut in the fabric of reality from one place to another, in this case, from the common room to Alric's office. Instant travel was yet another of the niceties of League membership, a necessity when you had to travel around the world on short notice, and one that League members designated as runners were particularly skilled at.

Alric smiled at the runner as the cut in the air closed behind him. "Bring me Berek Sted."

The runner raised an eyebrow. "Sted, sir?"

"Yes," Alric said. "And if he drags his feet, just tell him he'll finally get to test that bloodthirsty sword of his."

If possible, the runner's face grew even more sour. "Yes, Sir Alric."

The runner vanished, slipping through a new slit in space so quickly even Alric didn't see it open. Five minutes later, the enormous man with his sash of hideous trophies and a great, jagged blade worn naked at his side walked into the room.

"Ah," Alric said, turning to face his guest. "Just the man I wanted to see."

Sted didn't answer. He sat down on the heavy bench in the corner, glowering at Alric while the wood creaked under his weight.

"I have a job for you," Alric said. "A demon has appeared in Gaol. Most likely a girl. I want you to investigate."

"A girl?" Sted's voice dripped with disgust. "I don't fight girls."

Alric gave him a flat look. "I realize you're new to the League, but try to remember that what you're fighting is the thing inside the girl. Demons take the body that serves their purpose."

"I don't fight girls," Sted said again. "Send someone else."

"This is not open for debate." Alric's voice was as cold as a dagger in a snowbank. "If you want to keep your League privileges"—his eyes flicked to the sword at Sted's side—"I suggest you learn some discipline."

Sted narrowed his eyes, but said nothing. Alric let him stew a minute before continuing.

"Killing the girl may not be simple," he said. "She travels with a protector, a swordsman who wields a famous awakened blade."

Sted grinned and slapped the sword at his side. "Couldn't be better than mine."

Alric's thin mouth twitched. "This sword has had many names, but it is best known by the name it took for itself, the Heart of War."

Sted's eyes widened. "The Heart of War, the *real* Heart of War? Why didn't you say that earlier?"

"This isn't a pleasure trip, Sted," Alric snapped. "Your mission is to eliminate the demon girl and secure the seed inside her quickly and quietly. Avoid confrontation with her companions if at all possible. Even spirit deaf, your membership in the League gives you a sense for demons. If she's active, you should be able to find her easily enough."

"Aye, aye," Sted said, standing up. "Quick and quiet. Got it. I'm ready now, so go ahead and open me a door to Gaol."

Alric turned back to his ledger. "You're a fully initiated League man," he said. "Open it yourself."

Sted grumbled a long string of curses. Then a moment later, Alric heard the unmistakable soft sound of the cut in reality, and the grumbling vanished. When he glanced over his shoulder, the room was empty. Alric turned back to his ledger with a smile. Either way this gamble played out was good for him. If Sted lived up to his brutal reputation, Alric would have the Monpress demon out of his hair for good. If the girl or her swordsman defeated him, well, that wasn't really a loss either. He wouldn't have to put up with Sted's insubordination anymore, and, while the loss of the sword would be lamentable, Slorn could always make more.

That thought cheered Alric up immensely, and he set to work sorting through the rest of the day's business with a smile.

CHAPTER
15

The man Eli was looking for was not at the hotel he'd been listed under in the ledger. However, the desk clerk, after a little cajoling and a few carefully palmed coins, pointed Eli toward the docks where Mr. Richton was due to set sail for Zarin that afternoon.

"Are you sure this is our thief?" Josef asked as they walked down the curiously empty street toward the river.

"Positive." Eli grinned from under the brim of his large hat. It was his compromise, since his wig was dirty now, but he might as well have gone bareheaded. They hadn't seen a soul since leaving the clerk's office, a fact that was making Josef very nervous indeed.

They made their way along the back alleys to the dock the clerk had mentioned. There was only one ship moored on the long wooden jut, a large, respectable-looking trade vessel running low in the water, heavy with cargo.

Josef looked at it skeptically. "Kind of a slow getaway vehicle."

"Not if no one's looking for you," Eli said, jogging out onto the dock.

On the deck, barefoot sailors were tying off ropes and doing the final work of getting the barge ready to go. One of them, a large river man in a black shirt and red scarf, who seemed to be the leader, looked their way just long enough to glare.

"Shove off," he grunted.

"Now, now," Eli said, smiling warmly as he walked up the plank from the dock to the ship's deck. "Don't be so hasty. We're here to see Mr. Richton. It's very urgent."

"Oh yeah?" The man straightened up slowly. "Name?"

"Gentero," Eli said without missing a beat.

The sailor gave him a funny look, but he nodded and walked across the deck to the small cabin at the prow. He knocked once before sticking his head in. A few seconds later he waved them over.

"Mr. Richton says go in," he announced, going back to his work.

Eli thanked him, but the sailor didn't notice; he was busy tying off the rope he'd been working on when they arrived and grumbling about bloody merchants and their inability to keep a bloody timetable.

Eli, Josef, and Nico walked across the deck to the cabin. Without bothering to knock, Eli pushed the wooden door open, and the three of them ducked inside. The cabin was small, but very well decorated. A color-ful, gold-tasseled rug covered the plank floor and bright, mirrored lanterns anchored in the corners above flip-out seats filled the room with warm light. Bright paintings of exotic city skylines were nailed to the walls, making up for the lack of windows. A large desk was built into the wall directly across from where they stood, and sitting at it, dressed in a well-cut navy coat, was a handsome, older gentleman. Silver streaked his close-clipped fox-red hair and neatly trimmed beard, but his face was only lightly lined. He wore silver-rimmed spectacles low on his hooked nose and behind them, his quick, brown eyes missed nothing as he turned to face them.

"Gentero," he said thoughtfully in a soft, urbane voice. "The trickster. Wrong opera, but quite appropriate."

Eli shoved his hands in his pockets. "I never liked *Tragedy of the Scarlet Knight*, anyway."

"No," the man said, closing the fold-down writing table where he'd been working. "You never had any taste for subtlety." His eyes flicked from Josef to Nico. "Aren't you going to introduce me?"

Eli sighed. "Nico, Josef, meet Giuseppe Monpress. He is, for lack of a better insult, my father."

The man stood up and held out his hand. "Pleasure."

Josef just looked at him. "I thought we were here to find the thief who robbed the duke ahead of us?"

"We are," Eli said. "That's him."

"Bit of a family business," Monpress said, sitting down again.

"*You're* the one who stole the duke's treasury?" Josef said.

"What bits of it were worth the taking," Monpress said. "Quite honestly, when you factor in the setup costs and expense of fencing such well-known artifacts, I'm not sure I made any money at all on this venture."

"Then why did you do it?" Eli said.

The tone in his voice made Josef hesitate. He'd never heard Eli sound quite that sharp. Eli, however, wasn't paying attention to him or Nico. His focus was entirely on the smiling man sitting at the desk. "You never pull a job without running the numbers three times through. You used to say that anything less than fifty percent profit wasn't worth the breath to talk about. So why did you rob Gaol?"

Monpress gave him a dry look. "You mean, why did I take your target?"

"However you want to put it," Eli said, crossing his arms over his chest.

"Because it was made for you," the older Monpress said. "Come, you must have realized that this whole fiasco—the citadel, the bragging, the posters plastered on every wall for two hundred miles in any direction—was all bait in a trap for you. Of course you did, and yet here you are, ready to waltz in like an *idiot*, just like always."

"Traps aren't a bother if you go in with your eyes open," Eli said through clenched teeth. "It was a challenge. And I still don't understand why you felt the need to impersonate me."

"I did nothing of the sort," Monpress said. "I only robbed them. They decided it was you. And no wonder, with the way you carry on. I mean, a *challenge*? Did you listen to nothing I taught you? Thievery is about finesse, about getting in, getting out, and being long gone before anyone thinks to check the safe. It's *not* about having your face on every wall or being so well known that any noble with a budget shortfall can lure you into his lands."

Eli shot him a murderous glare, and the older Monpress took a deep breath. "I don't know why we're even having this discussion," he said, his voice calm again. "Like it or not, I still feel an obligation to watch out for you. I headed for Gaol as soon as I saw them putting up the posters in Zarin. The whole thing was so obvious that I knew it was only a matter of time before you came running. I *had* hoped to be done with the whole affair well before you crossed the border. After all, challenge or no, even you wouldn't bother breaking in when there's nothing left to steal. I thought if I couldn't stop you from taking the bait, I could at least disarm the trap." His eyes narrowed. "Obviously, I forgot how quickly you can move when your unfortunate flair for the dramatic makes you take leave of what little sense you have."

The two men glared knives at each other, and for a moment Eli looked as if he was about to turn on his heel and march out. Then he shook his head and shoved his hands in his pockets. "You know what?" he said. "I don't care. I don't even know why I was surprised to find you here. You always were a meddling old man who never knew when to leave well enough alone. But it doesn't matter. That 'thief-proof' citadel was a joke I wouldn't want to be known for breaking into anyway. However, we are here for something other than just the joy of breaking in. I need an item from the duke's collection, a Fenzetti blade."

Monpress looked appalled. "That thing? Why? Fenzettis are impossible to fence."

Eli smiled secretively. "Let's just say I have a buyer who's already paid in full."

"A buyer?" Monpress said, theatrically impressed. "That's a first for you. I was beginning to side with the popular opinion that you eat everything you steal."

"That's one of the nicest things they've said about me." Eli grinned. "Are you going to give us the Fenzetti or not?"

Monpress stood up with a long sigh and walked to the

far corner of the cabin. He lifted the plush carpet to reveal a hidden hatch, which he yanked open.

"After you," he said, nodding to the narrow ladder descending into the hold below.

After a skeptical look, Eli went first, then Josef and Nico. Monpress came down last with a lantern, which he hung from the hook on the low ceiling. The hold took up most of the ship's lower level. It was just tall enough to stand in and it was packed absolutely full of goods. There were bolts of fine cloth, casks of wine, enormous spindles of thread, wooden bowls, porcelain, all stacked in open-top boxes stamped with Gaol's label.

Josef looked around in disbelief. "Wait," he said. "If being a merchant is just your cover, where did all this stuff come from? Is it stolen too?"

"Powers, no," Monpress said, laughing. "It's all purchased from the duke's own shops. Every stitch of cloth or drop of wine on this vessel has been paid for in full, and then paid for again in tariffs, and insured."

Josef shook his head. "Sounds expensive and troublesome."

"For certain," the old thief answered. "But it's all part of a properly executed job. I stole the best of Gaol's family treasures, all of which are easily recognizable, and all of which the duke is probably searching for quite adamantly at this very moment. However, the Duke of Gaol is, before all else, a businessman. Even in crisis, the last things he'd want to search are his own insured goods."

Monpress reached over to the pile of cloth beside them and lifted the top bolt. There, nestled between the folds of burgundy damask, was a beautiful set of gold plates.

"White Tower Dynasty," Monpress said. "Probably

older than Gaol itself. Lovely design, too. I think those are my favorite pieces."

"Hiding stolen goods in purchased ones," Eli said, trying not to look impressed. "Classic. I have to say the insurance is a nice touch. Even if you did get stopped, the duke's guards wouldn't do more than a cursory inspection for fear of breaking something."

"First rule of thievery," the elder Monpress said, laying the cloth down again. "Always hide where it costs money to find you."

Josef burst into laughter, and Eli shot him a sharp look. "It wasn't that funny."

"No, no," Josef gasped between laughs. "It's just that I see where you get it now."

"Really?" Monpress smiled, gripping Eli's shoulder. "I'm so happy to hear he remembers *some* of what I taught him. If he can only learn to control his flamboyant nature, he might actually make a good thief someday."

"I don't know what you're talking about," Eli said, ducking out of the older man's grasp. "I'm already the greatest thief in the world, or haven't you heard?"

Monpress gave Eli a serious look, killing the mirth in the room. "If you were actually any good, I wouldn't have heard," he said quietly. "If you were actually the best thief in the world, no one would know you were a thief at all, even after you'd robbed them blind."

"What?" Eli said. "You mean like you? How many months did you play merchant to set this up? You had a tunnel into the treasury, so I'm guessing at least three. In the last three months I've stolen the Golden Horn of Celle, the original painting of the *Defeat of Queen Elise*, AND the King of Mellinor."

"Three months?" Monpress smiled. "That would have been a feat indeed, considering the posters went up only two weeks ago. And for your information, the tunnel was already there, one of the duke's many cost-cutting measures to save stone. All I had to do was cut the initial entry into the treasury and make the fake panels, which took about two days. I spent the next three moving everything before the duke found out."

"Well, it doesn't matter," Eli said. "The point is that the jobs I pull are—"

"I know, I know, very impressive. " Monpress sighed. "Your exploits are reported far and wide. But what do you have to show for it? You're hunted by everything that cares for gold, and yet look at you. Threadbare coat, worn boots, you look like a common cutpurse. It's embarrassing to watch you drag the name Monpress through the dirt and not even making a good living at it. If you wanted fame, you should have chosen another profession, or have you forgotten the most important rule of thievery?" His eyes narrowed. "A famous thief is quickly a dead one."

"Sorry if I don't put too much faith in that one," Eli said, crossing his arms. "I've been famous for years, and I'm still alive. My head is worth more than you've stolen in a lifetime, old man."

"Oh, I wouldn't count on that," Monpress said quietly. "I get by. But unlike some, I don't feel the need to turn every theft into a carnival."

"Uh-huh," Eli said. "A few hundred thousand more and my bounty will beat Den the Warlord. I'll be the most wanted man in all of the Council Kingdoms, and they *still* won't be able to catch me."

"Well," Monpress said icily, "that will be a red-letter day indeed."

The two men stared at each other, and the hold grew very uncomfortable. Just as things were getting really heavy, Nico spoke.

"The boat is moving."

Both Monpresses blinked in surprise.

"I guess our good captain decided it was time to go," the elder Monpress said. "River types can be so impatient."

"Well," Eli said, "not that it hasn't been a pleasure catching up, but I'm not interested in crawling to Zarin on a riverboat with you, old man. We'll just take that Fenzetti off your hands and be on our way."

Monpress arched an eyebrow, but led them to the back of the hold, stopping in front of a pile of rolled-up woven rugs in a rainbow of colors stacked against the wall. The old thief stood on tiptoe and reached for the one on the very top. He caught the edge with his fingers, then paused and looked over his shoulder.

"Sir swordsman," he said, "if you would be so kind. I'm afraid my arms aren't what they used to be."

Josef shrugged, and Monpress stepped back as the swordsman grabbed the rug. He swung it down with a grunt, and it landed hard on the wooden floor of the ship.

"Heavier than it looks," Josef said, panting slightly.

"Must weigh a ton to have you out of breath," Eli said, kneeling down. "Let's see it."

He gave the rug a push, and it began to unroll, dumping its hidden treasure onto the floor with a dull clatter. For a moment, they all just stared. The thing on the floor was whitish gray, metal, but not at all shiny, and a little longer than Josef's arm. Its matte surface had a strange, smooth texture, almost like it was made of soap. It was sword-shaped only in theory, and Eli had to look at it from several different angles to figure out which end was the point and which was the hilt.

Curious, Josef picked it up and gave the white blade a swing. It wobbled through the air, off balance and ungainly, and Josef stuck it into the deck floor, glaring when the dull point couldn't even pierce the wood.

"Fenzetti blade," he grumbled. "More like Fenzetti bat. It doesn't even have a sharpened edge."

"To be expected," the elder Monpress said. "There's not a force in the world that could put an edge on bone metal. That's part of why they're so hard to sell. Fenzettis are immensely rare, valuable historical pieces that demand a high price. But, in the end, who wants to pay through the nose for an ugly, dull sword?" He shrugged. "Hopeless situation."

"Good for you that we're taking it off your hands, then," Eli said, grabbing a folded square of crimson-dyed linen from the stack beside him and tossing it to Josef. "Wrap that thing up and let's get out of here."

Josef nodded and started to bind the cloth around the blade. But just as he was tying it off, the boat began to pitch. They all flailed for purchase as the hold lurched below their feet, listing high on the starboard side like a skiff at sea instead of a flat-bottomed riverboat loaded with cargo.

"What's going on?" Eli said, getting his feet back under him.

"I think it's the wind," Monpress said, holding onto a support beam as the boat started to level out again.

"Wind can't do that," Josef snapped, but Nico held up her hand.

"Listen," she whispered.

They listened. Sure enough, above the sailor's cursing and the creaking of the boat was another sound, a deep, howling roar.

Josef slammed his feet on the ground as the ship finally righted itself. "What kind of wind—"

He never got to finish because, at that moment, both Nico and Eli slammed their hands over their ears. Monpress and Josef exchanged a confused look.

"Powers," Eli gasped.

"What?!" Josef shouted.

"It's the spirits," Nico said, her voice strained. "They're all yelling. It's deafening."

Josef's eyes narrowed. "Demon panic?"

"No," Nico looked up, very confused. "They're shouting an alarm."

Josef's eyebrows shot up. "An alarm?"

"Yeah," Eli said. "And it gets worse. We've stopped moving."

He was right. Though the boat was still rocking from its sudden jump, they weren't moving forward like before. They weren't moving at all.

"Fantastic," Monpress said. "You know, the only time I ever have trouble like this on a job is when you're with me, Eli."

Eli rolled his eyes and walked over to the closest crate. He plunged his hand between the bolts of wool and came out with a jeweled cup. It was vibrating in his hand and, for those who could hear it, screaming like a banshee.

"Easy," Eli said gently.

The cup ignored him, squealing and spinning in his hand.

"Shut up," Eli said, loading a bit more force into his voice.

It was enough. The cup froze in his hand, looking slightly dazed, or as dazed as a cup could look.

"Thank you," Eli said. "What are you doing?"

"Raising the alarm," the cup said. "You're a thief."

"Am I?" Eli said. "And how would you know? You've been stuffed between textiles all morning."

"The wind was the signal," the cup said haughtily. "No one steals from the Duke of Gaol! He's already got you surrounded, and when he catches you, we'll finally be rewarded for years of loyal watching! Finally, after so long things will be—"

Eli shoved the cup back in the wool, muffling it.

"What?" Josef said, gripping the Fenzetti blade with both hands as if it was a bow staff.

"It's a trap," Eli said. "Looks like most of this treasure was awakened and set to report their thief's location. Apparently we're surrounded." He glared at the old Monpress. "Why do you never hire a wizard? If you'd just had someone to poke at all this before you hid it, you would have known."

The old thief folded his arms over his chest. "Not everything runs by wizard rules," he said. "And in case you haven't noticed, now is scarcely the time for blame." He glanced upward. Sure enough, boots were thumping on the deck above their heads. "Either my sailors have suddenly decided to wear shoes, or we should beat a hasty retreat."

"Right," Eli said. "Is there another way out?"

"Of course," Monpress said, beckoning them to follow him. "You're with me, remember?"

On the dock, Duke Edward watched the stopped ship with a satisfied smile. Below his feet, the river was perfectly still, holding the boat like a fly in amber as his soldiers swarmed over it.

"Excellent work, Fellbro."

"Thank you, my lord," the river said, its deep voice strained from the pressure of holding the water back. "Are the soldiers almost finished? I don't think I can keep this up for much longer."

"You'll keep it up until I tell you otherwise," the duke answered, motioning for another group of soldiers to move into position on the far bank.

"But"—the river began to tremble—"with all due respect, my lord, you're asking an imposs—"

"Fellbro," the duke said, staring down at the water, which had gone perfectly still, "do you remember when you first swore obedience? What happened that year?"

The water didn't answer, so the duke continued. "Do you remember how I dammed your flow and poisoned your water?" Edward leaned closer. "I do. I remember the great floating islands of dead fish, the stench, the flies. How anything that drank your water died within the day. Do you think that was pleasant for either of us?"

"No, my lord," the river said.

The duke leaned closer still, his voice a cutting whisper. "And do you think I would hesitate to do it again?"

The river's water sank away from him. "No, my lord."

"Then I suggest you stop complaining and find a way

to obey me," the duke said, straightening up. "Do not forget your station, Fellbro."

"Yes, my lord," the river murmured, its water dark and murky.

Satisfied, the duke turned to see his soldiers beat down the hold door while another group moved to secure the cabin. He was watching with pleasure when a strong wind blew down beside him.

"Everything's in place," Othril said, panting. "I must have flown across the duchy twice over, but everything is ready on your order. Though"—the wind turned to the boat, ruffling the duke's graying hair in the process—"we might not need it. The soldiers are almost into the hold, and there's no other way out. Maybe you overestimated his abilities."

"I overestimate nothing," the duke said, nodding toward the stern of the boat.

Right where the back of the boat met the water, something was shaking. Then, with a soft crack, the hull popped open and a plank splashed into the water a few feet from the long pier where the soldiers had boarded. The moment the plank hit the water, a small figure dressed in shapeless black jumped out, landing neatly on the dock. The figure was followed by a large man carrying a long, wrapped package, and then an older gentleman who jumped quite gracefully for his age. Last of all, a gangly, dark-haired man leaped from the boat. His jump was awkward, and he almost missed the dock altogether, but the larger man grabbed him at the last moment, pulling him onto the dock, and they started running just as a hail of arrows launched after them from the bow of the ship.

"Othril," the duke said quietly. "Close the trap."

The wind spun into the sky, shrieking like a kettle. The sound rang out to every corner of Gaol, and the city obeyed.

"Eli!" Josef shouted. "Now would be a good time for something impressive."

They were racing through backstreets. The soldiers weren't far behind, and though the narrow turns kept the arrows down, who knew how long that would last. But after that horrible, shrieking howl, the soldiers had become the least of their problems.

From the moment the sound rang out, the town itself had turned against them. The paving stones rumbled, trying to trip them, shutters unlatched themselves and swung freely, aiming right for their faces. Shingles flew from rooftops like arrows, forcing them to duck quickly or risk a caved-in head. Josef kept them moving, turning down smaller and smaller alleys, trying to get some cover. But whenever they changed direction, the street lamps, which suddenly seemed to be on every corner, began to flicker brightly, signaling their location to the soldiers chasing them.

"This is ridiculous," Josef shouted, parrying a flying butcher knife as they ran past an open kitchen window. He had both his swords out now, with the Fenzetti blade tied across his back. Nico was right behind him, batting roofing tiles, cutlery, and snaking clotheslines out of the air with the whiplike sleeves of her black coat. The awakened fabric moved with her like a living thing, growing and shifting its size to fit her needs. Eli would have been mightily impressed if he'd had the chance to watch, but he was crouched between Josef and Nico, shielding his head with his hands and stomping on the rattling paving stones whenever he could. Monpress jogged quietly behind them, seemingly immune to the onslaught.

"Eli," Josef grunted as he chopped a flying rake in half, "what are we dealing with here? Is it another wizard, like the one in the citadel? An army of them?"

"Nothing so simple," Eli said. "No one's giving orders. The spirits are just going crazy." He grimaced. "They're going on about taking me alive for the duke and all the things he's going to do to me. It's fairly disturbing, actually."

"Well, you're a wizard too," Josef shouted. "Do something!"

"I can't!" Eli snapped back. "The spirits here won't talk to me, remember? Anyway, they're so worked up I'd have to Enslave them just to get their attention. They keep shouting, 'For the glory of Gaol' and 'For the duke.'"

"So the duke's the wizard in charge?" Josef said, kicking over a beam before it fell on them.

"Either that or he's got the best propaganda program ever," Eli said. "Anyway, that still doesn't explain how he got the whole city to spontaneously awaken. It's actually kind of amazing. I've never seen anything like it."

"Save the praise," Josef said, cursing when the alley they'd been running down suddenly let out into a large square. Without missing a beat, Josef changed direction midstride, kicking a door that tried to open in his face so hard it fell off its hinges. "We need to get out of here *now*."

"Might I suggest we head north, then?" the elder Monpress said.

Josef whirled to look at him. The older man smiled patiently, jogging along to keep pace. "I have an emergency exit prepared," he explained. "It should still be open."

"Why didn't you say something earlier?" Eli said, exasperated.

"You always get upset when I try to help," the older thief pointed out. "You can't also get upset when I don't."

Eli opened his mouth to say something stinging, but Josef shut him up with an elbow in the ribs. "Save it," the swordsman growled, and then nodded to Monpress. "Lead on."

The thief smiled and took the lead, turning them down a breezeway between two houses. With Monpress leading, their journey was far less hectic. The man knew the city like the back of his hand, and every time their way seemed blocked, he found another path. In this way they reached the northern wall with comparatively little fuss. Getting past it, however, was another matter entirely.

"Oh, dear," Monpress said.

The city wall, which had been a thick wall of average height when they first entered the city, was now almost fifty feet tall. Even worse, the once simple, straight stones were stretched at almost impossible angles so that the wall was now much wider at the top than it was at the bottom, creating a curving slope that would have had them almost upside down if they tried to climb it. It was also covered in knife-sharp spikes that twitched as they watched, ready to spear any climbers.

"So," Eli said. "Where's your exit?"

"There." The older Monpress pointed at a squarish stone about thirty feet off the ground above them. "Of course, it was much lower before."

"Of course," Josef said, lowering his swords.

"Well," Eli said, looking at Josef, "if it's that tall, it can't be that thick. Can't you just break it down?"

"Sure," Josef said, "if I had the Heart, which I don't because someone said don't bring it."

Eli ignored the comment and looked at Nico. "Want to give it a punch?"

Nico shrugged and walked up to the wall. She stared at the stones for a few moments, and then, pulling her fist back as far as it would go, she punched the wall with all her might. A great cracking sound echoed through the town, and Nico spun back, gripping her fingers. The wall, however, stood firm. The spot where she'd hit was slightly dented, but otherwise whole.

"No use," Nico said, shaking her hand furiously. "The spirits are standing strong. Whatever convinced them to stand up straight also convinced them to hold tight."

Josef sneered at the stones. "I bet the Heart could still break it."

"I'm sure," Eli said, putting his hands on his hips. "But as you said, we don't exactly have it handy." He glared up at the wall. "Nice and trapped, aren't we? And the final blow should be showing up any moment." He nodded toward the lamp at the end of their alley, which was blinking like mad.

"*Surely* you've got some clever plan," Josef said, sheathing his swords.

"I'm working on it," the thief muttered.

"You may want to work faster," Nico said, feeling the ground. "If you believe the paving stones, we'll have soldiers here in less than a minute."

Eli frowned, glaring at the blinking lamp, then down

at the paving stones, and then back to the lamp. Finally, he shook his head.

"All right," he said. "We'll try this." He turned to the elder Monpress. "You've always got at least three safe houses. Do you think you have one that isn't compromised yet?"

"One, maybe," Monpress answered. "It won't stand up to a serious search, though."

"That's all right," Eli said. "It doesn't need to. Here's what we'll do. All of this noise is to catch me, right? So we'll split up. You three will go for the safe house."

Josef scowled. "And what will you do?"

Eli looked at him plainly. "I'm going to turn myself in."

Stunned silence was his answer. Josef was the first to recover.

"Are you crazy?" he shouted. "I don't know about wizard stuff, but I'm pretty sure there won't be any doors to charm this time, Eli. If the duke was good enough to trap us like this, he's certainly good enough to keep you in chains."

"Don't worry," Eli said. "Even without the spirits, I'm Eli Monpress. There isn't a prison in the world that can hold me." He winked at the elder Monpress as he said this, but the old thief just rolled his eyes.

"Anyway," he continued, "I'll break out and meet you at the safe house. Whatever the duke did to wake up the town, he can't keep it up forever or he would have done it the second he saw me, back at the treasury. I don't actually know how he managed this, but simple spirits need a huge amount of energy to stay awake, which I doubt the duke can provide indefinitely. The town will have to go back to sleep sooner or later, and that's when we'll run. Sound good?"

"No," Josef grumbled, "but I'll take it." He glared at Eli as he walked away. "Don't get yourself killed, idiot."

"Thanks for the encouragement," Eli called back, but the others were already jogging down the alley away from him.

Smiling, Eli began to jog the other way.

He ran along the wall, waving at each light as it lit up when he passed. The little alley he was on widened into a street as he reached his chosen destination, the city's northern gate. Sure enough, as he'd guessed, there was a small knot of conscript guards, half a dozen at least, standing at attention before the closed doors. They were rough-looking boys mostly, farmers' sons, Eli guessed, and all gripping their swords like fire pokers as they stared wide-eyed at the twisting, awakened city.

Moving silently along the wall, Eli snuck up behind the smallest boy and, after adjusting his clothes and smoothing back his hair, Eli tapped the young conscript on the shoulder. The boy jumped two feet with a deafening yelp, dropping his sword. The other guards held together more admirably, whirling to face Eli with their swords drawn. Eli, surrounded on all sides, leaned back against the gate and raised his hands with a charming smile.

"Congratulations," he said. "You've caught Eli Monpress."

He had time for one last grin before all six guards jumped him.

CHAPTER
16

The rest of the army arrived just as the guards threw Eli on the ground. The career soldiers were on him at once, pushing the conscripts aside and slapping enough iron on Eli's wrists to make a miner jealous. The boys protested and won the right to be the ones to march Eli to the citadel, which they did with great cockiness. Eli went right along with it, grinning and waving as best he could with his shackled hands. He actually liked getting caught a great deal. People were always so excited.

By the time they reached the steps of the citadel, every soldier in Gaol, conscript and professional, was marching with them, shouting and cheering. But the merry mood vanished when a tall man in somber clothes came down the steps to meet them. Eli gritted his teeth. It was the wizard from before, and he looked unpleasantly smug as he took Eli's chain.

"I want the conscript troops on patrol," he said, wrapping the chain around his hand. "Keep the city on lockdown until I give the signal to stop. Guardsmen, I want you inside the citadel. Double posts at all times."

"Yes, my lord." The response was a dull roar from a thousand throats as the soldiers saluted and began to break into units. The man watched them for a moment and then, keeping Eli's chain taut, turned and walked the thief into the citadel.

"Let me guess," Eli said, struggling to keep up. "You're the duke, right?"

"Correct, Mr. Monpress," the duke said. "I am Edward di Fellbro, Duke of Gaol, and your master now, so you will hold your words unless spoken to."

"I'm afraid there's a bit of a mix-up," Eli said. "The only master I answer to is myself."

The duke's answer to that was a long, thin smile as he led Eli up the stairs to the very top of the fortress. As they walked, the fortress responded. Doors opened on their own to let them pass, chairs scooted out of their way, and curtains pulled back to make room.

"That's an impressive trick," Eli said, marveling as a pair of washbuckets rolled themselves behind a corner, out of the duke's sight. "How do you manage it?"

"I am a firm believer in obedience," the duke answered. "You'll learn it as well, soon enough."

When they reached the smaller nest of towers and courtyards at the top of the citadel, the duke marched Eli around a garden and through a heavy door and into a well-appointed study. The large stone room had many windows looking out across the city and the countryside beyond. As soon as they were inside, however, every window but the last closed its shutters, and the heavy door locked itself behind them.

When the room was secure, the duke let go of Eli's chain.

"You may take off your manacles now, Mr. Monpress," the duke said, settling himself comfortably in a high-backed chair. "There is no need for this to be uncomfortable unless you force me to make it so."

Eli stared at the gray-haired man, not quite sure what to make of him. But the duke just sat there, waiting, so Eli turned around and fished a straight pin out of his sleeve with his teeth. He picked the manacle lock in five seconds flat and turned back around, tossing the irons on the carpet at the duke's feet.

"Any other tricks while I'm performing?" Eli said. "Should I dance?"

"You should sit," the duke said, gesturing to the stool in the corner.

Seeing no point in refusing, Eli sat.

"So," Eli said, "you've caught me. Congratulations! Shouldn't you be sending someone to the Council to collect your reward?" He looked around at the opulent study, the colorful tapestries and carved-wood tables. "I have to admit, I always hoped it would be a poor country that caught me, or some honest bounty hunter. Someone who could use the money. Gaol scarcely seems in need of sixty thousand standards."

"It's not an amount to scoff at," the duke said. "But you should know, Mr. Monpress, I didn't catch you for the bounty."

Eli stopped. "You didn't?"

"No," the duke said. "I must admit, Mr. Monpress, you've been an immensely interesting hobby. You first came to my attention three years ago, when you stole the crown jewels of Kerket. Since then I've been following you closely, and you've never disappointed, every theft grander than the last. It's really quite remarkable."

"I'm always delighted to meet a fan," Eli said with a pleased smile. "But you didn't have to go through all this effort if you just wanted to meet me. I do respond to letters, you know."

"I know," the duke said absently. "I have several of yours. Intercepted in travel and bought for a price higher than I was wise to pay."

Eli gave him a shocked look. "You *bought* my mail?"

"Yes," the duke said. "To learn more about you. To learn how to catch you. As you see, it paid off. Here you are."

"Here I am," Eli said. "And are you satisfied?"

"I must admit," the duke said, looking Eli over, "I didn't expect you to be quite so like the caricature you present to the world. You seem every bit as cocky and irresponsible as your deriders make you out to be. I had hoped to find the real Monpress a man of greater depth than the boy in the posters."

"Well, you did just trap and arrest me," Eli said. "I could hardly be expected to show my true colors under such conditions."

"Quite so," the duke said and nodded. "But we shall see what you are made of soon enough."

Eli swallowed. Something in the way the duke spoke hinted that he wasn't using the phrase in a figurative sense.

"So," Eli said, shifting in his chair. "If you didn't catch me for the sixty thousand, and you didn't catch me for the conversation, why am I here?"

The duke gave him a thin smile. "*Fifty-five* thousand, which is what the Council lists as your bounty, is hardly enough money to justify the great expense and enormous trouble of catching you. Especially once we factor in what the Council will take back in taxes, tariffs, and fees. I'd be surprised if there was enough left over to pay Gaol's Council dues."

"Then why bother?" Eli said. "Conscripting that army of millers, farmers, and shopkeepers outside must have been an enormous headache, and let's not forget the spirits." He glared at the duke. "I don't know how you got control over so many spirits at once, or what you threatened them with so that they won't talk to me, but I can guarantee that if the Spiritualists ever find out about your little dictatorship here, they will come down on Gaol like a swarm of locusts. Seems a great risk on your part for a reward you claim not to want."

"Don't flatter yourself too much," the duke said. "The spirits of Gaol have been mine since long before you appeared."

"So what then?" Eli leaned forward. "Did you just catch me to prove something? Personal challenge? If so, bravo and well done; can I go now?"

The duke chuckled and leaned back in his chair. "Catching the uncatchable thief does bring a certain feeling of accomplishment—pleasant enough, but meaningless in the end. I'm a duke, Mr. Monpress, and as a duke I must think as a country, not as a man."

He stood up from his seat, pacing back and forth like a professor expounding his theory. "As I said earlier, I've followed your exploits for some time now, and over the years, I've noticed something of a discrepancy. Let's

take your robbery of Kerket. The crown jewels consisted
of eight pieces, including the scepter of Kerket, which
contains the Sea Star, the largest sapphire in the world.
Technically priceless, though I imagine you would get
only around ten thousand standards for it on the open
market, and that's *if* you could find a buyer willing to take
the risk. Still, ten thousand standards, and that's just one
jewel in one piece of the set. Any normal thief would have
retired to a life of luxury after that, but you, you show up
in Billerouge not a month later to steal seven paintings
from the royal collection. Again, technically priceless, but
I estimate fifteen thousand for each at least, likely more.

"How strange, then," the duke said, fanning his fingers as he spoke, "that none of these famous items have
ever re-emerged. In fact, *nothing* you steal ever shows
up again. Every time you're spotted, you're wearing the
same threadbare clothing. You seem to have no lands, or,
if you do, you certainly spend no time on them, considering you're spotted in a different country nearly every
month. So far as I can tell, you travel mostly by foot,
primarily through wilderness, and of all the hundreds
of reports I've collected from the Council about your
exploits, not a single one has mentioned you ever spend-
ing more than twenty standards at a go." He stopped and
looked at Eli. "Do you see where this is headed?"

Eli shrugged, and the duke gave him a slow smile.

"You've been on the Council bounty list for what?" He
shrugged. "A little more than three years? I estimate that
in that time you've stolen approximately three hundred
and fifty thousand Council standards' worth of goods, not
counting what was stolen from my own treasury." His grin
widened. "To put that in perspective, three hundred and

fifty thousand standards is more than the entire yearly tariff income of the Council of Thrones. *That* is the number that caught my attention, Mr. Monpress, not the fifty-five thousand those idiots in Zarin say you're worth."

Eli tilted his head to the side. "It sounds so impressive when you put it like that. I never actually added it up myself."

The duke shot him a scathing look. "I find that very hard to believe."

Eli just smiled, and the duke moved on. "Now, Mr. Monpress, I have answered your question. I must insist you answer one for me."

"I'm a firm believer in fairness," Eli said, crossing his legs. "What do you want to know?"

The duke crossed over to the single open window and looked out at the rooftops and neat green fields of his country. "There is something I wanted to ask if I caught you," he said, his voice for once not commanding, but curious. "These thefts of yours are always elaborate, some quite dangerous. I've heard stories of you walking right past piles of gold brick to steal a wooden statue, simply because it was more famous. At first, I thought you must be a collector, but then you go and steal the payroll for the entire Marcheron Shipping Company."

"Oh, yes," Eli said, laughing. "I thought I'd really lose my neck that time. Those pirates are quick with a knife, and I didn't have my swordsman then."

"Yes, yes." The duke turned to look Eli in the face. "But what I want to know is why? Why do you steal these things? It's obviously not for the money. You've had more money than any one man could spend in his life for years now."

"Don't estimate what a man can spend," Eli said and chuckled.

"If you spent half of what you steal, you'd be your own economy," the duke scoffed. "You can stop the conceited-boy act. There's no audience for you here. Just tell me the truth. Why do you steal what you steal? Why do you live this"—he stopped, grasping for the right word—"this *vagabond* lifestyle? You're obviously intelligent, driven, not to mention a powerful wizard. So why? What is your motive? Why do you do it?"

"Well," Eli said slowly. "First, it's fun. A man needs something to do with his life. As for motive, mine is grander than most. That fifty-five thousand you didn't want to scoff at earlier? I can't even be bothered with such a number. Such a tiny sum isn't even a tenth of my ambition." Grinning at the duke, Eli leaned forward, his voice lowered to a conspiratorial whisper. "One day, this head on my shoulders will be worth one million in gold."

The duke's look narrowed to a glare. "I'd said you were driven, but now you prove to be delusional as well. One million in gold? You'd be worth more than any four kingdoms put together. The Council would never allow such a bounty. A sum like that could destroy the balance of power on the continent. It's an impossible goal."

"Perhaps," Eli said and nodded, "but an impressive one, nonetheless."

"But you have yet to answer *why*," the duke said. "Why set such a number for yourself?"

Eli paused, tapping his fingers thoughtfully against his knee. "A bounty is a unique thing," he said. "Some overly nice people would say that a man's life is priceless, but as you so eloquently pointed out, things are worth what people will pay. In that way, a bounty is like a price tag, isn't it? And who doesn't like large numbers? Especially when applied to one's self."

The duke tilted his head, his brow furrowing from effort to decide if Eli was being facetious. In the end, he must have decided it didn't matter, for he walked across the room and stopped in front of Eli with a patient smile. "Well, whatever you claim your reasons to be, your goal is tragically to die unfulfilled when I turn you in for the bounty."

"Come on," Eli said, scooting to the front of his chair. "Surely with all the money flying around, actually turning me in for the bounty would be superfluous."

"But I must turn you in," the duke said. "If I start selling your stolen treasures without turning you in, everyone will think we're in league together. Once you're caught, however, I can claim your treasures as my own. Finder's rights. Also, that fifty-five thousand, minus taxes, will just about cover the expense of catching you."

"Are you sure you should be telling me this before I tell you where I keep my treasures?" Eli said. "I mean, when you put it that way, I feel absolutely no inclination to help you. Shouldn't you at least pretend to offer me my freedom? Keep the carrot dangling?"

The duke gave him a withering look. "I do not lie, Mr. Monpress. Such fawning embellishment wastes my time and yours."

"Then I hope you have something spectacular planned," Eli said. "Because I can't think of a single reason why I should go along with you."

"Oh, you will," the duke said. He fixed Eli with a slow, cutting smile, and waved his hand. The second his fingers moved, the chair Eli was sitting in threw itself backward. Eli hit the wall with a thud that knocked his breath out, but he didn't bounce off it. The moment he touched the stone, the blocks changed shape. The stone moved like living clay, wrapping around his legs, arms, waist, and neck, pinning him spread-eagle to the bare wall of the study. He was still trying to blink the spots out of his eyes as the duke walked over and pressed a gloved hand against his shoulder.

"I have a great deal of experience with bringing objectors around to my point of view," he said softly. "You see, Mr. Monpress, everyone has something they find intolerable. All you have to do is discover what that is, and then, whether it's a Great Spirit or a man, it becomes your willing servant."

"Sorry to disappoint," Eli said, gasping against the stone's chokehold, "but I'm afraid life as a thief has made me remarkably tolerant."

"That's all right," the duke said. "Life as a duke has made me remarkably patient." He gestured at the stone. "We'll start with the simplest, physical pain."

Eli sucked in a breath as the braces holding him in place began to move slowly and inexorably away from one another, stretching him in all directions.

"The stretching is a slow buildup," the duke said calmly, a connoisseur explaining the intricacies of his art. "The pain will become greater and greater as the joints are stretched past their limits, disjointing the shoulders, knees, elbows, possibly the hips, though most never get that far. I don't normally go to these lengths. Most people find even the idea of pain intolerable, but I try to keep in practice."

Eli grunted in reply, panting as his arms stretched far-ther. The stone crushed into his skin as it pulled, stretch-ing him like taffy. He could feel his sinews pulling, his bones creaking at unnatural angles until he had to clench his teeth to keep from whimpering. The duke saw this, and gave Eli a pleasant smile.

"We can stop at any time," he said. "Just tell me what I want to know and this will all be over. Otherwise, the pain will continue to grow until you pass out. When that happens, we'll rest an hour and then start again. Just remember that this situation is completely within your control. One concession, that's all it takes."

"You know," Eli said, gasping as something in his shoulder began to make a horrifying creaking sound, "for someone who claims to have studied me as long as you have, you don't know me very well. If you'd paid any attention, you'd have stuck with the carrot. Being bullied just makes me more stubborn, and life with Josef has made me very blasé about pain."

"We'll see," the duke said, resuming his seat by the window. "I can wait."

A moment later, the something in his shoulder snapped, and even Eli's clamped teeth couldn't stop the scream that came next.

"Sorry about the cramped conditions," the elder Mon-press said, passing Josef a bottle of wine and a set of mismatched cups. "This place was never meant to hold more than one person."

"We've been in worse," the swordsman said.

They were crowded into an attic with a sloped ceiling that Josef had to almost double over to fit under. He and

Nico were sitting shoulder to shoulder on the wrapped Fenzetti while Monpress sat opposite, cross-legged on top of the trapdoor.

They'd made it to Monpress's hideout with relatively little trouble. Once the soldiers captured Eli, the streets had emptied to nothing. Now they were waiting for dark, and while, technically, everything was going according to plan, Josef couldn't shake the feeling that the situation was rapidly spinning out of control. For one, they hadn't received a signal from Eli. Whenever he'd let himself get caught before, he'd always sent a signal of some kind. This time they'd gotten nothing. It could be because Eli couldn't cajole the spirits in Gaol like usual, but Josef had a bad feeling about it.

Monpress, however, was keeping busy. He'd already changed clothes from his somber merchant outfit to what looked to Josef like a set of ragged black pajamas. The cloth looped and tied in a dozen places, held close to the old man's surprisingly lithe body by an intricate network of straps. Once he was dressed, Monpress began slipping tools into hidden pockets with a silent efficiency that impressed even Josef. In addition to two small knives, he had a host of crooked hooks, pliers, straight pins, and other metal objects Josef recognized from Eli's thief tools but couldn't put a name to. He was wrapping his feet in padded cloth when Josef finally gave up and asked him what he was doing.

"Isn't it obvious?" Monpress said. "I just took a large chunk from my schedule to keep Eli out of trouble. Yet here I am, Eli in jail, and myself trapped in an attic with no treasure at all for compensation. So, I'm going to do the only thing I can do to mitigate my losses. I'm going to spring him."

"Wait," Josef said. "Don't bother. I'm going for the Heart as soon as it's dark. I'll just get him then."

Monpress looked at him skeptically. "You're going to beat an entire army with one sword?"

"No," Josef said. "The sword is for the wall. I don't need the Heart to fight common soldiers."

"Is that so?" Monpress chuckled. "I hope you don't mind if I try my way as well? Just for variety's sake?"

"Do what you want," Josef said. "Whatever happens, we're getting out of here tonight."

"I couldn't agree more," Monpress said, pouring himself a glass of wine from the bottle in Josef's hands. "Drink up; it's a good bottle. Be a shame to waste it."

Josef eyed the bottle skeptically. "No, thanks. I'm sure it's good, but I don't drink when I have to fight."

"Wise man," Monpress said, sipping at his own glass. "I only hope Eli can pick up a little of your forethought."

"Not a chance," Josef said. "He's categorically against considering the consequences of his actions." He looked at the old thief. "You seem like a cautious man. How did you end up with a son like Eli?"

"Oh, he's been like that ever since I've know him."

Josef scowled. "That's an odd thing for a father to say."

Monpress shrugged. "Well, you need to understand that I'm not actually his father. He showed up on my doorstep ten years ago very much as he is now. Smaller, of course, but every bit as ridiculous. I don't know how he found me. I make it a point of not being findable—hazard of the business—but there he was, standing in the snow outside my mountain lodge, asking could I teach him to be a thief."

Monpress took a long drink from his cup. "I turned

him away, of course, but he wouldn't go. I don't even know how he got up there. I'd bought the lodge for its seclusion, so we were miles up in the mountains, but the boy had no horse or warm clothing. It was like he'd just appeared out of thin air. I turned him away several times, but he was so insistent about learning to be a thief, I realized I might have to kill him to get rid of him. Whatever my faults, I'm not a killer. Besides, there was a storm lurking overhead, and I'm not so heartless as to send a boy out into the weather. So I acquiesced and let him come in, just for the night. He's been my ward and apprentice ever since, and a sorry one at that." Monpress smiled, swilling the wine in his glass. "Still, infuriating as he is, one can't help getting attached to the boy, which is how I'm in the mess I find myself in today."

He raised his cup in salute and then downed the rest in one gulp. Josef scowled. He knew so little of Eli's life before they met, but it wasn't surprising to hear he'd been a thief's apprentice, and even less surprising to hear he'd sweet-talked his way into it. But who had he been before he'd taken the name Monpress? Just as Josef opened his mouth to ask, a strange, soft sound on the roof drove all talk of the past from his mind.

They all froze, listening. Josef motioned the others to stay quiet before leaning over to peer out the tiny, grimy window. Outside, he saw nothing but the same roofs and eaves he always saw. No strange movements, nothing out of place, just the last glow of the setting sun on the red tile. He was about to pass the sound off as something innocent, a cat maybe, or the house settling below them, when it sounded again, a low creaking, like something large was walking on the tile above them.

Very, very slowly, Josef opened the window and climbed outside. It was a tight fit, but he made it soundlessly, getting both feet on the roof before slowly peeking over the edge at the roof of their hideout.

The moment his eyes cleared the eave, it launched at him.

Josef flew backward, skidding down the tile. His short swords were in his hands before he knew what was happening, and it was a good thing, because the blades were his only protection from the ball of shifting white fur, claws, and teeth on top of him as they both slid down the roof.

"Oh, *Powers*," he growled through gritted teeth. "Not you again."

The ghosthound snarled, and Josef took the initiative, kicking the dog hard on the flat spot between his front legs. Gin yelped and jumped away, landing lightly on the roof's peak just as Nico winked in from nowhere and grabbed his neck. Gin howled and kicked, tossing her into the air, but she turned in flight, landing neatly beside Josef, who was sheathing his swords.

"Easy, puppy," Josef said. "I'd love to make a coat out of you, but this isn't exactly the best place."

As if to prove him right, the lamppost on the street below them began to flicker frantically and, a moment later, whistles sounded in the distance.

"If you're looking for Eli," Josef said, "he's not with us."

"I know," Gin growled, keeping low against the tiles. "I'm not here for him."

Josef glanced at Nico, who repeated what the dog had said. Gin, meanwhile, was watching the evening sky through slitted eyes.

"We need to move," he said. "That wind is coming. Follow me."

With that, he hopped off the roof.

Nico repeated this to Josef, who repeated it to Monpress, who was just climbing out the window to see what was going on.

"We might as well follow," the old thief said. "This hideout was blown the second you got out the window. We'll be up to our necks in guards in a moment."

"Or worse," Josef muttered, looking down at the tiles under his feet, which were beginning to rattle. "Come on."

He reached through the window to grab the Fenzetti blade, and they walked to the edge of the roof where Gin had jumped off. It was a two-story drop, but fortunately most of it was covered by a sturdy trellis. Nico climbed down first, then Monpress, who was remarkably agile for his age, and Josef brought up the rear. Gin was waiting at the bottom, and he led them around a corner to a large stone storehouse. It was an ancient thing, with great cracks between the stone overgrown with plants. Still, it was big enough for all of them, just barely, and they got inside just before the strange, howling wind passed overhead.

"All right, dog," Josef said, crossing his arms. "You lost us our hideout and nearly blew our cover altogether, so what do you want? Where's your master?"

Gin glared at him, then looked at Nico. "Don't tell me you're the only one who can understand me?"

Nico shrugged, and Gin rolled his eyes. "Fine," he growled. "Tell your sword boy that his second question answers the first. I'm here looking for Miranda. She went into town this morning and never came out. Then all the spirits started going crazy, so I decided to come get her. I know she's in the citadel, and I smelled the thief in there as well. It doesn't take a genius to put two and two together. But even I can't get into a castle crawling with guards and winds who do nothing but watch, so I sniffed you out, swordsman." Gin wrinkled his nose. "Not that I could miss you. Do you even know what a bath is?"

Nico repeated this, leaving out the bath comment, and Josef gave the dog a skeptical look.

"We didn't even know the Spiritualist was in town," he said. "She certainly didn't go in with Eli. She's probably helping the duke. Catching Eli is her job, after all."

"It's complicated," Gin growled. "But she's not with the duke. Miranda wouldn't help anyone who treated the spirits this way. Common little spirits were never meant to be awake this long. It's going to kill the town if it keeps up. Miranda wouldn't put up with something like that to catch a hundred Elis. However, she is in the citadel, along with your thief, and I don't imagine either of them wants to be there. So if you're planning a rescue, then I want in."

Josef listened as Nico repeated the dog's words, rolling his eyes when she got to the end. "If you just wanted to come along there was no reason to jump us."

Gin grinned, showing a spread of long, sharp teeth. "I figured my negotiating position would be stronger if I had your head in my mouth, but this works too."

Nico gave him a horrified look, and didn't pass the message on.

Monpress, however, was sitting back against the stones, stroking his neatly trimmed beard with a thoughtful calmness not usually witnessed in the presence of ghosthounds. "Dog," he said, "you can understand what we're saying, correct?"

"Of course," Gin snorted. "Human speech is the simplest form of communication."

The thief chuckled as Nico translated. "Well, then, if you're willing to follow directions, I think we can come to an arrangement."

"That depends on the directions," Gin growled. "Who are you anyway?"

Nico answered that one. "He's Eli's father. He's a thief too."

Gin gave her a sideways look. "He doesn't smell anything like Eli."

Nico passed that on to Monpress, who laughed. "I'll take that as a compliment. I am Giuseppe Monpress, and I have many occupations. For the last few days, I served as a masonry and antiques expert. This morning, I was a thief. Right now, I'm simply a mentor trying to save his lost charge from his own cockiness. Does that answer your question?"

"In a roundabout sort of way," Gin growled, but he nodded just the same.

"Excellent," Monpress said. "As I was saying, I'm no wizard, but I can guess that the Duke of Gaol is the one controlling the town. If there's one thing living in Gaol taught me, it's that the duke controls everything within his borders, no matter how trivial. The man doesn't know the meaning of the word delegate. I wouldn't be surprised if he had a personal contract with every paving stone in Gaol. This level of attention to detail has gotten him where he is, but it's also a tremendous handicap, which we are going to use to our advantage. Look here."

He leaned over and began to sketch an outline of the citadel on the shed's dirt floor with one of Josef's knives, which Josef hadn't even felt him take. "We'll create a series of catastrophes, each requiring the duke's attention. Mass destruction seems to play well to each of your strengths, so I don't think this will be a problem. While the duke is putting out fires, I will locate and free Eli and the Spiritualist. Can you tell me where they are in the citadel?"

Gin nodded. "Once I'm inside."

"You'll be with me, then," Monpress said after Nico translated. "Once we've set the first distraction, you'll point me toward our targets. After that, you keep the attention off me while I do the extraction and then provide us with a quick getaway. You can run faster than a horse, can't you?"

Gin's toothy grin needed no translation, and Monpress turned to Nico and Josef. "We'll be depending on you two after we finish the jailbreak. Your job will be to cause enough flash that any report of prisoners going missing is lost in the noise, but not bring so much heat down that you become prisoners yourselves, or die in the process."

"Shouldn't be a problem," Josef said. "Let me get the Heart and I'll put a hole the size of a wagon in that outer wall. Maybe a couple. That should solve both the getaway problem and the distraction."

"I leave that to your discretion," Monpress said, making a mark at the corner of the citadel closest to the river. "We'll exit here, at the stables, so make your first hole on the northern wall. We'll rendezvous at the northern border of Gaol. I've got one final hideout there. Nothing fancy, but it should last long enough for a simple switch. From what I've seen, the duke's reach ends at the Gaol border, so all we have to do is cross the line and we're free. Aside, of course, from the usual pursuing guards and whatnot, but I'm sure you have experience avoiding those."

"Tons," Josef said, grinning.

Nico frowned at the diagram. "It's kind of a blunt plan."

"Circumstances have given me blunt instruments. You do your best with what you're given."

Nico's mouth quirked at that, and she seemed satisfied. Josef, meanwhile, snatched his knife back and stood up, settling the blade back into his sleeve. "I'll need an hour to get the Heart and get into position."

"That's fine," Monpress said, standing up as well and dusting the dirt off his black, padded suit. "We'll need full dark anyway, so that gives us just the right amount of time. I won't be able to give a signal when we start. Can I trust you to be in position on time?"

"One hour," Josef said, walking to the rickety shed door. "We'll be there."

He paused for a moment, listening. Satisfied the coast was clear, he opened the door and slipped out into the alley, Nico right on his heels like a little shadow. Monpress watched them go, a skeptical look on his face.

"The girl I'm not worried about," he said and sighed. "But I have to admit, the thought of our success depending on that swordsman's ability to sneak to the river and back without causing a scene is not very reassuring."

Gin chuckled and settled down with his chin on his paws, his ears swiveling for any hint of sound. A moment later, Monpress sat down as well, and together they waited in silence for full dark to fall.

CHAPTER 17

Eli felt like a wad of kneaded dough. His breath came in ragged hiccups, his muscles ached, and his vision was almost black. The duke had called the first rest seconds before he passed out, but Eli wasn't sure he'd made it in time. Passing out still seemed like a valid option. Currently, however, he was awake, more or less, and being carried down a long hall suspended between the bulky arms of two enormous men. The duke ghosted ahead of him, a tall, dark shape among dark shapes.

They'd gone down a dozen flights of stairs, and the part of Eli's mind that wasn't whimpering in the corner realized they must be deep underground. The air was old, dusty, and cold enough to make his teeth chatter by the time they finally stopped in front of a deep-set iron door.

"My strongest prison," the duke said, standing aside as one of the guards unlocked the fist-sized padlock. "Also, my only prison. As most situations can be solved via the strategic use of force, I normally find them a waste of time. This one, however, I had made especially for you, Mr. Monpress, just in case you lived up to your reputation."

As he talked, the guard got the door open and carried Eli through and into a low, wide room. The only light came from the duke's own torch, but it was enough to make Eli wish he couldn't see. The dark stone walls were covered in strange metal objects, most of them sharp. There was a rack of hand and foot manacles in various sizes, as well as racks of other things he vaguely recognized from some of the more horrible dungeons he'd broken out of, but he had never worked up the courage to study the implements closely. There was also a large, locked grate in the middle of the floor, almost like a drain, and Eli shuddered to think what that was for.

But the guards walked past all that, dragging Eli to another iron door at the back of the room. This door the duke unlocked himself, standing in front so Eli could not see what he was doing and whispering something Eli couldn't make out. The door opened soundlessly to reveal a cell the size of a large closet stacked with bales of dark-colored hay.

Eli wanted to quip something about how nice it was of the duke to consider his comfort, but all he managed was a gurgling sound as the guards tossed him in. He landed on the hay with a grunt, the door clanging shut behind him.

"One hour." Eli could hear the duke's smile through the iron. "Then we'll begin again. Think on your answer."

Their footsteps faded away and the prison's outer door slammed shut, leaving Eli lying in the straw in utter black silence.

When he heard the outer door close, Eli sat up stiffly. His fingers went to his belt pocket and pulled out a small ring of heavy keys that had, moments ago, been in the guard's pocket. He felt them in the dark, and a small grin spread over his face. They'd have to beat him worse than that to slow his pickpocketing.

With a low groan, Eli pulled himself over to the door and set about looking for the keyhole. The duke had said one hour, but Eli wasn't about to wait that long. In one hour he intended to be with Josef and Nico as they plowed a hole out of the city. However, those happy thoughts were quickly put out of his head as his finger ran along the door's pitted metal surface from floor to ceiling, and found nothing. No lock, no hinges, just metal that jutted almost seamlessly into stone.

Eli bit his lip. He had to be missing something. What he needed was a light. So he closed his eyes and reached down, prodding the lava spirit that slept in the burn on his chest.

"Karon," he whispered. Then again, a little louder. "*Karon.*"

His chest warmed as the lava spirit stirred sleepily.

"Could I bother you for a light?"

The spirit mumbled sleepily, and a warm, orange light began to shine from under Eli's shirt. Now that he could see, he noticed the door did have an opening, a small slit right at eye level, probably for guards to check on prisoners without opening the door. Otherwise, the light only confirmed what his fingers had found earlier. No lock, no handle, no hinges, nothing.

"Come on," Eli muttered, running his hands along the door's edge, tapping it with his fingers. As he tapped, he felt the door move away. It was a tiny, stubborn motion, but Eli jumped when he felt it, and everything fell into place. Of course, he realized, rolling his eyes. The hunk of iron was awakened, and probably terrified loyal like everything else in this pit of a country.

With a frustrated groan, Eli sat back and contemplated his next move. Something dramatic would be a nice change. Maybe he could get Karon to blow the door down in a shower of fire. He was turning this idea over when his nose caught the hint of something odd, a grassy, chemical smell, almost like lamp smoke. At once, the warm light from his chest went out.

"*Powers*, Eli." Karon's deep voice made his ears ring. "What are you doing, calling me like this? I could have killed us both."

Eli scowled. "What are you talking about?"

"You're covered in oil," Karon said. "I nearly set you alight."

Eli reached down in alarm, patting his shirt with quick hands. Sure enough, his clothes were slick with something that smelled faintly of grain. He grimaced. Lamp oil, cheap smoky stuff too, but when . . . He reached down to the hay bales and gave an enormous sigh. He remembered thinking they looked dark when the guards threw him in. Now that he had his hands in them, and was thinking of something other than getting out, it was clear they were drenched in oil. No fire spirits.

"Fantastic," he muttered, flopping back into the straw. No point in avoiding it since he was already covered. "What a fine mess."

Fine mess was a pretty way of putting it. Royally screwed was more accurate, or completely bollixed. Eli folded his arms across his chest. They still hurt horribly;

so did his legs. Eli clenched his teeth. He hated pain. He also hated being trapped, but he had no one to blame but himself this time. He thought back to the duke's words in the library, before the pain had become too much. He'd let himself get predictable. How many times had he gotten himself caught? A dozen in five years? Two dozen? He shook his head. Far too many, that was for sure.

"You're getting lazy," he muttered at the dark. "Lazy and predictable."

Saying it actually made him feel worse, but he always tried to be honest with himself. First rule of thievery: If you can't be honest with yourself, you'll never fool anyone else. He rolled over, ignoring the horrible cramping in his back. Telling the duke what he wanted was out of the question. Even if he'd asked for something simple, Eli was categorically against bullies. He turned over again, trying to find a way he could lie without feeling like he was crushing something that had already been crushed too many times that day. It wasn't like he could take another round of the duke's questioning. He had to escape. Had to, and quickly, and he would get right on that as soon as breathing didn't feel like swallowing knives.

A while later he was still lying there, warring between making himself move and ignoring the necessity, when he caught a glimpse of light. It flashed red through his closed eyes, but when he snapped them open, the brightness was gone. Instead, the room, which had been pitch black, was now filled with cool, gray light. The itchy straw was gone from under him as well, and he was lying on something soft and yielding. Without warning, a gentle, cool hand touched his face, and Eli sucked in his breath at the burning touch the fingers left behind.

Just when he'd thought things couldn't get worse.

What? a lovely, musical voice chuckled behind him, *No hello?*

"Hello," he said through gritted teeth. "What are you doing here?"

Do I need an excuse? White hands, paler than fresh snow in moonlight, drifted down his chest to settle over his heart. *It pains me deeply to see you in trouble, dearest. Does love need a motive to come to the aid of the one she cherishes?*

Her voice was piercingly sad. Eli didn't fall for it for a moment.

The Lady sighed when he didn't answer, and her fingers ran over Eli's bruised body, leaving a burning feeling wherever they touched. *Look at what that man has done to my beautiful boy.* There was anger in her voice now, cold and sharp. *All you have to do is say the word and I will avenge you. Open yourself, show these common spirits whom you belong to, and this city will worship you as it should.*

"I don't belong to anyone," Eli said. "And I don't want your help."

The roving hands froze, and suddenly he found himself being whirled around. A terrible strength slammed him to his knees on the floor so that he was facing her as she stood before him, terrifying in all her glory. Perfectly straight white hair tumbled around a white face, spilling over her lovely shoulders, across her lovely body to the floor, where it flowed across the stones like moonlit rivers. Her eyes were pure white, the irises only defined by a shimmer of iridescent silver and the flutter of white lashes. She was naked, but her nakedness was not a shameful thing. Beside her inhuman whiteness, it was Eli who felt exposed.

Wherever her light touched, spirits woke, no matter how small or insignificant, and as they woke, they began to reverence her. The stones, the straw, the iron of the door, the tiny spirits of the air, everything, every bit of the world worshiped at her feet. Yet the White Lady ignored their praises. Her entire focus was on Eli alone. Slowly, gracefully, she reached forward and tangled her hands in his hair, pulling him close until his face was inches from her bare stomach.

You belong to me, she whispered, her voice shivering and terrible. *From the moment I saw you, you were mine. It was I who saved you, I who gave you everything you have. Because I love you, I have let you run free, but do not think for a moment that you are anything but mine.* She pulled his head up, almost breaking his neck as she brought his face to hers. *Do not forget what you are.*

"How could I?" Eli said, his voice wheezing with pain. "You keep showing up to remind me. But there's one thing you're wrong about," he said. "I don't belong to anyone but myself." The White Lady's hands trembled, and for a moment, Eli thought she was going to rip his head clean off. Then she began to chuckle. *So rebellious*, she cooed, ruffling his hair. *So arrogant. You haven't changed at all, have you? Refusing my help when I came all this way to save you. How selfish, but I always loved that about you, dearest boy.* She kissed his forehead. *Very well, beat yourself bloody if you must. But remember*— her hands gripped his head like a vice—*whatever you say, you do belong to me. I have been extremely tolerant, but push too hard, darling star, and I will take you back whether you like it or not. Then, things will be as they were before, when you were my darling little boy who loved me more than anything.*

"That was a long time ago," Eli said, leaning away from her touch. "Things change, Benehime."

Her hands caught him again and yanked him to his feet, putting his face inches from her own. She bent down with painful slowness, laying a cold kiss on his mouth. *I'll see you soon*, she murmured against him. *My favorite star.*

"Not if I can help it," Eli grumbled, but the room was dark again. The Lady was gone. Suddenly his legs felt as weak as jelly, and he flopped into the straw. For several moments, all he could do was sit there and adjust. Benehime's presence was intoxicating, and recovering once she left was a little like waking up after drinking an entire bottle of grain liquor. He was experienced with it, though, and recovered his mind with quick efficiency, especially when he realized he might still be able to take advantage of the awed spirits. But by the time he thought to try it, the door and the stones around it were already solidly ignoring him.

Of course, Eli sighed, flopping back over, she took the memory of her visit with her for everyone but him. She was too wise to be leaving him freebies like that. Her help never came for free. Well, she could wait forever, because there was no way he was ever going to come begging to her. Whatever she said, he was through being her pet.

Gritting his teeth against the pain of moving, Eli slid off the straw and knelt beside the door. No prison was perfect, he reminded himself. Even without his tools or wizardry, the duke was kidding himself if he thought he could keep Eli Monpress locked up. Feeling slightly better at this thought, he began patiently running his fingers along the door cracks, looking for the small oversight that would spell his freedom.

Miranda woke in the dark with her head throbbing. She was lying on her stomach with her arms under her, as if she'd fallen. She didn't remember falling, but her arms were asleep, so she must have been like that for a while. The memory of her capture was scattered and hazy, but she recalled Hern's face and the choking pain from the vines before everything had gone black. Even now, her head burned like someone was holding a brand to it. She tried pressing her fingers against her forehead, and a wave of blinding pain flashed through her. Miranda spat curses that would have made her mother faint and snatched her hand away. That bastard Hern would get what was coming to him, she thought bitterly, as soon as she got out of—

Miranda froze. Her fingers, the fingers she'd just pressed to her head, were empty. She held up her hands, waving them right in front of her face. It did no good; she couldn't see them, but then, she didn't need to. The feeling of bare skin against her cheek was enough.

"No," she whispered, curling over, her empty hands skittering across the unseen floor, desperately looking for what she knew was not there. "No no no no no."

Her rings were gone. All of them. So was Eril's pendant. And not just gone, but so far away she couldn't even feel the familiar tug of their connection on her spirit. Frantically, she flung her soul open, reaching out, calling for her spirits. Calling and waiting, but there was no reply.

Fear deeper than even the demon panic flooded through her, and her mind began to race. How long had she been out? How long had her spirits been without their connection? Where was Gin? Where was she, and how could she get out? She had to get out. She had to escape right now, before her rings died out.

"They won't die out," tsked a voice deep inside her. "Your spirits are stronger than that. Have a little faith, Miranda."

The low, watery voice in her ear made Miranda jump, and she cracked her head hard on the wall behind her.

"Sorry," Mellinor said.

"It's all right," Miranda whispered. "I've never been happier to hit my head in my life. Thank goodness you're still here."

"I live inside you," Mellinor said, matter-of-factly. "How would they take me?"

"Good point," Miranda said, sinking into a sitting position on the cold floor. "Did you see who took my rings?"

"No," Mellinor said and sighed, creating a strange feeling of water moving over her mind. "But I did get a lesson in the limitations of using a human body as a vessel. It turns out, if you're unconscious, I can't see anything. I heard them fighting, though."

"They fought for me?" Miranda was unexpectedly touched.

"Of course," Mellinor said. "As well as they could, anyway. Their abilities are very limited without you up to channel power to them. I couldn't even get out to help. I can't leave your body without injuring it if you're not awake to let me go. Yet another inconvenient lesson for today."

"This is kind of a new thing for all of us," Miranda said. "Let's get out of here."

"My thoughts exactly," Mellinor rumbled. "What first?"

Miranda blinked in the pitch dark. "How about some light?"

Mellinor made a bubbling sound, and Miranda felt cool water running through her. At once, soft light, like moonlight seen from deep underwater, began to fill the tiny cell, and she got her first good look at her prison.

"Good grief."

She was kneeling in a circular pit that might have been an old well. The walls were smooth, so either the prison had been cut into a solid block of stone, or they were deep underground, cut into the bedrock. The walls finally ended fifteen feet up at a metal grate sitting atop her cell like a well cap and held shut by a thick padlock. Above the grate, she could see nothing but darkness. The cell itself was more spacious than she'd originally thought, however. She had enough room to sit down, if not to stretch out. Other than herself there was a wooden bucket, presumably to be used as a toilet, and a great deal of gray dust. It covered everything: the floor, the walls, and even, she realized with disgust, her clothes where she had been lying.

Miranda stood up, slapping at her skirt, but the dust clung to the fabric almost like it was sticky. It was on her hands too now, gray and fine as dried silt. She rubbed at it fiercely, but the powder stuck to her, forming dark little rivers in the creases of her skin. She held her hands to her nose. The dust had an odd scent that was strangely familiar. Very lightly, and sure she was being very foolish,

Miranda licked her finger. The stuff had a horrid, alkaline taste, and that was all she got before the tip of her tongue went numb.

"Thought so," Miranda said, coughing. "It's graysalt. The servants used to put it down as a rat poison when I was a child."

"And you licked it anyway?" Mellinor said, horrified.

"Well, it's not lethal to humans," Miranda said, scraping her numb tongue with her teeth. "As a dust it's harmless, but get it wet and it becomes a paralytic. So the rats would run through and then get it wet when they tried to groom the dust off, and bam, dead rat."

"Good thing you're not a rat then," Mellinor grumbled.

"No," Miranda said, "but I'm trapped like one just the same. Look"—she pointed at the piles of gray dust on the floor—"there must be pounds of it down here. Sure, it's nontoxic now, when it's dry, but if we were to get it wet there's more than enough here to paralyze me from head to toe, maybe for good."

She peered up at the locked grate, high overhead. Even if she could reach it, she didn't think she could break the lock without Durn or one of her other spirits. Mellinor could, maybe, if he got enough pressure, but in her experience, lots of pressure meant lots of water, which was precisely what they couldn't have.

"Well," Miranda grumbled, "nice and trapped. I must admit I never expected something this ingenious, or cheap, out of Hern. Twenty pounds of graysalt probably cost less than one of those bottles of wine he had with dinner."

Mellinor shifted inside her. "Actually, I don't think we're in Hern's tower."

Miranda frowned, and the spirit explained. "Generally speaking, spirits who spend a lot of time around Spiritualists are pretty active, but it's quiet as the dead down here."

"That's no different from anything else in Gaol," Miranda said. "Hern's got a stranglehold on this place."

"You keep saying that," Mellinor murmured. "But something's been bothering me. You said before that Hern was always in Zarin, right?"

"Right," Miranda answered.

"Well," the water rippled in her head, "whatever's controlling the spirits in Gaol, it's acting like a Great Spirit. That kind of control doesn't work if the controlling power's not constantly in contact with the land, like a Great Spirit is. A land without a Great Spirit becomes sleepy and stupid, more so than usual. Just look at my old basin. But this land is disciplined, and easily woken. That's not something you see when the commanding power is always somewhere else."

Miranda bit her lip. Mellinor made a good point, and he would be the expert on this sort of thing. "But," she said, "if it wasn't Hern, then who? Who's running Gaol?"

"The duke, of course," said a cheery voice above her.

Miranda looked up in alarm, biting back a curse as she whacked her head again. She knew that voice, she realized, rubbing her poor, abused skull, but she certainly hadn't expected to hear it here.

"Monpress?"

"Who else?" Eli's laughing voice was muted, like he was behind something large and heavy.

"What are you doing in here?"

"I was caught." She could almost hear his shrug. "It happens from time to time. The trouble, as always, is keeping me caught. I was just exhausting my options when I heard your voice. Now, I think I can safely assume, unless your little oration about the powdered poison was a cruel and elaborate ploy, that you are also an unwilling guest of our illustrious host, Duke Edward?"

"Duke Edward?" Miranda stood up. "The Duke of Gaol?"

"No, the Duke of Farley," Eli said, sighing. "Yes, the Duke of Gaol. As I said, he's the one running everything. Whose castle do you think we're in?"

"Nonsense," Miranda said. "The duke isn't even a wizard."

"Who told you that?" Eli scoffed. "Just because a man doesn't wear rings or have WIZARD written across his forehead doesn't mean he isn't one."

Miranda shut her mouth. Now that she thought about it, everything she knew about the Duke of Gaol came from Hern's annual reports. This situation was getting stranger by the minute.

"So," she said slowly, "the Duke of Gaol is a wizard, and he's the one controlling the spirits, not Hern?"

"I don't know who Hern is," Eli said, "but that's correct. Now that you know, however, I can't imagine it makes you any happier to be locked up, so how about we work together and get out of here? It'll be just like Mellinor, only with less enslavement and near-drowning."

"*Me*," Miranda cried, "help *you*? Do you have any idea how much trouble helping you has caused me?"

"Not in the slightest," Eli said. "But think on this: I wouldn't be sitting here talking if I had a way out, would

I? I'm proper trapped, same as you. Now, the duke will be back in less than half an hour to take me away, and after that, I don't think I'll be coming back. Are you really going to let a wizard who runs his spirits through a system of fear and intimidation be the one to catch me?"

Miranda scowled. The thief had a point. She'd put Monpress to the side while she focused on getting dirt on Hern, and it had landed her in here. If circumstance had delivered the thief, and possibly her freedom, right into her hands, who was she to argue? Plus, she now knew who was behind the strange happenings in Gaol. If the duke had indeed set himself up as the tyrant Great Spirit of Gaol that would certainly fit the West Wind's concern. If she played things carefully, she could very well walk out of Gaol with everything she'd come here to get, and that was worth taking a risk. After all, she thought and glared at the grimy filth on her skin, what did she have to lose?

"All right," she called back up. "What do you want me to do?"

"Catch!" Eli shouted, and she heard the jingle of something metal flying through the air before a set of keys landed with a jangle on the grate to her cell. They tottered there a moment, and then fell. She caught them in her outstretched hand.

"I don't believe it," she said. "How did you get keys? And how did you know what cell I was in?"

"You *are* the only source of light in the room. It's kind of hard to miss," Eli said. "As for the first part, who do you think you're dealing with? I'm Eli Monpress, the—"

"Greatest thief in the world. Yes, I know," Miranda sighed, looking up at the lock high, high overhead. "How am I supposed to use these?"

"I can't do everything for you," Eli said. "Figure it out, and do it fast. The duke could come in at any moment."

"Right," Miranda grumbled. "No pressure." She looked around at the walls for anything she could use as a grip to climb, but they were smooth, almost glossy, and she couldn't find so much as a hairline fracture. Jumping was out of the question. Even standing on tiptoe on the wooden bucket, stretching with all her might, she couldn't reach the halfway mark. She put her fists on her hips, scanning the cell. There had to be a way.

Her roving eyes stopped on the bucket under her feet. It was wide and low like a wash bucket, which was probably what it had been before being repurposed. It was made of cheap, light wood, but the joints were tight and waxed to hold water. Suddenly, she began to smile.

"Mellinor," she said, "could you flood this cell?"

"Theoretically," the water answered. "It's dry, but I could probably get enough water out of the air to do it, but I thought we weren't going to risk the powder."

"We're not." Miranda grinned and clunked her heel against the bucket.

She felt the water's attention flit down to the floor, and then Mellinor heaved a sigh like a tide. "Miranda, be reasonable. I don't think that thing is buoyant enough to float, let alone support you. Even if it did, I'd be turning the cell into a pool of toxic sludge. One slip and you'd be paralyzed forever."

"That's just a risk we'll have to take," Miranda said. She patted her chest where the water's glow was the brightest and gave her spirit a confident smile. "If any water can float this bucket safely to the top, it's you."

"Flattery might work on the dog, but it gets you

nowhere with me," the water grumbled. "I'll try, but only if you understand that once we start, we can't stop. I can't just send the water away again if it has nowhere to drain."

Miranda flipped the keys over in her hand. "All you have to do is get me to the grate. I'll take it from there."

"All right," Mellinor said. "Brace yourself."

Miranda stepped into the bucket. "Ready," she said.

"The undersides of your wrists are clean, so I'll use those." Mellinor's voice was moving through her, collecting at her hands. "Roll up your sleeve and hold out your arm."

Miranda did as he asked, holding her hands out in front of her. What happened next was painless, but almost too intense to watch. The water spirit poured from the clean skin of her lower arms, flowing out of her pores like milk squeezed through cheesecloth. It hit the ground with a great splash, sending a splatter of the poison dust onto her skirt. Miranda closed her eyes and thanked whatever luck there was that she'd chosen the dress with thick, long skirts. Under her feet, the bucket groaned as water flowed around it, yet it did not start to float. Mellinor was completely out of her now, and she pulled her arms back, carefully holding them away from the parts of her dress that were still dry and dusty. The water kept rising as Mellinor pulled moisture from the air, the tiny specks of water too small to have consciousness, and into his body. When the water was less than a finger's width from the lip of the bucket, the wooden slats beneath her feet finally began to wobble. The bucket left the ground with a pitch that made Miranda scramble. After that, she braced herself against the stone with both arms, using the straight walls as a guide as Mellinor gently floated her bucket up.

Even with Mellinor's glow, the foaming water was filthy and foul smelling. Balancing became more and more difficult the higher they went, as the bucket began to bob on the swirling current. Miranda flailed her arms, keeping upright by pushing herself off the walls, first one way, then another, as the waves took her. Just when she'd finally gotten the rhythm of it, the game changed. She felt wetness in her boots. When she looked down between sways, she noticed about an inch of water on the low end of her makeshift boat.

Miranda gasped and jerked away, causing the bucket to pitch, and she almost fell in completely. She caught herself at the last moment, bracing against the wall as the water kept rising. Now that the water had found a way in, more and more of it was pushing up through the bucket's cracks. Miranda bit her lip. Another moment and it would be up to her ankles. It was time to take a risk.

The grate was right above her, though still a foot out of reach. Before she could psych herself out, Miranda jumped. She jumped straight up, toppling the sinking bucket with her momentum. For a moment, her reaching hands caught nothing. Then her fingers slammed into the iron bars of the grate and she held tight.

"Mellinor!" she cried, grabbing the bars with her other hand as well and pulling her legs up. "Stop the water!"

The water stopped instantly, and for a moment Miranda hung there, gasping for breath as she clung to the bars. Only a moment, though, and then she was on the move again, pulling herself along the grate until she was right beside the iron padlock. It took several tries to find the right key, and then a great deal of pushing once she found it, for the lock was trying its best not to give in. But, in the end, purpose overwhelmed even spirit determination, and the lock snapped open. Unfortunately, in her hurry to get out, Miranda had neglected to determine which direction the grate opened. As it happened, it opened inward, something she found out very quickly when the grate swung down, taking her with it.

She yelped as the grate swung wildly, slamming her against the wall and knocking her breath out. But the hinges hadn't been oiled in a while, and the grate, after its initial bout of movement, creaked to a halt, leaving her startled, upside down, and dangling mere inches above the foul water.

"Miranda," Eli whispered frantically. "Are you all right?"

"More or less," Miranda groaned, pulling herself around the grate. She climbed up the lattice of iron bars and then, with a final heave, onto the stone floor of the prison itself. The moment she hit flat rock, she flopped over, gasping, and didn't move for at least a minute.

"Well," Eli said, his voice floating through the dark, "at least it's never dull, being with me."

"Shut up," Miranda gasped, pushing herself upright. Mellinor's light was dimmer, thanks to the gallons of filthy water he had commandeered, but it was still enough to see by. As she'd expected, she was in a prison, though a strange one. It was all one long room with a wide variety of equipment, from a selection of manacles to things she didn't recognize and didn't want to, bolted to the walls. There were not, however, any cells she could see.

"Where are you?"

"Turn left," Eli said. "Your left. I'm the door at the far back."

Miranda turned as he said and found herself facing what she'd thought was an iron wall. Looking closer, however, she picked out a small rectangle cut at eye level and, peering out through the gap, a pair of familiar blue eyes glittered in the dim light.

"Hello," Eli said. "Mind letting me out?"

Miranda stumbled over to the door. It didn't seem to have a lock or hinges or a handle or anything normally associated with doors.

"I see why you had to give me the keys," she said, running her finger along the smooth door crack. "I suppose the door isn't in a talking mood?"

"No more than anything else in this country," Eli said with a sigh.

"We'll need to knock it down, then," Miranda said. "Wait here."

"Like I could wait anywhere else."

Miranda ignored him, walking back over to the pit where Mellinor was still swirling. She knelt by the edge and peered into the water, which was already looking clearer.

"Losing the sediment?"

"As much as I can," the water rumbled. "This stuff feels awful. It's all slick and heavy, and whatever personality it had before is long gone thanks to the processing. I see why they use it to kill rats."

Miranda grimaced. "Glad I didn't fall in it. Think you've got enough water to knock down a door?"

"That depends on the door," Mellinor said, swelling up in a wave and looking where she gestured. It studied the door for a moment and then vanished back into the pit.

"Tell the thief to get ready," he called, his watery voice echoing up from the bottom of the cell.

"I've been ready," Eli called back. His voice was farther away now, and Miranda guessed he was pressing himself against the back of his cell. "Just do it."

Mellinor gushed and thundered, but right before he erupted in a geyser, Eli cried "Wait!"

The water stopped and Miranda groaned in frustration. "What?"

"It occurs to me," Eli said, "that the duke was probably prepared for me, a trapped and notorious wizard thief, to do something desperate, like Enslave the door holding me in. Before you knock it down, you might check for traps."

"Traps?" Miranda said. "What kind of traps could he have against Enslavement?"

"Humor me?" Eli said sweetly.

Miranda shook her head and walked back over to the door. She didn't see anything, just the iron wall of a door set into the stone. Still, she ran her fingers along all the seams anyway, just to be sure. She was about to tell the thief he was being paranoid when she felt something unusual at the very top of the door. A thin bump, almost like a wire, ran up from the top of the door to the stone ceiling. Standing on tiptoe, she followed it with her fingers until she hit a loose brick in a wall that didn't have any bricks. Frowning, she reached up gently with both hands and gave the brick a tug. It came away easily, revealing a large metal tin attached to the wire she'd followed. She lifted the tin down gently. It was heavy in her hands and sloshing with a liquid she could already guess wasn't water. Sure enough, it was full to the brim with a black, inky substance Miranda recognized from when Mellinor's water first touched the powder in her cell. It was the poison, and from the look of it, very concentrated. If Eli had Enslaved the door or opened it or busted it down in any way, this stuff would have drenched him, paralyzing him completely. A good thief catch, she had to admit, much better than burning oil or anything that could kill or disfigure. The best bounty depended on him being alive and recognizable.

Very, very carefully, Miranda emptied the tin in the far corner of the prison, standing back as the black liquid pooled in a low spot on the stone. When it was all gone, she went back to Mellinor and told Monpress to get in position.

"Whenever you're ready," he called back.

Miranda gave the signal and the water burst up in a geyser, shooting out of the pit before turning in midair, like water in a pipe, and barreling straight for Eli's cell door. It hit the iron like a hammer and the metal squealed, but didn't give way. The water wasn't finished, though. Mellinor gathered himself in the door's cracks, pushing his water between the stone and the metal. With no hinges, the door depended on its resolve to stay upright, but no resolve was strong enough to hold with water in every crevice. It clung for a few moments more, and then, with a defeated squeal, the door fell forward, crashing to the ground.

Almost before it hit, Eli jumped out. He was dirty and pale, his short black hair standing up at all angles, but he was beaming as he grabbed Miranda's hand and gave it a vigorous shake.

"I knew I could count on you," he said, clasping her

hand tightly in his. "I always told Josef, if there's one Spiritualist with her head on right, it's Mira—"

He was interrupted by the clink of a lock closing. Eli looked down. The hand that was shaking Miranda's now had a manacle around its wrist, the other end of which Miranda was fastening around her own. It was one of the manacles from the rack on the wall, and she locked it in place with a key from the key ring he'd given her before tossing the entire ring into the pit of her former cell.

"Eli Monpress," she said, grinning like her ghosthound, "you are now under the authority of the Spirit Court."

Eli looked down at his wrist, wiggling his hand against the tight, sharp, metal band. "That was a dirty trick."

Miranda didn't stop smiling. She held out her hand, and Mellinor blasted himself against the prison's outer door, popping the hinges. The door fell over with a squeal of metal on stone, and Mellinor returned to Miranda, leaving the excess water he had gathered to drain away back into Miranda's cell.

Eli watched as the keys vanished under a layer of filthy, poisoned water. "A *very* dirty trick," he grumbled as she dragged him out into the hall.

"I don't want to hear it," she said, walking quickly and quietly, using Mellinor's light to guide her. "You're the master of dirty tricks."

"I thought you were above all that," he said, letting her drag him. "And you *know* it's not going to work."

"Maybe not for long," she said, "but if I can keep you under control for even an hour, it will be worth it." She came to a stop at another door, a wooden one this time, blocking the entire hall. It was locked, of course, with a padlock that looked very similar to the one on her cell.

"Well," Eli said. "I doubt your little spout spirit there has enough water to bash this one in. If only we still had the keys."

Miranda silenced him with a jab to the ribs and pressed her ear against the door. She could hear shouting on the other side, shouting and guard whistles. They didn't seem to be coming her way, though. She bent down lower to examine the lock when the door rattled softly. Miranda jumped, slapping her hand over Eli's mouth as she pressed them back into the wall. The door rattled again, and there was an almost inaudible click as the lock popped open.

Miranda dampened Mellinor's light to nearly nothing and then reached up to grabbed an unlit torch from the wall bracket above her. She brandished the torch like a bat as the door opened. The moment a head came into view, she braced herself and brought her makeshift weapon down with all the force she could muster.

A second before it would have conked his head, her target dodged. He spun, a shadow in the dark hall, grabbing her arm as he went. She barely had time to gasp before she was on the floor with her arm wrenched behind her and the stranger's knee in her back.

"Well," a cultured voice whispered just above her head. "Eli, what are you doing, letting the lady go first?"

The pressure vanished from Miranda's back, and she felt the chain jerk as Eli rolled over on the floor beside her.

"*Letting her go first?*" the thief sputtered. "Whose idea do you think this was?"

The man, whoever he was, ignored Eli completely, and a black-gloved hand swooped down to help Miranda to her feet.

"Apologies, my dear," he said kindly. "The boy never could learn manners."

Miranda took the hand gingerly, very confused, and lifted her head to see a tall, thin man in late middle age with a handsome, cultured smile wearing wrapped clothes in varying shades of black.

"Giuseppe Monpress," he said, before she could ask. "You must be Miranda. Gin has told us all about you."

"Gin?" she said, her voice rising in a rush of hope. "Is he here? What do you mean you're Monpress?"

"It's not a terribly uncommon name," the man said. "And your hound is currently making a fine distraction running circles around the duke's men. Now"—he took her arm, the one that wasn't chained to Eli, whom the man seemed to have forgotten—"we should hurry. The duke's a clever man. He'll tear away from the ruse soon enough. We've got a little time before Josef and Nico's cavalry shows up, however. Meeting you here has put me ahead of schedule."

"Well, good for you," Eli said, elbowing his way between them. "I, however, am in a hurry to miss my date with the duke, so if you don't mind..."

He made a series of gestures toward the door. The older Monpress shrugged and, gesturing for Miranda to go ahead, let Eli lead the way up the narrow stairs to the maze of tunnels that ran below the citadel, speaking up only to correct the thief when he was taking them in entirely the wrong direction.

CHAPTER
18

Josef and Nico snuck through the empty streets. Above them, lights flickered behind the wobbly glass windows in the upper stories of the lovely houses, but Josef and Nico saw no one. Though it was still early, all the restaurants were dark and closed, same with the taverns, and even the inns. Whatever command of the duke's had cleared the streets earlier was obviously still in effect, and now that Eli was caught, even the patrols were off the streets, leaving Nico and Josef to run in the shadows behind the watchful lamps and toward the dark river and the docks beyond.

"At least the paving stones aren't trying to trip us any-more," Josef grumbled, stomping harder on the cobbled street than was strictly necessary. "I guess Eli was right when he said the spirits couldn't keep it up forever."

"Or they just aren't looking for us," Nico said. "Spirits are famously bad at finding nonwizards. Humans all look the same to most spirits."

"Lucky us," Josef said, hopping up the stairs toward

the tall bridge that was the only way across the river. They kept to the back line of storehouses, ducking behind crates and barrels until they reached the dusty, neglected warehouse they'd slept in the night before. Josef flipped the rusty lock with impatient fingers. He could almost feel the Heart inside, waiting for him. The door opened with a groan, and they slipped inside.

With the docks empty, there were no fires burning in the braziers outside. Without the ambient light, the warehouse was ink black, forcing Josef to stop at the threshold and let his eyes adjust. Nico went on ahead of him, striding confidently into the dark. That was typical. The dark never seemed to slow her down, which was why he jerked to attention when her soft footsteps stopped.

His hand dropped to the sword at his hip. He could just barely see Nico in front of him, a spot of darker shadow gone completely rigid. Keeping one hand on his sword and the other on the dagger in his sleeve, Josef crept forward until he was pressed against Nico's back.

"Someone's here." Her voice was scarcely more than a breath.

Josef stared over her shoulders, but he saw nothing but shadowy outlines and dusty beams. She pointed at the darkness ahead of them, and Josef squinted. He could make out details now, the edges of crates, the forgotten tools lining the walls, and, directly ahead of them, the dark, solid shape of the Heart of War leaning against the corner, right where he'd left it. He was about to ask Nico to be more specific when something shifted in the dark, and then he saw it as well. Sitting on the stack of crates beside the Heart was an enormous, dark shape. At first Josef thought his eyes were playing tricks on him, that the shadows were stretched out, for no man could be that large. Then the shape jumped down, landing on the wooden floorboards with a crash that rattled the building to its foundation.

Josef stumbled, gripping the hilts of his sheathed swords, white-knuckled as the dark figure stretched out his hand, pointing one long finger, not at Josef, but at Nico, who was trembling in front of him. The man, for Josef could now see it was a man, smiled, his teeth glinting in the dark, and spoke a command.

Don't move.

Even Josef, spirit deaf, could tell the words were more than words. The moment they left the man's lips, Nico went down. She fell hard, straight down without catching herself, landing on the floor with a bone-splitting crack. Josef was at her side in an instant, but wherever he touched her, her coat was as hard as iron. Even the air felt like stone around her skin. Her body was rigid, the frantic darting of her eyes and the slight noise of her panicked breaths the only sign she was still alive.

Josef was still trying to get her up when he heard the clank of enormous footsteps coming toward him. Leaving Nico with a curse, he drew his swords with a singing scrape of metal and turned to face the enormous man closing the distance between them.

But the man wasn't looking at him. He didn't even seem to notice the blades in Josef's hands. He was staring at the girl lying on the floor.

"You were hard to find, little demon." His deep voice was still terrible, but it was at least mostly human this time. "I don't know how you hid yourself, but no matter. No one hides from the League forever."

Josef stepped over Nico and took up position between her and the approaching man. "What did you do to her?" he shouted. It looked like wizard stuff to him, but Eli had always told him wizards couldn't control other people.

"League benefit," the man said, walking slowly. "I gave the spirits around her something to do. The League is the arm of the White Lady, so their nature binds them to my command when it comes to demon hunting. They'll stay like that, squishing her down, until I tell them otherwise."

Josef had no clue what the man was talking about, but he had other worries. Now that he was out of the deep shadows, the man wasn't as large as Josef had initially thought, but he was no less a monster. He stood seven feet tall at least, and was wide enough to make his height seem normal. His head was shaved clean, and scars that stood out white against his deeply tanned skin ran from the top of his skull to the tops of his bushy eyebrows. A long cut had scarred his face into a permanent sneer, and his nose was crooked from multiple breaks. He looked like a man who'd spent his life brawling, and he carried his enormous frame with a fighter's grace. Across his bare chest, he wore a wide, red sash festooned with a host of strange objects—jeweled rings, sword hilts, necklaces, talismans, and even, Josef cringed, a preserved hand curled in a fist.

Above the ghastly collection, a long black coat with a high collar sat awkwardly on the man's monstrous shoulders. The sleeves were ripped off, revealing muscular arms covered in mismatched tattoos. The coat looked too small for him, but anything would look small on this man. Anything, that is, except the sword he wore at his side. That suited him perfectly. Its pommel was the size of an orange, and the hilt was wrapped in thick leather until it was almost as large as the guard above it. He wore it naked, with no sheath, the dark blade out and lying bare against his coat so that the wicked, toothed edge tore at the fabric until the dark cloth was nearly in tatters. It was eerily familiar, but the blade looked so at home on the man's hip that it took Josef a few moments to recognize it as the sword he'd seen in Slorn's workshop.

"Ah," Sted said, laying a hand on the sword's hilt. "You like my new baby, yes? You must be the demon's guardian." He looked Josef up and down. "Aren't you a bit puny to be the master of the Heart of War?"

Josef ignored him. "Who are you? What are you here for?"

"What kind of question is that?" Sted cackled. "Don't you see the jacket?" He flipped his torn collar. "I'm Berek Sted, best killer in the League of Storms, and I'm here to kill the demon."

Josef raised his swords. "You'll find that harder than you think."

"Really?" Sted laughed. "I like you, swordsman. Tell you what, I'll make you a deal. See, I kind of owe you. When I got to Gaol, I couldn't find the girl. I've never been good at finding demons and all that League mumbo jumbo. But I could feel the Heart." His scarred face grew almost wistful. "Any swordsman worth the name can feel a sword like that. It's a force of nature. So I followed it and waited and, sure enough, here you are. I hate owing people, so how about I make you a deal to call it even?"

Josef scowled. "What kind of deal?"

"A fighting chance," Sted said. "It goes like this: You

give me a good fight, something to make me remember why I put up with the League. If you beat me, I'll let the girl go and tell old Alric I couldn't find the demon."

Josef stared at the man. "Wait," he said. "You're a member of the League of Storms, and you're offering to let the demon go if I fight you and win?"

Sted shrugged. "The League is work, you know? You look like you know how to give a good fight, and I always say pleasure before work. Anyway," he chuckled, "it's not like I'll *lose*."

Josef glanced down at Nico. She was still on the floor, prone and flat against the boards. He did a quick calculation in his head. They had a little under half an hour before they were supposed to meet the elder Monpress and Eli at the wall. Not much time, but it wasn't like he could ask the man to wait. He'd just have to be quick. In any case, he thought as his hand tightened on his sword, wasn't this the kind of challenge he'd been looking for?

"All right," Josef said. He bent over, laying the wrapped Fenzetti on the floor beside Nico. "You've got your deal."

Sted's scarred face broke into an enormous grin. "Wonderful! If you put up a good enough show, I might even add something of yours to my trophies." He cackled and pounded his chest, making the grim collection on his sash clatter.

"I'll pass," Josef said, dropping into a defensive crouch.

"Suit yourself," Sted said. "Start whenever you're ready."

Josef balanced on the balls of his feet, swords out. The Heart was on the other side of the room still, but that was fine. He was going to win this without the Heart's help. Across the room, Sted watched him, arms slack at his sides. Josef chose his spot carefully, a stretch of unguarded muscle to the left of Sted's ribs, just above his stomach. When he could almost feel his sword cutting the man's flesh, he sprang.

He threw himself forward, moving with a speed that would have impressed Coriano had the other swordsman been alive to see it, and dashed hard to the right, making a feint toward Sted's leg. Then, at the last second, he swung his swords around to bite into his true mark, plunging the flashing steel straight into Sted's flesh. But as the blow came down, Josef knew something was wrong. Sted wasn't blocking. It wasn't that he'd seen through the feint; he hadn't even moved. The man just stood there, smiling as Josef rushed him, not even flinching when both of Josef's swords landed in his undefended side.

Josef felt a shock move up his arm as the strike hit, but it was all wrong. The impact was far too strong. It was like hitting stone, not flesh. Josef slid with the blow, letting his momentum carry him past Sted. The moment he was behind the larger man, Josef flipped his swords, turning and thrusting them into Sted's back. Again, the blades struck true, and again that horrible reverberation went up his arm, only this time it was accompanied by a sharp crack. Josef's eyes widened, and he jumped, landing in a crouch on a crate several feet away.

He held his swords in front of him, grimacing at the two inches missing from the top of his left-hand weapon. The tip had snapped clean off, leaving a square nub where the point should have been. But Sted, who had just taken four killing blows, stood the same as ever. He looked over his shoulder at Josef, and then reached behind him, picking the broken tip of Josef's sword out of his coat. Beneath the holes the swords had torn when they entered, his skin was smooth and whole.

When he turned, Josef saw Sted's side was also uninjured, the skin not even reddened from the strike. Sted's grin grew wider as he watched the realization sink in.

"You know," he said slowly, tossing the broken sword tip casually in his hand, "when you get an invitation to join the League of Storms, they give you a gift, sort of a consolation prize for leaving your life behind. Some guys choose a longer life, some choose an endless supply of beautiful women, some just want to get drunk with no consequences. *I* didn't want any of that. Instead, I asked for skin that couldn't be cut." He grabbed the sword tip midtoss and jabbed the broken end straight into the soft flesh below his wrist. Josef flinched, but the jagged metal slid harmlessly over Sted's skin without leaving so much as a scratch. Point made, Sted tossed the sword tip over his shoulder, where it clattered across the unseen crates and vanished into the dark.

"I probably should have told you that before you agreed to the fight," Sted said, sinking into a combat stance for the first time. "You can still run if you want."

Josef's answer to that was to lob his broken sword right at Sted's head. Sted dodged easily, but Josef was already moving, running along the crates. He flipped a knife into his empty hand and, before Sted could turn to face him, launched himself at the larger man.

Again, Sted didn't try to dodge. Josef came in high, aiming for Sted's shoulder. But then, at the very last second, he switched up and thrust his knife hand up, stabbing not for the shoulder, but straight at Sted's left eye.

Sted caught Josef's arm before the blow could land, and he heaved the swordsman off. Josef landed with a crash in a pile of crates, filling the air with dust. Sted watched where he had landed cautiously, but when the dust cleared, there was Josef. He was sitting cross-legged on the splintered crates with both his blades still in his hands, and looking enormously pleased with himself.

"So," he said, grinning. "Judging from that little display, uncuttable skin doesn't account for the eyes. I wonder what other parts your 'gift' missed?"

Sted grinned back. "Why don't you come see?"

Josef leaped forward. This time, he went for Sted's grinning mouth, holding his sword like a spear. Just as he was about to land, Sted drew his own sword, the great iron monster at his side, and met Josef's blow with one of his own. The two swords crashed in a shower of sparks, and Josef's blade shattered. Sted carried the blow, striking Josef straight across his now-unguarded chest.

Josef grunted as the jagged blade bit through his shirt and into his skin. He felt his ribs crack as the impact of Sted's strike blew through him, and then he was flying backward in free fall. He hit the wall with another blow that knocked what little breath he had left from his lungs and toppled to the ground. For a moment, he felt nothing, saw nothing, heard nothing but the blood pounding in his ears. Then, finally, his lungs thundered back to life, and pain exploded through him. He lay gasping for a moment, barely aware of Sted's hulking shape as the man came to stand over him, holding his enormous, jagged sword in one steady hand.

"The skin wasn't the only gift I got." Sted's voice was far away as Josef tried to roll over, tried and failed. He looked up, his blurry vision barely making out the shape of Sted's sword as he held it over Josef's prone body.

"Meet Dunolg," the enormous man grinned, "the Iron Avalanche."

Josef groaned and dropped his broken sword. Normal blades were no use against an awakened sword. He'd already learned that the hard way. Nothing for it now, he thought bitterly. He'd have to use the Heart. But the great sword was all the way across the room, and Sted was already raising his blade for the final blow.

Then, just as Josef was trying to think of a way to dodge, his fingers brushed familiar fabric, and he had an idea. Sted dropped his sword down on Josef's bleeding chest, but just before the blow landed, Josef grabbed the wrapped bundle of the Fenzetti blade and held it over him. Sted's sword crashed down, the jagged edge meeting the wrapped fabric with a deep, golden sound, like a great bell. For a moment, the swordsmen stared at each other as the sound rang through them, and the cloth fell away to reveal the bone-white blade holding back the jagged black one.

Josef used the moment of confusion to roll out of the way, sliding the Fenzetti's dull blade along Sted's with a shower of red sparks. He came up on his feet with the sword in front of him. His breath was back, his chest aching but bearable, and, most important, he was holding a sword Sted couldn't break. The Fenzetti sat awkward and heavy in his hands, but he held it steady, watching as Sted turned to face him.

"What kind of sword is that?" Sted spat. "It doesn't even have a cutting edge."

"A cutting edge is hardly necessary for you," Josef

answered. "Since I can't cut you, we'll see how you stand up to bludgeoning."

Sted glared at him. "I didn't give you this deal so that we could play-fight with dull sticks." He stood aside, pointing at the enormous black blade in the corner, still leaning where Josef had left it. "Pick up the Heart," Sted growled. "Stop this dancing and give me a real fight."

Josef just grinned and brandished the Fenzetti blade, leaning in to balance the skewed weight. "The Heart is my sword," he said. "I use it when I choose. You challenged me; you fight by my rules."

Sted stabbed his sword into the wooden floor. "That's how you want it?" He took off his coat, throwing it on the ground. It landed with a great crash, and Josef realized with a grimace that it was weighted, enormously so if the dent it made on the floor was any indication.

"That's how you want it," Sted shouted again, flexing his now-bare shoulders and rocking his head from side to side, cracking his neck in a hail of popping bones. "All right, little swordsman." He grabbed his sword again. "Here I come."

Josef barely had time to raise his sword before Sted was on top of him, the jagged blade flashing and flying across the Fenzetti's bone-white surface. He pushed Josef back, and back again, raining a flying onslaught of jagged teeth across the dull blade of the Fenzetti. It took every ounce of Josef's skill just to keep away, and even when Sted's openings were enormous, which was common, the man was throwing everything into his attack, and Josef couldn't break away from his defense long enough to take advantage of them. Sted was laughing now, pushing Josef back faster and faster with each blow, taunting him endlessly.

The Fenzetti, however, was living up to Slorn's promise. No matter how hard Sted attacked, no matter what angle his blade hit the uneven, bone-colored edge, the Fenzetti never faltered. It formed an impenetrable wall in front of Josef, so long as he was fast enough to block. That, Josef thought, gritting his teeth, was the hard part. The sword's unevenness and bad balance pulled at his muscles, but he didn't dare slow down. Still, he was quickly using up his strength, and at this rate it was only a matter of time before he made a mistake. When that happened, it would be over.

"Yes," Sted said, laughing, as his sword flew. "I know what you're thinking. I've seen it in every man's eyes, right before the end." He thrust straight and then cut left, forcing Josef to overreach in the scramble to guard his shoulder. "It's just one missed block, and down you go." Sted switched up his attack again. "After that, there's nothing left to do but butcher the girl. I'll cut the seed right out of her heart." Sted followed his words with a thrust that sent Josef spinning backward from the force.

Josef stumbled, looking for footing, and his feet touched something yielding. He threw his weight at the last minute and glanced down in surprise to see that he was standing over Nico. He hadn't realized they'd come back around the room. She was still exactly as she had fallen. Only her eyes moved. They looked at him, bright and wide and filled with an emotion he couldn't name but that he felt all the way to his core. The desperate need to fight, to live.

Sted was charging again, and Josef jumped to the side, leading him away from Nico, but the look in her eyes followed him, and, slowly, shame began to grow in his mind.

All this time, from the moment he first found her dying in the mountains, she'd struggled to keep living, to never lose the battle against the dark creature that lived inside her. And here he was, playing, throwing that struggle away because of his pride. Because he didn't want the Heart to win for him again.

He looked down at the crooked sword in his hands, at the white metal that turned awkwardly in his grip. He couldn't win like this. He wasn't good enough to win like this, not yet, but that didn't mean he was free to lose. After all—he turned, letting Sted drive him toward the far corner of the warehouse—this wasn't just his battle anymore.

On Sted's next blow, Josef let go of the Fenzetti. It flew out of his hands, and Sted, not expecting the sudden lack of resistance, fell off balance. It was only a moment, but it was enough. Josef sprang backward, reaching for what he couldn't see but knew was there. For a moment he felt nothing, and then his fingers closed around the wrapped hilt of the Heart of War. Grinning, he brought the black blade around. The cloth unraveled like a veil, fluttering away into the dark to reveal the black, pitted blade. Its matte surface was impossibly old, crisscrossed with the scars of ancient battles no one but the blade itself remembered anymore. It sat confident and comfortable in Josef's hand, the blade perfectly balanced against his weight, ready.

Sted grinned like a mad dog and, swinging his sword in an arc, took up a fencing position, the first Josef had seen him use.

"Now," Sted growled. "Now we will fight. Now we will have the kind of battle worth dying for."

As he spoke, his sword began to glow brighter. Its light swelled red-silver, the color of blood in cold water, filling the room. The Heart, however, stayed as dark as ever, but the feel of it, the endless strength, flowed in a torrent down Josef's arms as he raised the blade for a swing.

What happened next happened in an instant. Josef charged forward, gripping the Heart's long hilt with both hands. He was moving with the Heart's impossible speed now, the kind of speed where the air is like jelly, and everything, every step, every heartbeat, slows to a painful crawl. Even so, even as he barreled down on top of him, Josef saw Sted lift his sword, setting it across his chest to block the Heart's blow. It was the first defensive position he'd taken in the entire fight, and he took it just in time as the Heart, and the mountain of force behind it, crashed into him.

Time snapped back as they collided, and there was an enormous crash. Sparks flew from the clashing blades while wood and debris went everywhere as Sted's braced feet ripped the floorboards to pieces, fighting to stop Josef's momentum. Finally, halfway across the room from where Josef had struck, they stopped in a great cloud of dust. Josef stood panting. He could barely see anything, but the Heart was still in his hand, and he could see Sted's crouched outline below him. It was over. No sword, awakened or not, had ever taken a full-on blow from the Heart and survived. And yet, even as the thought floated through his head, the dust began to settle, and his eyes widened. There, beneath the Heart's blade, was Sted's jagged sword, bent where the Heart had struck, but not broken. Its light shone brighter and hungrier than ever, and behind it was Sted, baring his teeth in triumph.

"Is that all?" he roared.

And then he pushed back, throwing his tremendous strength into his sword until Josef was the one crouching under him.

Josef rolled before the man's weight could crush him completely, his mind spinning wildly. How had his attack not worked? The Heart was unbeatable. It never lost. Sted should be dead, but he was on the attack wilder than ever, and Josef had to scramble to knock his blows away. Once again, Josef was falling back, but the Heart was not the unbalanced stick the Fenzetti had been. It danced in his grip, blocking Sted's blows and then snaking up to strike the gaping openings in Sted's defense. But even the Heart's blows slid off Sted's impenetrable skin. Josef struck again and again, harder and harder, but it did no good. Sted's skin remained unmarred. Sted's attacks, however, were beginning to get through. The long fight with the Fenzetti, his earlier wound, the enormous initial blow with the Heart, it was all taking its toll. Josef could feel himself getting slower, and cuts began to appear on his body as his parries grew closer and closer.

With every new cut, Sted's smile fell farther, and his blows grew more vicious. "Come on," he said, dragging his jagged sword across Josef's shoulder, leaving a deep trail of jagged cuts. "Come *on*. You're just swinging your sword. Fight me! Show me the Heart of War!"

He crashed an overhanded blow down on Josef's head as he said this, forcing Josef to duck and roll. Josef was openly panting now. Blood ran down his sides, hot and slick under his shirt, but there was no time to stanch it. Every ounce of strength went into keeping Sted's sword away.

"How disappointing," Sted sneered, catching the Heart's edge and dragging Josef up until they were eye to eye. "You're not even a swordsman, are you? You're just a man with a *sword*."

He screamed the last word, matching it with a thrust at Josef's unprotected stomach. This time, it was too fast. Josef couldn't dodge. The jagged sword bit into him, and pain exploded. His vision went dark, his mind blanked out, and only his clenched muscles kept the Heart in his hand. Breath came in ragged gasps as he struggled to keep his eyes on Sted, yet he couldn't do anything, couldn't even raise his sword to block as Sted slowly, languidly, tossed him aside.

Josef landed on his stomach, the air crushed out his lungs, the Heart of War landing with a deep, resounding gong beside him. For a moment, Josef just lay there, not breathing, not moving, not knowing if he was dead or alive. Then air thundered back into his lungs, and reflex took over. He pressed his hand to his bleeding side, trying to stop his lifeblood from washing out onto the floor. He steadied his breaths and looked for his sword. It was right beside him, inches from his fingers. He forced himself to reach out. The Heart could get him through almost anything. All he had to do was touch it.

But when his fingers were a hair's breadth away from the Heart's hilt, an enormous boot came down on his wrist, crushing his hand and pinning it to the ground.

Sted looked down at him, his scarred face disappointed. "Just a man with a sword," he spat. "And to think the Heart of War chose someone like you." He knelt down and grabbed Josef by the hair, lifting his head up to whisper in his ear. "This next blow is for your sword. An act of mercy. I'm going to set it free from such an unworthy master. Who knows"—he grinned against Josef's skin—"maybe it will choose me."

"The Heart wouldn't have anything to do with you," Josef growled, spitting the words.

Sted dropped him back onto the floor. "How would you know?" he said, turning Josef over with his foot so that he was lying on his back. "You aren't even strong enough to protect a little girl."

And with that, he brought his jagged sword down on Josef's stomach. Josef cried out in pain, a hitching, sobbing sound. Sted just held him down with his boot, pushing the sword in deeper. When Josef stopped struggling, Sted pulled his blade out and slung it in an arc, flinging Josef's blood across the room.

He picked up his cast-off coat and wiped his blade clean. Then he turned and started toward Nico, the clomp of his boots the only noise in the warehouse. He walked with his sword out, the curved blade awake and glowing hungry red. Yet, for all that he was her death walking to meet her, the girl wasn't looking at him. Her eyes were focused on the swordsman's body.

Subtly, almost imperceptibly, her hand twitched. Her head moved very slightly off the ground before being slammed down again. Her leg kicked a fraction, like a child's in the womb. Sted saw this, and walked a little faster.

"I'm impressed you can move under the weight of the command," he said. "I'm told that takes a tremendous amount of will. You must have been a very strong wizard before the demon took you."

Nico didn't even look at him as he spoke, but her hand

edged forward, her short nails digging into the wooden floor.

"You'll only hurt yourself if you keep trying," Sted warned. He was a dozen feet from her now. "I'm no wizard, but the order you're under has nothing to do with spirit talking. It's a tool given to League members by the Lord of Storms himself, a sharing of his gift from the Shepherdess, or some such. I'm told it commands the spirit world's inborn hatred of demons to create a crushing weight. Supposedly, with practice, a skilled League member can control its strength, make it less painful on the victim." He stopped just short of her outstretched hand, grinning wide. "I never saw much point in that."

He nudged her with his boot, turning her over, and held his sword above her exposed throat, just above her silver collar, which, for once, lay perfectly still against her skin. "Time to go to work," he said, sighing. "May whatever is left of your human soul find peace with your precious swordsman in the next life."

He swung his sword up in a whistling arc, and then brought it down. A great cloud of dust and debris went up as the jagged blade crashed through the girl and into the floor, obliterating everything. The deed done, Sted straightened up, swinging his sword back to inspect the damage. But as the dust began to clear, his confident smile faded. He could see the black outline of the girl's body, clearly crushed by his sword, and yet there was no smell of fresh blood. He waved his arms frantically to clear the last of the dust, and his teeth clenched in a snarl. There, in the crater his sword had made, flat and empty as a shed skin, was the girl's coat.

He whirled around just in time to see the girl,

surprisingly thin and bony in her torn shirt and threadbare trousers, clutch the swordman's body before vanishing again into the shadows.

Sted snatched the shed coat with the point of his sword and tossed it away. "What are you?" he bellowed. "A damned cicada? Come out and fight!"

Silence was his answer.

On the other side of the warehouse, behind a stack of crates she'd scouted out yesterday as a potentially useful hiding place, Nico gently set Josef's body on the floor. At some point after Sted's final blow, his hands had managed to grip the Heart, which was the only way she'd been able to move it. The black sword followed no hand but Josef's.

Quiet as a shadow, Nico pulled a length of dyed silk out of the crate beside her and wrapped Josef's wounds as best she could. She worked quickly, tugging the bandage with shaking hands. Even though he was spirit deaf, Sted was a League hunter. Without her coat, it was only a matter of minutes before he found her.

She looped the crooked bandage over Josef's chest one last time and tied it tight. The blood was already seeping through, but it would have to do. She was out of time.

Nico ran her hand over Josef's face, feeling his dim, ragged breath on her fingers. "Keep breathing," she whispered. "This time, I'll save you."

With that, she vanished, skipping through the shadows to the far end of the warehouse. She reappeared behind the pile of splintered wood Josef had crashed into earlier. Sted's back was to her. He was standing near where she'd hidden Josef, studying the crates. Soundlessly, Nico reached up to the line of dusty tools hanging from the rack above her and took down a heavy iron hammer. It woke instantly at her touch, and she could feel it getting ready to scream.

"Don't." The command was a whisper, but it was more than enough. The hammer froze in place, terrified, and Nico lifted it to her mouth, her lips moving against the cold, trembling metal. "Strike him quietly and true," she whispered, "or I'll eat you whole."

She felt guilty as she spoke, and the image of Eli's serious face as he held her sleeve flashed through her mind. Nico crushed the feeling. The thief had had it easy. He didn't understand that survival meant doing what had to be done. Anyway, beating Sted and saving Josef meant far more to her than a stupid hammer. Decision made, she drew back her arm and, taking careful aim, threw the hammer as hard as she could. It flew unnaturally straight, balancing itself as it spun, and landed right at the base of Sted's skull.

The swordsman stumbled and roared, whirling around to face his attacker. This time, Nico didn't blink away. She stood her ground, staring Sted straight in the face as he raised his arm to throw the immobilization on her again.

"You said you wanted a fight," she growled, dropping into a crouch.

Sted's arm fell. "I don't like to fight girls," he said with a sneer. "But for that"—he kicked the fallen hammer—"I'll make an exception. I only hope you're more of a challenge than your guard, demon."

Nico's answer was to flit behind him and slam her fist into his back, right below his liver. Josef had already learned Sted was uncuttable, but every human had the same organs. Still, punching Sted was like punching a rock, and about as effective. The League man didn't even grunt. Instead, he spun with his blade, forcing Nico to skip away through the shadows or get sliced in half. She emerged panting on the other side of the room, shaking her hand to get the feeling back. Sted turned slowly to face her, looking cockier than ever.

Nico clenched her fists, pressing her buzzing manacles against her skin. Without her coat she could feel the spirits all around her, easy prey, easy power. She could feel the demon inside her waking, scenting food. The spirits were beginning to wake as well, to notice what she was, and she could feel the panic growing. She couldn't fight like this much longer, and from the look on his face, Sted knew it.

"Jump while you can," he said, walking toward her with terrible, slow steps. "Every power you use gives me more allies. Soon, you won't even have a place to stand."

As if to prove him right, the boards beneath her feet began to groan, working up the courage to snap and trap her. Nico leaped before they got the chance, blinking through the dark to the air above Sted's head. Sted just laughed and raised his sword to block.

At that moment, deep inside Nico, in the places she never went, something woke, and the wailing demon panic exploded all around her.

CHAPTER
19

The outside of the duke's citadel was utter chaos when Eli, Miranda, and the elder Monpress finally emerged from the tunnels below. Soldiers were running everywhere, carrying rope and spears, far too busy to notice three people in the shadows as they rushed to get to the square. Squinting into the dark, Miranda could see why. Even from this angle, she could see the cobblestones moving like waves, chasing something she couldn't see. There were clouds overhead as well, winds ripping across the sky, forming a tiny tornado right in front of the citadel. From the top battlements, she could hear the duke shouting orders, his voice carried far and wide by the spinning wind. He was shouting for them to catch something.

"Ah," Monpress said, locking the door again behind them. "Splendid."

"Splendid?" Miranda said, looking in horror as a sheet of roofing tiles flew off a nearby house at whatever was circling in the front courtyard. "This is utter madness."

"Chaos is the thief's best friend," Eli said with a shrug. "Where's our ride?"

"Busy, from the looks of it," Monpress said, pointing at the courtyard.

"Ride?" Miranda said. "Do you mean—"

She cut off midsentence as Gin appeared around the corner, followed by a hail of clay roofing tiles. He was running full tilt. They barely had time to jump out of the way before he barreled past. He gave Miranda a wink as he flashed by, and she saw at once what he was planning.

"Get in a line against the wall," she said, jerking Eli's chain and pushing Monpress with her other hand. "Be ready to jump on when I say so."

"Jump on?" Eli said. "You mean throw ourselves at the dog when he comes around again?"

"Pretty much," Miranda said, hiking up her skirt and tucking it under her belt so it wouldn't get tangled. "Get ready, here he comes."

They all whirled to look at Gin. He was still running full tilt away from them with the stones right on his tail. But just as he was about to hit the tall bank that separated the castle grounds from the river, he dropped to a crouch and skidded to a stop. The stones, not made for high-velocity anything, sailed straight over him, landing with a splash in the river beyond. The moment they were over his head, Gin was back on his feet racing toward Miranda. She held out her hands, motioning for Eli and Monpress to do the same. The ghosthound ran low, and as he passed they grabbed on to the thick fur of his back. Gin's momentum took them off their feet, and suddenly they were flying along with him down a side alley while the wind howled overhead.

"Letting yourself play decoy," Miranda said, digging her fingers in a little harder than was necessary as she climbed into position on his back. "That was a foolish thing to do, dog."

"Well, hello to you too," Gin panted. "Ask the old man if we're still going for the wall."

Miranda glared at him, but turned and relayed the question to the elder Monpress, who was helping Eli get into place.

"So far as I know," he said. "I haven't heard anything from Josef or Nico."

"You probably won't," Eli said, grabbing Gin's fur with both hands as the dog raced through the night. "Even if he sent a message, we'd never get anything through all this mess. I can barely hear myself think with the town like this."

He was right, Miranda thought with a grimace. The whole town seemed to be shouting all at once. And not just spirits, but guards and alarm whistles too. Gin had his ears back as he ran, taking a crazy path through the back alleys as he ran north and a little west, toward the wall.

"Wait," Miranda shouted. "We're escaping? What about my rings? I can't leave without my rings!"

"We can't go back for them now," Eli shouted over the din. "Not unless you want to fight the entire town."

"The duke took your rings?" Gin panted, alarmed.

"No, I think Hern did," Miranda answered. "We have to go back."

"Well, look at it this way," Eli said. "Now that you're out, those rings are the only power this Hern fellow has over you. He's certainly not going to risk them on something trivial."

"Oh, that's comforting," Miranda said, bending low on Gin's back. But the thief had a point. They couldn't turn around, not without getting killed. She didn't like it, but for now she'd get out, maybe try and make contact with the West Wind, get some backup. Maybe she could get word to Banage. Even if it came from an exile, the Spirit Court couldn't ignore something like this, and then the duke would *really* have something to worry about. Of course, she thought as she ducked under a shop sign that was swinging wildly at her head, they'd have to get out first.

Gin hopped over a low shed, and suddenly they were at the wall, still stretched to an impossible height and bristling with spikes. They ran along it, looking for some sign of Josef and Nico, a bashed-in bit of wall, some knocked-out guards, anything, but there was nothing. Gin slowed, panting, and sniffed the air.

"No good," he growled. "Neither the swordsman nor the girl has been anywhere near this place for hours."

"They've got to be somewhere," Eli said, looking around frantically. "It's not like Josef to be late for anything."

"Well, something must have happened," Gin snapped back, "because he's not here, and we shouldn't be much longer. This city's on the verge of tearing itself apart trying to do that man's bidding. I'd hate to see what it'd do to us."

"Wait," Miranda said suddenly, her eyes bright. "Hold on, you just gave me an idea." She stood up on the dog's back, looking out over the dark city. The streets glowed, some with lampposts, some with torch light from the pursuing guards, but in the distance, the river glittered dark and slow, strangely peaceful in the light of the half moon.

"Gin," she said, "we're going back to our first plan."

"What?" he said, then he paused. "Oh, I get you."

Miranda nodded. "Take us to the river."

"The river?" Eli cried as Gin launched himself back the way they had come. "Are you mad? The river's at the center of the mess we're trying to get out of!"

"You want to solve a problem," Miranda said, "you start at the top. Now be quiet." She jerked the chain holding them together. "Prisoners shouldn't talk this much."

The elder Monpress laughed at that and tipped his head to Miranda, who smiled back. Eli, seeing he was getting nowhere with these people, folded his arms over his chest and focused on not falling off as Gin wove a crazy path down to the river.

The Duke of Gaol stood on his battlements, shouting orders to his spirits as the lampposts signaled the ghost-hound's position. They had reached the wall already, but were turning back, probably realizing they were trapped.

Good, he thought. Let them scramble. He had other problems at the moment, starting with the one standing directly beside him.

"For the last time, Hern," Edward said, "go back to your tower."

Beside him, Hern went pale with anger, gripping the battlements with clenched fingers. "I will not," he said. "You promised me, Edward! You promised to keep that girl locked up, and then you go and throw her together with Monpress? What were you thinking?"

"If anyone should be angry, it's me." He glared at the

Spiritualist. "Helping you almost cost me my thief. If I hadn't taken precautions by keeping the city secure on multiple levels, both of our quarries would have flown by now. So save your bluster for your Court and kindly get out of my way. In case you haven't noticed, I have other problems besides Monpress slipping his leash."

As if on cue, a wind rose up from the south, and he turned to meet it.

"Othril," he said when he felt the wind on his face. "Report."

"The south docks are in a full demon panic," the wind said quickly. "Big one, too, though not as flashy as the treasury. I put up a quarantine as you ordered. Not even a cockroach is going to cross the boundary without your say-so. That should contain the panic somewhat, but you know we can't keep a lid on these things for long."

"We won't need to," Edward said. "This is a ploy by Monpress, a distraction for his escape. Now that he's out, it should be calming down."

Hern shook his head. "What kind of reckless idiot uses a demon panic to cover his escape?"

"When you hunt Monpress, you must be prepared for everything," Edward said. "Othril, follow Monpress and the Spiritualist girl. Now that they've realized the wall is trapped, they might try the river."

"That would be good for us," the wind said. "Fellbro's water will catch them like flies in honey."

"With Monpress you can only corral, never anticipate," Edward said. "Watch him and report to me at once if they change direction."

"And check for the girl as well," Hern added. "She must be contained."

Othril stopped midgust, and Hern felt the strange, itchy sensation of a powerful wind spirit staring at him. Edward, however, waved the wind away, and it blew into the night.

"Hern," Edward said when the wind was gone. "Never presume to give orders to my spirits again."

"Well," Hern said, shifting his hands so that his rings glittered menacingly, "you hadn't mentioned it, and I wanted to be sure you did not forget what you owed me, Edward."

The duke spun around and grabbed Hern's hands before the Spiritualist could move, squeezing his fingers until the gemstones dug painfully into Hern's flesh.

"You forget yourself," the duke whispered, his voice low and dangerous. "Never forget where you are. You might have sway in Zarin, but *I rule Gaol*. So long as you are on my lands, you obey *me*."

Hern was gasping in pain, his rings flashing under the duke's hands, but the duke's spirit was like a vise across them, and they could not leave. He held the Spiritualist like that until Hern nodded, falling to his knees. Only then did Edward release his grip.

"Do not make me remind you again," he said quietly, turning back to the battlements.

Hern retreated, grumbling empty threats under his breath as he slunk back to the far wall with as much dignity as he could muster. Edward ignored him. Hern's lot was firmly entrenched in Gaol. He could alert the Spirit Court to Gaol's activities, but it would mean the end of his own career as well, and Hern was far too selfish for that. That settled, Edward dismissed the Spiritualist from his mind, focusing instead on the blinking lamps that marked the ghosthound's position as it ran a winding path through the back alleys of his city and toward the black line of the river.

Gin burst out of the cover of the narrow alley and onto the dock and turned sharply, leaving the pursuing hail of roofing tiles and weather vanes and other trash to soar out past him, straight into the river. Panting, Gin slowed down a fraction, bringing them right up beside the water, which flowed dark and murky in the flashing lamplight.

"We're here," the dog growled. "Now what?"

"Now we do what I should have done this morning," Miranda said, getting into a crouch on his back. "Put control of the city back where it belongs, with the Great Spirit." She glanced skeptically at the river as they ran along with it. It didn't look like an enraged spirit, but maybe the duke had some kind of binding on it. Well, she thought, reaching back to tie her hair tight, she'd know in a second.

"I'll meet you on the other side," she said, scratching Gin's head. "Don't get caught."

"Never do," Gin snorted.

"Wait," Eli said, tugging on the chain that connected them. "Before you do anything rash, aren't you forgetting something?"

"Not that I can recall," Miranda said, turning toward the river. She gave Eli one last smile. "Hold your breath."

And then she jumped, taking Eli with her. For a moment they soared through the air, Miranda tucking gracefully, Eli flailing to keep his head upright, and then they landed with an enormous splash in the dark water. The moment they hit, Mellinor was there, surrounding them in a clear, bubbling flow, forming a protective pocket of air around them as they sank down into the muddy river. It was deeper than Miranda had expected, going down a dozen feet between the docks. All light from above vanished after the first foot, leaving only Mellinor's own watery glow to light their way as they sank deeper, coming to rest on the black silt at the bottom.

Miranda stood inside the bubble Mellinor had made. Eli followed more slowly, shaking the water out of his hair.

"Why is it every time we get together, I get drenched?"

Miranda ignored him. They had limited time before their air ran out, and considering the duke certainly knew where they were, she didn't think things would end well if they had to surface. It was now or never, so she put Monpress out of her mind and, standing very still, opened her spirit.

It was like stepping into another world. She could feel the enormity of the river's spirit flowing around her, dark and slow and inexorable. Yet even as she marveled at the size of it, she could feel that something was wrong. The flow of the water felt pinched, hobbled, almost like it was being squeezed through something, yet there was nothing there. Stranger still, and more alarming, was the water's silence. Though she could feel the power of the river, she heard nothing, no threats, no demands for her to state her identity or purpose, nothing but the quiet sound of the water as it crept by.

"Mellinor," Miranda whispered. "What's wrong with it?"

"I'm not sure," the glowing water answered. "There's

no Enslavement, but what kind of river doesn't respond to a wizard with a blazing open spirit standing at its heart?"

"Maybe it's shy?" Eli offered.

"Or maybe it's under a binding we can't feel." Miranda stepped forward until she was at the very edge of Mellinor's bubble. She hated doing this. Not only did it feel like a vaguely abusive display, it was unspeakably rude. Still, they were on a strict timetable, and the river certainly wasn't going to cooperate on its own.

"River Fellbro!" she cried, pouring the weight of her spirit into the words until they buzzed with power. The water around them hitched as her voice struck it, and for a moment, the river was still. Then, as though nothing had happened, the water began flowing again, darker and murkier than ever. Miranda, panting from the power she'd put into her call, looked around in confusion. She'd thought for sure even a Great Spirit wouldn't ignore something like that.

She was gathering herself for another try when Eli's hand brushed her shoulder. She looked at him, startled and scowling, but he just pointed at a spot in the water behind where she was standing. There, in the clouds of swirling silt, was a face. It was large, about as wide as Miranda was tall. Its features were murky, shifting in and out as the water flowed, and it did not look pleased.

The dark, silted eyes roved over them as a muddy, brown mouth opened. "Go away."

Its voice was like a wet slap against their ears, but Miranda reached out with her spirit, catching the river as it tried to fade. "We will not," she said firmly. "Great Spirit Fellbro, I come before you as a representative for all the spirits of Gaol currently under the thumb of Edward di Fellbro, Duke of Gaol. It is the Great Spirit's duty to protect those in its charge, yet your spirits live in fear and slavish obedience because their Great Spirit will not stand up for them. I feel no Enslavement on you, no madness. Why, then, do you ignore your duty?"

The silted face glowered and turned away. "How easy it is for you to talk," it grumbled, "coming here at the end of things. We're the ones who have to live with the duke day in and day out." The river looked at her, and Miranda shuddered as the weight of years pressed against her through his gaze. "There are worse things than being Enslaved."

"I don't think you know what that means," Mellinor growled, his water flashing brilliant blue. But Miranda raised her hand.

"What kind of threat could the duke use," she said softly, "to make you abandon your duty?"

"All kinds," the river said. "He is a powerful man with all of humanity's destructive nature at his aid. He's threatened to dam me up, pollute my water, reroute my flow to another river, the worst kind of things you can think of. With all that, Enslavement seems kind of superfluous, don't you think?"

"So you abandoned your spirits?" Mellinor roared. "All to save yourself?"

"Not forever!" the river roared back. "Judge all you want, but you never lived with the duke. We have to, and we suffer every day for it. Our only consolation is that, awful as he is, the duke is only human. He'll die sooner or later, and then we'll be free. But for now, we do as he says, all of us, even me, because no humiliation, no suffering he puts us through is worse than what he would do to us if we disobeyed."

Miranda opened her mouth to answer, and so did Eli, but it was Mellinor who spoke first, his water almost boiling with rage.

"You rivers," he sneered. "Always flowing downhill, always taking the easy way out. You let him walk all over you just because he won't live forever?"

"Don't talk so mighty, lost sea," the river rumbled, sending ripples through their bubble. "What right do you have to judge us? It's not like you're so pure. I know you, Mellinor. We've all heard of your failure, the sea defeated by a wizard. Rage all you want, but I had no mind to follow your path into madness. A few years of shame is nothing compared to hundreds trapped under a dead wizard's thumb. I just did what you should have done, and I have kept my lands."

"Then your lands are poorer for it," Mellinor rumbled, his water spinning faster and faster, "saddled with such a coward!"

"Live a year in Gaol and you'd understand!" Fellbro shouted. "I only did what I needed to survive!"

"Mellinor!" Miranda said sharply. "Enough! This isn't—"

A great tide of power cut her off. Mellinor's spirit welled up inside her, choking her breath, pushing his way free. He poured out of her, pushing the black water of the river back in a great, shining wave. Through it all, Miranda could only stand there, the conduit of his power, until, all at once, he was gone. The emptiness hit her like an avalanche, and she toppled over. Eli caught her just before she hit the mud, pushing her back onto her knees.

But even like that, Miranda could barely keep her balance. She clung to his wet shirt, staring up at the great white wave above them as it invaded the river.

"What is he doing?" she said, her voice trembling. "Why didn't he listen? We're supposed to be *helping* the river."

Eli gave her face a little slap, startling her back into the present. "He's being a Great Spirit," he said, nodding up at the glowing water. "I warned you about this, back in Mellinor, but you were the one who wanted to be his vessel, as I recall. You can't complain now when he acts according to his nature."

"He's going to ruin everything," Miranda groaned, staring helplessly as Mellinor's white water invaded the dark river. "We need the river on our side. This isn't the time for fighting!"

"I think Mellinor knows a lot more about being a Great Spirit than either of us," Eli said softly. "Trust him."

Miranda gave him a sideways look. "Must you be so smug about everything?" she grumbled. "I should have left you up top."

"I told you to," Eli said. He pointed up with a grin. "Now things are getting going; watch."

Miranda looked up. Mellinor's blue water was invading the dark river in every direction. She could feel Fellbro's fear as it fought the sea for control of its water, but Mellinor's rage was ironclad, and he did not fall back.

"Mellinor!" The river's roar had a pleading edge to it. "Don't do this!"

"You have betrayed your station, Fellbro." The blue water foamed and flashed.

"You have no right!" the river shrieked, its murky

waters racing away. "This is my land! Mine! I will run it as I see fit!"

But Mellinor's water pressed on without mercy or hesitation, and when he spoke, his voice echoed from all directions. "You relinquished your right to rule the moment you gave your powers away to save your own water. You have acted in a way unbecoming of a Great Spirit, and you know the price for that, same as the rest of us. Therefore, as Great Spirit of the Inland Sea, I, Mellinor, claim your rights as restitution on behalf of your spirits." The river trembled and fought, but Mellinor's wave ate everything as his final decree rang out. "Your water is now mine."

With that, the river's face shattered, and the entire river flashed the color of sea foam. The wave of power took Miranda and Eli off their feet, tumbling them along the river bottom as the bubble collapsed. But before they could come to harm, the water caught them gently. It carried them in a swell up from the depths, and they broke the river's surface with a gasp, sucking clean, fresh air into their lungs.

All around them, the river had changed. What had been a dark, stagnant flow now glittered a deep, deep blue. The water glistened with its own blue light, and she could feel the familiar weight of Mellinor's spirit all through it, comforting and a little apologetic.

"I am sorry," the water whispered. "I know you wanted a peaceable solution, but we spirits have our own laws that must be upheld."

"No," Miranda said, shaking her head. "Being a Spiritualist means understanding and respecting my spirits' natures. But"—she slapped the water, sending a splash up in the air—"I *wish* you'd *told* me what you were going to do *before you did it*."

She felt a wave of power that was distinctly like a shrug. "I didn't know I needed to until I was doing it."

"I see," Miranda said. "Well, at least no one can argue that I Enslaved you now. Not after that display."

"Only idiots argued it in the first place," Mellinor said. "But"—she felt a motion that could only be the spirit equivalent of a grin—"you'll like this next part."

Miranda sank into the water, suddenly alarmed. "What do you mean?"

"He means he's the Great Spirit of Gaol now," Eli said beside her. "And everyone knows it."

Miranda looked at him, confused, and he nodded toward the shore. She followed his gaze, and her eyes widened. The city, which had been a knot of controlled chaos, was perfectly still. The lamps were all burning steady, not flashing, and the dark clouds were frozen in the night sky. On the bank across from them, Miranda saw the army of conscripts standing with their torches. The archers drew their bows when they saw the two floating in the water, but even as they notched their arrows, Mellinor gave a warning rumble, and the bows went limp. The soldiers scrambled, but the bows had lost their tension and refused to draw.

"Was that you?" Miranda said in awe.

"Partially." Mellinor sounded extremely pleased with himself. "Most of it is the spirits." He laughed. "Let's just say they didn't particularly like being under the good duke's thumb, and now that I'm here to back them up, they're not feeling particularly charitable toward his forces."

As if to prove him right, at that moment every sword of the enemy army cut through its sheath and clattered to the ground, some of them going straight through the feet of their previous owners. A great cry of fear and surprise went up, and, sensing the chaos, the torches they carried chose that moment to erupt in great geysers of flame. Suddenly, fire was everywhere, and the army broke into a mob. Men in flames screamed and dove into the river, which pulled back at the last moment to let them land in the mud. Others ran away, disappearing down the alleys and leaving the wounded gripping their bleeding feet.

"That's what I call a complete rout," Eli said cheerily. "Though I can't say I've ever seen an army defeated by its own swords before."

Miranda grinned. "Come on," she said, turning to swim for the far shore. "Let's get your swordsman and my dog and we'll finish the duke before he does something drastic."

"Sounds marvelous," Eli said, swimming beside her. "See, we can agree on occasion."

"Don't push it," Miranda said, giving him a sideways look. "Swim faster; you're dragging me down."

"Yes, mistress," Eli quipped, earning himself a baleful glare, which he ignored completely, swimming in long, easy strokes toward the shore.

High overhead, Othril watched the battle of the Great Spirits with a growing sense of terror. This was bad, very bad. He needed to warn the duke before things got completely out of hand. He spun around to start toward the Duke's citadel, but as he turned, something inside him hitched, and he froze motionless in the air. For a moment, panic completely overwhelmed his mind. Had a wizard caught him? Was the duke angry? Then he felt a familiar cold breeze, and he realized what was wrong. He was blowing west.

"Othril."

The voice blew through him, cold and salty and enormous as the western sea. Frozen in place, he could only tremble as he answered.

"All hail the West Wind."

A laugh gusted past, and he felt other winds slide up beside him. Strong, powerful winds, and all blowing from the west.

"Othril," the great voice of the West Wind chuckled. "Did you honestly think that allying yourself with a wizard who coerces Great Spirits would end well?"

"How are you even here?" Othril said with as much authority as he could muster. "Fellbro told you to get out! I don't care how strong you think you are, you can't ignore a direct dismissal. Winds are forbidden by the Shepherdess from interfering in the affairs of other Great Spirits within their own domains!"

"But Fellbro isn't the Great Spirit anymore," the wind said. "You were riding high as the duke's right hand, weren't you? Far more power than a spirit of your level would ever gain in the usual course. I can see how you were tempted, but your days of playing spy and weathermaker for the the duke are over."

Othril began to dispute that, but clawed hands, airy but sharp and cold as iced iron, interrupted him, digging into the core of his spirit.

Panic sent him rigid. Being caught is the greatest fear of all winds, and Othril was no exception. It was how the duke had convinced him to serve in the first place.

A laughing breeze blew over him, but the words it whispered in his ear were as cold as the claws that held him. "It's time to remember your true loyalty, little wind."

Othril struggled one last time, and then he was gone, tumbling off to the west. The other winds watched until his spirit winked out of sight. Then, without a word, they spun up high into the cloud layer and began to carry out their lord's commands.

Slowly, the sky grew dark and heavy with clouds. And then, in long sullen sheets, a night rain began to fall on Gaol for the first time in twenty years.

CHAPTER
20

Duke Edward stood at the top of his citadel. The soft rain fell on him, trickling down his clenched jaw and trembling fists. He was staring at the river, its water shining silver in the night, and the last of his routed soldiers beside it. Behind him, his officers stood uncertainly, waiting for orders, but no orders came. The duke just stood there, staring at the river, growing paler and paler as his rage set in.

It was Hern who dared to speak first, stepping up to stand beside the duke.

"Edward," he said, very softly. "That water spirit is Miranda's. We still have her rings. That's all the leverage we need on a girl like her. We still have control."

"Control?" The duke's voice was low and sharp. "What do you know about control?" His hand shot out, grabbing Hern's collar with alarming strength, dragging the Spiritualist until they were an inch apart.

"I have devoted my entire life to shaping Gaol," he

whispered. "Every moment, from the first moment I heard a spirit's voice, I knew that this was my purpose, to turn this ragged hash of spirits into a land of order, discipline, and prosperity. I did not work all those years to lose it now."

"Edward!" Hern gasped against his grip. "I know what you're thinking, but be reasonable. Sometimes controlled retreat is a victory. We still have—"

"There will be no retreat!" the duke roared, tossing Hern to the ground. "I rule Gaol! It is not a matter of that girl controlling the river, but of my spirits disobeying me!" As he spoke, his spirit surged through the words until Hern could barely hear them over its roar. "I rule here," the duke said, turning back toward the river, "and disobedience will not be tolerated."

"Edward!" Hern shouted, but it was too late. A massive wave of Enslavement rolled out of the duke. It hit Hern full force, and he toppled over, dragged down by his rings. The Enslavement surged up the connection he shared with his spirits until he was writhing on the ground. But even as the overwhelming pressure threatened to crack his mind, he reached up and began to pluck his rings one by one from his fingers. With each ring removed, the pressure grew less. He kept taking off rings until he could stand again, and then, using a leather pouch to grab them so the terrified spirits did not touch his skin and reopen the connection, Hern gathered his spirits and fled.

Edward had gone too far. Hern shook his head, making his way quickly down the shaking stairs. He wouldn't help the duke Enslave his country. He was a Spiritualist still, and there were limits to what even he would do. Besides, if word ever got back to Zarin that he'd been involved in this in any way, no amount of politics could save him. So, with that, Hern vanished into the night, running for his tower as the city began to go mad around him.

Miranda pulled herself out of the river, grinning from ear to ear as she bent over to help extract Eli from the glowing water. Gin was waiting for them on the dock, looking as pleased as she was, which didn't seem to be making the elder Monpress more comfortable. Gin's toothy smiles were difficult to appreciate unless you knew him.

"I never thought that would work half as well as it did," he said, lowering his head to help Miranda climb onto the dock. "The city literally leaped at the chance to look for a new master."

"Anything would be better than the old one," Miranda said, pulling herself up by the tough fur on his ruff. "Actually, I don't see how things could have gone better, the duke's control broken, Eli on a chain; all I need now is for Hern to come begging for mercy and I think I'll have just about everything I could want in the world."

"As pleased as I am to be included in such happiness," Eli said, climbing up onto the dock behind her, "I would like to remind you—"

But he never got to finish. At that moment, an ear-splitting howl drowned out all other sound. Miranda, Gin, and Eli all shielded their ears, and even the elder Monpress looked up, startled. The cry went on and on, shaking and changing pitch, like it was being passed from one voice to another, full of terror and wailing and crushing despair.

"Is that Nico?" Miranda shouted. It was certainly desperate enough to be demon panic.

"Nico's panics don't sound like this," Eli shouted back. With a wince, he glanced up at the city, and his face went bone pale. Startled, Miranda looked, too, but even she didn't quite recognize what she was seeing until Gin named it.

"It's an Enslavement," he whimpered. "I've never seen one so large."

Miranda straightened up, forcing herself to ignore the horrible noise and look. Across the river, the city was twisting like a trapped animal. Buildings writhed and screamed, their bricks cracking from the pressure. Fires were breaking out everywhere, shooting up chimneys as their spirits fought the wizard's will. But it was too strong. Even as she watched, the city began to settle down, the buildings crouching low like beaten animals, trembling. Yet for all the flash, Mellinor's captured river seemed unaffected by the crushing force. So did Gin, who was on his feet, teeth bared.

"It's the duke," Eli said beside her, answering her question before she spoke it. "His Enslavement is only for his spirits. He's taking his city back."

"Oh, no, he's not," Miranda said, grabbing hold of Gin's fur and pulling herself up. But as she settled on Gin's back, she jerked violently. Her eyes widened, and she doubled over as if she'd been punched in the stomach.

Eli, one arm pulled up beside her anyway from the chain linking them together, caught her as she wobbled. "What's wrong?"

"It's my rings," Miranda whispered, her voice shaking and terrified. "They're gone."

Eli frowned. "I thought that was already established."

"No," Miranda snapped. "I mean they're *gone*. Before

they were there, but far away, but just now..." She shrugged helplessly. "It's like a door closed. I can't feel anything."

"Miranda," Gin growled, "calm down. It's way too early for them to flicker out. Get a hold of yourself before you panic Mellinor."

Miranda blanched and glanced over at the river. Sure enough, the water was washing toward her. She waved it away frantically and sat up straight, wiping her eyes with her hands.

"You're right," she said quietly. "But why can't I feel them?"

"Well," Eli said, "who did you say had them?"

"Hern," Miranda said. "He's another Spiritualist. A nasty one."

"Sounds like most Spiritualists," Eli said, nodding sagely. "Present company excluded, of course."

Miranda didn't even bother with the nasty look for that one. Instead, she sat, brow furrowed in furious thought, until all at once she groaned.

"I know what happened," she said, turning to Gin. "Hern sealed himself in his tower. He's too much of a coward to try stopping the duke's Enslavement, so he's separated himself to wait it out. I bet my rings are in there, too, and whatever he's using for a seal is blocking my connection as well."

"Then we have a problem," Gin said. "So long as there's some connection, the spirits can hold out by staying deeply asleep. But if the connection is gone entirely, they'll die within the hour."

"I know, I know," Miranda said frantically. "But I can't just ignore the Enslavement of an entire town!"

"Might I suggest something?" Eli interrupted.

Spiritualist and ghosthound turned to glare at him, but Eli's cool smile didn't falter. "You need to get your rings back before they expire, right? That's part of your oath, isn't it? Protection?"

"Of course it is," Miranda growled.

"But at the same time, you, as a Spiritualist, need to stop this Enslavement before the entire town is driven mad, or else you violate your oath to protect the Spirit World."

Gin snapped his teeth together. "Get to the point, thief."

"The point should be clear," Eli said. "Even you can't be two places at once, so why don't we split our efforts? You go rescue your rings and I'll take care of the duke."

"Do you think I'm stupid?" Miranda scoffed. "What's to say you won't just turn tail and run? Isn't 'get while the getting is good' one of your rules of thievery?"

"It is," Eli said. "Though not quite in those words. But consider this, dear Miranda"—he rolled up his sleeve—"you're not the only one out for payback tonight."

Miranda gasped. Eli's arms were covered in horrible bruises. Most were red and angry; others were starting to turn a deep purple. She stared at them in disbelief. How had the thief kept up with her? She wouldn't have been able to move with bruises like that, but the whole time that she'd been dragging him along, Eli had given no sign he was injured. Now she felt almost guilty for being so rough with him.

"Anyway," Eli said, letting his sleeve drop again, "it's not just vengeance for me." He glared at the town, which was now almost totally still in submission. "I have no love for bullies and Enslavers."

Miranda believed him on that. From what she'd seen of his tactics, spirit goodwill played an enormous part. He must have been going crazy not being able to talk to the spirits in Gaol. Eli might be a scoundrel and an embarrassment to the dignity of wizardry, but when it came to protecting the well-being of spirits, they were almost always on the same page.

Of course, once she let him go she might never get him back, but at this point surrendering Eli was a small price to pay for not having to choose between the town and her spirits.

"Are you sure you can do it?" she asked, looking him straight in the eye.

"Nearly positive," Eli said. "You already broke Gaol free once. How hard can it be to do it again?"

"Right," Miranda sighed. She was suddenly feeling less confident. "I guess we'll have to break this chain."

"That won't be necessary," Eli said. He held up his wrist and did a quick flipping motion that made her own hands ache to see, and the iron manacle slid neatly off his hand.

"There," Eli said, rubbing his reddened wrist.

Miranda stared at him, deflated. "You could have done that at any time, couldn't you?"

"Of course," Eli said. "But no other escape would have been nearly as enjoyable as seeing your face just now."

Miranda put her head in her hands. "Just go do your part," she said. "I'll be there as soon as I get my rings back. If you can't take the duke, just stall him or something until I arrive."

"As you command," Eli said and bowed.

Miranda gave him one last dirty look. Then, shaking

her head, she tapped Gin's sides with her heels. The ghosthound sprung forward, and then they were flying down the dark docks beside the glowing river.

"Think he'll keep his word?" Gin growled.

"I have no idea," Miranda said. "But we've already made our choice; no time for second-guesses."

"Never is," Gin said.

She ducked low on Gin's back as Mellinor parted his waters to let them cross. When they reached the other side, Gin turned north between the silent, trembling buildings and headed toward the tower where, somewhere, her spirits were waiting.

Eli waved until the dog dove into the riverbed, and then sat down with a long, pained sigh to rub his poor, aching wrist.

"There was no need for disjointing," Monpress said, sitting down beside him. "You could have just borrowed my lock pick."

"What," Eli said, "and ruin the show?"

Monpress sighed. "When will you learn there's more to life than theatrics?"

"About the same time you learn there's more to theft than money," Eli said, slapping the old man across the shoulders.

Monpress grunted at the impact. "We should be going," he said. "Will your companions be along soon?"

Eli looked sideways at him. "The Heart's going strong, and I can hear the demon panic from here, so I think Josef and Nico are a little busy. Even if they weren't, I'm not going anywhere. Weren't you listening? I have a crazed Enslaver duke to bring down."

Monpress gave him a surprised and disappointed look. "You're actually going through with it? Have you forgotten *everything* I taught you?"

"I know, 'the best revenge is a clean getaway,'" Eli said. "But this isn't about revenge, old man, not entirely. It's about principle. Not letting the tyrant win."

Monpress shook his head. "Since when are you a man of principle?"

"Since always," Eli said, getting up. "My principles were just never anything you cared about. Anyway, I didn't volunteer you to come. Isn't it about time for you to make a quiet exit?"

"Past time," Monpress said, standing as well. "But I just lost ten thousand gold standards worth of stolen art trying to save your neck. I'm not about to let you go off and ruin my investment completely."

Eli rolled his eyes. "Thanks for the fatherly concern."

Monpress nodded graciously. "So, I assume you have a plan."

"The beginnings of one," Eli said, scratching his chin. "Can you still throw a clawhook and line two stories?"

"Of course," Monpress said, insulted. "I'm old, not infirm."

"Good," Eli said, starting toward the bridge. "Then this just might work. Come on, I'll explain on the way."

Monpress shrugged and jogged after him, moving silently over the glowing river and toward the cowering city.

CHAPTER
21

Nico crouched, panting. Sted was walking toward her, panting as well, but his sword didn't waver. They'd been going around the room for what felt like hours, neither able to land a finishing blow. Nico was too fast, and Sted was, so far as she could tell, uninjurable. He didn't even defend when she leaped at him, but always went on the offensive, and the maze of long, bleeding cuts running across her body was all she had to show for her efforts.

But it wouldn't last much longer. Already she'd dipped too deep into the demon's power. The blackness was swimming over her vision, and she could feel her eyes burning, which meant they were glowing with the unnatural light. She was getting very close to the edge.

Normally she wouldn't be concerned. She'd gone over the edge and come back before, and it was worth the risk if it meant she could do what needed to be done. But this time was different. This time there was no Josef waiting to bring her back. She slid between the shadows, watching as Sted circled in the dark, racking her brain for a way to finish this quickly, when a voice whispered deep in her ear.

Why not let go?

Nico froze midstep. The words echoed in her mind, but the voice wasn't Sted's. It came from inside her ears, from the dark blotch deep behind her conscious mind.

Embrace what you really are. We could crush him like a bug in one blow, him and that rabid dog sword of his.

Nico began to breathe heavily. The voice was cold and soft and somehow nostalgic, but she couldn't actually remember hearing it before. In answer to that thought, the voice began to chuckle, and Nivel's warning came back to Nico in a cold rush of sudden understanding: Never listen to the voice. Never acknowledge it.

Nico fled the shadows and dropped to the ground behind a crate, slamming a wall down between her mind and the voice. It was happening. She was losing control, just as Nivel had said she would. But Josef was relying on her. She had to hold on, had to beat Sted. Now was not the time to go soft.

As if to prove the point, the boards on the other side of her hiding place began to creak. Sted was moving toward her, dragging his sword along the crates, methodically breaking up every hiding place. Nico crouched in the shadow, examining her options, but any way she came at it, the situation looked hopeless. She'd matched Sted strength for strength, bashed his skull hard enough to crumple it to dust, but even after her best blows, Sted was uninjured. His skin was still whole and without so much as a bruise. Nico bit her lip. He couldn't be unbeatable. No one was unbeatable, but she'd tried everything.

Everything? The voice chuckled. *You haven't begun to try. What are you doing, anyway? Dancing around in circles, trying the same things over and over, like they'll somehow come out differently this time. How stupid.*

Nico slapped her hands over her ears, but unbidden, driven by a force other than herself, her eyes flicked to Sted's shoulder and the narrow sinews bending under his impenetrable skin.

Nico closed her eyes. This was too much. She couldn't fight Sted and the voice. She cracked her eyelids, and her vision snapped back to Sted's shoulder.

The strongest are only as strong as their weakest point, the voice said, smooth as honey. *One hit and you'll have the victory even Josef couldn't manage.*

Nico frowned. For all that she knew she shouldn't listen, it was a good idea. Certainly better than her other options. Knowing she would probably regret this, but seeing no other option, she slid forward. Sted was nearly on top of her, though still clueless. For a League member, he was laughably bad at finding demons. She held her breath, waiting until the very last moment, as his hand was reaching for the lip of the crate that covered her. The moment his fingers wrapped around the splintered wood, she leaped.

She grabbed his sword arm and swung up, moving so quickly he could do nothing but watch as she landed feet-first on his shoulder. As soon as she had her footing, Nico reached down and grabbed Sted's arm at the elbow with both hands, planting her feet on his shoulder, just like the image the voice had shown her in her mind. Pressing her feet against his straining shoulder right at the joint, she brought his arm up and back with all her strength until, with a sickening pop, she felt his shoulder snap through her boot.

Sted screamed, and there was a great crash as his sword fell to the ground from his limp hand. It was a temporary victory, however. Sted's shoulder was only dislocated, not broken. Before he could recover, she needed to do some permanent damage. So, almost before the sword had hit the ground, she swung sideways, wrapping her legs around his thick neck and, using her motion as torque, threw him sideways. Overbalanced from his huge bulk, Sted slammed to the ground. He tried to catch his fall with his uninjured arm, but Nico was too quick. She kept moving, grabbing his arm and stepping sideways so that he landed on his stomach with her on his back, her foot stamped on his remaining good shoulder and his arm bent backward in her grip.

He was trapped beneath her, unable to move without breaking his own arm. Slowly, pleasurably, Nico bent his arm back over her knee, grinning as the bones groaned under the pressure, ready to snap. But as she bent his arm toward the breaking point, something deep inside her smiled, and her fingers began to move on their own. Her nails stabbed into Sted's arm, digging into the flesh. Panic-blind and terrified, Nico tried to let go, but her limbs weren't listening. Deep in her mind, the voice began to laugh, and, a second later, her fingers broke Sted's iron skin.

Sted's power flooded into her. His thoughts, strength, memories, and experiences flashed through her mind before vanishing into the maw of the dark thing clawing its way up out of the well of her soul. The manacles on her wrists beat against her, the metal glowing white hot, searing her skin. But the pain was far away, overwhelmed by the torrent in her mind. Beneath her feet, she could feel Sted screaming, but she heard nothing. The entire world had shrunk to the power flowing into her and the creature that ate it, leaving no room for Nico at all.

Her mind was being squeezed, her consciousness trampled beneath the demonseed as it devoured Sted. She was slipping away from her own soul, and as she scrambled to stay in her skull, she could hear the demon laughing. The moment the sound touched her, fear turned to anger and, without knowing what she did or how, Nico slammed the full force of her wizard's will down on the connection holding the demon to Sted. The voice cried out in pain, the sound of it threatening to tear her skull apart, and her hand ripped free of Sted's arm, and the connection of power snapped shut.

The enormous man collapsed, and Nico flew off him, thrown by the force of her own command. She landed hard on her back, gasping for air, and in her head, she could almost hear Nivel's voice shouting at her—*never* take the demon's advice.

Never take my advice? the voice said crossly. *My advice brought us closer to victory in five minutes than the last half hour of your jumping around. You were the one who wasted our chance, all because you're too cowardly to embrace your true power.*

But Nico wasn't listening anymore. Slowly, painfully, she sat up. Sted was still on the ground, clutching his bleeding arm. He looked up when he heard her move, his eyes murderous.

"That's it, *monster*," he growled, pushing himself up. He rolled his neck, popping his dislocated shoulder back into place. "No more running. Now you die."

I can finish him for you if you get behind him now, the voice whispered. *Don't be an idiot.*

Nico clenched her fists and held her ground, watching Sted's approach with glowing eyes.

Why keep pretending you have a chance without me? the voice said softly. *Everything that makes you worthwhile, your speed, your toughness, your strength, the ability to move through shadows, it all comes from me. Do you think Josef would keep you around if I wasn't with you? The thief certainly wouldn't. He tolerates you only so long as you're useful. Face it, little girl, I am what makes your life worth living. Without me you're nothing but a stupid, weak, ugly creature. No one likes you. No one cares if you live or die, except me.*

Nico pressed her eyes closed, willing the voice away, but it went on, smooth and dark, seeping into her mind. *You think that by ignoring me you can somehow change things? Do you think you've done any of this on your own? No. I have given you everything, gifts beyond measure, power beyond your deserving. I have saved your life more times than I can count. You've been using my power from the very beginning. Why deny it now? I want to live just as much as you do, so let me help you. All you have to do is let me in, let me control you, take care of you, and you'll never have to be weak again.*

"Shut up!" Nico screamed. The words ripped out of her, and even Sted paused, taken aback.

"This is my body," Nico said. "Since I can remember, all you've done is make everything think I'm a monster. There's no place for you here. So just shut up and go away!"

The warehouse fell silent. Sted was watching her

warily, looking for a trap, but Nico couldn't have attacked even if she'd been planning to. Her body was lead beneath her, frozen in place as the dark thing began to crawl back into the well of her soul.

No place, you say? The voice was haughty and cold, sliding like wire through her mind. *After everything I've given you...* It sighed in disgust. *I think it's time for you to learn, little girl, just how worthless you are without me.*

She felt a faint pressure, like a hand on her mind, and then the voice was gone. Suddenly, Nico could move again, and scarcely in time, for Sted was standing over her, his glowing sword washing everything with its blood-red light. Nico flinched and slid sideways to escape into the shadows.

Nothing happened. She blinked in confusion. Jumping through shadows was something she did as easily as breathing. She'd never really thought about how she did it, but now...it was like a door had closed. Even as this realization took root in her head, she felt something else she wasn't accustomed to feeling—pain. Crippling pain shot up her limbs, running in long, burning lines across her chest, her arms, her face as the cuts Sted had landed during their fight, cuts that had healed instantly, reopened. All at once, blood was everywhere. Her head felt heavy and dark, and even the red light of Sted's sword began to dim as her vision darkened, yet she could not escape. The shadows were closed to her. Her body felt small and weak and beaten, and she knew without testing that her strength was gone as well, along with everything the demonseed had given her.

She had just one moment to look up and watch the shadow of Sted raise his blade before the jagged sword tore into her. Pain exploded through her body, and Nico felt herself flying, carried by the force of the blow. She landed on her back, skidding across the floor until, finally, she hit a crate and lay still. The pain was blinding, overwhelming, and it was all she could do to keep breathing in tiny wheezing gasps. The world was getting darker, colder, and further away.

She gasped, choking on her blood. But even as she desperately fought for breath, the voice spoke in her ear.

It doesn't have to end like this, it whispered, sweet and soft. *All you have to do is surrender. Give yourself over to me, and I will save you. You will have everything you lost and more. You'll never be weak or alone again.*

Nico closed her eyes and focused on her breathing.

The thing in Nico's mind gave a long, deep sigh as Sted's fingers wrapped around her neck. *A failure to the end. This is twice now you've failed me. And to think, you used to be the strongest demon in the world.*

With one final, desperate shove, Nico pushed the voice away. When her eyes met Sted's, they were dark and human again.

"It's over," he hissed.

Nico set her jaw and pinned her hands at her side so her demon couldn't try eating him again. This was it, she knew. After trying so hard, this was it. Still, she'd never give in to the demon, not even to keep living. Tears welled up in her eyes at that thought, and she murmured an apology to Josef. She'd tried to keep going, to cling to life, but the price was just too high. Still, she kept breathing as Sted raised his sword, pressing the sharp tip against her ribs, just below her heart. So long as she was alive, she had hope, even now.

Hope, the demon sneered. *A stupid, human concept.*

"That's the idea," she whispered back.

Her last thought before closing her mind was Josef as she'd first met him, leaning over her on the snowy mountain slope, telling her to breathe. Then the sword came down, and the world vanished.

Josef floated in darkness. He was in pain, horrible pain, but he couldn't see where. His body was missing, lost somewhere in the blackness. It was just him and the pain and the darkness that went on and on and on forever.

"I'm dead," Josef said. It was as much an experiment to see if he could speak as a test to see how that statement felt. The words made no sound, which made sense, considering, but they felt very real when he said them.

Don't be stupid, a voice answered from the darkness. *If you were dead, you wouldn't be in pain.*

Josef flinched. It was the Heart's voice, and if he was hurt enough to hear it, things must be really bad. On the other hand, if the sword was talking, it probably knew what was going on, which meant it was time for some answers.

"If I'm not dead," Josef said, "where am I, and how do I get out?"

You are almost dead, the Heart answered. *I caught your life a moment before it flickered out. I am keeping it alive by holding it next to my own until you decide what you're going to do.*

"What do you mean, 'I decide'?" Josef said. "What's there to decide? I'm not going to die to someone like Sted."

I'm afraid things are no longer that simple, Josef Liechten, the Heart said and sighed. *We were defeated utterly. Struck down. And do you know why?*

Josef felt a twinge of shame. "Because I'm not strong enough."

Correct, the Heart thundered.

Josef choked. The Heart's answer struck him harder than any of Sted's blows.

The Heart sighed. *I've been waiting for a defeat like this to make you understand. You think you know what it means to be strong, but every time a fight pushes you, you wait until the last moment to draw me, then treat my blade as a guaranteed victory, an undefeatable weapon.*

"I have to," Josef said. "You're too strong. You agreed I'm not good enough, but how can I get better if your power blows everything away? You're the greatest awakened sword ever made, but I'm the one bleeding to death on the floor, not Sted. Obviously, the weakness is with me. I have to fix it before I can move forward."

Fights you can win with dull swords are not the ones that make you better, the Heart said. *Every time you fight you handicap yourself, pushing me aside for your dull blades, thinking that doing so will make you stronger. But real strength doesn't come from such cheap tricks. Real strength comes from fighting at the edge of your ability, pushing yourself past the last inch of your resolve with everything you have.*

Rage filled Josef, and he started to answer, but the Heart cut him off.

I chose you as my wielder because I thought you understood this. But from the moment I allowed you to grasp my hilt, you've done nothing but avoid my powers. Not once have you used me to my full potential. You draw me only as a last resort, a final blow.

"But—"

I did not bind myself to you to stay cooped up in a sheath!

Josef flinched at the anger in the sword's voice, but he could not deny what it said.

These last few years we've been together as two parts, the Heart said, *sword and man, without understanding. If you wish to leave this place, if you wish to defeat Sted, this must change. I am not your trump card, not your guaranteed out. I am a sword, your sword. You've come this far on your own, but no farther. If you want to survive, Josef Liechten, then we must emerge from this together, as a swordsman, or not at all.*

"But I don't understand," Josef said. "You want us to work together? How? I hear you only at times like this, when I'm almost dead. Am I going to have to take a mortal wound every time I want to fight, just so we can talk?"

The Heart rumbled. *Do you think you're my first non-wizard wielder? Do you think I would have chosen you to carry me if I thought you were incapable of truly being my swordsman?*

Josef shook his head. "I don't see—"

Do you always need to speak to know why a person fights?

"No," Josef said. "But—"

Do you need words to understand why a sword cuts?

Josef took a deep breath. "No."

Good. He could hear the Heart smile. *You begin to understand. Listen well, Josef Liechten. If we are to fight together, you must see me for what I am, a part of yourself, another facet of your own power. To do that, you must push aside your thinking mind, the mind that requires words, and understand me with what lies deeper.*

Josef clenched his teeth. The Heart was starting to sound like Eli's wizard talk. "You mean like a wizard?"

No, the Heart said in disgust. *I mean like a spirit.*

Josef shook his head. "I still don't understand."

You will, the Heart promised. *Open your eyes.*

"What?" They were open, or he thought they were.

This close to death, even you should be able to see. The Heart's words were an avalanche. *Open your eyes!*

Josef did. The darkness was gone; the pain was gone. He was floating high in a blue sky filled with clouds, and before him, rising like a great wave from the land, was a mountain like none he had ever seen. It was taller than anything in the world, its edges sharp and straight as a blade. Its snowcapped peak cut the sky, slicing clouds as they passed, while its wide base spread for miles and miles in all directions, its roots deeper than humans could comprehend. It stood perfectly sharp, proud and tall, unmovable, unbreakable, and the moment Josef saw it, he understood.

The mountain vanished, and he felt something in his hand. He looked down and saw he was holding the Heart of War. The black sword looked the same as ever, and yet different. When he looked at the blade, the memory of the mountain flashed across his mind.

You have seen my true nature. The Heart's voice was deep and warm. *Do you still need words, Josef Liechten?*

"No," Josef said, tightening his grip on the sword.

The Heart of War laughed, a deep, rumbling sound, and Josef woke.

He was alone, and in a different place from where he'd fallen. Crates were stacked high around him and his wound had been bound, though the bloodstains told him how useful that would have been if the Heart had not intervened. He looked down at the sword in his hand for a long moment, like he was seeing it for the first time.

The path to true strength is not easily walked. The Heart's voice was more like a memory than a sound now. *Now that we've started, there's no going back. I hope you're prepared to bet your life on this.*

"I always have," Josef whispered. "Every single time."

A great feeling of laughter welled up in his head, and the sword's hilt settled hard in Josef's hand. He gripped it with a grin and, using the sword as a prop, began the long, painful process of sitting up. When he was about halfway there, he heard a crash. He froze, listening. It was the sound of something hitting the floor, something small and human. He was on his feet at once, creeping up the pile of crates just in time to see Sted panting over something on the floor. It was dark, but he would know that shape anywhere, the slender back, the long, thin arms lying limp on the floor, the pale, pale skin.

Rage filled him to boiling, painting the room in a wash of angry color. Rage at Sted, at himself for letting this happen, at Nico for not running from a fight she couldn't win. Hadn't he taught her anything? But the sword weighed heavy in his grip, bringing him down, telling him what must be done.

Even so, Josef wasn't the kind of man to fall on an opponent from behind with no warning.

"Sted!"

The cry echoed through the warehouse, and the enormous swordsman looked up just in time to see Josef leap, the Heart of War held high over his head. The sword felt heavy in his hands, yet Josef could swing it with ease, even more so than before. The blade answered his every movement like it was part of his hand rather than something clasped inside it, and Josef felt a rush like never before as the Heart's triumphant cackle rolled through him.

For a moment Sted just stood there, staring, and then he started to raise his sword to defend. But this time he was too slow. Josef was already on top of him, swinging the Heart with all his rage. The black blade hit Sted in the side with the weight of a mountain. There was a great iron *gong*, and Sted flew backward, slamming into the front wall of the warehouse with a crash that cracked the wooden supports.

Panting from the force of the blow and keeping one eye on Sted's slumped body, Josef limped over to Nico. He'd seen plenty of violence in his time, but she was still hard to look at. An enormous wound ran down her chest, as though Sted had been trying to gut her. Still, he told himself, this was Nico. She was about as killable as a rock wall.

Josef knelt down to check her breathing. Sure enough, he could feel it, a faint breeze on his fingers, and he let out the breath he didn't realize he'd been holding. She was alive. He let himself savor the realization before forcing it down again, turning to face Sted's twitching body. She was alive, and it was his job now to make sure she stayed that way.

Across the warehouse, Sted groaned and retched, coughing up a streak of bright blood. He stared at it in shock before turning his hateful glare on Josef. Keeping a hand to his side, he stood slowly, pushing himself up by painful inches.

"I'm impressed," he gasped, spitting out another mouthful of blood as he got to his feet at last. "You broke a rib. How long has it been since someone did that? Not for years now." He bared his bloody teeth at Josef. "You'll pay for that."

"If we're paying blood for blood," Josef said, "I think you owe us far more."

Sted grabbed his sword again. "What does it take to kill you?" he grumbled. "This time I'll cut off your cursed head!"

His threat turned into a scream as he began to charge. Instinctively, Josef turned to jump out of the way, but the Heart would not move. For one panicked moment, he stared at the blade. Then he quieted, and understood. Josef planted his feet firmly, in the position shield troops call Bracing the Mountain, and held the Heart in front of him, broad side out, like a shield. There, firm as bedrock, he met Sted's charge.

The swords clashed in a scream of twisting metal and flashing sparks. Sted was snarling, his sword red as fresh blood, pushing with all his strength. The blood rage crashed into Josef, but the swordsman did not break his stance, and he did not move an inch.

Realizing his assault was useless, Sted began to swing wildly, using his superior height and reach to try and get around Josef's iron guard. But everywhere Sted swung, the Heart was there. The great black sword and the man carrying it moved together, flicking from one position to the next with a speed unlike anything they'd shown earlier. Sted struck harder and harder, faster and faster, but

Josef and the Heart met him blow for blow, each block flowing seamlessly into the next, and try as he might, Sted could not break the sword's wall.

Finally, desperately, Sted lashed out with his entire body, throwing all his weight into his attack. This time, when the jagged sword met the Heart's dented surface, the glowing blade snapped. It broke with a squeal of metal that made Josef's ears ache, and Sted stumbled back. He held up his sword, now just a foot of toothy metal above the absurdly large hilt, and stared at it like a bewildered child. Then, with a cry of despair, hatred, and utter, devouring rage, he threw himself at Josef.

It was a wild charge. Sted thundered toward him, flailing with the broken sword as though it were still whole, running with his whole body to crush Josef beneath his weight.

It was then, in the madness, that Josef struck. He turned the Heart deftly in his hand, sliding the enormous blade around to meet Sted's flailing arm. He didn't look at the man's bared teeth or his twitching muscles. He didn't look at his own footwork, or how Sted was poised to crush him without the Heart as a barrier. Instead, he focused on the image the Heart had shown him, of the mountain's peak cutting the clouds. He held it in his mind until the picture was burned into his vision, until the need to cut, the way of cutting, not as a sword cuts, but as a mountain cuts, was all he could feel. Only then did he swing his sword, *his* sword truly, for the first time, catching Sted in the left arm, just above his elbow.

The black, blunt blade of the Heart met Sted's impenetrable skin, met and sliced it clean. The Heart cut straight through the flesh, through the bone, with no more resistance than a razor through spider webs. Then it met the air again, and Sted was falling, his arm cut clean off.

The enormous man collapsed on the floor, clutching the space where his arm had been. Josef spun around, taking up his guard again, but he didn't need to. Sted was curled in a fetal position, clutching his broken sword with the only arm he had left while blood poured out of his wound onto the floor. Josef lowered his guard, resting the Heart's tip on the floor, and Sted's head whipped around to face him, his eyes burning with pure, horrible hatred.

"No," he panted. "We're not finished." He forced himself up with his one remaining arm and grabbed the top of his broken sword, clutching the pieces together against his chest. "It's not over."

"No," Josef answered. "It is. You are defeated, Berek Sted."

Sted laughed, a horrible, wheezing sound. "You, you couldn't defeat me in a hundred years," he muttered. "You were lucky, that's all. My sword broke. There's no way you could have defeated me otherwise."

"Luck had nothing to do with it," Josef said. "Get out or bleed to death on the floor, your choice." He swung the Heart over his shoulder and started toward Nico. "I'm finished with you."

"I decide when we're finished!" Sted roared. "Your name, swordsman of the Heart of War. Tell me your name!"

Josef stopped, looking back over his shoulder with a cold, dull glare. "Josef Liechten."

Sted pushed himself to his knees. "See you soon, then, Josef Liechten."

He gave Josef a final, bloody grin, and then said

something Josef heard but could not understand. Suddenly, the light twisted around Sted, and a cut opened in the air. It was as though someone had taken a knife to the fabric of the world and cut a hole to another place, somewhere dark and lined with black stones. Sted fell backward, letting the tear in the world devour him, and then he was gone. No sound, no smoke—he simply was not there anymore.

Josef stared for a full minute at the bloody place where the swordsman had been. Even his cut-off arm was still on the ground, but the man was gone. He would have stared longer, but the Heart was heavy in his hand, pulling him toward Nico. Taking the hint, Josef decided to just ask Eli about it later, and he walked over to where Nico had fallen.

He had expected her to be sitting up by now. Nico's ability to heal herself was something he took as a truth of the world. Yet Nico had not moved from where he'd left her, and even in the dark, he could see a darker stain on the floor around her. Fear began to grow inside him, and his walk turned into a run.

The first thing he checked was her breath again, which, though faint, was still there. His relief at that vanished when he looked at her chest. The wound from Sted's sword was still open and bleeding. For some reason, her healing didn't seem to be kicking in. He looked around frantically, searching for anything to use as a bandage to stop the bleeding when he felt something grasp his wrist.

He looked down to see Nico's hand clutching his. Her eyes were open, dark and pleading as they looked at him, and her lips moved in a whisper he couldn't understand.

"Say it again," he said, leaning so that his ear was against her lips.

"My coat," she whispered. "Find my coat."

Josef nodded and glanced around. Her coat was piled on the floor not far from where she lay, and Josef grabbed it. He handed it to her, but the moment the black cloth touched her hand, it began to move on its own. The coat flowed around Nico's body, wrapping itself across her like a cocoon, binding her wound and stanching the bleeding. In the space of a breath, she was completely bound, and Nico gave a long, relieved sigh.

"It protects me," she whispered, looking at Josef again. "Just like Slorn said."

Josef clutched her shoulders. "Nico, what's happening?"

The girl looked away. "I'll tell you"—she breathed—"later."

And then she was out, and the coat slithered over her head, wrapping her completely, leaving Josef alone and confused.

"Powers," he muttered. This was getting worse and worse. Nico was a bundle, he had no idea what was going on, and he had completely missed his part of old Monpress's plan, which, if the growing sounds of chaos outside were any indication, was going very badly.

Nothing for it, he thought, standing up. He had to find Eli. If anyone could tell him what was wrong with Nico and get them out, it was the thief. Mission firmly in mind, Josef set to work. Using a length of fine table linen from one of the shattered crates, he wiped Sted's blood off the Heart and tied it across his back. After settling the sword in place, he took a deep breath, bracing for the rush of exhaustion that always followed. But even when his hand let go of the hilt, he felt the same. Tired, beaten up, but no worse than he had when he was still holding the blade. On his back, the sword settled smugly into place, and Josef arched his eyebrows. Whatever had happened in that black place, it had done more than just bring him closer to his sword. Their partnership had changed; he was sure of it, though understanding the exact extent of the changes would have to wait until he had more time.

Next, because he knew he'd never hear the end of it if he forgot, he grabbed the Fenzetti blade from the corner where it had landed and hefted it on his shoulders. Finally, he gently lifted the black bundle that was Nico and held her against his chest. Going slowly so he wouldn't jostle her too much, Josef walked to the door of the warehouse, which, miraculously, was whole and untouched. He opened it with a swift kick that took it off its hinges and stepped into the night. Clutching Nico carefully, he ran across the one remaining bridge over the now inexplicably glowing river. Soft, cold rain splattered on his shoulders, and he could hear people far away yelling, but the streets he could see were dark and empty. Ordinarily, this would have put him on his guard, but Josef was in too much of a hurry to worry about threats he couldn't see. Instead, he picked up the pace, moving toward the citadel, Eli's most likely location.

He only hoped the thief was alive to get them out of this.

CHAPTER
22

Gin ran through the silent, rain-soaked streets of Gaol with Miranda crouched low on his back. The city cowered around them, crushed under the duke's will. It made Miranda ill just passing by, but she ignored it as best she could. Her duty right now was to get her rings back, then she could help Monpress put the duke in his place... assuming he even intended to carry out his end of things.

She looked back over her shoulder at the river, and Gin growled. "Don't even think about it," he said, picking up the pace. "We've got our plan and we're sticking to it. If we start second-guessing things now, we won't save the town or your spirits."

Miranda nodded and let him run. Hern's tower was on the northern edge of the city, an ornate stone spire surrounded by wealthy houses. Or at least that's how it had looked that afternoon. What met them now as they came to a stop at the end of the charming little street leading up to Hern's private domain was not an elegant tower but an enormous spike of rough stone. Gin slid to a stop and Miranda jumped off for a better look. Hern's tower looked like a boulder had fallen on it. Miranda walked up and put a hand against the stone and then snatched it away again with a grimace.

"It's Hern's stone spirit," she said, shaking her hand where the stone had bitten it. "He's wrapped it around the tower like a shell to shield himself and his other spirits from the Enslavement."

"He has a spirit powerful enough to stand up to the duke?" Gin snorted.

"Normally I'd say no," Miranda said. "But he's got the same advantage we have right now, namely that the duke is stomping on his own spirits, which leaves the Enslavement too thinly spread to press down much on Spiritualist servants."

Gin crouched down, nosing the spot where the rough stone met the cobbled street. "Does it go all the way down?"

"It would have to," Miranda said, tapping the stone with her fingers. "I hate to say break it, but I don't see any other way we're getting in. Of course"—she opened her spirit a fraction, putting a warning edge of power into her voice—"I'm not feeling particularly charitable toward spirits who willingly help Hern stamp out mine."

The stone shuddered, and high above them in the tower, something made a low grinding noise. A second later, the smooth rock face in front of them cracked, and a gap just wide enough for Miranda to slip through opened up.

Miranda and Gin exchanged a look, and the ghost-hound sat down firmly.

"No," he said. "That might as well have 'trap' written

out in glowing letters. You're not going in. Especially not without me."

Miranda put her hands on her hips. "Who was it who just said we're sticking to our plan?"

"That plan didn't include you facing Hern alone on his own turf," Gin growled. "You might as well hand him the knife to stab in your back."

Miranda glanced at the opening. Inside was pitch blackness, but for the first time since that moment by the river, she could feel the wisps of her spirits through their connection again. Very faint, but there, and that made her decision for her.

"Keep watch, Gin," she said, turning toward the tower. "If you hear anything strange coming from the keep, go and help Eli."

Gin reached out and slapped his paw down on the hem of her skirt, pinning her to the pavement. "What part of 'you're not going in' didn't you understand?"

Miranda took a deep breath and turned to face the hound. This wasn't a card she played often, but sometimes Gin was too protective for his own good.

"Gin," she said stiffly. "They're my spirits, just as you are. Let me go."

It was an order, not a request, and Gin, despite not being a formally bound spirit, had to obey. Slowly, begrudgingly, he lifted his paw, and Miranda walked toward the cleft in the tower.

When she reached the entrance, she stopped and looked over her shoulder. "I'll make it up to you, mutt," she said. "Promise."

"*If* you ever come out of there," Gin growled, looking away, "I will hold you to that."

Miranda smiled, then turned and vanished into the cleft of stone. The rock face sealed instantly behind her.

Hern's tower reminded Miranda more of a wealthy townhouse than a Spiritualist's working office. The inside was all polished hardwood and stone hung with tasteful, expensive tapestries, oil paintings, and fine porcelain. Small oil lamps burned in the dark, giving just enough light to make the elegant hall feel claustrophobic. The lamps were lit in a line leading her toward the stairs, painting an obvious path to Hern. Any other turning was blocked with heavy doors Miranda didn't bother trying. She was already in the trap; she might as well follow it through. In any case, her rings were upstairs. She could feel them strongly now, and they were pulling her toward the spiral stair to the tower's high second floor.

When she reached the foot of the stairs, she spotted something that made her stop. Nestled in the space beneath the stairs was a small pump room. Buckets and clothes were stacked neatly, and below the pump was a large bucket of soapy water probably left by Hern's cleaners, for Miranda couldn't imagine the Spiritualist scrubbing his own floors. Still, it gave her an idea. She stepped sideways, scooping up the sturdy bucket by its wooden handle and holding it carefully behind her back as she began to climb the spiral stairs.

Though they might vary greatly in style according to the individual, all Spiritualist towers were built the same. The first floor was cut into multiple rooms for private living, while the second, connected by a wide spiral stair, was one open room that served as the Spiritualist's office, work floor, meeting room, and library. Hern's tower was no exception. Miranda emerged from the spiral staircase at the center of an enormous room. Dozens of lamps hung from the pointed ceiling, and Miranda had to shield her eyes from the sudden brightness. Even so, it was immediately obvious that Hern's taste for nice things didn't stop at his professional space. This room was every bit as elaborate as the rooms below. Fine silk furniture clung to the rounded walls, arranged in little, inviting clusters perfect for confidences. The wooden floor was smothered in fine rugs and the walls were strewn with paintings, mostly cityscapes of Zarin and lovely lounging women wearing very little.

But what caught her attention the most wasn't the glitz or the opulence, the fine statues or the heavy bookcases filled with leather volumes seemingly arranged by color rather than author or subject. Instead, her focus was instantly drawn to a wooden box sitting on a stone end table just in front of her. It was a simple thing, rough-hewn wood and an iron latch with a heavy lock, but Miranda's heart leaped to see it, or rather to feel what was trapped inside. In answer, something inside the box rattled, a beautiful, tinkling bell sound of gold on gold as her rings clattered together.

"Not another step, if you please," a charming, hated voice sounded from somewhere on her left.

Miranda turned, slowly. There, lounging in a chair beside an opulent liquor cabinet, with a sifter of something golden dangling from his jeweled hands, was Hern himself. The arrangement was so contrived Miranda couldn't help wondering how many setups he'd experimented with before settling on this one. He was dressed in a lounging jacket and soft silk pants, more like a gentleman enjoying an evening at home than a Spiritualist whose land was being Enslaved, and he met her glare with an indulgent smile.

"Now," he said, "don't look like that. You should be happy I didn't just catch you in stone and cart you back to Zarin. I'd be well within my rights, considering the trouble you've caused."

"I don't think you'll have any rights once the Court hears about this," she said. "Having a drink in your tower while your lands are crushed beneath the boot of Enslavement? Have you given up even the pretense of being a responsible Spiritualist, Hern?"

"That is a delicate political situation," Hern said. "Not that you'd understand anything about those, seeing how, yet again, you've barged in and upset a stable and delicate system to satisfy what?" He sneered at her across his glass. "Some childish need for revenge? Or do you just enjoy helping Monpress upset kingdoms?"

Below the edge of the stairwell, out of Hern's line of sight, Miranda clenched her bucket of water. "Enough lies, Hern," she said. "Hide here all you want, but I'm taking my spirits back, and then I'm going to put a stop to this. If you won't do your duty to your lands, I will."

She took a step toward the box containing her rings, but she stopped at the familiar whoosh of flame. Hern was standing now, his outstretched hand wreathed in blue fire.

"You forget yourself, Miranda," he said, grinning from ear to ear. "You are in my tower, on my land. You are powerless, spiritless, and trapped. You are in no position to be making demands."

The flames licked at his fingers in long, threatening waves. It was just what Miranda had been waiting for. In one sweeping motion, she flung the bucket at him. Hern barely had time to understand what had happened before the bucket, and the wave of water flying out of it, struck him straight across the chest. The flames on his hands sputtered out and Hern yelped, leaping back and toppling his heavy chair as he did so.

It was only a momentary interruption, but it was enough. From the second the bucket left her hands, Miranda was running for her rings. By the time Hern had his feet back under him, she had the box in her hands. Roaring with rage, Hern made a throwing motion, and a wave of fire leaped from his hand.

Clutching the box to her chest, Miranda dove behind a long couch upholstered in gold and blue silk. The fire flickered out inches from the couch's surface, and Miranda grinned. She'd known Hern would never risk his nice furniture, not even to get her, and that hesitation would be her victory. She looked at the box in her hands. It was small, about the size of a hat box, and she could feel her rings inside jumping and clattering against the wood, trying to get to her.

Miranda checked the lock, but it was enormous, heavy, and dead asleep. So were the hinges, and the wood itself. Still, she thought, grimacing, there was no point in being subtle anymore. So with a whispered apology to the sleeping box, Miranda closed her eyes and opened her spirit. Power flowed into her, and she caught it as it surged, sharpening the raw wizard's will to a needle-thin point that she forced through the crack in the box and into her spirits.

The moment the surge of power hit her rings, she felt their power echo back along the connection. The box in her hands burst into a shower of splinters as Durn, her stone spirit, exploded out of his ring. He rose to his full height in the blink of an eye with her rings clutched gently in his enormous stone hands. Almost sobbing with relief, Miranda took her spirits and slid them back onto her fingers, quaking as the connections roared open again as they met her skin. Durn stood guard until she'd fit every last one back on her fingers. Then, her rings awake and flashing like embers on her hands, Miranda stood again and turned to face the man responsible for all of this.

Hern, however, was ready. He stood across the room, his rings blazing like small suns, and a calm, concentrated look on his face.

"So," he said. "It's come to this."

"You were the one who started it," Miranda growled, standing firmly beside Durn's hulking form. "If you're too scared to finish it, then you shouldn't have called that trial in the first place."

"Oh, I'm not worried about the finish," Hern sneered, lifting his hand so Miranda could see not only his rings but the glittering bands of his bracelets set with large, colorful stones, all sparkling with suppressed power. "You might be Banage's protégé, but I'm the older Spiritualist, more experienced, and master of a larger retinue of spirits. No, I know exactly how this will finish. I'm only sad because I'll probably have to kill you, as that seems to be the only way to keep you down." He sighed. "I was so looking forward to parading you in shame before Banage and the Court, but at this point, I'll take what I can get. However"—his face broke into a thin, hateful smile—"with you dead, I can probably blame this whole Enslavement mess on you, seeing as you won't be around to defend yourself, so the situation is not without its silver lining."

"Don't count your victory so easily," Miranda growled, planting her feet and raising her glittering, jeweled hands. "You may have more spirits, but even if I had only one I would count it against all of yours. It's quality and loyalty of spirits that matters, Hern, not quantity, and we have no intention of losing to a man like you."

"Well, then," Hern said, "let's not waste any more time."

He clapped his hands and then thrust them apart, and every stick of furniture in the room suddenly slid back to the tower walls, leaving a large, open space at the center of the room. Hern, the blue fire still flickering on his fingers, took up position on the far end, while Miranda stepped up to stand opposite, Durn hovering over her. They stood for a moment, studying each other, and then, sick of waiting, Miranda attacked.

Durn launched forward on her signal, skidding across the floor in a wave of spiked stone straight for Hern. The Spiritualist flicked his finger, and vines, the same vines that had trapped Miranda earlier, exploded across the rock spirit's surface. Durn's charge ground to a halt as the plants doubled and tripled, trapping him beneath a swirling nest of woody growth. But Miranda was already moving. She crooked her left thumb where Kirik's ruby flashed. At her signal, the stone glowed like a forge and crackling heat poured off of her hands. A moment later, Durn, and the vines tying him down, burst into a pillar of orange flame that blackened the tower's peaked stone roof. The vines fell away instantly, shriveling in a cloud of resinous black smoke and tiny screams before pouring back into the deep green stone on Hern's middle finger. Hern paid them no attention, raising a large blue-green stone on his opposite hand that began to flash blue-silver as he whispered to it.

Miranda jerked Kirik's fire away just in time, as a massive torrent if icy water drenched the place where the pillar of fire had been. The fire poured back into her ring, but Durn, now free from the vine trap, ignored the water that was raising great clouds of steam from his scorched surface and went straight for Hern. Just before the enormous, enraged rock pile reached him, Hern grabbed a heavy crystal hanging from his neck and shouted a name Miranda couldn't make out. As the word left his lips, the entire tower shook, and the stone wall behind Hern burst open, punched open by a great stone fist. Miranda could only stare in amazed horror as she realized what it was. That hand belonged to the stone spirit that was wrapped around Hern's tower. With amazing speed, the enormous stone hand grabbed Durn midcharge and lifted him in a crushing grip. Durn cried out as the hand tightened and chunks of him began to crumble and fall to the ground.

Miranda thrust out her hand, calling the rock spirit frantically back, but as she moved to help him, Hern made a throwing motion with both hands, and a ring of blue fire roared up around her. Miranda shrank back from the blistering heat and shouted for her wind spirit. Almost before she'd said his name, Eril burst from his pendant and hit the fire full force. He spun in a circle, crushing the flames under a roaring wall of wind so that Miranda could jump out. As she jumped, a cool mist flowed out of the round sapphire on her ring finger. The mist fell like a blanket, smothering the blue fire in an oppressive curtain of water. By the time Miranda landed, the inferno was nothing but a circle of scorch marks on the floor. Panting, she whirled to face Hern, bringing her right hand up. Skarest, her lightning bolt, was already crackling. But as she prepared to launch him, Hern snapped his fingers and a wall of water sprang up in front of him.

Miranda hesitated. Striking water was dangerous for her lightning. At best, it would be horribly painful for the spirit; at worst, it could diffuse Skarest permanently.

Hern caught her hesitation and seized the opportunity. "Enough!" he said. "With that lightning bolt, you're out of spirits, unless you're going to bring your little moss spirit into the fight. I, on the other hand, am just getting started. I've already shown I can counter everything you throw at me. If we keep going, I'm going to have to start breaking your spirits one by one, beginning with that pile of rocks."

As he spoke, the enormous fist holding Durn tightened, and the rock spirit made a gritty, pained sound. Miranda clenched her teeth, but did not lower her hand or stop the arcs of lightning crackling over it. From behind his wall of water, Hern arched an eyebrow at her.

"Fire at me," he said, "and your little lightning spirit will fizzle before he gets ten paces." He crossed his arms over his chest. "You know that, and so for all your posturing, you won't shoot. I'm calling your bluff, Miranda Lyonette. The day of your trial, you were willing to throw away everything to save your spirits. You wouldn't risk killing one of them now, just to get to me. Lower your hands and I'll let the rock spirit live."

"Don't do it, mistress!" Durn cried, struggling against

the larger stone spirit's grip. "You fought for us; we'll fight for you!"

"The rock is right," Skarest crackled. "You came for us like we knew you would. We're not going to be the ones to let you down. Shoot me."

"No," Miranda whispered. "Hern's right; you'll die. We'll find another way."

"We don't need another way," the lightning snapped back. "Look at the water. The spirit he's using as a shield is trembling. For all hitting the water will hurt me, it'll hurt the water twice as much."

Miranda glanced at Hern's water shield. Sure enough, its surface was trembling, warping Hern's smug face behind a lattice of terrified ripples. Her hand crackled. Skarest was gathering power, obliviously intending to shoot whether she gave the order or not, and so Miranda decided to trust him. She focused on her lightning spirit, letting her power flow through their connection until his arcs were painfully bright. Hern must have felt the power building, for his smug expression began to fall, but it was too late. With an enormous burst of blinding light and terrible power, Miranda let Skarest fly.

What happened next was almost too fast to see. Skarest arced toward Hern, flying in a thousand branches of spidering, flashing bolts. Hern raised his hands to brace the water, but then, a moment before the lightning struck his spirit shield, the wall of water vanished. It fell away in a terrified rush, leaving Hern open, unprotected. He had no time to raise another spirit, no time to get out of the way, no time to do anything but stare unbelieving at the white-hot arc before Skarest struck him square in the chest.

There was a tremendous crack, and Hern flew backward, slamming into the stone wall behind him. Deafening thunder clapped a split second after as Skarest returned to Miranda. Now that Hern's power was interrupted, Durn broke away from the great stone hand that held him, smashing the enormous grip to rubble as he fought free and went to stand beside Miranda.

Thus, flanked by her spirits, Miranda stood her ground and watched Hern's slumped body. But the other Spiritualist didn't move. All around them, the tower was shaking as the stone shell fell away, and a stream of sand returned to the crystal around Hern's neck. But still, he did not move.

"Did you kill him?" Miranda whispered, looking down at her lightning bolt.

"No," Skarest sounded very smug. "But he won't be getting up for a while."

Miranda let out a breath and cautiously walked over to Hern. She knelt down beside him and, very gently, turned him over. His chest was burned, but not badly. His hair, however, the long blond tresses he prized so highly, was singed beyond recognition.

Miranda stifled a giggle, covering her nose against the stench of burned hair. "How did you know the water would move?"

"Easy," Skarest crackled. "From the very beginning Hern was a peacock, a liar, and a coward. I knew that a wizard like that couldn't possibly have a bound spirit willing to take a real killing blow from me on his behalf."

"Good guess," Miranda said, standing up.

"Guess nothing," Skarest said. "If I've learned anything from you dragging us to the Spirit Court, it's that bound spirits take after their Spiritualist. If the wizard's good for nothing, the spirits won't be either, doesn't matter how big or how many."

Miranda shook her head. She was endlessly amazed at how her spirits could still surprise her. But before she could start giving orders to secure Hern, there was a horrible clatter from the floor below. Miranda jumped and fell into a defensive position, visions of Hern trapping some sort of vindictive, wild spirit to avenge him if he went down running through her head. He was narcissistic enough to do something like that, she thought, gritting her teeth as she turned to face the top of the stairs, which the whatever-it-was was climbing with astonishing speed. But what popped out of the stairwell wasn't a vindictive spirit, or at least not one of Hern's. It was Gin, and he burst into the room in a flurry of shifting fur and claws.

"Are you all right?" he snapped, looking her over, then looking at Hern. "Oh, good, you did win. I thought you had when the rock barrier went down, but I had to be sure."

"What, so you tore all the way up here?" Miranda winced, imagining the beautiful, decorated halls smashed to pieces in Gin's frantic wake.

Gin gave her a sharp look. "See if I come to help you again."

Miranda just laughed and shook her head. "Sorry, sorry, I'm very happy to see you. Now"—she shoved her arms under Hern's shoulders—"help me get this idiot secured."

Together they got Hern into one of his chairs and tied him tight with a curtain pull. Once he was secure, Miranda plucked off every bit of his jewelry. It was quite a pile, ten rings, five bracelets, and a half dozen necklaces, all humming with power. These she put in the bucket that she'd thrown at him earlier and gave them to Durn.

"Watch him," she said, giving the rock spirit a firm look. "If he starts to wake up again, club him, but gently; don't crack his skull. Just keep him asleep, away from his rings, and out of trouble."

"Very well, mistress," Durn said. "Where are you going?"

Miranda looked out through the enormous gaping hole in the side of Hern's tower, where the city of Gaol lay dark, silent, and frozen under the Enslavement. "I'm going to make sure that thief keeps his promise."

Durn bowed, and Miranda climbed onto Gin's back. As soon as she was on, he leaped through the hole in the wall, landing neatly on the roof of the house next door. The moment his feet hit the rain-soaked tiles, he was running, jumping along the roofs toward the citadel.

CHAPTER
23

Duke Edward stood soaked and alone on the battlements of his citadel. His guards were gone; so were his servants. He didn't know where and he didn't care. He had larger problems. He stood very still, his eyes closed, his face twitching in a concentration deeper than any he'd ever had to maintain. Below him, spread out in a dark grid, was the city, his city, and every spirit, every speck of stone, cowered in homage to him. Their fear bled through the raging spread of his own spirit, making him feel ill and weak, but he did not loosen his grip. Such unpleasantness was necessary if he was to preserve the perfection he'd worked his whole life to achieve. This was just another test, and though he'd never been pushed to Enslavement before, he'd always been ready to do what he had to do. Perfection was not something that could be achieved through half-measures.

Out on the edge of his control, he could feel the sea spirit that had taken over his river surging. It was gathering water from farther upstream, increasing its size and power. It had doubled since he began the Enslavement, swollen with water until he could no longer feel the Spiritualist girl's hold on it. Maybe she had died, or maybe the water spirit had grown too large for her and broken away. Whatever the case, Hern's idea of catching and forcing her to remove her spirit had never been an efficient option. The river was growing too quickly. In another ten minutes it would have enough water to flood the whole city, an outcome that could break his already tenuous hold on his spirits and ruin his town, neither of which was an option he was willing to consider. No, his path was clear. Reestablishing control meant getting the sea spirit out of his river, and Edward was going to do just that, even if it meant destroying the water.

He reached out, his focus sliding across the cowering city to the warehouses on the northern stretch of the river, where he kept his tanneries. Long ago, when he was just a boy, he'd brought the river to heel by threatening to dump the tannery waste into its waters. Now, forty years later, he made good on that threat. With a great thrust of his spirit, the side of the tannery burst open, and five enormous metal barrels of stinking hide soak, their tops frothy with flies and decay, toppled into the river's newly clear water. He grinned when he felt the Great Spirit's power shudder and cringe as hundreds of gallons of rancid, black-green sludge slithered across its surface.

Still, it wasn't enough. The river surged beneath the layer of poison, denying Edward's control of the area, refusing to retreat. He needed something more drastic, but he was already panting from the effort of controlling spirits so far away. Fortunately, the next step was easy.

Even Enslaved, fire needed little encouragement to burn. All he had to do was nudge one of the fallen torches that lay on the docks, dropped by his retreating army, and the flame leaped into the polluted water.

The sludge caught instantly, and the night lit up as hot red fire streaked across the river's surface. The water screamed and churned, raising great waves as it tried to break the surface film of floating sludge and smother the flames, but all it managed was to fan them higher. The duke smiled in triumph, but never let his control waver. Even this might not be enough to drive the invading spirit out.

"My lord?" a small voice whispered beside him. It was plaintive and hoarse, as if it had been calling a long time. He would have ignored it, but if a spirit had gotten up the courage to interrupt him under these circumstances, it was probably important.

"What?" he said, turning only a tiny fraction of his attention from his battle with the river.

The spirit flickered, and he saw it was the castle fire, the single large fire that moved the treasury door and cooked the castle's food and heated the rooms, speaking through the chimney. The fire had remained loyal even when the river had been compromised, which was why he turned to listen more closely.

"The thief, Eli Monpress," it said, its voice crackling. "He's out in the front square."

The duke's patience vanished instantly. "Don't bother me with such rubbish," he said, turning back to the river.

"But sir," the fire said again. "I really think you should look. He's doing something..." It paused, throwing a puff of nervous smoke into the air. "Odd."

"Odd?" The duke looked sideways at the chimney. "Odd how?"

"It looks like he's giving a speech, sir," the fire finished in a rush, its light ducking back down the chimney just in case the duke decided it was wasting his time. But Edward was frowning, considering his decision. The river demanded his attention, but ignoring Eli Monpress was a risk only fools took. He tried it one way, then another, and came to the conclusion there was nothing to be done but to have a look himself. Keeping the back of his mind on the burning river, the duke walked through the small knot of buildings at the top of the citadel to the battlements on the opposite side, which overlooked the square.

The moment he looked down he understood why the fire had called him. There, standing on a pile of barrels and crates he'd scavenged from who knew where, was Eli Monpress. He was standing in plain sight in the middle of the square, and he seemed to be yelling. Very cautiously, the duke shifted a bit of his spirit away from the river and toward the city center. As his spirit moved over the square, he suddenly heard the thief's words loud and clear, and his hands clutched the edge of the battlements in white-knuckled fury.

Eli stood atop his mountain of borrowed barrels like a general in a war monument. Light rain soaked his shirt and plastered his black hair to his scalp, which added nicely to the desired effect. Beleaguered heroes always looked better in the rain.

He threw out his hands dramatically as he spoke, pouring every ounce of every scrap of everything he'd ever learned from a lifetime of unconventional wizardry into his voice. "Spirits of Gaol!" he cried, layering just enough power so that his words flowed smooth and strong over the quivering panic around him. "Look at what's been done to you! Look at the situation you've allowed yourselves to be put in! What has happened in Gaol? Free spirits are beholden to no one save their Great Spirit, and yet here you are, cowering while your river is out there fighting the duke for your freedom!"

"That's not our river!" one of the lamps shouted. "It's that Spiritualist's spirit!"

"All the more reason to be ashamed!" Eli answered, his voice harsh. "That an outsider came and risked their neck to save you, and you won't even help."

A great round of shouts went up at this, calling him wizard thief, and demanding why should we listen to you? Finally, one voice rolled over the rest. It was the door, the great iron door from the treasury, now standing sullenly at the corner of the square, propped up with sandbags.

"What do you know?" it said. "This is all your fault, anyway. Things were fine until you got here. And now you stand there and tell us to what, rise up? Bah, easy for you! You're a wizard. You never lived with the duke!"

Eli stared at the door, his eyes wide. When he spoke next, there was a tremor in his voice. "You think I don't know the duke's cruelty? You think I just waltzed into Gaol to make empty speeches? Look then!" he shouted, ripping off his coat. "Look for yourselves and then say that I don't know what it's like to cross the Duke of Gaol!"

He unbuttoned his shirt and peeled it back, and a great sound went up from the gathered spirits as his bare shoulders came into view. Eli's skin, always pale, was now a horrid mottle of black and purple bruises. Angry red marks stood out on his lower arms, and his joints were red and swollen until they were painful to look at. All around the courtyard, the spirits who could see the physical world were whispering to those who couldn't. Those in turn whispered to their neighbors, and Eli's injuries got worse with every telling. For his part, Eli stood perfectly still, letting the soft rain splash on his injured skin as the story grew around him.

"So you see," Eli said, gritting his teeth as he gently replaced his shirt, "I, too, have felt what it means to defy the Duke of Gaol."

But the door was not impressed. "Bah," it growled. "What are a few bruises? You're human. You're free from the true horrors. You can't even feel the Enslavement, the duke putting his boot on your mind. If you could feel what we feel, you'd be terrified. You wouldn't last a day living the life we live."

A general murmur of agreement went up at this, but Eli kept his eyes on the door. "And this life," he said calmly. "Do you like it?"

"Of course not," the iron said. "We hate every day, but what can we do? This is our domain; we can't leave it."

"You don't need to leave to be free!" Eli stood up straight, filling his voice with power until it swelled through the entire square. "Listen up, all of you. You're right that, as a human, I can never know the humiliation of Enslavement. But, as a human, and a wizard, let me tell you a secret: *No* wizard, not even the Duke of Gaol, is strong enough to simultaneously Enslave an entire city. The only reason he was able to do it is because you're all afraid of him. It is your own fear that Enslaves you, not the duke! If you want to be free of this life of fear and subservience, then stand up and fight back! His control is already broken, or he wouldn't have had to try an Enslavement in the first place. The only thing standing between you and a free life is yourselves!"

A great murmur went up across the square as the last of Eli's words echoed off the tall buildings. Lamps flickered and houses leaned their eaves together, whispering. Eli remained on his barrels, listening, marking the difference in tone. Fear was being replaced by something else—energy, anticipation, and a raw urge to get out of an intolerable situation. Then, like the tide shifting, the fear came roaring back. In a single instant, the square fell silent. Eli squinted a moment in the dim lamplight, confused, and then he turned around and looked up. Two stories up on the battlements of the square citadel stood the Duke of Gaol.

He looked down over the square in utter contempt, but he didn't say a word. He didn't need to. At that moment, the full weight of his crushing will slammed down on the square. All around Eli, spirits began to squirm frantically, lowering themselves and begging for forgiveness. The duke just sneered, and the Enslavement grew until the weight was unbearable. It was at that moment, when it looked like the spirits would be under that crushing weight forever, that Eli crooked his fingers behind his back. Suddenly, a sound broke the silence. It was a thin, soft whistling noise, as of a rope being spun, and then, out of the dark, something small and black launched from the alley between two houses. Everything in the square turned to look as a stone roofing tile shot through the air, flying in a beautiful, straight arc high over the houses and the cobbled square, straight toward the duke.

What happened next seemed to unfold in slow motion. The duke stared at the tile in disbelief as it whistled toward him. Then, belatedly, he threw up his hands and began to shout a command, but he never got the words out. The tile struck him on the shoulder with a loud, solid *thwack*.

The duke stumbled back with a pained gasp, clutching his shoulder. The tile's impact wasn't a blow to kill him, or even injure him beyond inconvenience. His Enslavement hadn't even wavered, but the change in the square was immediate. All at once, spirits straightened up, gazing in wonder as the duke, the untouchable, terrible, unbeatable Duke of Gaol, lurched from the blow of a single tile.

For a long second, everything was silent, and then, with a great cry, another roofing tile launched itself at the citadel. It fell short, clacking off the stone wall, but the next one whizzed just past the duke's head, forcing him to duck for cover. The moment his head disappeared below the battlements, the square went crazy.

Houses shook, tossing off the drainpipes, shutters, and overhangs that had been their mouthpieces for reporting to the duke's wind. The lamps flared up like tiny, glass-trapped suns, spreading the story of what had just happened down the dark streets in a wave of light. Everywhere, spirits were casting off the duke's order, shouting and carrying on and doing what they wanted. The cobblestones slid out of their perfect geometric alignment to lie comfortably crooked. The tiny flowers in the pristine window boxes sprouted in absurd abundance, spilling leaves and seedpods into the street. Inside the empty houses, whose residents had fled for the walls the moment the conscript army was routed, tables flipped themselves over, chairs fell backward, and neat piles of table linens threw themselves like streamers over everything, creating dancing shapes behind the wobbly glass windows.

It was, in short, beautiful chaos, and Eli could not have been happier. He hopped off his pile of now-jittering barrels and waved at them as they rolled off to wherever they wanted to go. He was sliding his wet jacket back over his sore shoulders when Monpress jogged over from his alley, an anxious look on his usually calm face.

"Excellent job," Eli said with a wide grin, slapping the old man on the back. "Beautiful arc, too. You haven't lost an inch on that throw."

Monpress gave him a sideways look. "Glad to hear you're so happy about it," he said, glancing at a pack of wooden benches as they gallivanted down a side street. "From my point of view, it looks like we just kicked off the end of the world."

"Hardly," Eli said. "We were merely the catalyst for something that had been brewing for years." He smiled up at the empty battlements. "People and spirits aren't all that different in their fundamentals. When the circumstances are primed, all it takes is one act of defiance to set off a revolution."

"I see," Monpress said, frowning as a line of barrels rolled out of a shop on their own accord and emptied themselves into the street, dumping gallons of dark red wine into the gutters. "Remind me never to take you into a country I like."

Eli just grinned and settled back to watch the show.

The Duke of Gaol ran down the spiral stairs of his citadel, taking the broad stone steps two at time. He could hear the chaos through the thick stone walls, and rage like he had never felt burned in his mind, tightening the grip of his enslavement even as more and more of the city's spirits slipped free. Well, he thought as he burst into the great hall of the citadel, not for much longer. He was the Duke of Gaol still. The rebellious spirits would remember who their master was before the sun rose.

The last of his soldiers had already fled, leaving the great hall empty. The duke marched past the scattered benches and to the enormous hearth. The fire was banked for the night, awake and quiet under a blanket of ash. Without hesitation, the duke thrust his hand into the glowing embers, and the fire sprang up with a piteous, crackling roar.

"You're coming with me," the duke growled. "We're putting an end to this."

The fire bowed, shuddering under the Enslavement that roared down the duke's arm. It rose heatless from its bed and settled itself in his hand, flickering across his skin without so much as singeing his white cuffs, too cowed even to burn. Satisfied that this spirit was still loyal, for the moment at least, the duke turned on his heel and walked toward the great racks of weaponry on the far wall. He grabbed an ax with a great, curving moon for a blade. Hefting it in one hand, he mastered the small, stupid spirit with one blast of his will. Thus armed, he marched to the front of his citadel. The great doors flung themselves open as he approached, and he stepped into the chaos that was once his ordered, beautiful, perfect city to face the man responsible.

"Monpress!" he roared, his voice cutting through every other sound.

Across the square, two men looked up, and the duke, one hand wreathed in orange fire, the other gripping his ax, went out to reclaim his authority.

"Eli," Monpress whispered, watching the black figure with the flaming hand and the gleaming ax stalk toward them. "I say this as your teacher. You should run. That man cannot be reasoned with."

"You think?" Eli said quietly. "However, considering the little speech I just made, running doesn't seem like an option."

Monpress sighed. "Do you see the trouble principles get you into? If I'd known you were this eager to throw your life away, I wouldn't have bothered coming here to save you."

"Thanks for the encouragement." Eli sighed, turning to face the duke. "If you don't want to fight, I suggest you leave. This could get ugly."

He expected some sort of protest at this, maybe a dry stab at his supposed inability to do anything without help. But all he got was a hand squeezing his shoulder. "Good luck," Monpress whispered. Then the hand was gone, and so was the feeling of having someone beside him.

Eli gritted his teeth. Couldn't blame the old man, really. He was just living by the rules that had kept him alive through his decades as a thief. The rules he had taught Eli, and which Eli was ignoring right now as he stood at the end of the chaotic square, lounging with his arms crossed as the duke marched toward him.

"I should point out," he said when the duke was ten feet away, "that if you kill me, you'll never know where I stashed all the money I've stolen."

"You've made yourself more trouble than any money could pay down at this point." The duke's voice was an icy knife.

Eli swallowed and took a step back. His back was to the line of houses on the far side of the square, directly across from the citadel. Though the ruckus of rebellion was raging loud and strong around them, the houses facing the duke were silent and crouching. The show of obedience didn't save them. The duke glared up at the wooden structures and raised his left hand, the one wreathed in flame.

"Stop!" Eli cried. "If you burn it, it'll never serve you again."

The duke glared murder at him. "Understand, *thief*," he said. "I'd rather rule a smoking pit than be disobeyed by my city."

He waved his hand in a great, glorious burst of orange sparks, and the house behind Eli exploded in flames.

"Let this be a lesson!" the duke cried, his voice booming through the Enslavement that was, even now, still grabbing at order. "The price for disobedience is death!"

The house screamed and writhed as enormous flames raced across its timber frame, devouring the old hardwood with unnatural speed. But then, as fast as the flames had started, they flickered out. The duke's eyes widened, and he turned to the fire in his hand. It flared up, flickering in terror and pointing wildly at Eli.

Eli was standing at the house's door, one hand gripping the wood of the door frame. He had his back to the duke, and his figure was shimmering with heat. Steam rose from his wet jacket and with it smoke curled from his shoulders in long white wisps, forming a cloud above his head that flashed and sparked. The cloud grew, clinging

to him, and by the time the last of the house fires flickered
out, Eli's shape was almost invisible behind the thick
smoke. A great sound roared up in the sudden darkness,
and a giant burst from the sparking smoke. It stood as tall
as the house it clung to, glowing and liquid, like flowing
fire, in a bulky and almost human shape, complete with
a great, grinning face. Little puffs of steam rose from
the giant's surface as the soft rain brushed against it, but
the fiery monster ignored the water, grinning down at the
duke with monstrous glee.

"You see, Edward," Eli said, his voice hoarse with
smoke but still mocking, still triumphant as he grinned over
his shoulder, "you don't get to set the price anymore."

The duke's eyes narrowed. "So your fire spirit appears
at last? I was beginning to think it was a rumor after all
when you failed to bring it out during out little talk."

"Come on," Eli said. "You weren't nearly scary enough
before for me to bring out my trump cards."

"Really?" The duke scowled. "Well, let's see how
many more I can make you play before you die."

"Now," Eli said, turning around, "be reasonable—"

A blast of fire was his only answer. Eli dove sideways
as the duke lashed out, sending fire out in great waves,
burning anything that would burn. All around them the
houses burst into flame, and the wood began to shriek in
terror. Eli shouted to Karon. The giant nodded and began
moving from house to house, sucking up the fire as he
went. But even he wasn't fast enough to stop it all. The
duke's enslaved flames leaped with singular purpose, eating up the wet wood like sparks on dry grass, turning the
square into a trap of flames.

Grim and grinning, his ax gleaming in the firelight, the

duke began to advance on Eli, and Eli, not keen on traps or axes, decided it was time to run. In a burst of speed, he shot past the duke and ran flat-out toward the far side of the square, where the fire had not reached. But hard as he ran, he could hear the duke behind him. The duke moved with amazing speed for a man his age, and just as Eli was about to duck down a fireless alley, the duke gave a shout. There was a flash of light, and a stream of flame leaped over Eli's head, singeing his hair. A moment later, the houses on either side of the alley burst into a hungry fire.

Eli skidded to a stop and turned to find the duke right on top of him, swinging wildly with the ax. The old man held it like a stick of firewood, but with a blade like that, he didn't have to be good. Eli shrieked and jumped out of the way, careful to keep his back to the open square and not the burning buildings.

The duke recovered instantly, hurling a wave of flame, not at the houses, but at Eli himself. The thief was gone before it landed, running along the edge of the square and back toward his lava giant, his last refuge. Before he'd gone a dozen feet, the duke landed a blast of fire on his back, and Eli fell. He rolled across the wet cobbles, smacking the giggling flames with his hands until they were smothered, but while he was putting himself out, the duke had closed the distance, and when Eli looked up again, he saw that he was trapped. They were back where they'd started, at the farthest end of the square from the citadel. Eli jumped to his feet as the duke advanced, ready to run again, but there was nowhere to go. He was right up against the burning doorway of a storefront, with the duke in front of him and everything else in flames.

By the time Eli realized that he was truly trapped, it was too late. The duke's burning hand closed on his shoulder and tossed him to the ground with surprising strength. Eli hit the doorstep hard, crying out as the skin on his shoulder blistered from the duke's burning grip. He started to get up again, but the duke's boot slammed down on his chest, pinning him to the ground. Edward stood above him, a black silhouette against the burning night.

"Go on," the duke whispered. "Call your lava spirit. It won't do you any good. Your head will be off your shoulders before the words leave you."

Eli swallowed, and the duke's boot pressed harder on his chest, crushing the breath out of him.

"I've won, Monpress," the duke said, raising his ax in a shining arc. "I *always* win."

Eli couldn't even think of an answer for that. He could only watch as the ax whistled through the air, flying straight for the exposed area between his collarbone and his neck.

A moment before it struck, something strange happened. The blow, which had been straight and true, turned sideways, landing not in Eli's flesh, but deep in the wooden doorstep beside him. For a moment, both Eli and the duke just stared at the blade. Then Edward ripped it free with a roar of rage and raised the ax again, using both hands this time, the fire from his flame-wreathed fingers scorching the ax's wooden handle. But as he swung again, Eli saw the ax blade flip in the duke's hands. It flipped on its own, and Eli heard a small, terrified voice cry out in defiance, "Death to tyrants!"

With that cry, the metal head of the ax let go of its

shaft. It flew into the house behind Eli, burying itself in the burning door. Edward, robbed of the ax's weight, stumbled into his swing. He was still staring at the blade-less hilt in disbelief when another extraordinary thing happened. The wooden shop sign, its painted surface blistered and illegible from the fire's heat, let go of its hinges. Nothing had broken, for the nails were still there, still strong. The wood simply had stopped holding on to them. The sign fell with a fearsome cry of vengeance and struck the duke square in the back.

"Go!" the sign shouted, bearing down on the duke with all its weight.

Eli went. He shot up, kicking the duke out of the way and running past him. But the duke was not done. With tremendous strength, he threw the sign off and made a grab for Eli as he passed, catching the thief's leg and sending them both sprawling on the wet cobbles. Eli kicked, but Edward was too fast. He surged forward, his hands going for Eli's neck, but just before he reached the thief, the ground beneath them began to rumble. At the corner of the square, the iron treasury door launched off its supports with a great, ringing cry. It rolled like a wheel, bouncing over the cobblestones that swiveled to guide it.

"For the cause!" it cried, its iron voice filled with decades of bottled anger. "Death to tyrants!"

The duke had just enough time to look up, his face pale and disbelieving, as the door flipped itself around and, with a final wordless cry of vengeance, fell flat-side down on top of him.

With a great, iron crash, the enslavement over Gaol vanished. The duke's control winked out like a snuffed candle, and all at once spirits were everywhere, piling themselves on top of the door, which was ringing like a gong in triumph. Unfortunately, in their exuberance, they weren't watching for Eli, who was still lying on his back where the duke had tripped him, staring in amazement. When the second hail of roofing tiles nearly took his leg off, he realized he'd better get out.

He rolled over with a groan, moving stiff and slow where the running and the falls had battered his poor bruises, looking for somewhere safe to lie. But everywhere he looked, spirits were rushing forward, trampling him under a wave of pent-up rage. Eli beat them back as best he could, but it was like fighting the tide, and he realized that he was going to be crushed to death under a riot of celebrating barrels, cobblestones, and roofing tile.

He had just enough time to appreciate the inglorious and ironic nature of such an end when a pair of strong arms burst through the jabbering spirits and grabbed him by the shoulders, hauling him up and out in a single motion.

"You all right?" said a blessedly familiar gruff voice, and Eli nearly burst into tears. He'd never been so happy to hear Josef in his life.

"Better than the other guy," he said, but the words turned into a choking cough. Even with the rain, the square was still black with smoke.

"He's fine," Josef said, slapping him on the back.

Somewhere behind them, Eli heard Giuseppe Monpress's familiar sigh. "Glad I found you, then. If he'd died here, he'd have been too burned to turn in for the bounty."

"Thanks for the sympathy," Eli coughed out, slapping his chest to get his lungs clear. He was just thinking about maybe trying to stand on his own when he felt the court-yard rumble and looked up to see Karon coming.

"I've kept the fires confined as best I could," the lava spirit rumbled. "But I think it's time for me to go. The river seems to be taking matters into its own hands."

As if to prove his point, a great crashing sound rose up in the distance, the sound of water washing over things it shouldn't. Eli opened his arms and let Karon's smoke pour into him again, wincing as the pain of the burn on his chest flashed like a fresh wound. But the pain faded quickly, and he pushed off of Josef just before a wave of white water burst into the square. It flooded up the street, surging over the burning houses in absurd, gravity-defying waves. Even the great pile of spirits marking where the duke had fallen was washed under, and everywhere the fire vanished beneath the cool, blue-white surge.

With the water came a stiff wind. It blew from the west, driving the stench of burned wood away. By this point, Eli and the rest had slogged through the water to the steps of the duke's citadel, where they were out of the flood. The wind hit them head-on, chilling their wet clothes and fill-ing the air with the smell of the cold, rocky shore. Then something landed with an enormous splash just around the corner. Eli jumped at the sound, and Josef's hand went to the Heart, but he dropped his grip when the source of the sound came around the corner. It was a little old man, thin as whipcord and with a genteel, scholarly appearance that was only slightly ruined by the way he was wringing the water out of his billowing white robes.

He stopped when he reached the stairs, staring at the huddled group with trepidation as he settled his spec-tacles on his nose.

"Excuse me," he said, leaning forward inquisitively. "Which of you is Eli Monpress?"

"That would be me," Eli said, stepping forward. "Might I ask who's asking?"

"My name is Lelbon," the man said with a dry, polite smile. "I am a scholar and general errand runner for Illir, the West Wind."

He paused, as if this should mean something to them, but Josef just stared at him, and the elder Monpress leaned back against the doors, keen to see where this would go. Eli, however, broke into a grin.

"The West Wind, you say?" Eli scratched his chin thoughtfully. "And what is the West Wind doing sending representatives here? Gaol certainly doesn't count as the western coast."

"My employer is interested in the well-being of all the lands he blows over," Lelbon said stiffly. "We've been aware of the situation in Gaol for some time, but were unable to interfere due to the local Great Spirit's refusal to allow outside aid. The Spiritualist Lyonette has been investigating for us and, as you can see, has rectified the situation."

"By flooding the whole place," Eli said, laughing. "That's Spiritualists for you."

Lelbon just gave him a sour look. "I was sent to you with a warning. Spiritualist Lyonette is currently speaking with my master, but she will be heading in this direction shortly. I am instructed to relay that it would be wise of you to move on."

"Would it?" Eli said. "And where exactly does your master get off giving me orders?"

"It's only a suggestion," Lelbon said with a shrug. "The

great Illir is merely concerned for your welfare. After all, even for as great a spirit as the West Wind, interfering in the affairs of the favorite is politically unadvisable."

"Favorite?" Josef said, looking at Eli. "Favorite what?"

"Forget it," Eli said. "All right, you heard the little old man. Let's get out of here."

"What, just like that?" Josef asked. "We're not going to steal anything?"

"What's left to steal?" Eli said, nodding at the smoldering town and the great empty citadel. "Besides," he said, grinning at Monpress, "according to everyone, *I* already stole the entire treasury from the thief-proof fortress. That's quite enough for one country. We've got the Fenzetti; we're done here."

That's when he noticed that Josef wasn't carrying anything.

"You *do* have the Fenzetti, don't you?" Eli said. "It's with Nico, right? Where is she, anyway?"

"I've got it," Josef said flatly. "Nico's another matter." He turned around and walked into the shadowed doorway of the citadel, coming back with the Heart strapped across his shoulders and two wrapped bundles. One was sword-shaped and wrapped in cloth, the Fenzetti. The other was small and dark and carefully cradled in Josef's arms.

"Wait," Eli said, going very, very pale. "She's not—"

"No," Josef said. "But it isn't exactly good. I'll tell you on the way. Let's go if we're going."

"Right," Eli said quietly, putting his smiling face back so fast Josef didn't even see his expression change. He turned to the elder Monpress, who was still lounging on the dry step. "You're welcome to piggyback on our escape, old man. It makes me feel useful to assist the elderly."

"Your concern is touching," Monpress said, "but I've still a little unfinished business here. Anyway, even your quiet escapes are too flashy for me."

"Suit yourself," Eli said. "See you around."

"Hopefully not," Monpress answered, but Eli and Josef were already splashing across the soggy square. They vanished down a side street headed toward the north gate, where the panicked crowds of people, who had fled to the city border the first time the city went mad, were now surging through the newly opened doors and over the walls, which had shrunk back to their original size and shape on the duke's death.

When the thief and his swordsman had vanished completely into the dark, Lelbon and Monpress exchanged a polite farewell and went their separate ways, Lelbon down the road toward the river, and Monpress, very quietly, into the citadel. That was the last Gaol saw of either of the Monpress thieves.

CHAPTER
24

Gin raced through the streets and toward the burning square, Miranda clinging to his back, urging him on. Minutes ago, she'd felt the pressure of the duke's Enslavement vanish completely. Since then, everything had been in chaos. The spirits of the city were rioting in their new freedom, and the entire town seemed to be moving as it saw fit. Mellinor's water was everywhere, putting out fires, moving through the streets, but the water's spirit was too large for her to touch now, and their link felt thin and distant. By contrast, her rings felt closer than ever, the connection woven thick and heavy up and down her arms.

A wind rose as she rode, stiff and cold and smelling of the sea, though they were a hundred miles inland. It grew stronger as they went until Miranda could feel it through her clothes, pressing on her skin like a weight. Unbidden, Gin began to slow down, falling from a run to a trot, then a walk, then nothing, standing still on the broad street that opened into the square at the front of the citadel.

"What's wrong?" Miranda whispered. "Keep going."

"I can't," Gin growled. "The wind is blocking the way."

Miranda glanced up, staring at the empty road ahead. The wind was to their back now, buffeting ghosthound and rider from side to side. Then, all at once, the air fell still. High overhead, the clouds peeled back, brushed aside to reveal the moonlit sky, and in the stillness, the air grew lighter. Miranda smelled wet stone, salt, and sea storms, and then, without warning, the West Wind itself was upon them.

Though she couldn't see it, Miranda didn't need to. Playing host to Mellinor had made her an expert at feeling the special nature of the Great Spirits. Still, even if she'd never met one before, she would have known the West Wind for what it was. There was simply nothing else the enormous spirit surrounding her could be. It was the essence of a sea wind, endless, wet, salt laden, and powerful, blowing ever upward. It covered the city, missing nothing, and yet Miranda could feel its attention focus on her as an approving ripple, almost like a chuckle, ran through the enormous, invisible river of power.

"A pleasure to meet you at last, Spiritualist," the West Wind said. "You and Mellinor have undone a great wrong against the spirits of this place. For this, you have our gratitude."

Miranda nodded, dumbstruck. The wind's voice was like a gale in her head. The words ricocheted off the buildings, garbled, and yet there was no mistaking them for anything other than what they were. When she did find her own voice at last, however, she asked a question.

"What of the duke?" she said. "Did Eli succeed?"

"He did," the wind said, "and disappeared shortly thereafter. I am sorry, Spiritualist."

Miranda felt like the wind had punched her in the stomach. She slumped over, letting the crippling feeling of defeat work its way through her. There went her reputation, her ticket back into the Spirit Court. There went her career. *Why* had she let Eli go off on his own?

"Don't look that way," the wind said. "I had Lelbon promise you great rewards for your assistance here, and I keep my word. Already I have sent winds to the Spirit Court Tower in Zarin to speak with the Rector Spiritualis. Banage and I have met before, and I am sure he will listen with an open mind. I have also sent winds to each tower to inform the Keepers of your deeds today, and the great debt I owe you." Miranda felt something in the wind slide, and she could almost imagine that the West Wind was smiling. "Surely, such words of praise will smooth over any remaining rough politics."

Miranda could only nod stupidly. Most Spiritualists had only heard of the West Wind in stories. To actually be directly contacted by such an enormous and powerful spirit would be the experience of a lifetime. They'd forgive just about anything for a chance to curry its good favor.

Seeing her expression, the wind chuckled. "Is it enough, Spiritualist?"

"I suppose," Miranda said, still dumbstruck. "What happens now?"

"Now, I must leave," the wind said. "Winds are not meant to be lords over land. I have received a special dispensation from those who care for this sort of thing to allow Mellinor to remain as temporary Great Spirit for the next few weeks until the river Fellbro's soul can be cleansed and reinstated."

"Fellbro is still here?" Miranda asked. "You mean he's not—"

"What?" the wind said. "Dead? Of course not. It takes more than losing some water to kill a river. Mellinor only pushed it aside for a while. Right now Fellboro's slinking in the mud and sulking. Too long spent living in fear has made his water bitter, but we'll soon have him to rights. In the meanwhile, Mellinor will put the land back in order. Once a Great Spirit, always a Great Spirit. You should stay here as well. I imagine the human side of Gaol also needs fixing."

Miranda looked around at the empty town. "That it does, but I'm not exactly a lady of the manor."

The wind laughed, rippling over her. "I'm sure you'll manage. I'm leaving Lelbon here to help. Try not to be too hard on the little river spirit when it comes back. And Miranda?"

This last bit was whispered, a bare breeze in her ear. "Good luck and thank you. I won't be forgetting your usefulness."

That struck Miranda as an odd way of putting it, but the wind was already blowing past her, rising in a gale and blowing west, clearing the clouds out of the way as the sun began to peek over the horizon.

"Well," Gin said. "Now what?"

"I'm not sure," Miranda said. She was feeling a bit deflated, but happy. If anyone could get her back into the Spirit Court without Eli, it would be a spirit like the West Wind. Still, first things first. "Erol," she said clutching the pearl pendant at her neck. "Go and tell Durn to bring

Hern to the citadel so we can lock him up somewhere more comfortable."

The wind tittered at this and left, blowing out in a whistling gust. When it was gone, she nudged Gin forward. He trotted off toward the citadel, tongue hanging out.

"We need to find the second-in-command," Miranda said, running her hands through her hair as her brain scrambled. "Send a runner to the Council and to the King of Argo to find out who's supposed to be taking over, and to explain what happened. I'm not looking forward to that. Plus, there's cleanup, getting the people back in line and back into their homes, rebuilding, so much to do."

"You'll manage," Gin said. "First, let's get some breakfast. I don't think anyone would begrudge me a pig after all that running."

Miranda laughed, and together they picked up the pace, loping past the burned-out buildings and into the great, empty citadel of Gaol.

All in all it took two weeks for the King of Argo to declare the Duke of Gaol's successor. Edward of Gaol had no wife or children, and though his nephew was the obvious choice to inherit, the nature of the duke's death prevented a smooth transition. He'd been murdered, that was certain. Still, the King of Argo couldn't levy charges against a shop sign, roofing tiles, and an iron door. So, after much deliberation, the duke's death was written down as an accident. Once that was out of the way, the nephew showed up almost immediately and proceeded at once to instigate a full inventory of Gaol's wealth and property, a task that left him exceedingly unhappy.

"This is intolerable!" he cried, shoving the account books under Miranda's nose for the fifth time that hour. "Not even counting the water damage done to my priceless treasures, which we're still dredging out of the river, the old goat spent almost forty thousand gold standards on his ridiculous Eli Monpress obsession, ten thousand of which was spent making that brick of a citadel look impressive from the outside! Honestly, it's not even a citadel, just a garrison with overly thick walls and an absurd little mansion stuck on its head."

"Well," Miranda said, "look at it this way: at least Gaol's not in the hole, which is more than I can say for most kingdoms. So why don't you count yourself lucky? You are, after all, one duchy richer than you were last week."

"That's hardly the point!" the nephew cried. "Look here! Here's a check written out to one Phillipe di Monte for 'consultation and advice involving the actions of Eli Monpress.' Written out *the day my uncle died*, no less! It's scandalous!"

"Phillipe di Monte," Miranda said thoughtfully. "Isn't he the villain from Pacso's *The Piteous Fall of Dulain*?"

"I don't care if it was Punchi the puppet!" the nephew shouted back. "I just want to know why *he's* getting almost twenty thousand standards of *my* money when his advice obviously didn't work!"

Miranda didn't have an answer for that. Fortunately, Lelbon appeared at that moment to tell her that Fellbro was almost ready to take his river back.

As it turned out, by the time the duke's nephew contacted Gaol's money changer in Zarin, the gold had already been paid to the mysterious Phillipe di Monte. This sent the poor boy into a rage, and convinced it was

Eli himself making a fool of him, the new duke then sent off a letter pledging another twenty thousand to Monpress's bounty, just on general principle.

"That will show the no-good thief!" he said, sealing the letter to the Council Bounty office.

Miranda wisely kept her comments to herself.

Just when she was sure she could take no more, an envoy from the Spirit Court arrived to fetch Hern and Miranda and take them back to Zarin. The wind's words must have had a better effect than even Miranda had anticipated, for the Spiritualists treated her as if she was the Rector Spiritualis himself. This infuriated Hern to no end, which put Miranda in very high spirits as she rode down to the river.

She'd spoken to her sea spirit very little while Mellinor had inhabited the river. He'd simply been too large and too busy to talk with. Now the blue water was gone and the river was back to its usual cloudy green. As Miranda walked out on the dock, Mellinor rose in a pillar of water to greet her, his water cloudy with fatigue.

"I was almost afraid you wouldn't come back," Miranda said. "Not after you'd gotten a taste for being a Great Spirit again."

"Of course I came back," the water said. "I'm a sea, not a river. All this flowing and silt was driving me mad. Besides"—his voice grew wistful—"no river could replace my own seabed. But I'm already resigned to that, and anyway, you're my shore now, Miranda."

She smiled at that, and held out her hands. "Ready to come home, then?"

"More than you know," he said and sighed, sliding back into her with a relieved, sinking feeling.

He sank to the bottom of her spirit and fell asleep almost instantly. When he was completely settled, Miranda turned around and walked back to Gin, who was waiting on the road.

"Come on." She grinned, sliding onto his back. "Let's go home."

"I thought we'd never leave," Gin sighed, loping back toward the citadel where the other Spiritualist waited with Hern, now ringless and bound in chains, to journey with them back to Zarin where, Miranda had the feeling, she'd get a much warmer welcome this time around.

ACKNOWLEDGMENTS

Thank you to Aaron, Matt, Krystina, Steven, Andrea, and everyone who read my books back when they were really terrible. Your feedback got me to where I am today.

extras

www.orbitbooks.net

about the author

Rachel Aaron was born in Atlanta, GA. After a lovely, geeky childhood full of books and public television, and then an adolescence spent feeling awkward about it, she went to the University of Georgia to pursue English literature with an eye toward getting her PhD. Upper-division coursework cured her of this delusion, and she graduated in 2004 with a BA and a job, which was enough to make her mother happy. She currently lives in a '70s house of the future in Athens, GA, with her loving husband, overgrown library, and small, brown dog. Find out more about the author at www.rachelaaron.net

Find out more about Rachel Aaron and other Orbit authors by registering for the free monthly newsletter at www.orbitbooks.net

if you enjoyed
THE SPIRIT REBELLION

look out for

THE SPIRIT EATER

The Legend of Eli Monpress: Book 3

also by

Rachel Aaron

The great hall of the Shapers had been flung open to let in the wounded. Shaper wizards, their hands still covered in soot from their work, ran out into the blowing snow to help the men who came stumbling onto the frosted terrace through a white-lined hole in the air. Some fell and did not rise again, their long, black coats torn beyond recognition. These the Shapers rolled onto stretchers that, after a sharp order, stood on their own and scrambled off on spindly wooden legs, some toward the waiting doctors, others more slowly toward the cold rooms, their unlucky burdens already silent and stiff.

Alric, Deputy Commander of the League of Storms, lay on the icy floor toward the center of the hall, gritting his teeth against the pain as a Shaper physician directed the matched team of six needles sewing his chest back together. His body seized as the needles hit a sore spot, and the Shaper grabbed his shoulders, slamming him back against the stone with surprising strength.

"You must not move," she said.

"I'm trying not to," Alric replied through gritted teeth.

The old physician arched an eyebrow and started the needles again with a crooked finger. "You're lucky," she said, holding him still. "I've seen others with those wounds going down to the cold rooms." She nodded toward the three long claw marks that ran down his chest from neck to hip. "You must be hard to kill."

"Very," Alric breathed. "It's my gift."

She gave him a strange look, but kept her hands firmly on his shoulders until the needles finished. Once the wounds were closed, the doctor gave him a bandage and left to find her next patient. Alric sat up with a ragged breath, holding his arms out as the bandage rolled around his torso and tied itself off over his left shoulder. When it had pulled itself tight, Alric sat a moment longer with his eyes closed, mastering the pain. When he was sure he had it under control, he grabbed what was left of his coat and got up to find his commander.

The Lord of Storms was standing in the snow beside the great gate he had opened for their retreat. Through the shimmering hole in the world, Alric could see what was left of the valley, the smoking craters rimmed with dead stone, the great gashes in the mountains. But worse than the visible destruction were the low, terrified cries of the mountains. Their weeping went straight to his bones in a way nothing else ever had and, he hoped, nothing ever would again.

The Lord of Storms had his back to Alric. As always, his coat was pristine, his sword clean and sheathed at his side. He alone of all of them bore no sign of what had just occurred, but a glance at the enormous black clouds overhead was all Alric needed to know his commander's mood. Alric took a quiet, calming breath. He would need to handle this delicately.

The moment he stepped into position, the Lord of Storms barked. "Report."

"Twenty-four confirmed casualties," Alric said. "Eighteen wounded, eight still unaccounted for."

"They're dead," the Lord of Storms said. "No one else will be coming through." He jerked his hand down and the gate beside him vanished, cutting off the mountain's cries. Despite himself, Alric sighed in relief.

"Thirty-two dead out of a force of fifty," the Lord of Storms said coldly. "That's a rout by any definition."

"But the objective was achieved," Alric said. "The demon was destroyed."

The Lord of Storms shook his head. "She's not dead."

"Impossible," Alric said. "I saw you take her head off. Nothing could survive that."

The Lord of Storms sneered. "A demon is never defeated until you've got the seed in your hand." He walked to the edge of the high, icy terrace, staring down at the quiet, snow-covered peaks below. "We tore her up a bit, diminished her, but she'll be back. Mark me, Alric, this isn't over."

Alric pulled himself straight. "Even if you are right, even if the creature is still alive somewhere, we stopped the mountain's assault. The Shepherdess can have no—"

"*Do not speak to me about that woman!*" the Lord of Storms roared. His hand shot to the blue-wrapped hilt of his sword, and the smell of ozone crept into the air as little tongues of lightning crackled along his grip. "What we faced tonight should never have been allowed to come about." He looked at Alric from the corner of his eye. "Do you know what we fought in that valley?"

Alric shuddered, remembering the black wings that blotted out the sky, the screaming cry that turned his bones to water and made mountains weep in terror, the hideous, black shape that his brain refused to remember in detail because something that horrible should never be seen more than once. "A demon."

The Lord of Storms laughed. "A demon? A demon is what we get when we neglect a seed too long. A demon can be taken out by a single League member. We kill *demons* every day. What we faced tonight, Alric, is something I have not seen in a thousand years. A child of the Dead Mountain itself."

"A child…" Alric swallowed against the dryness in his throat. "How is that possible? The Dead Mountain is under the Lady's own seal. Tiny slivers may escape to form seeds, but a child of the creature itself?" Alric shook his head. "Such a thing cannot be."

"You keep telling yourself that," the Lord of Storms said. "But it is the Lady's will that keeps the seal in place, and when her attention wanders, we're the ones who have to clean up." The Lord of Storms clenched his sword hilt as the smell of ozone intensified. "Thirty-two League members and a ruined valley are *nothing* compared to what this could end up costing us. We have to find the creature and finish her."

Alric was looking for a way to answer that when the soft sound of a throat clearing saved him the trouble. He turned to see a group of old men and women in fine, heavy coats standing in the doorway to the great hall. Alric nodded graciously, but the Lord of Storms just sneered and turned back to the mountains, crossing his arms over his chest. Undeterred by the League commander's rudeness, the figure at the group's head, a tall, stern man with white beard down to his chest, stepped forward.

"My Lord of Storms," he said, bowing to the enormous man's back, "I am Ferdinand Slorn, Head Shaper and Guildmaster of the Shaper Clans."

"I know who you are," the Lord of Storms said. "We'll be out of here soon enough, old man."

"You are welcome to stay as long as you need," Slorn said, smiling benignly. "However, we sought you out to offer assistance of a different nature."

The Lord of Storms looked over his shoulder. "Speak."

Slorn remained unruffled. "We have heard of your battle with the great demon as well as its unfortunate escape. As Master of the Shapers, I would like to offer our aid in its capture."

"Guildmaster," Alric said. "You have already helped so much providing aid and—"

"How do you know about that?" The sudden anger in the Lord of Storm's voice cut Alric off cold.

"These mountains are Shaper lands, my lord," the Guildmaster replied calmly. "You can hardly expect to fight a battle such as you just fought without attracting our attention. Our great teacher, on whose slopes we now stand, is enraged and grieving. His brother mountains were among those injured by the demon, many beyond repair. We only ask that we be allowed to assist in the capture of the one responsible."

"What help could you be to us?" The Lord of Storms sneered. "Demons are League business. You may be good at slapping spirits together, but what do Shapers know of catching spirit eaters?"

"More than you would think." The old man's eyes narrowed, but his calm tone never broke. "We Shapers live our lives in the shadow of the demon's mountain. You and your ruffians may be good at tracking down the demon's wayward seeds, but it is my people, and the great mountains we honor, who suffer the most. Tonight several beautiful, powerful spirits, ancient mountains and allies of my people, were eaten alive. We cannot rest until the one responsible is destroyed."

"That's too bad," the Lord of Storms said, stepping forward until he towered over the old Guildmaster. "I'll say this one more time. Demons are League business. So until I put a black coat on your shoulders, you will stay out of our way."

The Guildmaster stared up at Lord of Storms, completely unruffled. "I can assure you, my dear Lord of Storms, we will avoid your way entirely. All I ask is the opportunity to pursue our own lines of inquiry."

The Lord of Storms leaned forward, bending down until he was inches away from the old man's face. "Listen," he said, very low, "and listen well. We both know that you're going to do what you're going to do, so before you go and do it, take my advice: Do not cross me. If you or your people get in my way on the hunt for the creature, I will roll right over you without looking back. Do you understand me, Shaper?"

Slorn narrowed his eyes. "Quite clearly, demon hunter."

The Lord of Storms gave him one final, crackling glare before pushing his way through the small crowd of Shaper elders and stomping back across the frozen terrace toward the brightly lit hall.

Alric thanked the Shaper elders before running after his commander. "Honestly," he said, keeping his voice low, "it would make my life easier if you learned a little tact. They were just trying to help."

"Help?" the Lord of Storms scoffed. "There's nothing someone outside the League could do to help. Let them do whatever they like, it'll end the same. No seed sleeps forever, Alric. Sooner or later, she's going to crack, and when that happens, I'll be there. And this time, I won't stop until I have her seed in my hand." He clenched his fists. "Now get everyone out of here, including corpses. We burn the dead tonight at headquarters; I want nothing of ours left in this mountain."

And with that he vanished—just disappeared into thin air, leaving Alric walking alone through the center of the Shaper hall. Alric skidded to a stop. It was always like this when things were bad, but the only thing to do was obey. Gritting his teeth, he walked over to the best mended of the walking wounded and began giving orders to move out. His words were met with grim stares. Most of the League was too wounded to make a safe portal back to the fortress. But they were soldiers, and they obeyed without grumbling, working quietly under Alric to bring home the dead through the long, bloody night also look out for

THE ACCIDENTAL SORCEROR

Rogue Agent: Book One

by

K. E. Mills

CHAPTER ONE

The entrance to Stuttley's Superior Staff factory, Ottosland's premier staff manufacturer, was guarded by a glass-fronted booth and blocked by a red and blue boom gate. Inside the booth slumped a dyspeptic-looking security guard, dressed in a rumpled green and orange Stuttley's uniform. It didn't suit him. An ash-tipped cigarette drooped from the corner of his mouth and the half-eaten sardine sandwich in his hand leaked tomato sauce onto the floor. He was reading a crumpled, food-stained copy of the previous day's *Ottosland Times*.

After several long moments of not being noticed, Gerald fished out his official identification and pressed it flat to the window, right in front of the guard's face.

"Gerald Dunwoody. Department of Thaumaturgy. I'm here for a snap inspection."

The guard didn't look up. "Izzat right? Nobody tole me."

"Well, no," said Gerald, after another moment. "That's why we call it a 'snap inspection'. On account of it being a surprise."

Reluctantly the guard lifted his rheumy gaze. "Ha ha. Sir."

Gerald smiled around gritted teeth. *It's a job, it's a job, and I'm lucky to have it.* "I understand Stuttley's production foreman is a Mister Harold Stuttley?"

"That's right," said the guard. His attention drifted back to the paper. "He's the owner's cousin. Mr Horace Stuttley's an old man now, don't hardly see him round here no more. Not since his little bit of trouble."

"Really? I'm sorry to hear it." The guard sniffed, inhaled on his cigarette and expelled the smoke in a disinterested cloud. Gerald resisted the urge to bang his head on the glass between them. "So where would I find Foreman Stuttley?"

"Search me," said the guard, shrugging. "On the factory floor, most like. They're doing a run of First Grade staffs today, if memory serves."

Gerald frowned. First Grade staffs were notoriously difficult to forge. Get the etheretic balances wrong in the split-second of alchemical transformation and what you were looking at afterwards, basically, was a huge smoking hole in the ground. And if this guard was any indication, standards at Stuttley's had slipped of late. He rapped his knuckles on the glass.

"I wish to see Harold Stuttley right now, please," he said, briskly official. "According to Department records this operation hasn't returned its signed and witnessed safety statements for two months. I'm afraid that's a clear breach of regulations. There'll be no First Grade staffs rolling off the production line today or any other day unless I'm fully satisfied that all proper precautions and procedures have been observed."

Sighing, the guard put down his soggy sandwich,

stubbed out his cigarette, wiped his hands on his trousers and stood. "All right, sir. If you say so."

There was a battered black telephone on the wall of the security booth. The guard dialled a four-digit number, receiver pressed to his ear, and waited. Waited some more. Dragged his sleeve across his moist nose, still waiting, then hung up with an exclamation of disgust. "No answer. Nobody there to hear it, or the bloody thing's on the blink again. Take your pick."

"I'd rather see Harold Stuttley."

The guard heaved another lugubrious sigh. "Right you are, then. Follow me."

Gerald followed, starting to feel a little dyspeptic himself. Honestly, these people! What kind of a business were they running? Security phones that didn't work, essential paperwork that wasn't completed. Didn't they realise they were playing with fire? Even the plainest Third Grade staff was capable of inflicting damage if it wasn't handled carefully in the production phase. Complacency, that was the trouble. Clearly Harold Stuttley had let the prestige and success of his family's world-famous business go to his head. Just because every wizard who was any wizard and could afford the exorbitant price tag wouldn't be caught dead without his Stuttley Staff (patented, copyrighted and limited edition) as part of his sartorial ensemble was no excuse to let safety standards slide.

Bloody hell, he thought, mildly appalled. *Somebody save me. I'm thinking like a civil servant . . .*

The unenthusiastic security guard was leading him down a tree-lined driveway towards a distant high brick wall with a red door in it. The door's paint was cracked and peeling. Above and behind the wall could be seen the slate-grey factory roof, with its chimney stacks belching pale puce smoke. A flock of pigeons wheeling through the blue sky plunged into the coloured effluvium and abruptly turned bright green.

Damn. Obviously Stuttley's thaumaturgical filtering system was on the blink: code violation number two. The unharmed birds flapped away, fading back to white even as he watched, but that wasn't the point. All thaumaturgical by-products were subject to strict legislation. Temporary colour changes were one thing. But what if the next violation resulted in a temporal dislocation? Or a quantifiable matter redistribution? Or worse? There'd be hell to pay. People might get hurt. What was Stuttley's playing at?

Even as he wondered, he felt a shiver like the touch of a thousand spider feet skitter across his skin. The mellow morning was suddenly charged with menace, strobed with shadows.

"Did you feel that?" he asked the guard.

"They don't pay me to feel things, sir," the guard replied over his shoulder.

A sense of unease, like a tiny butterfly, fluttered in the pit of Gerald's stomach. He glanced up, but the sky was still blue and the sun was still shining and birds continued to warble in the trees.

"No. Of course they don't," he replied, and shook his head. It was nothing. Just his stupid over-active imagination getting out of hand again. If he could he'd have it surgically removed. It certainly hadn't done him any favours to date.

He glanced in passing at the nearest tree with its burden of trilling birds, but he couldn't see Reg amongst them. Of course he wouldn't, not if she didn't want to be seen. After yesterday morning's lively discussion about his apparent lack of ambition she'd taken herself off in a huff of ruffled feathers and a cloud of curses and he hadn't laid eyes on her since.

Not that he was worried. This wasn't the first hissy fit she'd thrown and it wouldn't be the last. She'd come back when it suited her. She always did. She just liked to make him squirm.

Well, he wasn't going to. Not this time. No, nor apologise either. For once in her ensorcelled life she was going to admit to being wrong, and that was that. He wasn't unambitious. He just knew his limitations.

Three paces ahead of him the guard stopped at the red door, unhooked a large brass key ring from his belt and fished through its assortment of keys. Finding the one he wanted he stuck it into the lock, jiggled, swore, kicked the door twice, and turned the handle.

"There you are, sir," he said, pushing the door wide then standing back. "I'll let you find your own way round if it's all the same to you. Can't leave my booth unattended for too long. Somebody important might turn up." He smiled, revealing tobacco-yellow teeth.

Gerald looked at him. "Indeed. I'll be sure to mention your enthusiasm in my official report."

The guard did a double take at that, his smile vanishing. With a surly grunt he hooked his bundle of keys back on his belt then folded his arms, radiating offended impatience.

Immediately, Gerald felt guilty. *Oh lord. Now I'm acting like a civil servant!*

Not that there was anything wrong, as such, with public employment. Many fine people were civil servants. Indeed, without them the world would be in a sorry state, he was sure. In fact, the civil service was an honourable institution and he was lucky to be part of it. Only . . . it had never been his ambition to be a wizard who inspected the work of other wizards for Departmental regulation violations. His ambition was to be an inspec*tee*, not an inspec*tor*. Once upon a time he'd thought that dream was reachable.

Now he was a probationary compliance officer in the Minor Infringement Bureau of the Department of Thaumaturgy . . . and dreams were things you had at night after you turned out the lights.

He nodded at the waiting guard. "Thank you."

"Certainly, sir," the guard said sourly.

Well, his day was certainly getting off to a fine start. *And we wonder why people don't like bureaucrats . . .*

With an apologetic smile at the guard he hefted his official briefcase, straightened his official tie, rearranged his expression into one of official rectitude and walked through the open doorway.

And only flinched a little bit as the guard locked the red door behind him.

It's a wizarding job, Gerald, and it's better than the alternative.

Hopefully, if he reminded himself often enough, he'd start to believe that soon.

The factory lay dead ahead, down the end of a short paved pathway. It was a tall, red brick building blinded by a lack of windows. Along its front wall were plastered a plethora of signs: *Danger! Thaumaturgical Emissions! Keep Out! No Admittance Without Permission! All Visitors Report To Security Before Proceeding!*

As he stood there, reading, one of the building's four doors opened and a young woman wearing a singed lab coat and an expression of mild alarm came out.

He approached her, waving. "Excuse me! Excuse me! Can I have a word?"

The young woman saw him, took in his briefcase and the crossed staffs on his tie and moaned. "Oh, no. You're from the Department, aren't you?"

He tried to reassure her with a smile. "Yes, as a matter of fact. Gerald Dunwoody. And you are?"

Looking hunted, she shrank into herself. "Holly," she muttered. "Holly Devree."

He'd been with the Department for a shade under six months and in all that time had been allowed into the field only four times, but he'd worked out by the end of his first site inspection that when it came to the poor sods just following company orders, sympathy earned him far more co-operation than threats. He sagged at the knees, let his shoulders droop and slid his voice into a more intimate, confiding tone.

"Well, Miss Devree – Holly – I can see you're feeling nervous. Please don't. All I need is for you to point me in the direction of your boss, Mr Harold Stuttley."

She cast a dark glance over her shoulder at the factory. "He's in there. And before you see him I want it understood that it's not my fault. It's not Eric's fault, either. Or Bob's. Or Lucius's. It's not any of our faults. We worked hard to get our trans-mogrifer's licence, okay? And it's not like we're earning squillions, either. The pay's rotten, if you must know. But Stuttley's – they're the best, aren't they?" Without warning, her thin, pale face crumpled. "At least, they used to be the best. When old Mr Horace was in charge. But now . . ."

Fat tears trembled on the ends of her sandy-coloured eyelashes. Gerald fished a handkerchief out of his pocket and handed it over. "Yes? Now?"

Blotting her eyes she said, "Everything's different, isn't it? Mr Harold's gone and implemented all these 'cost-cutting' initiatives. Laid off half the Transmogrify team. But the workload hasn't halved, has it? Oh, no. And it's not just us he's laid off, either. He's sacked people in Etheretics, Design, Purchasing, Research and Development – there's not one team hasn't lost folk. Except Sales." Her snubby nose wrinkled in distaste. "Seven new sales reps he's taken on, and they're promising the world, and we're expected to deliver it – except we can't! We're working round the clock and we're still three weeks behind on orders and now Mr Harold's threatening to dock us if we don't catch up!"

"Oh my," he said, and patted her awkwardly on the shoulder. "I'm very sorry to hear this. But at least it explains why the last eight safety reports weren't completed."

"But they were," she whispered, busily strangling her borrowed handkerchief. "Lucius is the most senior technician we've got left, and I know he's been doing them. *And* handing them over to Mr Harold. I've seen it. But what *he's* doing with them I don't know."

Filing them in the nearest waste paper bin, more than likely. "I don't suppose your friend Lucius discussed the reports with you? Or showed them to you?"

Holly Devree's confiding manner shifted suddenly to a cagey caution. The handkerchief disappeared into her lab coat pocket. "Safety reports are confidential."

"Of course, of course," Gerald soothed. "I'm not implying any inappropriate behaviour. But Lucius didn't happen to leave one lying out on a table, did he, where any innocent passer-by might catch a glimpse?"

"I'm sorry," she said, edging away. "I'm on my tea break. We only get ten minutes. Mr Harold's inside if you want to see him. Please don't tell him we talked."

He watched her scuttle like a spooked rabbit, and sighed. Clearly there was more amiss at Stuttley's than a bit of overlooked paperwork. He should get back to the office and tell Mr Scunthorpe. As a probationary compliance officer his duties lay within very strict guidelines. There were other, more senior inspectors for this kind of trouble.

On the other hand, his supervisor was allergic to incomplete reports. Unconfirmed tales out of school from disgruntled employees and nebulous sensations of misgiving from probationary compliance officers bore no resemblance to cold, hard facts. And Mr Scunthorpe was as married to cold, hard facts as he was to Mrs Scunthorpe. More, if Mr Scunthorpe's marital mutterings were anything to go by.

Turning, Gerald stared at the blank-faced factory. He could still feel his inexplicable unease simmering away beneath the surface of his mind. Whatever it was trying to tell him, the news wasn't good. But that wasn't enough. He had to find out exactly *what* had tickled his instincts. And he did have a legitimate place to start, after all: the noncompletion of mandatory safety statements. The infraction was enough to get his foot across the factory threshold. After that, well, it was just a case of following his intuition.

He resolutely ignored the whisper in the back of his mind that said, *Remember what happened the last time you followed your intuition?*

"Oh, bugger off!" he told it, and marched into the fray.

Another pallid employee answered his brisk banging

on the nearest door. "Good afternoon," he said, flashing his identification and not giving the lab-coated man a chance to speak. "Gerald Dunwoody, Department of Thaumaturgy, here to see Mr Harold Stuttley on a matter of noncompliance. I'm told he's inside? Excellent. Don't let me keep you from your duties. I'll find my own way around."

The employee gave ground, helpless in the ruthlessly cheerful face of officialdom, and Gerald sailed in. Immediately his nose was clogged with the stink of partially discharged thaumaturgic energy. The air beneath the high factory ceiling was alive with it, crawling and spitting and sparking. The carefully caged lights hummed and buzzed, crackling as firefly filaments of power drifted against their heated bulbs to ignite in a brief, sunlike flare.

A dozen more lab-coated technicians scurried up and down the factory floor, focused on the task at hand. Directly opposite, running the full length of the wall, stood a five-deep row of benches, each one equipped with specially crafted staff cradles. Twenty-five per bench times five benches meant that, if the security guard was right, Stuttley's had one hundred and twenty-five new First Grade staffs ready for completion. The technicians, looking tense and preoccupied, fiddled and twiddled and realigned each uncharged staff in its cradle, assessing every minute adjustment with a hand-held thaumic register. All the muted ticking made the room sound like the demonstration area of a clockmakers' convention.

At either end of the benches towered the etheretic conductors, vast reservoirs of unprocessed thaumaturgic energy. Insulated cables connected them to each other and all the staff cradles, whose conductive surfaces waited patiently for the discharge of raw power that would transform one hundred and twenty-five gold-filigreed five-foot-long spindles of oak into the world's finest, most prestigious, expensive and potentially most dangerous First Grade staffs.

Despite his misgivings he heard himself whimper, just a little. Stuttley First Graders were works of art. Each wrapping of solid gold filigree was unique, its design template destroyed upon completion and never repeated. The rare wizards who could afford the extra astronomical cost had their filigrees designed specifically for them, taking into account personal strengths, family history and specific thaumaturgic signatures. Those staffs came with inbuilt security: it was immediate and spectacularly gruesome death for any wizard other than the rightful owner to attempt the use of them.

Once, a long long time ago, he'd dreamed of owning a First Grade staff. Even though he didn't come from a wizarding family. Even though he'd got his qualifications through a correspondence course. Wizardry cared nothing for family background or the name of the college where you were educated. Wizarding was of the blood and bone, indifferent to pedigrees and bank balances. Some of the world's finest wizards had come from humble origins.

Although . . . not lately. Lately, Ottosland's most powerful and influential wizards came from recognisable families whose names more often than not could also be heard whispered in the nation's corridors of power.

Still. *Technically*, anybody with sufficient aptitude and training could become a First Grade wizard. Social standing might influence your accent but it had nothing to do with raw power. *Technically*, even a tailor's son from Nether Wallop could earn the right to wield a First Grade staff.

Unbidden, his fingers touched his copper-ringed cherrywood Third Grade staff, tucked into its pocket on the inside of his overcoat. It was nothing to be ashamed of. He was the first wizard in the family for umpteen generations, after all. Plenty of people failed even to be awarded a Third Grade licence. For every ten hopefuls identified as potential wizards, only one or two actually survived the rigours of trial and training to receive their precious staff.

And even for Third Grades there was work to be had. Wasn't he living proof? Gerald Dunwoody, after a couple of totally understandable false starts, soon to be a fully qualified compliance officer with the internationally renowned Ottosland Department of Thaumaturgy? Yes, indeed. The sky was the limit. Provided there was a heavy cloud cover. And he was indoors. In a cellar, possibly.

Oh lord, he thought miserably, staring at all those magnificent First Grade staffs. It felt as though his official Departmental tie had tightened to throttling point. *There has to be more to wizarding than this.*

An irate shout rescued him from utter despair. "Oy! You! Who are you and what are you doing in my factory?"

He turned. Marching belligerently towards him, scattering lab coats like so many white mice, was a small persnickety man of sleek middle years, clutching a clipboard and looking so offended even his tea-stained moustache was bristling.

"Ah. Good afternoon," he said, producing his official smile. "Mr Harold Stuttley, I presume?"

The angry little man halted abruptly in front of him, clipboard pressed to his chest like a shield. "And if I am? What of it? Who wants to know?"

Gerald put down his briefcase and took out his identification. Stuttley snatched it from his fingers, glared as though at a mortal insult, then shoved it back. "What's all this bollocks? And who let you in here? We're about to do a run of First Grades. Unauthorised personnel aren't allowed in here when we're running First Grades! How do I know you're not here for a spot of industrial espionage?"

"Because I'm employed by the DoT," he said, pocketing his badge. "And I'm afraid you won't be running anything, Mr Stuttley, until I'm satisfied it's safe to do so. You've not submitted your safety statements for some time now, sir. I'm afraid the Department takes a dim view of that. Now I realise it's probably just an oversight on your part, but even so . . ." He shrugged. "Rules are rules."

Harold Stuttley's pebble-bright eyes bulged. "Want to know what you can do with your rules? You march in here uninvited and then have the hide to tell me when I can and can't conduct my own business? I'll have your job for this!"

Gerald considered him. *Too much bluster. What's he trying to hide?* He let his gaze slide sideways, away from Harold Stuttley's unattractively temper-mottled face. The thaumic emission gauge on the nearest etheretic conductor was stuttering, jittery as an icicle in an earthquake. Flick, flick, flick went the needle, each jump edging closer and closer to the bright red zone marked *Danger*. In his nostrils, the clogging stink of overheated thaumic energy was suddenly stifling.

"Mr Stuttley," he said, "I think you should shut down production right now. There's something wrong here, I can feel it."

Harold Stuttley's eyes nearly popped right out of his head. "Shut down? Are you raving? You're looking at over a million quids' worth of merchandise! All those staffs are bought and paid for, you meddling twit! I'm not about to disappoint my customers for some wet-behind-the-ears stooge from the DoT! Your superiors wouldn't know a safe bit of equipment if it bit them on the arse – and neither would you! Stuttley's has been in business two hundred and forty years, you cretin! We've been making staffs since before your great-grandad was a randy thought in his pa's trousers!"

Gerald winced. By now the air inside the factory was so charged with energy it felt like sandpaper abrading his skin. "Look. I realise it's inconvenient but—"

Harold Stuttley's pointing finger stabbed him in the chest. "It's not happening, son, *that's* what it is. *Inconvenient* is the lawsuit I'll bring against you, your bosses and the whole bleeding Department of Thaumaturgy, you mark my words, if you don't leg it out of here on the double! Interfering with the lawful conduct of business? This is political, this is. Too many wizards buying Stuttley's instead of the cheap muck your precious Department churns out! Well I won't have it, you hear me? Now hop it! Off my premises! Or I'll give you a personal demonstration why Stuttley's staffs are the best in the world!"

Gerald stared. Was the man mad? He couldn't throw out an official Department inspector. He'd have his manufacturing licence revoked. Be brought up on charges. Get sent to prison and be forced to pay a hefty fine.

Little rivers of sweat were pouring down Harold Stuttley's scarlet face and his hands were trembling with rage. Gerald looked more closely. No. Not rage. Terror. Harold Stuttley was beside himself with fear.

He turned and looked at the nearest etheretic conductor. It was sweating too, beads of dark blue moisture forming on its surface, dripping slowly down its sides. Even as he watched, one fat indigo drop of condensed thaumic energy plopped to the factory floor. There was a crack of light and sound. Two preoccupied technicians somersaulted through the air like circus performers, crashed into the wall opposite and collapsed in groaning heaps.

"*Stuttley!*" He grabbed Harold by his lapels and shook him. "Do you see that? Your etheretic containment field is leaking! You have to evacuate! *Now!*"

The rest of the lab coats were congregated about their fallen comrades, fussing and whispering and casting loathing looks in their employer's direction. The acrobatic technicians were both conscious, apparently unbroken, but seemed dazed. Harold Stuttley jumped backwards, tearing himself free of officialdom's grasp.

"Evacuate? Never! We've got a deadline to meet!" He rounded on his employees. "You lot! Back to work! Leave those malingerers where they are, they're all right, they're just winded! Be on their feet in no time – *if* they know what's good for them. Come on! You want to get paid this week or don't you?"

Aghast, Gerald stared at him. The man *was* mad. Even a mere Third Grade wizard like himself knew the dangers of improperly contained thaumic emissions. The entire first year of his correspondence course had dealt with the occupational hazards of wizarding. Some of the illustrations in his handbook had put him off minced meat for *weeks*.